Praise for *New York Times* bestselling author Lori Foster

"Lori Foster delivers everything you're looking for in a romance."

—*New York Times* bestselling author Jayne Ann Krentz

"Foster hits every note (or power chord) of the true alpha male hero."

—*Publishers Weekly*

"Bestseller Foster…has an amazing ability to capture a man's emotions and lust with sizzling sex scenes and meld it with a strong woman's point of view."

—*Publishers Weekly* on *A Perfect Storm*

Praise for *USA TODAY* bestselling author Sarah Morgan

"Each book of [Sarah Morgan's] that I discover is a treat."

—*Smart Bitches, Trashy Books*

"Morgan's brilliant talent never ceases to amaze."

—*RT Book Reviews*

Lori Foster is a *New York Times*, *USA TODAY* and *Publishers Weekly* bestselling author with books from a variety of publishers, including Berkley/Jove, Kensington, St. Martin's, Harlequin and Silhouette. Lori has been a recipient of the prestigious *RT Book Reviews* Career Achievement Award for Series Romantic Fantasy, and for Contemporary Romance. For more about Lori, visit her website at lorifoster.com.

USA TODAY bestselling author **Sarah Morgan** writes hot, happy contemporary romance. Her trademark humor and sensuality have gained her fans across the globe and two RITA® Awards from the Romance Writers of America. Sarah lives near London with her family. Visit her at sarahmorgan.com.

New York Times Bestselling Author

LORI FOSTER

IN TOO DEEP

&

USA TODAY Bestselling Author

SARAH MORGAN

ONE ENCHANTED MOMENT

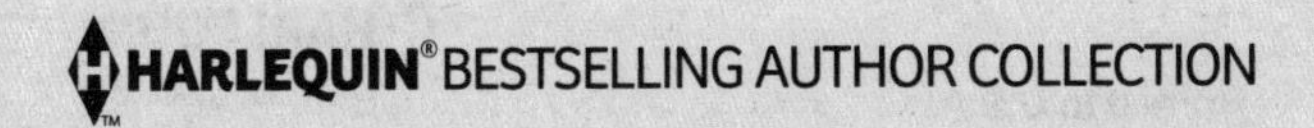

If you purchased this book without a cover you should be aware that this book is stolen property. It was reported as "unsold and destroyed" to the publisher, and neither the author nor the publisher has received any payment for this "stripped book."

ISBN-13: 978-0-373-01040-0

Recycling programs for this product may not exist in your area.

In Too Deep & One Enchanted Moment
Copyright © 2016 by Harlequin Books S.A.

The publisher acknowledges the copyright holders of the individual works as follows:

In Too Deep
Copyright © 2000 by Lori Foster

One Enchanted Moment
Copyright © 2015 by Sarah Morgan
First published as Christmas Ever After by Harlequin (UK)

All rights reserved. Except for use in any review, the reproduction or utilization of this work in whole or in part in any form by any electronic, mechanical or other means, now known or hereinafter invented, including xerography, photocopying and recording, or in any information storage or retrieval system, is forbidden without the written permission of the publisher, Harlequin Enterprises Limited, 225 Duncan Mill Road, Don Mills, Ontario M3B 3K9, Canada.

This is a work of fiction. Names, characters, places and incidents are either the product of the author's imagination or are used fictitiously, and any resemblance to actual persons, living or dead, business establishments, events or locales is entirely coincidental.

This edition published by arrangement with Harlequin Books S.A.

For questions and comments about the quality of this book, please contact us at CustomerService@Harlequin.com.

® and TM are trademarks of Harlequin Enterprises Limited or its corporate affiliates. Trademarks indicated with ® are registered in the United States Patent and Trademark Office, the Canadian Intellectual Property Office and in other countries.

HARLEQUIN®
™ www.Harlequin.com

Printed in U.S.A.

CONTENTS

IN TOO DEEP 7
Lori Foster

ONE ENCHANTED MOMENT 221
Sarah Morgan

Also available from Lori Foster and HQN Books

The Ultimate series

Hard Knocks
No Limits
Holding Strong
Tough Love
Fighting Dirty

Love Undercover

Run the Risk
Bare It All
Getting Rowdy
Dash of Peril

Men Who Walk the Edge of Honor

Ready, Set, Jett
When You Dare
Trace of Fever
Savor the Danger
A Perfect Storm
What Chris Wants
(ebook novella)

For a complete list of books by Lori Foster, please visit lorifoster.com.

IN TOO DEEP

Lori Foster

To Malle Vallik.
Though you'll no longer be editing Temptations,
you'll be forever remembered as
"one of the great ones." I take comfort in the fact
that your Temptation novels will go on,
pleasing readers for years to come.

CHAPTER ONE

SHE HAD THE SOFT, sweet mouth of a woman. And as she bent slightly at the waist, peeking out the front window of the quaint grocery shop, he inspected her bottom—and found it equally sweet. His palms itched, and he wasn't certain if it was with the need to caress—or swat.

Maybe she was a cross-dresser. Or she just had really bad taste in clothes. But she was definitely female, of that Harry was certain. He hadn't even noticed her until she'd gotten too close to him, and then he'd picked up on her scent. It made him feel like a buck in mating season, it hit him so hard. He stared, unable to help himself, until she noticed he was staring. Then she gave him a sour look and moved away.

And still he stared. The battered brown leather jacket was a couple sizes too big, ripped at one shoulder seam. And the flannel beneath it was baggy and hanging loose over ill-fitting, patched jeans. Scuffed, low-heel boots with chains on the back gave the impression she was trying for a bad-boy biker look. *Absurd.* Even her slicked back, glossy dark hair, held in a short blunt ponytail at her nape looked more female than rebel male. She had only one pierced ear, a small spent bullet dangling from the tiny silver hoop.

She kept her hands in her back pockets and a sneer

on her face. Harry wondered what she'd done with her breasts, for they weren't noticeable through the bulky clothing. Of course, maybe she was naturally small. He wouldn't mind. He was a bottom-man himself, and he liked petite women, he…

Harry drew up short, appalled at the direction his wandering mind had taken. He wanted nothing to do with the woman, absolutely nothing.

Whatever her excuse for aping a man, she didn't need to be here now, at this precise moment, possibly screwing things up for him, definitely distracting him.

Harry Lonnigan eyed the unfortunate female with annoyance, now dividing his attention between her and the two men working their way to the cash register. He had a job to attend to. Yet there she was, trying to saunter like a man, trying to sneer in a manly way. Harry snorted, then despite himself, he breathed deeply, trying to detect her sweet scent again. Not the smell of perfume, but the smell of warm woman, a smell proven to drive men crazy.

He wanted to ignore her, but couldn't. Who was she and what was she up to with her outrageous costume and bizarre acting? Only a complete imbecile would believe her to be male.

But just then one of the two men turned, eyed her, and gave credence to her costume by dismissing her without so much as a raised eyebrow. Harry was stupefied.

He came out from behind the rack of chips and strolled casually forward, in no hurry to draw attention to himself, but the female was getting entirely too close to the two men, trying it seemed, to keep surveillance out the front display window without being seen. Whatever she was up to, she apparently wasn't aware of the danger. Harry had no claims on being a hero, far from it, but he also wasn't callous enough to watch a woman get injured, not if he could stop it.

"Go away."

Harry halted, then blinked. The little imposter—she barely reached his shoulder—had hissed at him out of the corner of her mouth. How had she known he was behind her? He hadn't made a single sound!

The two men looked up. They were cocky and obnoxious young men, overly confident because they'd been running their scam in this area for far too long, at least that's what Harry's friend, Dalton, had said. He owed Dalton, and stopping these ruffians from their petty extortion would be adequate compensation, but it was a nuisance. Especially if some stray with a weird agenda was determined to interfere and complicate matters.

One of the men turned to face them, propping his elbows on the counter and giving them both an assessing look. "What are you doing?"

Harry pretended not to understand. He stared at a shelf filled with canned goods, finally selecting some potted meat. He shuddered. Nasty looking stuff, potted meat. The little female remained frozen beside him.

After an extended silence where no one seemed willing to move, Harry looked up. "Hmm? You were talking to me?"

The guy pushed off the counter and started forward through the narrow, crammed aisles. His blond hair was long and greasy, like the rest of his body, and his eyes were a pale, washed-out blue, red-rimmed and with lashes so light they were nearly invisible. Scraggly whiskers dotted his chin, a discredit to every manly beard ever grown. His partner, heavier and darker, also turned to watch while the proprietor, a man close to seventy, seemed to grow more agitated by the moment.

"Yeah, you. Who did you think I was talking to? The kid?"

Harry smiled. So the guy was a dolt, believing she was a man. Or rather a boy. Was he myopic? Couldn't he *smell* her, for God's sake? Harry cocked an imperious brow. "I didn't hear the question."

Irritation flashed on blondie's face as he struck an insolent pose, one hip thrust out, his arms crossed on his narrow chest. "I asked what the hell you're doing."

Bells jingled as a customer started in, then jingled again as the woman took in the situation in a glance and hurried back out. Obviously the denizens of this area were well aware of what went on. They were all simply too old or too wary to stop it on their own. Harry wasn't old or wary. He stared down at the man with utter disdain.

"I'm shopping. What concern is it of yours?"

Blondie's face darkened and he straightened slightly. "You've been hanging around since we got here. Why haven't you bought anything yet?"

Harry raised both brows. Pushy little bastard. "I'm selective."

The young man scowled, his pale eyes going even paler, then he obviously decided not to pursue it, probably given the fact that Harry stood a good six foot five, nearly half a foot taller than him. Though Harry dressed like a gentleman, few people ever thought of him as one. It was something, they said, to do with his eyes, though he tended to disregard such nonsense.

"Well, get done and get out. I don't like you hanging around."

Harry was willing to play along—up to a point. Right up until the punk turned to the girl and poked her in the chest with his finger, almost knocking her over. "Same goes for you. Beat it."

Harry wasn't a hero, he truly wasn't, but he detested bullies. Beyond that, he couldn't tolerate violence of any kind toward females, regardless of the fact the fellow was too dense to realize she *was* a female.

When he started to add an additional poke, snickering at the way she'd stumbled, Harry dropped the potted meat—no big loss there—and snatched the fellow's finger into his fist. Harry squeezed.

A loud wail of outraged pain filled the store.

Unconcerned, Harry asked, "Now, why would you want to inflict abuse on someone smaller than yourself?"

The guy's knees were starting to give way as Harry ruthlessly tightened his grip. Blondie stared up at him, his face pinched in a grimace. "He's almost as tall as I am!"

"Not an adequate excuse. You're obviously older. And moreover, I've decided I don't like you." Using a deft movement of his own hand, Harry twisted the hapless finger, attached to an equally hapless arm, until the man was forced to go on tiptoe, high-pitched curses winging from his mouth.

Pandemonium broke out.

The little female overflowed with umbrage. "I

don't need your help, you pompous ass!" The men either ignored her, or didn't hear her.

The bully's dark friend rushed forward. "Floyd!" he called out, as he pulled a gun from his pants. His gaze lifted to Harry, narrow-eyed and mean. "Turn him loose before I shoot your head off!"

The hard nose of a gun barrel poked into Harry's ribs. He cast a wry expression on the friend. "Now, that'd be rather difficult, with you aiming there. My head's a bit higher up."

His ill-advised insult got the gun immediately raised, and now he felt the cold metal against his ear. This comedy of errors was getting out of hand. Slowly, he loosened his grip.

Floyd shook his hand and cursed, then shook it some more. He looked up at Harry with red-rimmed eyes. "Shoot him."

"What?"

"Damn it, you heard me, Ralph! *Shoot him.*"

Harry said a quick prayer. The girl, finally showing some small signs of intelligence, began inching her way nonchalantly toward the door.

"Get back here, damn it." Floyd wasn't about to let her, or rather him, get away. "I think you two are working together to distract us. Who sent you here?"

The little female blinked and her smooth cheeks were suffused with color. "No one sent me! And I never saw that guy before in my life."

Harry waited for a gasp, waited for the recognition because her husky voice had obviously been that of a female's, despite her efforts to lower it accordingly.

He waited in vain.

"We can't jus' shoot him, Floyd. You know what

Carlyle said. Keep it tidy. Besides, it'll be easier if we jus' let him go. He's nobody."

"Then what was he buttin' his nose in for?"

Ralph lowered his brows in thought, all the while keeping the gun steady on Harry's head.

Trying to placate them, Harry shrugged and said, "I simply can't abide a bully."

The gun smacked against his head, making his ears ring. "You can *abide* anythin' Floyd tells you to! That's how it's done in these parts."

Floyd grinned, and Harry was amazed to see he had fairly even, white teeth. "So you didn't like me pushing the scrawny runt around?"

Knowing he'd handed Floyd his revenge on a silver platter, Harry almost groaned. Damn his mouth anyway. He started to speak, his brain searching for words to defuse the situation, and in that instant Floyd backhanded the woman. She went sprawling, landing with a clatter in a stacked display of canned tuna.

Harry growled, discretion forgotten, and lunged forward to grab Floyd by the neck. The proprietor shouted. Ralph, the only one thinking at this point, snatched the woman up and held the gun on her. "Stop now or the little bastard's gonna be in some serious trouble."

Harry stopped. The woman was dazed, he could see that, a bruise already coloring her jaw, but she was otherwise unharmed. Breathing hard with his anger, Harry slowly opened his hand and Floyd stumbled back two steps—and threw a punch. Harry caught the fist an inch from his nose, then made "tsking" sounds of disapproval. "I do believe your associate said to stop."

"He was talking to you, not me!"

Harry heaved an annoyed sigh. "Look, gentlemen, you obviously had business here and it's gotten side-tracked. Perhaps you should let us innocent bystanders go and finish up whatever it was you started?" Rather than observing, as he'd wished, Harry had managed to complicate things hideously. Now he only hoped to salvage what he could.

The proprietor nodded his head in frantic, disgruntled agreement. His low, scratchy voice was that of an aged sailor, used to taking command. "Yeah, take the damn cash. But put the gun away."

"Shut up, old man, and let me think."

Harry considered that an unlikely prospect given that Floyd obviously had very little brain to work with, but he held his peace. He didn't want to rile anyone further, especially the proprietor who looked ready for violence. That would be all he'd need to tip the scales into the never-imagined.

After a considerable amount of time, Floyd nodded. "I think you're a cop."

That straightened his spine. Harry blustered. "Don't be ridiculous."

A low whistle slipped past Ralph's drooping mustache. "Now that you say it, Floyd, he does look like a cop. Check out that coat he's wearing."

Rolling his eyes, Harry said, "You've been watching too much TV. It's drizzling today, therefore I wore a trench coat. I hardly think it's standard dress for the police force."

"Come to that," Ralph added, "you speak damn fancy for someone from these parts."

"I'm not from these parts."

Floyd jutted his chin forward. "Then what are you doing here?"

"I was in the area on business and I remembered I needed to pick up something for my dinner. It's no more complicated than that, I assure you."

"I don't believe you."

Well, hell, Harry thought, eyeing the female who now remained blessedly silent, her eyes downcast. Was he to be done in by a damn coat?

"Just to be on the safe side," Floyd said, grinning, "I think we'll take the boy with us. You call the cops, or try to follow, and I'll kill him."

The situation had gotten completely out of hand. "No, you can't do that."

Ralph tilted his head, his smile taunting. "And why not?"

The woman began to struggle. "I'm not going anywhere with you two! If you want a hostage, take him!" Her slender finger pointed in Harry's direction, disconcerting him for just a moment.

"Somehow I think you'll be easier to handle."

She kicked at Ralph's shin and he neatly sidestepped her, but Harry could see he was nonplussed by her somewhat feminine, awkward reaction. "What the hell?"

She tried to run. Harry was helpless, seeing the gun held steady, knowing any move on his part could get her injured. He wanted to curse at her theatrics, since she only complicated things further.

Floyd made a grab for her, and after his arms circled her chest, he too stopped, stunned. He released her as if burned, his eyes wide, going over her entire body in a single sweep.

"Take off your jacket."

"Go to hell!"

Floyd began to laugh. "I'll be a son of a… He's not a boy at all."

Dryly, for he was tired of the whole thing, Harry muttered, "How very astute of you."

Floyd swung around to glare at Harry, his voice a sneer. "I suppose you knew?"

"Of course."

Ralph drew a deep breath. "I don't like you much, mister."

The woman crossed her arms over her chest. "I don't like him at all."

Of all the nerve! Here he was, trying to preserve her ungrateful slender neck, and she—

"I said take off your jacket. Now. I want to get a better look at you."

Ralph held the gun pointed at her chest while Floyd did his ordering. Gently, buying some time, Harry said, "Better do as they ask."

She glared at him. "Go to hell."

Trying to be reasonable, Harry said, "There you have it, gentlemen. Surely you can see you're wasting your time."

The elderly owner, fairly bristling in outrage, slapped an envelope down on the countertop, offering it like a bribe. "Here's your damn money. Forget the girl and get the hell out of my store!"

"Be quiet, Pops. Now, even if you don't take off the jacket, I won't shoot you. That'd be too messy and would probably ruin the fun of this. And Ralph and I do like a little fun every now and again, don't we Ralph?"

Ralph snickered.

"But if you don't take the damn thing off, and right now, I'll have Ralph shoot *him.*"

The gun dutifully switched so once again it pointed at Harry.

After the briefest of hesitations, the girl shrugged, her chin elevated. "Go ahead, shoot him. What's it to me?"

Harry's chin hit his chest. Why that miserable little… "Now, see here!"

Enjoying himself, Floyd laughed. "So maybe you two aren't working together after all. It doesn't change anything. I want to see what you have under there, girlie. What are you hiding?"

She seemed to calm, and her eyes, which Harry just noticed were a very deep, dark blue rimmed with thick lashes, held steady. "Touch me and I'll kill you."

Both men laughed at that. Even Harry felt a small grin. The girl was so tiny, she couldn't hurt anyone, yet she had her fair share of bravado. He shifted, moving a little closer to the front window. No one noticed.

"Maybe I'll just have you get naked."

The owner was outraged. "You'll do no such thing! I have customers who come in regularly this late. It's not a quiet time. You need to take the money and—"

"I told you to shut up."

Harry moved another few inches toward the window. Between the girl and the store owner, things were far too unpredictable. Was he the only one to realize how grave this situation had become? If he could just get in view and signal Dalton that things had gone wrong, they'd have backup in a matter of moments. Dalton's jewelry store sat directly across the street and was likely next on Floyd's list of stops.

He could see Floyd getting agitated, and besides being stupid and a bully, Floyd could well be trigger-happy. Harry didn't consider it wise to push him too far.

To distract the men from his subtle movements toward the window, he suggested, "You don't want my death plaguing your conscience, sweetheart. Remove the jacket. You can't have anything all that singularly special to hide."

"Huh?"

Floyd wasn't as confused as Ralph. "Yeah, it ain't like all of us men here, even Pops, haven't seen a woman naked before. And I really will have Ralph shoot him. Hell, I'm looking for a reason."

Her brows beetled down and her eyes narrowed. "It's no skin off my nose what you do with him."

At that moment Ralph looked out the window and cursed, then cursed again. "There's a couple of cops over at the jewelry store."

He was distracted for that moment, and Harry started forward, only to be brought up short as Ralph swung around, the gun moving wildly in his hand from Pops to the girl to Harry. "What do we do now, Floyd?"

But Floyd was already moving, snatching the envelope from Pops with a muttered warning, then pulling his own gun. He pointed it at Harry. "Out the back. You're coming with us."

Harry's first thought was, *Thank God, they're taking me instead of the girl.* Not that he was a hero, but he was trained for this, knew how to handle it. But then Floyd grabbed her, too.

Harry's muscles tightened all the way down to his toes. "Stop and think, Floyd. You don't need her. She'll just slow you down."

"If she tries that, she'll be sorry." And he sounded deadly serious, all fun and games over.

"One hostage is more than adequate."

"Be quiet, damn it. I've heard all I want to hear from you. Now move."

With guns at their backs, Harry and the girl were forced to exit out the rear of the store. Was Dalton still waiting for a signal? He wouldn't get one, not now. But why were the police there? Had Dalton somehow known things had gone wrong even without Harry's signal?

There were no answers to be found, and no more time to consider the circumstances as they were led through a light rain to a rental truck left parked in the dark alley. The sun was all but gone, and the mid-June air felt cool and thick. Floyd waved his gun, directing them into the open back of the truck. After hopping in, Harry turned to assist the woman, but she scrambled awkwardly in on her own, disdainfully ignoring his hand.

"You drive, Ralph. I'll ride in here with the little lady." His grin was more of a leer. "You two, into the corner. Sit and keep your mouths shut."

Harry took off his long trench coat and gallantly spread it over the dusty bottom of the empty truck floor, then signaled for the woman to sit. She gave him a furious look and perversely retreated into an opposite corner, slumping down and wrapping her arms around her bent legs. Her position pulled the jean material tight around her thighs and he could see she was slender, her bottom rounded. He forced his gaze to her face.

She looked dejected and in deep thought, but not, thankfully, as frightened as she should be. Her cheek was dark and swollen where she'd been hit, spurring his anger. Harry carefully lowered himself, keeping his eyes alternately on Floyd and the woman.

He hadn't counted on such a predicament when he'd agreed to take care of things for Dalton. He certainly hadn't counted on his attention being diverted by a woman. Any woman, but much less one who was trying to be a man and had an attitude problem. Out of all the female types in the world, headstrong, bossy, controlling women were his very least favorite. He'd had his fill of them long ago.

Yet he couldn't seem to keep his eyes off her.

Dim illumination filled the back of the truck as a small, battery-operated light came on. Ralph pulled the door down from the outside, sealing the three of them in. Harry knew he had to adjust his plans. He couldn't risk the possibility of being taken among the conspirators. The odds wouldn't be good and now he had an outsider to think about.

He eyed the woman again. Why was she involved? He didn't doubt for a moment that she'd been up to something, but his brain couldn't dredge up a single plausible motivation. She hadn't been aware of what she'd blundered into until it was too late, of that he was certain.

Floyd paced the back of the truck, agitated, for a good fifteen minutes while the truck raced farther and farther away from the police. No sirens sounded in the distance; there was nothing but the gentle patter of the rain and the grinding of the shifting truck gears.

"Sit together," Floyd said as he slid down the opposite wall and propped the gun on a knee. "I want to be able to keep you both in my sights."

Harry merely raised a brow at the woman and with a muttered oath, she stood and came to him, then plopped back down. "Bastard," she whispered.

Taken aback, Harry said aloud, and with a good deal of annoyance, "I beg your pardon?"

Suddenly she turned and slugged him in the arm. "This is all your fault! They were paying me no mind until you drew their attention to me."

He rubbed his arm where she'd socked him, more out of indignation than actual hurt, as he eyed her furious expression. "How was I to know Floyd and Ralph were too ignorant to recognize a woman when she presented herself?" Unaccountable female hysterics. He knew he was frowning at her, knew his frown was enough to frighten most grown men, and didn't care one whit. If he scared her, it served her right.

She slugged him again. "I was disguised, you fool!"

He caught her fist and held it, careful not to hurt her, then leaned so close their noses almost touched. Through clenched teeth, he growled, "Obviously not well enough since I picked you out right away."

He heard her swallow. Her eyes shifted on his face, nearly crossing, then finally narrowed in suspicion. "How?"

Knowing he held Floyd's fascinated attention, Harry saw no reason not to explain. In fact, he relished the moment. "Actually, you have a woman's mouth."

He looked at her mouth again—now set in a mulish line—and felt his stomach muscles tighten. He swallowed. *Damn her.* His gaze came back up to hers and stayed there. "You have a woman's bottom," he said with a taunting smile, "despite the baggy jeans. You also move like a woman."

He grinned, pulling her slightly toward him, primed for his last tribute. "And you smell very much like a woman."

The hit was direct; she stiffened and sputtered. "Don't be stupid! I'm not wearing perfume."

He searched her face, amazed by his own reaction. He answered softly. "I know."

Floyd laughed, once again showing his perfect white teeth. "I hadn't looked at her butt." He shrugged. "I thought she was a guy."

Effectively distracted, Harry blinked and moved a little away from her, but maintained his grip on her punching arm. "Yes, well, she afforded me an unimpeded view. And since I'm a...*healthy* male, and I noticed, I knew she had to be female."

"Warped male logic," she accused with excessive heat, and tried to jerk her hand away. He held firm. "So why did you have to make my sex known to the other two idiots?"

"Careful." Floyd was no longer amused.

"That was unintentional." When she huffed, he added, "I was trying to protect you, you ungrateful child."

"I'm not a child."

“How old are you?” Floyd asked. It amazed Harry that Floyd could be so easily diverted.

“None of your damn business!”

The rain began to come down in earnest, sounding like gunshots on the roof of the truck. Gears shifted, throwing Harry slightly off-balance and completely toppling the girl.

Floyd stretched out his legs to brace himself. “I’d say you’re young, but not too young.” He frowned in consideration. “No one’s following us and we have a ways to go yet. Maybe you should just get naked now so I can judge for myself. You look a little too flat for my tastes, but you never know.”

The truck shifted again and they were all three caught scrambling for balance. Floyd crudely cursed Ralph’s driving abilities. The woman landed on her hands and knees and, looking comparable to a rabid dog, she shouted, “For the last time you miserable worm, I am *not* taking anything off!”

Harry silently applauded her bravado, misplaced as it seemed.

Judging by the incredulous look on Floyd’s face, he wouldn’t be patient much longer, and with each mile that passed, their odds of getting out of this unscathed decreased.

They rode steadily uphill. From what Harry could tell they were heading out into the farming area. No residential homes there, and people would be scarce. He had to do something before they covered too much ground.

Harry got an idea. Risky, but he had to make an effort.

He bent a stern look on the woman and demanded,

"Why not? For heaven's sake, your bosom can't be so spectacular that it's worth my life. Don't think I've forgotten you were willing to see me die to protect your dubious modesty."

She looked surprised, frozen, for only a heartbeat. Slowly, she turned to face him, her back to Floyd, her hands on her hips. Then to his shock, she gave him a wink, no smile, just that understanding wink that nearly floored him. At the same time she yelled, "I should have known you weren't really a hero! You're as bad as the other two."

He almost grinned. He did surge to his feet to tower over her. "Almost as bad? I'll have you know they're babies compared to me."

Floyd sputtered, no longer enjoying their show.

The woman leaped at him, the truck veered sharply left and they went down in a welter of arms and legs. Floyd yelled for them to stop, but they paid no heed. Their bodies rolled toward Floyd, twisting and fighting.

Harry made feigned attempts to subdue her while she did her best to bludgeon him with fists and feet. He caught himself alternately chuckling and struggling to keep from getting his nose broken. A sharp elbow in the ribs made him grunt.

Finally, finally Floyd got within reach, determined to end their scuffle. The woman neatly tripped him, and as he stumbled Harry snatched his gun hand and raised it to the roof, then clipped him hard in the chin.

He had very large, solid fists and Floyd went down without a whimper.

Breathing hard, the woman turned to him, stuck

out her hand and said, "Thanks. I was starting to worry. My name's Charlie."

Harry laughed. "Charlie? I suppose that fits as well as anything else. You may call me Harry." He took her hand, noticing how slim and warm her fingers felt, then asked, "I didn't hurt you, did I?"

She snorted rudely as her eyes darted around the truck. "I say we toss his sorry butt out the back. I have things to do and they don't include going…wherever the hell it is we're going. Plus I have no desire to meet their pal, Carlyle."

Harry studied her, again stupefied. "You're not at all upset? You weren't frightened?"

"'Course I was."

She didn't look frightened. She looked determined to drag poor Floyd's body to the edge of the truck bed so she could throw him out. Never mind that it would probably kill him. Wasn't she squeamish about such a thing?

"Don't just stand there, give me a hand here. He's heavy."

Nope, not squeamish. Damn vicious female.

She could at least pretend *some* feminine qualities. He *really* didn't like bossy, overbearing women. Harry crossed his arms over his chest and studied her. "I'm sorry to disappoint you, miss, since you do seem rather set on your course, but I'm not up to killing a man."

"Coward." She heaved and pushed and dragged the body closer to the edge. "Besides, who says he'll die?"

"Now listen here—"

She jerked upright, her face flushed, one thick wisp of glossy black hair now hanging over her right eye.

"No, you listen! You got me involved in this with your damn nosiness and misplaced heroism. This is all your fault. The very least you can do is…is…" Her voice dropped off and she covered her face with her hands. Her shoulders shook.

Harry had the horrible suspicion she might be crying.

Good God. He hadn't wanted her to be *that* female.

CHAPTER TWO

"DON'T YOU TOUCH ME." Charlie stared at the behemoth coming toward her, his expression now bemused. She drew a deep breath, absolutely refusing to give in to her tears, her disappointment. She felt humiliated and decided most of it was his fault. She lifted her chin in the air and said with disdain, "You've done plenty, already."

He held up his hands—very large, capable hands. "I'm sorry. But we don't have time for this." She started to speak, but then he put the gun in the back of his belt, and she wanted that gun, damn him. She didn't trust him, didn't trust anyone at this point, and needed to be able to protect herself. Whoever would have thought a simple Monday could get so dastardly confused?

After all her efforts to move Floyd—and she really did want to toss his body out—it took Harry only a second to heave him to the other end of the truck bed, well out of danger from falling out.

He pulled a knife from his own pocket, stripped off Floyd's jacket, and proceeded to cut it up. He used the cloth strips to tie and gag Floyd in record time.

"Now." He stood and dusted off his hands.

He seemed to have things well in control and that

annoyed her anew. At first, he'd seemed too pretentious to get involved in a scuffle. But once he'd gotten involved, he'd been beyond impressive. It wasn't what she'd expected of him at all.

She was used to being the one in control, the one people came to for help. This man acted as though getting kidnapped and held at gunpoint was a regular part of his workweek. "Now what?"

The truck shifted again and Harry braced himself before giving her a wary, probing look. "You're not going to cry?"

"No." Charlie almost laughed at his look of relief. She hadn't figured him to be the type to fall apart over female tears. She gave him a sideways look. "How about you?"

He paused, stared at her a moment, then raised his brows. "I'm holding up. Completely dry-eyed."

"Good, because I can't stand blubbering men."

He gave her a small smile—a very charming smile actually, and she was beyond shocked that she noticed. She ducked her chin to avoid looking at him.

"We're on an incline," he noted thoughtfully. He picked up his coat from the corner, shook it out, then slipped it back on. "Let me get the door open and see where we're headed."

Charlie bit her lip and mustered up a calm tone. Nothing ventured, nothing gained, she'd always heard. "Since you have the knife, I'll hold the gun."

"No."

She bristled at his blunt reply. "Why not?"

Harry carefully lifted the door a foot or so, then lay on his belly and peeked out. He kept looking at her over his shoulder, as if he expected her to push him out as she'd planned to do with Floyd. It wasn't a bad idea, except that it'd be impossible; he was twice as big as Floyd and very alert. Besides, she didn't particularly want to get that close to him.

His thick brown hair dripped with rain when he pulled his head back inside. "We're near the Wayneswood exit."

Charlie gasped. "Wayneswood!" She hadn't realized they'd traveled quite so far. Her heart started an erratic pounding. "I have to get home."

"Come here." Harry lifted the door a bit more and sat, hanging his legs over the edge. He took the time to overlap his long coat, protecting his trousers as much as possible from the pounding rain.

Once Charlie had settled beside him—accepting whatever his plan might be, because she had none of her own—Harry took her hand. She jerked and had to struggle not to pull away. She didn't want to look like a wilting ninny.

"As the truck travels uphill," Harry explained, "it will have to slow down even more. We can jump out then. Luckily the rain will help conceal us, in the event Ralph glances out his mirror."

"It's too dark for him to see us."

"Perhaps. But a flash of movement might draw his attention and we can't take the chance. So lie low as soon as you can. Just flatten out on the road and we'll hope the truck keeps going. I don't relish the idea of getting into a shoot-out."

"Coward. Give me the gun."

He grinned and shook his head at her. "Valiant

try, but I don't provoke that easily, so you can hold the insults."

He completely ignored the rude sound she made. "Besides, I have experience in handling guns."

His large hand felt so warm, and his muscled thigh pressed hard against her own. She shivered. Hand-holding with an appealing man was definitely not on the agenda for today. For the most part, it hadn't been on the agenda for her entire life. Raising her free hand, she flicked her earring with the flattened bullet attached. "So do I."

"You mean that trinket is real? And here I thought it was part of your costume."

She ground her teeth. He was humoring her, and she wouldn't put up with it. "It's real."

"Hmm." She was very aware of his thumb rubbing along her knuckles, and his close scrutiny. "Whatever could you possibly be involved in that would require a gun?"

To ease her own tension, and defuse his attentions, she said, "I own a bar. Usually it's as dull as dishwater, but one night things got too rowdy and there was gunfire. This particular bullet missed my head by an inch. I decided it was lucky. You?"

He watched her too closely and far too long before he answered. With an elegant shrug he said, "I'm a private investigator." And that was that.

With no more confidences forthcoming, Charlie turned her attention back to the weather. "We're going to be drenched." Already her jeans were wet at the bottom. Her legs didn't extend nearly as far as his, but the rain blew furiously in all directions.

"True enough. However, it's not all that cold yet and the rain helps to mask the noise we make in the truck. I'm grateful to Mother Nature for her assistance."

Charlie made a face at him, though he didn't see it. So calm, so sure of what he planned to do. She wanted to know what was going on, who he was and what he'd been up to, why Floyd and Ralph had taken money from the store owner and what a private investigator had to do with it. Her curiosity was pricked, even though she had no room for other mysteries, other ventures. And now definitely wasn't the time. First she had to get back to Corsville. All her plans, shot through.

"You'd truly have let them shoot me?"

She lifted her face to see Harry studying her. He was so sure of himself, so arrogant. *So damn good-looking.* "Of course," she lied, disconcerted with his stare and just annoyed enough to goad him. She evidently used enough sincerity because his fierce frown reappeared.

Despite his obvious polish, he looked almost demonic with that evil glare. His incredible light brown eyes seemed scorching hot and far too probing, as if he could see inside her. She shivered, then shook off the fanciful thoughts. He was just a man like all the others, bigger, definitely stronger and more eloquent, but still fairly basic and ruled by simple motivations. She could, and would, control him.

His gaze lowered to her chest. "I can't imagine why. You don't appear to have anything all that spectacular to conceal."

He was going for the jugular, but Charlie, having worked in a bar for the past seven years, wasn't even tempted by the familiar baiting. At least her disguise had worked well. She was wearing enough layers to keep her warm and conceal any feminine curves at the same time.

Harry squeezed her hand to regain her attention and his expression was still too intent. "It's not that I haven't been shot before, you understand, but—"

"You should be more careful with your gun."

His eyes darkened, grew hotter. "Not with *my* gun, you little—"

"Listen. Isn't he shifting now? And if I'm not mistaken, the truck is slowing."

Harry gave her a long look of promised retribution. "Yes." He pulled his long legs up against the bed of the truck, bracing himself. "Time for us to go."

Charlie gulped. She looked down at the passing roadway beneath her and winced. True enough the truck had slowed, but the road still flew by them.

"One…"

"Ah, maybe—"

"Two…"

"Wait a second!"

"…three."

"Harry!"

"Go." And with that, he gave her a shove while using his muscular bulk to propel them out. They landed together, their hands still linked, and somehow Harry managed to get beneath her so that he cushioned much of her fall, not that his hard body felt much more giving than the roadway. They tumbled before coming to a dead stop, her on top, their legs tangled together. But just as quickly he rolled to the left, putting her beneath him—and into a very large icy puddle. She sucked in her breath with the shock of it.

His enormous body covered her completely, unmoving, heavy and hard. For the moment she was unable to think with any clarity. It felt as though her teeth had been jarred loose and with his great hulking weight on her, she couldn't draw a deep breath. Rain struck her face, icy cold and stinging against her flesh.

After a moment he lifted his head and looked behind them. Rain ran in rivulets from his hair to her chest. "The truck lights are going around the bend. I do believe Ralph is totally unaware that he's lost his guests."

When she didn't respond, he looked down at her. Charlie stared at his shadowed features in the darkness, struck again by his perfect handsomeness. He seemed such a contradiction. A fancy-pants, but with a lumberjack's body. A gallant hero, but still a bit earthy. She couldn't help but be awed by him, and she hated it.

His head lowered until he blocked the worst of the rain from her face, until she could feel the warmth of his breath on her lips. Her chest constricted the tiniest bit more.

It was absurd! She'd long ago learned the truth about men and their deceptions. But now, at the most unlikely of times, her mind had gone wandering along wayward paths.

Still, she could feel him from breasts to knees, and

he was firm and muscled and *big.* The wet ground and the danger seemed to fade for just a moment.

"Are you all right?"

His voice was low and deep and she wondered at it, even as she felt her belly curl in response to his tone. "I can't breathe."

His gaze dropped to her mouth and lingered for long moments. He closed his eyes and turned his head away. "My apologies." Gingerly, he removed himself, groaning every so often. He offered her a hand and together they sat there in the middle of the road. "I lingered in the hopes of feeling something worthy of my life, but you seem to be all pointy bones."

"What are you whining about?" As she stood, forcing her wobbly legs to support her, she squished. The puddle had seeped beneath her leather jacket to the layers of padding beneath. She was soggy as an old dishrag and probably holding about a gallon of water.

"Your breasts, sweetheart, those magnificent assets that are worth my life."

Oh for pity's sake. "Are you still harping on about that?" She looked around and saw nothing but darkness and endless stretching highway. The rain continued to fall, but luckily there was no traffic. None at all. "Where are we?"

"Yes, I'm still harking. It is my life, after all, though it obviously means little enough to you. And I'd say we're in the middle of the damn road, somewhere between Corsville and oblivion, getting more sodden by the second."

She started walking, leaving him behind. With every step, her boots, two sizes two large and now slick with the rain from the inside out, rubbed against her heels. It wasn't a pleasant feeling and she knew before long she'd have horrible blisters. But what else could she do? Stand around and wait for Ralph to return? Miss the grand performance she'd waited a lifetime to witness?

Probably, her thinking continued, she'd already missed it. That prospect angered her so much, she ignored Harry when he called to her.

"Hold up." His large hand closed on her arm and pulled her to a halt. "We can't just traipse down the middle of the road. In case it's escaped your notice, Floyd and Ralph are not nice men. They could double back looking for us. We need to get out of sight."

True enough, she thought, and nodded. "Yeah, and I suppose that means the woods." She glanced down at his dress shoes. "And with this downpour, it'll be a swamp." Her smile wasn't entirely nice. She started in that direction, and Harry followed. Both sides of the highway were lined with thick trees and little else.

"I can see by your snide expression you expect me to have a certain aversion to mud?"

She kept walking. "I hope not, 'cause big and heavy as you are, you'll sink up to your knees."

Harry turned up his collar and swiped the rain from his face, then shaded his eyes. "With all those trees acting as an umbrella, the ground might not be as saturated as you think."

"You hope."

He ignored her. "And likely the woods abut a farm or some sort of residential dwelling. We could get access to a phone."

She turned to face him. "All right, have you convinced yourself?"

His look of condescension had her grinning again. "I was attempting to reassure you, but I see the effort was wasted. Allow me to lead."

"Sure thing, Harry." At least his big body would block some of the rain. She stumbled along behind him in her heavy, soaked clothes, more miserable than she'd ever been in her life—not that she'd let him know it.

Harry took her arm. "You surprise me. I didn't expect you to be so agreeable."

She hunched both shoulders against the rain and trod onward, pulled along by his hand on her arm. "I'm easy."

His chuckle could be heard even over the rainstorm. "No grand confessions here, if you please. Not when I can't do anything about them."

She tried to stare at him, lost at his words, but he more or less dragged her behind him. "What's that supposed to mean?"

He grinned again; she couldn't see it, but she could hear it. "I appreciate an *easy* woman as much as the next man. But these conditions aren't exactly conducive to seduction."

Appalled, she forgot to watch her step and tripped over a tree root. Harry pulled her upright before her face hit the mud. *Of all the outrageous!...* "I wasn't talking about sex, you idiot!"

They continued a few more feet, and luckily, though the mud did suck at her too-big boots, it was drier, the rain not so blinding, filtered by the many trees.

"That's for the best, I suppose, since I don't as yet know what you have to offer. All I know is that you apparently think it's worth a man's life."

She rolled her eyes and decided to ignore him. Several minutes later, she was wincing in pain.

Harry stopped and turned to frown down on her. Without the rain lashing her face, her eyes were able to adjust to the darkness, and once again she found herself scrutinizing him.

He was by far the biggest man she'd ever seen, tall and thickly muscled, but with grace, if such a thing was possible. And he had the strangest eyes, a shade lighter than his medium brown hair, almost a whiskey color, but bright and thick lashed. Intense, bordering on wicked. When he looked at her, she actually felt it; she'd felt it even back in the store. That's how she'd known he was creeping up on her, intent on telling her something. She hadn't wanted his attention or anyone else's. She'd wanted to be able to concentrate on her first small victory in her private war.

But the plan had fallen through. Damn Dalton Jones.

Harry touched her chin, his fingers gentle. "What's the matter? I expected a tenacious little mug like you to keep up, not lag behind."

She sighed. Showing a weakness to this man, any weakness, went against the grain. He was the one out of his element, yet he hadn't offered a single complaint. But there was no hope for it. "My feet are killing me."

"Ah, I see. Well, since I may want to retain that pleasure for myself—killing you, that is—why don't you explain to me exactly what the problem is?"

The threat didn't alarm her. She was already used to his wry sense of humor and didn't fear him at all. "My boots are too big and now that they're wet they're sliding up and down and I can feel the blisters on my heels. It hurts."

He stared down at her, those eyes of his bright in the darkness, like a wild animal surveying prey, making her shiver with a strange and exciting feeling. But his voice, in comparison, was soft, inquiring. "Why are your boots too large?"

She scowled, attempting to ignore the fluttering in her stomach. "Because I hadn't exactly planned on trudging through the woods in them."

Coming down on his haunches in front of her, he said, "Give me your foot."

"The bottom is covered in mud."

"I'll survive."

He lifted her foot and wiggled her boot, judging the size while ignoring her cry of pain—the jerk.

"I have some knit gloves in my pocket. Do you think you could stuff them into the heels as a little padding?"

Her sore feet loved the idea. "Yeah, thanks."

To her surprise, he picked her up.

To her further surprise, he cursed and hastily set her back down again when streams of rainwater squished out of her clothing to run down his chest. "What in the world are you wearing? You feel like a sodden mop and weigh a ton."

She flushed, both from his initiated gallantry and his censure. She wasn't used to either. No man tried to schmooze her, and they sure as hell didn't try to boss her around. Through gritted teeth, she explained, "I have a few…layers on."

Though she tried to duck away, one large hand reached beneath her jacket and clutched at the material over her rib cage. He squeezed, and it was like wringing out a rag. "Ah. I assume this is why your precious breasts are invisible?"

Overcome with embarrassment, ready to drown him in the nearest available mud puddle, she nodded. "And you can shut your mouth on any more questions because it's none of your damn business anyway!"

"My curiosity grows in leaps and bounds."

"I hope you choke on your blasted curiosity."

He laughed. "Come on, and no, I won't carry you regardless of how your feet hurt."

"I wasn't going to ask!"

He assisted her to a fallen log amidst tons of greenery. Charlie prayed it wasn't poison ivy vines twining everywhere. Harry crouched in front of her again and tugged off the boots.

"I'm sorry. I know it hurts." He pulled the gloves from his pockets, folded one in half and put it inside her sock. "Let's try this and see how it works." After both feet were repaired and her boots back on, she stood.

"How does it feel?"

The gloves were soft and thankfully dry. She took a few careful steps, then smiled. "Much better. Thanks. You're a handy man to have around, Harry."

He opened his mouth and she said, “If ever again I find myself kidnapped and then abandoned in a rainstorm on an empty highway bordering the woods while wearing boots that are too big, why then, you’re just the man I’d want to…”

A chirp sounded, interrupting her teasing, and they both jumped. Harry started to shove her behind him and she laughed. “I appreciate your efforts to save me from my phone, but I think I can handle it.”

He muttered a low curse.

Charlie looked at the display and added her own, more heated and descriptive curses to his.

He tsked her language, then asked, “An important call?”

“My sister. But the battery just died.”

“Will she worry about you and send someone to find you? Did she know where you were today?”

“Yes and no and no.”

“I forgot the order of my questions. Care to clarify?”

Charlie felt like crying. Her poor sister. She hadn’t wanted Charlie to go through with her scheme. She’d said it didn’t matter. And now she’d be sick with worry.

“Charlie?”

It was the first time he’d called her by name and she liked the way his cultured tones made it sound. Everyone she knew called her Charlotte, despite her protestations. Her mother had set the example, and everyone had followed it. Except for her sister, but then her sister loved her.

“I hate to say it, Harry, but no, no one will look for

us. My sister will worry when I don't call her back, but she won't know what to do, or where to check."

She fell silent for a long time, her thoughts dark and troubled, when Harry touched her arm. "Are you all right?"

That particular tone was new coming from him, and it surprised her. No one worried about her. "Of course."

"You're quiet and I don't like it." His hand touched her cheek, her ear. "I don't want you to turn too brooding on me. It unnerves me and won't help anything."

"So distract me."

She saw the flash of his grin before he tried to hide it. "I'd be glad to oblige you, even though you're too short and your assets are still rather questionable, regardless of the high value you've put upon them—"

"Harry."

"—but again, it's just too messy out here. Too much mud and too many weeds I don't recognize and don't want my more private body parts to come into contact with. Plus, I don't know anything about you, why you're dressed as a male, if you're possibly gay—"

"I'm not gay."

"Well, being that we're alone for who knows how long, that's a comfort of sorts I suppose."

Charlie stopped. She turned to face him, her hands fisted. "Will you stop blathering on. And what possible difference could it make to you if I'm gay or not?"

"We may never find civilization again. Or at least, it could take more hours than I'm willing to ponder. Feminine company might come in handy. Think about it. It's almost romantic. All alone in a dark woods, silence all around us. Only my body to keep you warm and protect you."

Though she knew he was being sarcastic, her stomach tingled at his words. She could almost feel his heat.

Men *never* flirted with her, if indeed that's what he was doing. Men threw lewd comments her way on occasion, but she doubted Harry could sound lewd if he tried.

She dredged up her own sarcasm to mask her response. "All we need is candlelight and wine?"

His voice lowered to a sexy rumble. "I never imbibe when with a woman. It dulls the senses, you know, and I prefer to feel everything as it's supposed to be felt."

Despite herself, she drew in a long breath of surprise.

He laughed, then flicked her nose. "Also a flashlight is more economical. Candlelight is far too vague." He pulled a small penlight from his pocket, dangling with his keys from a key chain. "I think I'd like a nice sharp beam of light so I can fully explore things. Especially these mysterious breasts of yours." A skinny beam of light flashed over her shoulders and she jerked around, giving him her back. She saw the light coast lower.

"Harry," she warned.

"Hmm?"

"You're being outrageous." She started walking again, no better reply forthcoming.

"Thank you." When she snorted, he said, "I did manage to distract you, didn't I?"

She paused in her stride, but just for a moment. "I suppose. Now tell me why you were in that store, what a private investigator has to do with Floyd and Ralph. And, oh yeah, who's Carlyle?"

"If I tell will you tell?"

"Kind of like, show me yours and I'll show you mine?"

"I'm willing if you are. Of course, I don't have the added pressure of having to produce something worth a man's life."

Charlie laughed, she couldn't help herself. For several years now, she'd disdained men, her supposed father especially, though she didn't remember the man all that well anymore, the long ago memories and her mother's words mixing together in confusion. Today might have been the day to end the confusion, but everything had gone worse than wrong.

As to the others, the men who sat in her saloon night after night, drinking themselves into a stupor, claiming their wives were responsible or irresponsible or dull. And her mother's old boyfriends, no accounts without a future or the urge to motivate. They were all jerks and users and she had nothing but contempt for them all.

Harry was different. He was outrageous, true, but he made her laugh and his outrageousness wasn't a threat or an insult, but rather a game, a certain charming wit that he employed with skill. She had no fear he would force her, or that he'd actually try to humiliate her as Floyd had. He was big and brave, and something of a hero, a fact she couldn't deny since she'd seen herself the efforts he'd made to try to protect her, even with a gun to his head.

"How old are you, Harry?"

"An odd question, coming out of the blue like that, but why not? As a conversational gambit, it beats the obvious chitchat of weather, and it's as good as any other. I'm thirty-two. And you?"

"Are you a good private eye?"

"Meaning?"

"Do you make much money at it?"

He cleared his throat. "Less of a gambit, but yes, I support myself nicely if that's what you mean."

He was probably expensive, too expensive, but maybe she could figure something out. "How long have you been in the detecting business?"

"Detecting? Well, let's see. About six years now."

"Are you kind to animals?"

He laughed. "There's a purpose to this interview? All right, I'll trust there is. I have two dogs and a cat and they love me or at least they pretend to in order to get me to do their bidding or sometimes when I find a chewed up shoe or a mess in the corner. Does that answer your question?"

"Are you married?"

"Did you have an unemployed dog in mind that you're hoping to foist off on me?"

A small lump of dread formed in her stomach and she struggled to keep her tone light. "So you are married?"

"Divorced, actually, not that it should concern you."

She turned to face him. He was big and gorgeous

and funny and a hero. He might well be the man she needed. God knew her level of success on her own hadn't been anything to boast about, especially given today's incredible fiasco. "I think I like you, Harry."

"Look there," Harry said, pointing over her head and studiously ignoring her last statement. "A building of some sort. I do believe salvation is at hand."

Charlie looked in the direction he indicated. They'd wandered completely through the woods to another road. A small block building, bludgeoned by the rain, sat close to the road, looking indeed like salvation.

Harry, his face averted, plodded onward and Charlie gladly let him lead the way, content to follow behind. To say she trusted him now would definitely be going too far, but he'd made her laugh and that was a huge accomplishment. As to the rest, she'd just have to wait and see.

CHAPTER THREE

"WELL WHAT DO you know, it's an abandoned gas station."

Harry stood in a spot of grease, thankfully out of the rain, and studied their little Eden. He'd had to kick in the door, which had proved remarkably easy given the rotting wood and rusty lock. Likely inhabited by any number of critters, it was still dry and safe and a block against the growing breeze. The rain finally began to taper off, but with that concession came a chill that sank bone-deep. The temperature had dropped by several degrees and he could see Charlie's lips shivering. Nice lips, sort of pouty in a seductive way, especially for a woman who wasn't all that attractive and seemed to have a problem with cordial behavior. Would she have really let them shoot him?

Damn her, he just didn't know.

"How long has it been empty do you think?"

She stood huddled in the middle of the floor, her arms wrapped tight around herself, her knees knocking together, determined not to utter a single complaint, as if admitting to the cold was a weakness. Strange woman.

A growing puddle formed around her. Her hair

had mostly come loose from the rubber band and was starting to curl just the tiniest bit.

"Perhaps from the time they put in the highway some five years ago. This is the old county road. No one travels it anymore, which is, I presume, the reason this particular station closed up."

"The road must still lead somewhere though, to a house or two."

"No doubt, but we won't be finding any help in this storm. You're the picture of misery, half-frozen and too tired to budge. Time to get as dry as possible." He looked at her, saw her staring back wide-eyed, and added, "That means removing your ridiculous costume."

She froze in the process of rubbing her arms, sluicing off more water. "Is that the only tune you know? All right, damn it, I lied. I wouldn't have let them shoot you, not if I could help it. But I knew if they thought I cared, they'd think we were together. I wanted them to take you and forget about me."

Well, that was brutal honesty of a sort. Not quite what he'd had in mind, but… "Believe it or not, Charlie, it was my wish as well." He found a crate, tested it for sturdiness and sat down with a deep groan of pleasure. "I had no desire to be responsible for you, and in fact I could have defused this entire situation if you hadn't screwed things up."

"It was you—"

He held up a hand. "No more bickering. And no more ridiculous modesty. Your belated concern for my safety has nothing to do with anything. I don't want to be lugging a half-dead woman back to town tomorrow, and that's what you'll be if you don't make some effort to warm yourself. It has nothing to do with my curiosity over your precious body parts."

"You have only my welfare in mind?"

"Quit sneering." He felt a smile tug at his lips and firmly repressed the urge to grin at her. "Come now, you must be in your mid-twenties at least. Surely you can't claim all that much modesty. I promise not to be impressed no matter what you unveil."

She looked ready to strike him, so he quickly added, "I'll make the grand sacrifice. My coat is still fairly dry on the inside, given that it's made for this weather and water repellent. You can wrap up in it after you've gotten out of your wet clothes."

She chewed her lips, thinking of heaven knew what, and finally shaking her head. More hair slipped free and clung to her forehead and cheeks. She didn't look like a boy now; she looked like a drowned rat. A wide-eyed, nervous rat. "No."

"What if I insist?"

She went stiff as a poker. "Insist all you want! I'm not taking anything off and I'm not—" Her voice dwindled into a very ratlike squeak when he started toward her. "Don't you dare touch me!"

"You're being unreasonable, Charlie. I hadn't thought you the type to submit to hysterics, but what else can it be? You can't be comfortable and if there was enough light to see, I have no doubt you'd be a pale shade of blue." He caught her arm and she tried to jerk away. He easily caught the neck of her jacket and stripped it off her, despite her efforts and the volume of her rank curses. The woman had the vocabulary of a sailor. "It's too dark in here for close observation anyway. What exactly do you suppose I'll see?"

"You'll see nothing because you're going to take your hands off me right now."

That calm tone of hers should have given him a warning, but he was too intent on forcing her to accept his benevolence. He was wet also, yet he'd offered her his coat, which would leave him with only his dress shirt and undershirt. Contrary to popular female opinion, men were not impervious to the cold. She should be thanking him, not cursing his ancestors. Why were women always so stubborn?

And then he felt the gun press into his ribs. He almost laughed. She'd done nothing but surprise him since he'd first spotted her. It was entertaining when it wasn't so annoying.

"Ah, you're fast. Don't tell me. You were a pickpocket once, weren't you, as well as a saloon girl? No, don't lie to me."

"I wasn't going to lie! I'm not a *saloon girl,* I'm the owner, and no, I was never a pickpocket. It's just that you weren't paying attention." She pressed the gun harder against him. "And you're *slow.*"

In the next instant he jerked up her wrist and snatched the gun from her hand. In the process, it fired, the sound loud and obscene, sending particles of ceiling plaster to rain down on their heads. They both heard a flurry of scurrying from around them.

The shock left them still as statues. "Good grief, what was that?"

Harry was aware of her uneasiness, even her breath held. "Rats. And at the moment, they're the least of your worries." This time he stuck the gun a good distance inside his pants, then dared her with a look to try retrieving it. "Now."

She quickly regained her aplomb. "You're lucky you didn't shoot me!"

"I'd say you were luckier, being that you would have been the one shot." He took a firm step toward her.

"All right." She held up her hands. "Give me your coat, then turn your back and close your eyes."

"No." The silly woman persisted in her belief that he was an idiot.

"You're not going to watch, Harry."

"In case it's escaped your notice, it's exceedingly dim in here. What miserly moonlight there is can hardly penetrate the rain and the dust on the broken windows. I can't see my own hand in front of my face." That was an exaggeration; he could see just fine, but she didn't need to know that.

"I'll give you the coat, and if you'll promise not to do anything else foolish, I'll try to find a propitious spot for us to nest in until this storm completely blows over."

She curled her lip at him. "Your diction is astounding."

"Thank you." He handed her the coat and turned away, kicking debris with his feet as he carefully walked.

"It wasn't a compliment!" she called out, her voice heavy with sarcasm. "You're what the regulars at my bar would call a *fancy-pants*."

"I'm wounded to my soul by their censure." The station stunk, literally. He could smell oil and rotting vegetation and heaven only knew what else. He preferred not to ponder the possibilities. He retrieved his tiny flashlight, flicked the light around in a wide arc, avoiding Charlie's dark corner, then settled on an area that would have to do.

"I've found a spot that's fairly dry and empty, and there's an old car bench seat. I suppose it'll support us and keep us off the cold cement floor."

He heard a "plop" and knew she'd dropped part of her disguise. He smiled in the darkness. "What exactly did you have on under your shirt?"

"Some old linen, pinned in place." Another plop. "Why don't you sit on the bench just to make sure nothing else is nesting there. I'm not keen on sharing with rats."

"I'm sure they feel the same about you." He kicked the seat with his foot. Nothing happened. Holding the flashlight in his teeth, he lifted one end and dropped it. And then did it again. "Nothing but an abundance of dust."

Another plop.

He turned off the flashlight before the temptation became too overwhelming. His eyeballs almost itched with the urge to peek. "Exactly how many layers did you have on?"

"Enough to get rid of any lumps or bumps, which was easy since my femaleness isn't all that noticeable anyway."

Temptation swelled. He looked toward her voice, but could only see a vague outline. He felt cheated and stared harder, but still only got shifting shadows and a stinging sense of guilt.

A wet length of toweling slapped up against his face. "You can use that to wipe off our nest."

Grumbling, he did as instructed then turned to her again. "I beg to differ. About your femaleness, I mean." He noticed her voice shook when she talked, more from cold now than anything else. His concern doubled. "If you'll recall, I knew right away that you were a female sort of person."

"I don't understand that. No one else noticed."

He could hear the chattering of her teeth. Definitely the cold. "Come here, Charlie. Let me warm you."

Not a sound. Not a movement. The irritating little twit.

"Oh for pity's sake." Though he tried to hide it, his irritation came through. "Charlie? Come on, I've proven myself by now, haven't I? We may have the entire night ahead of us, with nothing but the rain and the rats for company. Regardless of how stoic you might be, I don't mind admitting I'm cold. Let's at least make the attempt to get warm."

She took a step out of the shadows and he could see her vigorously rubbing her hair with her discarded shirt. His coat covered her from neck to ankles, enormously big on her petite frame. "What, exactly, did you have in mind?"

"A little cuddling." He smiled, already feeling the anticipation which was surely odd considering she really wasn't all that attractive and she had a penchant for insulting him with every breath. It was a unique feeling for him, being insulted by a woman. Even his ex-wife had refrained from that, at least until the very end. Before that, she'd been cajoling and sweet, even as she tried to manipulate him. Unaccountably, Charlie's bluntness piqued his interest. There was no understanding the workings of male hormones. "I'm willing to sacrifice myself by being on the bottom.

You can sit on my, ah, lap and with our combined body heat we should stay warm enough."

"I don't know."

Her hair was a tousled dark mass of shining black, some locks hanging down to her eyes, others flipping around her ears. She looked almost cute, in a disheveled, bedraggled way. "Charlie, did you take everything off?" Now *his* voice shook. Damn it.

"No, of course not! My jeans are wet, but that can't be helped. I did remove those muddy boots, though, so you don't have to worry about them."

"My gratitude knows no bounds."

"What about you?"

He cleared his throat. "Just damp around the collar. Except for my pants, which are soaked."

"Leave them on."

He grinned again, but kept his tone mild. "I have no intention of lacerating your dubious sensibilities by strutting around naked. Now come here."

The stillness was palpable.

Harry sighed. "If you're hesitating because I said you smelled nice, well, keep in mind I feel the same about new leather and burnt sugar, but neither has ever inspired me to levels of uncontrollable lust."

He heard her grousing and mumbling, heard her shifting, then she moved a little closer. And damned if he didn't catch a whiff of her elusive scent again, now mixed with the dampness of the rain and the fresh outdoors. With his eyes closed, he breathed deeply.

"Why burnt sugar?"

She'd sidled close, near enough that he could see her clearly, could reach out and touch her. He did, his fingers first landing on her narrow shoulder, and when she didn't bolt, he let them slide down to her slender wrist. His coat sleeves had been rolled up but still hung down to her fingertips. She'd buttoned up all the way, but the coat was so big on her, the neckline hung disturbingly low. All in all, she looked adorable in his coat, all wet and stubborn and mulish. *Only, he didn't like stubborn, mulish women.*

He sat on the bench and tugged her down to his lap, giving her a moment to get used to the feel of that and giving himself a chance to calm his stampeding heart.

Ridiculous. There was absolutely no reason to react so strongly to her. She was just a woman, caught up in the same bizarre circumstances as he. Masculine interest hadn't prompted his offer to share body warmth. No, his motives were altruistic, they were—

"Harry?"

He could feel her breath on his throat when she spoke, feel her shivers. His awareness of her as a woman was acute. Slowly, wary of getting slugged at any moment, he wrapped his arms around her. "A friend of my father's used to make me this candy. He called it burnt sugar, and I suppose that's exactly what it is. He puts plain white sugar in a small buttered metal dish, melts it in the oven until the edges are dark brown, then lets it cool and harden. It's sort of like a sucker without the stick, and has a different taste since it isn't flavored at all. As a child, I forever had sticky fingers from eating burnt sugar."

She relaxed slightly, her body settling more closely into his and he could feel her heartbeat, could hear her breathing. "I can't imagine you as small, or with sticky fingers. You're so big now, and you seem so… fastidious."

"Yes, well, we all must grow up." Hoping to catch her off-guard, he asked, "What were you doing there, Charlie? And why the cross-dressing costume?"

She turned her face inward, doing the cuddling he'd suggested. Moments before he'd been cold and uncomfortable. But now he felt abundantly warm, almost too much so. He wouldn't be at all surprised if his damp clothing started to steam.

She was a very soft, very feminine weight nestled into his lap. And he really did enjoy her scent; something about it hit him on a gut level, very basic and primitive, forcing him to react in spite of himself. Overall, it was the kind of thing men fantasized about. Except for the kidnapping and the irritating storm.

"I was there to spy on someone."

He hadn't expected that, and the immediate conclusion he came to had a volatile effect on him. He stiffened, his voice sounding cold and hard even to his own ears. "A lover? A husband?"

She chuckled. "Nah, I have no interest in either of those, thank you very much." There was a heavy silence, then she added, "I suppose you could say I was actually spying for someone else."

"A friend?"

"Mmm. I didn't want anyone to recognize me."

"Well, you blundered into a mess and now I have to rescue you."

"Just like a fabled hero?" Her hair tickled his chin as she shook her head. "Not likely. I can take care of myself."

"I'm the first one to admit I'm not hero material. But I am bigger and stronger and I know the situation, whereas you're small and weak—"

She punched him in the stomach and he wheezed, then immediately flattened her against him so she couldn't retaliate further.

"—and you obviously don't know what you've gotten yourself into."

"Okay, so tell me. Who are these clowns who grabbed us and what are you going to do about it?"

He twisted to look down at her, and she lifted her face at the same time. Their noses bumped. Harry's thoughts scattered, and he struggled to bring them back to order. It wasn't easy.

"First I'm going to get you home and safe and out of my way. Then I'm going to get Floyd and Ralph, on my own ground, and pound some sense into them." He hesitated, pondering his own words and the probability of enacting them. "Maybe. I still have to weigh my personal vendetta against a promise I made to get them both legally stopped."

"A promise to who?"

"The friend who makes burnt sugar. He owns a shop in the area. Floyd and Ralph work for Carlyle as petty extortioners, and my friend refuses to pay. He's been threatened, and I don't take kindly to that sort of thing."

"What had you planned to do today?"

As she asked it, her gaze dropped to his mouth and one small hand opened on his chest. She looked vaguely confused, as if dealing with unfamiliar feelings. Harry understood completely, since he was in a similar predicament.

He forgot to answer her for the longest time. He could feel that small palm, warm and still, like a brand against his flesh. It aroused him, and surely that was insanity.

"Harry?"

He forcibly shored up his flagging wits. "Today I was just sizing things up." He touched her cheek where the bruise was visible, along with a little swelling. His tone lowered with regret. "Damn, I'm sorry you got hit."

"I've had worse."

Given her backbone and courage, he didn't doubt she'd led a hard life, but hearing of it made him want to hold her closer, to protect her. They stared at each other while Harry's fingers gently coasted over the bruise. If for no other reason than this, Floyd deserved to feel his fist, Harry decided.

"Answer me something, Charlie." His hand cupped her cheek and she didn't protest. He smoothed wet tendrils of hair away from her face, marveling at how soft her skin felt. Surely all women were as soft, but he couldn't seem to remember.

She didn't move away and he felt his heartbeat thud, felt his muscles harden. "Did you mean what you said about not being interested? Not at all?"

Her gaze met his, so close. "Interested in what?"

"A lover."

"I don't know." She frowned, then looked at his mouth again. "I've never given it much thought."

He drew a slow breath, filling himself with her scent. "And now?"

She looked away, then back up again with a sort of daring grin. "I admit I'm thinking about it."

She was so bluntly honest, he smiled. Charlie might be demanding, but she would never be manipulative.

Her arms looped around his neck. "You know, Harry, this is turning into a romantic moment after all, isn't it?

Harry gently kissed the bruise on her cheek, his lips just grazing her skin, his nose nuzzling her temple. "Hmm. And I don't even have my flashlight out."

She chuckled. "I'm starting to like you, Harry."

It was the chuckle that did it, low and husky. He turned his face and she met him halfway and their mouths met, open and hot and devouring. *Oh damn,* Harry thought with some surprise. He hadn't expected this, hadn't thought she'd be this way, avaricious and hungry, clinging to him as if she'd never been kissed before or was starved for it. He was the starving one, and the hunger had come on him so suddenly.… It turned him on so much he groaned.

Sweeping one large hand down her back, he fondly cupped the adorable backside he'd admired earlier. Soft and sweet, the feel of her made him want more.

But before he could allow things to progress, he felt he owed her a measure of honesty. "Charlie, honey, listen a minute. I have to tell you something."

Her eyes narrowed. "Getting discriminating on me again, Harry?"

He swallowed hard. Did she actually think he'd want to back out when he was shaking with lust? Not likely. "I'm not interested in a romantic relationship."

She blinked at him in surprise. "Okay." She tried to kiss him again, her hands clutching his shoulders.

He held her back with one hand, putting breathing space between them. "Charlie, I can't make you any promises."

She blinked twice, then frowned at him. "What are you talking about?"

She looked so confused he wanted to shake her. He realized his hand still held her bottom and he gave her a gentle squeeze, then shuddered with the effects of that caress. Damn, he wanted her. *Insane.*

"Marriage." He cleared his throat and managed to explain. "All those questions earlier. You were hinting about marriage and I want you to know, my plate is full right now. I have no intentions of getting even mildly involved with a woman."

One side of her mouth quivered, and she bit her lip. *Oh God, don't let her cry,* Harry thought, his body so tense he hurt, his mind feeling like mush.

She covered her mouth with her hand and a chuckle escaped. Harry frowned. In the next instant, her chuckles turned to uproarious laughter. "You," she said between hiccups, "thought I was sizing you up for marriage material?" She laughed some more, not dainty feminine laughter. No, this was boisterous, unrestrained hilarity. "Good grief, I hardly know you!"

Disgruntled with her misplaced mirth and his unabated lust, Harry demanded, "Then why all the questions?"

"Actually, if you must know," she said, trying to get herself under control and failing miserably, "I had thought to *hire* you."

"Hire me for what, damn it?"

"To find out more information on my father." She wiped her eyes, perched primly on his lap with her midnight hair hung over one eye giving her a seductive look. "That's what I was doing there today. Spying on him. I haven't seen him in almost eighteen years."

Harry wanted explanations and he wanted them now. Who was her father? And why the long separation?

His arms were still around her, one hand still splayed over perfect buttocks. When she smiled, her dark blue eyes seemed to smile, too.

He wished now that he'd kept his big mouth shut.

She traced his mouth with a delicate fingertip. "You really are a wonderful kisser, Harry."

Hope rose that he might be able to salvage this debacle, but then car lights hit the window of the gas station, and every thought other than protecting her slipped from his mind.

He shoved her off his lap and onto the dirty floor. "Stay there and don't make a sound." In the next second he was gone.

CHAPTER FOUR

CHARLIE SAT ON the floor, her backside bruised, her lust squelched. Where had Harry gone? On hands and knees she crawled to the window to peek out. Just as her head lifted, Harry snatched it back down.

Hissing close to her ear, he asked, "Is there a particular reason you want to offer up your brains for target practice?"

"Where did you go?" Her words were muffled against his fly, and while there, she noticed he'd suffered quite a reaction to their kisses. Heaven help her, the man was hard.

"I was surveying our options, of course. Now be still."

She quit squirming and sighed. Having her cheek pressed to an erection, her nose smashed against a muscled thigh, with no hope of any loveplay, seemed like a terrible waste, especially since this was the first time in ages she'd been interested in such a thing. "Do you have any suggestions?"

"Yes, as a matter of fact, I do."

At that moment, Floyd called out. "You might as well come on out of there!"

Charlie whispered, "He certainly sounds furious."

"Yes, well, maybe he knows you planned to toss him off the truck."

"Ha! I think it's probably his aching jaw where you slugged him that has the bastard madder than hell."

He tsked. "Your language is a disgrace."

"You have my face buried in your lap, but you're worried about my language?"

Harry groaned, and his fingers contracted on the back of her head. "This is no time for your unregulated tongue, so keep quiet if you please."

"We know you're both in there!" Floyd growled. "There wasn't no place else for you to go. Now come on out and maybe we won't shoot you. We'll just take you to Carlyle."

Harry kept one large hand mashed against her head, forcing her to stay low, as he yelled out, "I have your gun, remember? Come anywhere near here and I'll be obliged to put a bullet in you! At the moment, the thought doesn't distress me at all."

Curses exploded from outside the garage.

"He really doesn't like you, Harry."

"The feeling is mutual, I assure you."

Unable to help herself, she nuzzled slightly into his lap. Harry jerked away. "Keep your head down, and no, don't say a thing. In case you've failed to notice, we're in something of a situation here. I need to keep my wits collected." When she dutifully remained silent, he nodded. "Good. Now, I'm going to draw them to the back of the garage. There's a door back there, and when they think we're escaping out the back, we'll make a run for the truck. Understand?"

He was all business, his eyes bright, his voice low, his body hard, poised for action. He impressed the hell out of Charlie, being so urbane one minute and so lethal the next.

"How can I help?"

"By not getting yourself killed. Now, do you understand everything I told you?"

"I'm not an idiot."

He sighed. "I suppose I'm to take that as a yes." He started to move away, then suddenly leaned forward and grabbed her by the neck. His mouth landed on hers, hot and hard, for the briefest second, and then he disappeared into the shadows. He managed to move without making a sound, causing her admiration to grow.

Charlie plopped down onto her backside and waited. She didn't like waiting. She felt ineffectual and cowardly and the feelings didn't rest well with her at all. She was used to taking action, to controlling things.

Floyd evidently didn't like waiting, either. "I'm losing patience!" he shouted. "I'll give you to the count of ten, then we're coming in and shooting any damn thing that moves. Carlyle would rather have you dead than loose."

Hurry up, Harry, she thought, listening as Floyd started a loud, monotonous recitation of his numbers.

Glass shattered at the back of the garage, followed by the sound of running footsteps. Cautiously, Charlie peeked over the edge of the window above her head. Floyd and Ralph stood frozen in the moonlight for a single heartbeat, then they cursed and ran hellbent for the back of the garage.

She waited until they were out of sight before she slithered toward the door Harry had kicked in, proud of the fact that she, too, made no discernible noise. She'd barely edged outside before a rough, hot hand clamped over her mouth and a steely arm closed tight around her waist. She would have panicked if it hadn't been for Harry's height, assuring her he was the one who'd accosted her.

Without struggling, she got dragged to the truck and roughly thrust inside through the driver's door. Harry slid in beside her.

Seething, Charlie restraightened the huge coat she wore, holding the throat closed with a fist, and leaned close to whisper, "What? You thought I'd refuse your rescue and opt to stay with my buddy Floyd? Is that why you felt you had to manhandle—"

"No keys, damn it."

She squeaked. "What do you mean, no keys? How the heck are we going to—"

He thrust the gun into her hand. "Watch out for the two stooges while I hot-wire this barge."

Bemused, Charlie looked down at the gun in her hand, then to where Harry bent low beneath the dash, then dutifully out the window.

Hmm. There was something innately sexy about a man who could hot-wire.

It took him mere seconds. He'd just managed to fire the engine when Floyd and Ralph came stumbling back around the garage, their curses so hot Charlie's ears felt singed, and that was surely impressive given she'd been raised hearing curses all her life. The two men literally jumped up and down in rage as gravel and mud slung off the spinning tires, embellishing Harry's daring getaway. Ralph fired, and Charlie thought she heard a bullet or two hit the side of the truck bed, but it didn't slow Harry. She waited, wondering if, because of the gunshot, he'd feel it necessary to put her head back in his lap.

She was slightly disappointed when he didn't.

Harry didn't say a word, concentrating instead on finding the main road and figuring out how to turn on the lights, the wiper blades, the heat. Charlie was just about to tuck the gun into her pocket when he retrieved it from her without a word.

She knew a struggle for the gun was useless, and she scowled. "Now what?"

Harry rubbed the back of his neck, glanced at her, his gaze moving over her from head to toe, then cursed slightly. "I think we'll abandon this truck outside town. No sense in taking a chance that Carlyle or one of his cronies will recognize it and want to pull us over. We'll grab a taxi to my apartment."

"Why your apartment?" Not that she'd complain. Her curiosity over Harry grew more rampant with every moment she spent in his company. From his place, she could call her sister, and then maybe they could finish what they'd started at the garage. She glanced down at Harry's lap, but the interior of the cab was too dark to tell if he still reacted to their little interlude. She liked it a lot that she'd turned him on. In all her life, she'd seldom had the opportunity, or the desire, to indulge in lust. But with Harry, well, she was more than a little intrigued.

"I think we need to talk, to figure out what we're going to do."

Charlie sighed, then carefully ventured a suggestion. "I don't think we should call the police."

Harry stilled for a moment, smoothly switched gears, then nodded. "Okay, I'll bite. Well, not really, not unless you wanted me to, and then it'd be more appropriate to say nibble—"

"Harry."

"Why don't you want to contact the police?"

"Because I can't see any way for you to explain this without telling them I was there, dressed as a guy, spying. And I'd just as soon no one knew about that."

"I can see where that would be a tale you'd hesitate to broadcast. But as it so happens I don't relish involving the police, either."

"And your reasons are?" When he only slanted her a look, she poked him in the side. "No way, Harry. I told, now it's your turn."

"You told very little, actually."

"I'll get into more detail once I'm warm and dry and have time to reason a few things out."

"I suppose that'll have to appease me."

"Give it up, Harry."

He didn't want to, she could tell that. He gave her a grudging look that almost made her smile. "I promised my friend I wouldn't involve any of the other people in the area. They're older proprietors, like Pops, and they aren't excessively fond of the police right now."

"You mean Pops—the guy who runs the store we were in before Floyd decided to play kidnapper?"

"That's right. They've contacted the police a few times in the past over other situations—loud music, loitering, things like that. They were pretty much told that since they're in a run-down, high-crime area, they have to expect a certain amount of that sort of thing. The police offered more surveillance, but the elders didn't think that was enough. They were determined to take matters into their own hands, which of course would be dangerous."

Even as she nodded, Charlie wondered if her father was one of the men being bothered. It seemed likely. She felt a moment's worry before she firmly squelched it. Her father deserved nothing but her enmity, and that's all he'd ever get. He'd never been there when she needed him most, but she'd found him now, and he could damn well pay. What she wanted from him—financial assistance to get her sister through college—had nothing to do with emotions or family relationships.

The rain started again, and they settled into a congenial quiet. Harry reached over and pulled her to his side. It wasn't quite as nice as his lap, but he was warm and firm and secure, and she took comfort from his nearness, though she'd never have admitted it.

As they neared the outskirts of town, Harry nudged her with his shoulder. "It's regretful things got interrupted back there."

"Yeah."

He cleared his throat. "If you're interested…"

"Yeah."

Laughing, Harry pulled the truck up to the curb and turned the engine off. He tilted Charlie's face up and kissed her softly. "There's nothing coy about you, is there?"

She raised a brow. "Should I pretend I'm not interested? That'd be dumb, Harry, since I don't get interested all that often."

Harry fought a smile, and lost. "So you're telling me you're not easy after all?"

Charlie snorted. "Most of the men that frequent my saloon could tell you I'm usually damn difficult."

"No! You? I'll never believe it."

Charlie smacked his shoulder. "Smart-ass."

Chuckling, Harry said, "Wait here. I'll call us a taxi."

He left the truck and trotted to a pay phone across the street. Charlie watched him go, admiring his long-legged stride, the way he held his head, the natural confidence and arrogance that appeared as obvious as his physical attributes. He was a strange man in many ways, his lofty wit and cultured diction in opposition to his easy acceptance at being kidnapped, shot at and holed up in a greasy garage. He'd stolen a truck as easily as if such a thing were a daily occurrence. Though it was apparent to Charlie he'd led an expensive, well-bred life, he hadn't so much as sniffed at her admission to owning a saloon, or the fact that for the most part, she was an obvious gutter rat, born and bred on the shadier side of life.

And he didn't hesitate to call her Charlie.

Most of the regulars at her saloon called her what she told them to, wary of getting on her bad side. They weren't, however, great examples of masculine humanity, so their concessions counted for very little. She had a feeling Harry, with all his grins and arrogance and stubbornness, was a true hero, even if he'd chosen to deny it.

He watched her from the phone booth while he placed the call, alert to any possible danger. With a smile, Charlie turned away to view their surroundings. They were near a park, but not one she recognized. Of course, she had little time or interest for dawdling in parks, so that wasn't a surprise.

Seconds later, Harry returned. His wet dress shirt clung to his upper torso, showing a large, smoothly muscled chest and shoulders, and even through his undershirt, she could see a sprinkling of chest hair. The shirt opened at the collar and his strong throat was wet, a couple of droplets of rain rolling down into the opening. Charlie swallowed.

His damp hair stuck to his nape and one brown lock hung over his brow. His light brown eyes, framed by spiked eyelashes, darkened as he watched her inspect his features. Harry leaned back on the seat and the corners of his mouth tipped in a slight smile. "Have I sprouted horns?"

Charlie shook her head. "You're a real looker."

One brow lifted as his smile turned into a grin. "Thank you."

"I bet you hear that a lot."

"Seldom enough to keep me humble."

She choked on a laugh. "There's not a humble bone in your big body, Harry, and I bet women fawn over you all the time."

He didn't deny it. He did tilt his head to look at her, then slowly reached out to touch the top button of his coat, where it rested low on her chest. "I don't suppose you'd want to pass the time by appeasing my curiosity over these mysterious breasts of yours, would you?"

Charlie gaped. She should have been used to his boldness by now, especially since his brain did seem to stay focused on her upper assets—or lack thereof. "You expect me to just flash the coat open for your entertainment?"

He shrugged, shifted to his side to face her. His finger trailed over the deep V at the neck of the coat, tickling her skin, raising her body temperature by several degrees. "I'll admit I'm vastly interested, and while you're indulging in more temperate humors, I thought this might be the ideal time. Besides, what else have you got to do right now other than model for my delectation?"

He certainly had a way with words. And his gentle touch and tone, compared to the coarseness she was accustomed to, was a major turn on. But she shook her head. "I'm not putting on a show for you, Harry, so forget it."

Harry fought his grin. "Ah, well, you do like to vex a man, don't you?"

Before she could answer, headlights flashed against the windshield of the truck. For a second there, Charlie panicked, thinking somehow Floyd and Ralph had found them. But then Harry leaned forward, gave her a swift kiss, and said, "Our ride is here. Faster than I'd anticipated, but evidently the cabbie was in the area. Come on. Other than seeing your elusive bosom, dry clothing is the most appealing thing on my mind."

The cabbie, a seasoned veteran, made no comment on her lack of shoes or bedraggled appearance, much to Charlie's relief. Harry somehow managed to be imperious, despite their circumstances, and the driver gave him due deference.

Harry held her hand all the way to his apartment, which wasn't all that far, taking a mere fifteen minutes. But it was long enough to make her edgy, to make her ponder several different things, mostly how enticing the thought of having an affair with him seemed.

He paid the cabbie, refusing to let her dig money from her own pocket to pay half. In fact, he seemed insulted by the very idea. Charlie shrugged. She needed her money, and if he wanted to play the gallant, that was fine by her.

Harry led her to the first floor of an exclusive complex, and Charlie wasn't at all surprised to see, once he'd gotten the door unlocked, that his apartment wasn't an apartment at all, but rather an expensively decorated, immaculate and beautiful town house. She couldn't help herself, she felt intimidated.

Then the barking began, startling her half out of her skin.

Harry relocked the door and switched on more lights. A miniature collie and a small, stocky, mixed-breed mutt darted out around a large leather sofa. The collie's entire body quivered with happiness at the sight of Harry and he laughed as the dog jumped up and down in near berserk joy. The mutt, a little more subdued, ran circles around Harry and howled. Harry immediately knelt to rub the dog's scruff. He glanced up at Charlie. "Meet Grace and Sooner. Grace has been with me a long time, but Sooner has only been in the family a couple of years."

She stared at the dogs, who stared back, one sitting on each side of Harry, heads tilted, expressions alert, like sentinels guarding the king from a scourge. She grinned, and the dogs seemed to grin back.

"I can understand the name Grace, since she looks so refined. But Sooner?"

Harry shrugged. "He'd 'sooner' be one breed as another."

"Ah."

Harry patted the dogs. "She's entirely acceptable, guys, so you may as well present her with the royal treatment."

Once he said it, both dogs trotted over to sniff her, lick her hand, bark a few times in a doggy greeting. Then they each gave Harry a quizzical look, as if her presence made no sense at all, and retreated. Grace leaped up to lie on the sofa, resting her head on a black and beige motif throw folded over one end. Sooner went over to flop onto the floor in front of a white stone electric fireplace. He gave a loud groan and closed his eyes.

The town house was very sleek, and as Charlie looked around, she saw marble-topped oak end tables, bare wood floors with thick area rugs, and windows with streamlined blinds rather than curtains. All in all, she thought the room was gorgeous and suited Harry to a T.

She was afraid to move. Her bare feet were muddy, grime from the garage between her white toes. Water still dripped from her hair, her nose, Harry's coat. She felt like a flea-ridden squirrel turned loose in a palace.

No wonder the dogs thought her curious.

"Make yourself at home. I'll locate us some dry clothes. Would you like something to drink?"

All the social niceties. Charlie shook her head, fighting the urge to fidget. "I'd really like to call and check in with my sister, if you don't mind."

He went to a desk situated in front of a long window that looked out over the backyard. It was partially separated from the living room by a wide arched doorway. Charlie could see oak file cabinets and office equipment. She heard Harry curse.

"What's wrong?"

"The electricity evidently went out with the storm. My answering machine is dead, meaning I've missed any calls that may have come in."

"Were you expecting an important call?"

"Several, actually." He walked back to her. "You'll have to use the phone in my bedroom. The portable is out."

His bedroom?

Harry crossed his arms over his wet chest and frowned at her. "Surely that look doesn't mean you're afraid of me? Not the woman who challenged Floyd and Ralph, the woman who did her best to bait two miscreants. I assure you, you're safe enough with me."

"Me, fear you? Ha!" She was more afraid of herself at the moment. She felt like tossing his gorgeous self to the floor and having her way with him. But she would never do such a thing in front of the innocent dogs. "It's just that my feet are dirty. The dogs are cleaner than I am. I don't want to track mud all over the place."

Harry looked down, took in her bare feet and growled. "I forgot you'd removed those hideous boots. You could have cut yourself on something when we ran for the truck. I can't believe I didn't notice sooner. Well, actually I can, given my attention was somewhat fractured by other things, but not so much so, I shouldn't have noticed naked feet. I am a P.I. after all, usually very alert to small details."

"Uh, Harry?"

He still stared at her feet. "Hmm?"

"The phone?"

"Oh, yes, of course. Okay, no help for it. I suppose I'll have to play the martyr."

"No! Don't you dare… Harry, put me down."

"You're really very slight, now that we've rid you of your ridiculous waterlogged costume." As he made his way up a flight of carpeted stairs, he looked down at her, their noses almost touching, and the smile he gave her made her catch her breath. His gaze dipped lower, and Charlie glanced down to see the coat had slipped some and she had a modest amount—all she possessed really—of cleavage showing. She tried to make a grab for the coat, but then Harry lowered her, and she realized she was in a taupe and black tiled bathroom, more specifically, he stood her in the black tub.

"Don't move. I'll play lady's maid and get you a towel and dry clothes and you can clean up just a bit before we progress any further."

Progress to what, she wondered? Another part of his home, or another level of intimacy? She knew where her vote would be, but she didn't say so. She did need to clean up, and dry clothes sounded heavenly.

Harry reappeared with two plush white towels, a long polo shirt, and silky boxer shorts. He grinned as he laid the items on the marble vanity. "The thing is, you're something of a squirt, so nothing I have would be small enough to fit you. However, I wear a "tall" so my shirt should make do for a dress, only I couldn't bear the thought of you being naked beneath it, not if you expect me to exhibit my more civilized tendencies, so I determined the boxers would serve as well as anything." He lifted his hands. "I'm fresh out of ladies' panties."

She drew a blank, except to ask, "You wear silk boxers?"

"Actually no. They were a gift from a friend."

"Ah."

He headed for the door. "Go ahead and wash up. You can hang the coat on the back of the door and I'll take care of it later. There's a hamper under the cabinet where you can stick your muddy jeans. I'll be in the kitchen making coffee after I've changed."

The second he was out the door, Charlie rushed through her bath. She stripped off the coat, praying it wasn't ruined, and then spent several minutes working her wet, worn jeans down her legs. She didn't know what to do with her panties—no way would she put them in his hamper for him to find later. After giving it some thought, she washed them out and hung them on the side of the tub.

She disdained a full shower for simply cleaning herself off. Calling her sister was a priority.

Once she'd pulled on the dry clothes Harry'd brought her, she found his comb and worked the tangles out of her short hair. The polo shirt hung almost to her knees, looking, as he'd predicted, like a dress. It adequately covered her, but the silky boxers tickled. Rather than toss her dirty jeans in the hamper as he'd suggested, she folded them, put her panties in the pocket along with her money, and left the bathroom.

Harry sat on a corner of a colossal bed, head bent forward while he towel-dried his hair. He had on clean khaki slacks, and nothing else. His back was broad, muscled, lightly tanned. His feet were long, narrow, braced apart on the thick carpeting. Charlie stood there gawking, appreciating what a spectacular sight he made.

Oh yes, she definitely wanted to explore these unique feelings he inspired. She'd been around men all her life, but she'd never, not once, felt this much interest in one.

Her sigh caught his attention. He lifted his head, surveyed her tip to toes, then slowly stood. "You are an adorable sight, Charlie..." He paused, looking much struck. "I just realized I don't know your last name."

"Jones," she squeaked, breathless over the way he watched her. She cleared her throat. "Charlie Jones."

He held out his hand in the formal, time-honored tradition. "Harry Lonnigan." Smiling, she stepped forward, shifted her wet jeans to one arm, and took his hand. With a mere glimpse of evil intent, Harry tugged her forward. He took her small bundle from her and dropped it to the floor. His hands lifted to cradle her face, she caught her breath, and then he kissed her.

HARRY COULDN'T BELIEVE the way she made him feel. It was a simple kiss, damm it, and heaven knew he'd kissed plenty of women in his time. And among those women, Charlie was likely the least proficient at it. So her lips were soft? So she smelled incredibly sweet?

She looked like a rumpled child in his shirt, the shoulders bagging almost to her elbows, the hem skimming her knees—very sexy knees actually, followed by shapely calves. He shook his head. She'd combed her hair straight back, evidently not the least interested in impressing him with her feminine attributes. She'd made no effort at all to make herself more appealing. Yet he already had an erection and he practically shook with lust. All because of a simple kiss.

It was so unexpected, he almost grinned.

That happened a lot with her; hell, he'd grinned more since first spotting her in that small grocery, all decked out like an adolescent thug, than he had in the past six months.

Beneath his palms, her skin warmed and she felt so incredibly silky, so vibrant, he wanted to devour her. *He never devoured women!* He was suave and controlled and applauded for his technique.

She had him so turned on, he couldn't even remember his touted technique.

His thumbs stroked over her temple, her jaw. He kept the kiss easy, letting her lead, though he wanted badly to taste her, to slip his tongue into her mouth, to feel her tongue on his.

With a groan, he pulled back the tiniest bit and looked at her. Eyes almost closed, she swayed toward him, her pale, flushed skin in striking contrast to her glossy black hair and dark blue eyes. Her lips were slightly parted, and unable to help himself, he kissed her again, this time giving in to the urge to explore. He licked over her lips, and when she gasped, he slipped inside, coasting over her teeth, mating with her soft tongue.

He pulsed with need, he was so aroused.

Charlie's hands opened on his naked shoulders. She moved against him, and he could feel her stiff little nipples, could feel the plumpness of her breasts, small, but very feminine and sweet. He started to lift a hand, to cup her, tease her and himself, and his honor came knocking, just barely nudging aside the need.

Unspoken invective filled his brain. He wanted so badly to feel her breasts, but…

Once he got started, he knew good and well it would be hours before he got his fill. He should be getting in touch with Dalton. He had no doubts the man would be worried, wondering what had transpired, whether or not Harry had been able to make any headway. He owed Dalton that much.

"Charlie."

"Hmm…" She nuzzled his throat, took a small nip of his chin.

"Sweetheart, we need to talk."

She blinked up at him, her look dreamy. "You called me sweetheart."

Sighing, he said again, "We need to talk. Now."

She stiffened, her gaze searching his. "Oh good grief. Please, don't give me the old 'you're not that kind of guy' routine."

He took two steps back, and commended himself for accomplishing that much when he wanted so badly to feel her flush against him.

"I'm absolutely that kind of guy," he assured her, staring down into her sweet face. "I'm the kind of guy who is nearly desperate to strip you to your very sexy naked hide. I'm the kind of guy that once I got started, especially on the unveiling on these stupendous breasts of yours, I wouldn't want to stop until we were both insentient and without wit. I wouldn't stop until you begged me to. Unfortunately, what happened tonight probably has several people worrying about us."

The changing expressions on her face were almost comical. She went from openmouthed surprise, to blushing, to wide-eyed with realization. “My sister!”

“Yes. And I have a friend to contact. They deserve to know that we’re still alive and kicking.”

She rudely shoved him aside to snatch up the phone, and Harry admired the smooth rounded lines of her delectable backside. Nobility was surely a curse.

“I can’t believe I forgot about my sister.” She sent him a grave look of accusation and dialed the phone, muttering how it was his fault for distracting her, leaving off his shirt, showing his bare feet.

His bare feet? Harry shook his head. There was no accounting for her strange twists of reason. “I’ll finish dressing while you make your call.”

She’d barely finished dialing when Harry heard a shouted, frantic “hello” through the earpiece. Her sister had evidently been waiting for the call.

“Jill… I know, and I’m so sorry. I’m fine, really—*Jill, I’m fine,* I promise. Well, it’s a long story. I met a guy… No, Jill, it’s not *that* long.” Charlie glared at him, and Harry took the hint. He grabbed the rest of his clothes and left the room with a salute.

As he bounded down the stairs, he could hear the animated conversation, along with the occasional hushed, whispering tones, which he assumed meant the two women were discussing him. He entered the kitchen and because he was distracted, he almost tripped over his cat, Ted, now twisting around his bare ankles. It didn’t matter where Ted might be, if Harry entered the kitchen, Ted showed up.

He smiled down at the cat as he added some fresh

food to his dish—always the first order of business. "I wonder how much Charlie will actually tell of our adventure."

The dogs heard him talking and sauntered in. Harry reached for the back door that led to a tiny yard with a privacy fence. "Hey, why don't you guys go out and run around a little, maybe give me some privacy?"

Doggy tails wagged, but actual bodies didn't move. The cat looked thoroughly indignant at such a suggestion and continued to eat.

"So it rained a little. Don't you have to go?"

Sooner woofed an agreement and ran out. Grace took a little more coaxing, until she heard Sooner bark again and trotted out to investigate. Ted, with a look of disdain, licked his whiskers clean and leaped up to sit in one of the kitchen chairs.

Harry had the coffee ready, two cups poured, when Charlie came striding in. Harry handed her a cup and motioned for her to sit at the round table. Unfortunately, she tried to sit in Ted's chair.

Ted could be very theatrical when it suited him. He made a horrid hissing sound, arched his back, fuzzed out his tail and made a general threatening display until Charlie had backed up a good five feet.

"What the hell's wrong with your cat?"

Harry smiled fondly at his pet. "That's Ted. He doesn't like females."

"Ted? How'd you come up with that name?"

Shrugging, he said, "He's just Ted. Here, use this chair."

Cautiously, keeping her gaze on the cat, Charlie

circled to the chair Harry held out. "Is he always so mean?"

"With women, yes. He behaves well enough for me. Or maybe I behave well enough to suit him. Whatever, the arrangement works." Harry smiled at her.

"The dogs don't bother him?"

"Actually, they all get along fairly well. On his first day here, about a year or so ago, Ted explained things. We haven't had a real ruckus since."

"You've only had him a year? He looks older."

"He is. I found him in an alley while I was on a job. He saved me by making a grand distraction when he objected to our invasion of his private space."

"He threw a hissy like he just did to me?"

"Exactly, which effectively distracted the fellow who'd been holding a gun on me. I was able to… get the upper hand. So I brought Ted home. The vet treated him, despite Ted's vicious complaints, and as long as I keep him well fed and his litter box clean, he doesn't destroy my home."

"A fair enough trade-off, I suppose." She still eyed the cat warily, but Harry was pleased to see there was no dislike in her eyes. She understood, and he liked that.

"Cream or sugar?"

She snorted at such a suggestion, then took a healthy sip of her black coffee.

Harry scrutinized her as he liberally sweetened his own. "So you drink yours like a trucker, hmm? Now why doesn't that surprise me?"

After another sip, she asked, "For the same reason that seeing you turn yours into syrup doesn't surprise me?"

"Your insults are getting sloppier. You must be tired." He glanced at the clock, saw it was after midnight, and wondered if he should call Dalton after all. He hated to wake the older man if he'd already gone to bed. And Dalton did know Harry could take care of himself, so perhaps he hadn't been worried at all. "Is your sister appeased by whatever story you told her?"

She frowned at that. "I told her the truth, and yeah, she's appeased, but far from happy. She told me she's going to wait up for me."

Charlie offered that last small tidbit with a wince, which told Harry the night was going to get a whole lot shorter. "I assume this means you want to head home soon?"

"I'm afraid so. Jill is only eighteen, and she worries more than she should."

That brought out a snort, which appalled him. Good God, he was beginning to pick up her less discriminating habits. Harry cleared his throat. "More than she should? With a sister who muddles into extortion and gets herself kidnapped, I'd say she's justified."

Charlie shrugged. "She wants me to give it up, my spying that is, but I'm determined."

"Charlie—"

"No, before you start any lectures, I have a few questions for you."

"Please, don't keep me in suspense."

"I know you said you wouldn't want to see me again—"

Before he could correct her, because at this point he had every intention of seeing her, all of her, as many times as was necessary to get the fever out of his system, she held up a hand and continued.

"Don't worry. I'm not going to get clingy. A little hanky-panky would have been…nice. But the night has gotten way too complicated, and I can see why you wouldn't want to get involved with me beyond the night. I mean, we're hardly two peas from the same pod." She tried a smile that looked more like a grimace. "But… Well, I was hoping we could work out a different arrangement."

Harry leaned back in his seat, positively prostrated. "You think a rendezvous with me would be merely *nice?*"

She looked startled by his tone. "*Very* nice," she clarified, as if that made it better.

He felt smote to his masculine core. Here he'd been dredging up pagan images too erotic to bear, and she'd relegated the possibilities to merely *nice.* "I'll have you know—"

"I'd like to hire you, Harry."

That effectively put the brakes on his righteous diatribe. Hire him? Did she consider him a gigolo? Did she dare think she could afford him if he *was* for sale? The nerve.

But in a lusty sort of way the idea genuinely appealed to him. His body tensed until his muscles cramped. He was so hard, he could be considered a weapon.

Carefully, in case he misunderstood, he asked, "Hire me for what?"

"Detecting, of course. What else would I mean?"

Disappointment flowed through him. Nevertheless,

he contrived to look merely curious. "Of course. And what would you need a P.I. for?"

"I told you." she said with exaggerated patience. "To find out information on my father. He abandoned my sister and me ages ago, and that's fine by me because from what I know of it, we were better off without him. Except now I think it's time he accepted a few responsibilities. I figure since your friend has hired you to look into the extortion, and my father is one of the proprietors in that area, it shouldn't really be too much trouble for you to find out a few things for me."

A sick feeling of dread started to choke him. He remembered their most recent introduction, when she'd given him her last name. His belly churned, and he forced the question out. "Your father is?"

"Dalton Jones."

CHAPTER FIVE

HARRY STARTED TO CHOKE, picked up his coffee to take a large gulp, then choked some more. Coffee spewed out his nose and Charlie jumped up to pound on his back with surprising force. The cat hissed and loped out of the room. Harry fumbled for a napkin, and while Charlie tried to drive his ribs through his chest, he cleaned his face.

"You okay?"

Wheezing, he said, "If you'd quit bludgeoning me, it's possible I'll survive."

She quit. In fact, her small hand opened, and rather than pounding, she smoothed her palm over his back. Harry stiffened. "What are you doing?" he asked carefully.

"You feel nice. Hard. And real warm."

He started to choke again, and Charlie reseated herself. "That was the strangest damn thing, Harry. I've never seen coffee shoot out someone's nose before. And it was still steaming." She looked vaguely impressed when she added, "That had to hurt."

"You frightened Ted, attacking me that way—"

"Yeah, right." She gave a hearty snort. "Nothing would scare that beast."

"—*and* you don't sound the least bit sympathetic, so just be quiet." His brain throbbed not only from her interested, caressing touch, but with ramifications of her admission. Dalton Jones, his best friend, the man who'd always been there for him, emotionally supported him, got him through his divorce-from-hell, was Charlie's father? And she didn't appear to have any fond feelings for the man. No, she literally sneered when she said his name, leading Harry to believe her feelings bordered more on contempt than anything else. Harry dropped his head to a fist and sighed.

"Sheesh. What's got you so all-fired dejected, Harry?" She lounged back in the chair, at her leisure. "If you don't want the job, just say so. It's not like I was trying to coerce you or anything. I just thought since you'll be checking things out there anyway, it'd be no big deal to let me know if you heard anything."

Feeling himself duly cornered, Harry sighed again. "Let me get this straight. You want to get reacquainted with your father?" It was a shock, but Dalton would certainly be thrilled. Harry knew he'd spent a good portion of his life chasing after his ex-wife, doing his best to locate his children, to reclaim them, but the woman had always eluded him for reasons of her own.

Charlie bristled like an offended porcupine. "Hell no! I personally don't want anything to do with him. And if I had any other choices, he could rot for all I cared. But…well, my mother passed away not too long ago and between her never-ending medical bills and the funeral, I'm flat broke. I need some cash to get my sister through college. The bar is mortgaged through the roof, and I can't handle another personal loan."

Harry started to tell her that Dalton would gladly help her in any way he could. But he held back. It wasn't his place to make promises for Dalton, so he decided to talk to him first. Besides, Charlie's attitude was less than promising, and explaining away the past was a chore Dalton could better handle.

Still, Harry felt he had to soften her just a bit, to perhaps suggest she modify her assumptions until the facts could be presented. "I'm sorry to hear about your financial difficulties, but—"

Her fist smacked the tabletop, causing him to jump. "Why should my sister have to settle for less than the college of her choice, just because my father was too low, too deceitful to own up to his responsibilities? Why should he get off leaving the entire burden to me… I mean, my mother?"

Harry heard the slip, of course, but he let it pass. All he knew about Charlie's mother was what Dalton had shared, and he imagined from what he'd heard, Charlie's life hadn't been an easy one. That had been one of the biggest motivators for Dalton, the main reason why he'd refused to give up the search. He'd worried endlessly for the well-being of his daughters.

The dogs chose that propitious moment to want in, giving Harry a few minutes to think. He automatically went into his laundry room first to get an old towel, then opened the back door and knelt down. The dogs, well used to the routine, waited while Harry cleaned their muddy paws.

Charlie gawked at him. "Do you do that every time they go out?"

"When necessary, yes. I have fastidious dogs."

"Gee, I wonder where they get it from?"

There was just enough sarcasm in her tone to tell Harry she was nettled. Very slowly, he looked up at her. "You're not, perchance, making fun of my animals, are you?"

Her brows lifted.

"Because while I'll accept aspersions thrown at me, I don't take kindly to insults of my pets."

She rolled her eyes. "You're defending an old collie, a mutt and an alley cat?"

His eyes narrowed and she muttered, "All right. Sorry."

She didn't look overly sincere. In fact, she still looked angry. Well, there was nothing he could do about it, not yet at least.

Harry reseated himself. Sooner lay on the floor, resting his head on Harry's feet. Grace went to her dish to eat. "Perhaps your father has a legitimate excuse—"

"Ha! If he does, then he can damn well keep it to himself, because I'm not interested in hearing it. Years ago I might have…" Her voice trailed off and she looked away. Sooner stared at her, picked up on her distress, and abandoned his master to go lick her hand. Charlie smiled and scratched his head.

After an audible swallow, she continued. "All I want to know is if he's got any money, if I can count on him to do the right thing. He owes it to my sister to help her, to give her the opportunity to do her best in this world."

Harry saw her stubborn pride, her visible struggle to keep herself together. Something inside him softened, and that tender feeling made him uneasy. "What about you? Doesn't he owe you, too, Charlie?"

She stared him straight in the eye and said, "If it

was just me, I'd gladly survive in the gutter with the moldy rats before giving him the time of day."

Well. Harry leaned back in his seat, nonplussed. She certainly had a visual way of getting her point across. "Things aren't always as they seem, you know."

She stood, and both Grace and Sooner flanked her. "If you don't want to help out, that's fine. But spare me the lectures on goodwill. My charitable attitude died a long time ago."

She turned away and the dogs followed, forming a small parade. Harry felt abandoned and left his seat to hurry after them. Since his legs were so long, he only had to hurry for two steps. "Where are you going?"

"To call a cab. It's time for me to head home."

"Charlie." He caught her arm and turned her back around to face him. But she looked up at him, and her face was so innocent, despite her bravado, her eyes dark and searching, he felt that damn tender feeling swell up again. It seemed to explode inside him, filling him up, choking him when he hadn't even touched his cursed coffee.

He released her and backed up. The dogs frowned at him, but with the facts of her parentage dropped at his feet, all carnal tendencies would have to be forgotten. He couldn't see her as a sexual being, as a woman he wanted so badly his muscles ached. No, she was the daughter of his friend, a man who'd always been like a father figure to Harry. Touching her would mean betraying Dalton, and he couldn't do that.

Charlie was definitely off-limits.

That little truism annoyed his libido and gnawed at his control, but he stiffened his resolve.

He shook his head, verifying to himself, if not to her, that he couldn't, *wouldn't,* be tempted. Not now. "I'll drive you home. You can't very well get into a cab alone this time of night, especially not dressed like that."

She summoned a look of such scorn, he felt his ears burn. "I know how to take care of myself, Harry. I've been doing it most of my life. You can rest easy. Your duty is over."

He looked down his nose at her, being deliberately intimidating, which sent the dogs slinking off, though the effect on her seemed minimal. "Your shoulders are too narrow to support such an enormous chip, Charlie. No, don't flog me with your insults. I *am* taking you home and that's all there is to it. Since I'm of a greater size, and you're rather piddling in comparison, it stands to reason I'm more capable of carrying through with any threats, veiled or otherwise. It'll be better for both of us if whatever you're thinking remains unsaid."

She rolled her eyes. "Half the time, Harry, I have no idea what the hell you're saying."

"And..." he added, knowing he was jumping into a muddy creek when he had no idea how deep it might be, "I will check into things for you."

There, he'd committed himself. But even as he'd reluctantly uttered the ill-fated words, Harry wondered what else he could possibly have done. He couldn't just let her leave; Dalton would never forgive him. He'd looked for his children, spent a small fortune on the chore, for a great many years. Now here was his daughter, despising Dalton without knowing him, resenting him on hearsay, condemning him without knowing all the details, and Harry had the chance to find out where she lived, to assure Dalton that his daughters were alive and thriving.

He thought of everything at stake, and added softly, "Please, Charlie."

It was the "please" that did it, causing the rigidity in her shoulders to relax, her attitude to soften enough that she could agree. "Oh, all right," she muttered, without an ounce of feigned graciousness. "I suppose it doesn't make sense to give up what I want just because I'm pissed off."

She was certainly direct. "Ah…exactly." He retrieved her jeans and found her another jacket to keep her warm on the ride to her place. They both said goodbye to the dogs, who wanted badly to go along but Harry explained to them there wasn't room. "Just guard the place until I come home."

The dogs went back to sleeping in their self-appointed spots.

Ted was nowhere to be found.

"He sulks when it's dark," Harry explained, "because more than anything, he likes lazing around in the sunshine. When there is none, Ted hides. Which is good, because when he doesn't hide, he makes his discontent known to everyone."

Charlie gave him a soft, feminine look that took him completely off-guard. "You're very good to them, Harry."

He didn't like that look, didn't want her thinking soft, feminine things about him, not when he couldn't do anything about it. So he hustled her out to the parking garage where he kept his car before temptation could get the better of him, or before she could start disagreeing with him again. She truly was a most contrary woman.

He worried about her being barefoot, but he certainly had no shoes that would stay on her small feet, and she'd disdained the socks he offered her. Luckily, the complex was kept tidy, with nothing strewn about the grounds to injure her tender skin. No broken glass or debris.

She had very cute feet.

"You know, Harry, I figured you'd left your car at the grocery today."

Distracted from her pink toes—hardly a source of sexual stimulation, even if his body tended to disagree—he looked up at her and made a face. "My car wouldn't have survived three minutes parked at that curb. I took a taxi. What about you?"

"The bus. Cabs are a little out of my price range."

As he stopped next to his car, a shiny black Jaguar convertible, she dug in her bare heels, stiffened up again, and whistled low. "*These* are your wheels?"

"Yes." He noticed her horrified expression and patiently asked, "Now what's the problem?"

She turned to him, beautiful blue eyes wide, jaw dropped. "I can't afford you! First that luxury town house, and now this. You must make a killing as a P.I. to afford this car. I mean, these suckers go for over eighty grand a pop!"

Her phraseology alternately amused and irritated him, but her meaning was always quite clear. After another heartfelt sigh, Harry opened the door and practically thrust her inside. "Put on your seat belt." He closed the door, circled the car and slid behind the wheel.

Her frown was ferocious. “I mean it, Harry. We need to reevaluate here. I thought it’d cost a few hundred bucks at the most to get your help. I had no idea—”

The car started with a throaty purr. “I’m not charging you, Charlie.”

He was in the middle of backing up when she opened her car door and literally leaped out. He slammed on the brakes. “What in the name of—”

She leaned in and growled across the seat, “I don’t take charity, Harry Lonnigan!” He opened his mouth, and she said, “And before you bother sighing again, let me tell you, this is *not* negotiable!”

Since Harry had lost all semblance of patience, he barked, “Fine. Have it your way. But a few hundred will more than cover it, so get your sweet little posterior back in the damn car!” He ended on a shout, and shouting was something Harry had seldom done since his divorce. He liked it that way, liked his life calm and orderly, dished up to his specific design, without interruptions and disturbances and ill-mannered females throwing things into a whirlwind and stirring up unaccountable lust.

He sucked in a deep breath, sought for lost control, and continued in a forced icy-polite tone, “I have inherited money from my father, and that’s how I bought the car. Now, will you please quit making a spectacle of yourself and let me drive you home?”

She gingerly reseated herself, as if the leather seat could bite her. She also looked around the garage, then snorted at him. “I can hardly be a spectacle when there’s no one here to see.”

"I'm here, and your show is beyond distressing. A little decorum wouldn't kill you, you know."

She relatched her seat belt, then waited until they'd entered the nearly abandoned roadway before saying, "So you come from a rich family, huh? I could have guessed that."

Harry looked at her with acute dislike. His father had been rich, and he'd also been unfeeling. He'd given Harry very little during his life, certainly no real emotion or pride or concern. Taking his wealth after his death had been beyond difficult. At first, all Harry'd wanted to do was give it away. But Dalton convinced Harry to accept his father's legacy, to acknowledge and use the one thing his father had been capable of sharing.

He didn't discuss his father with anyone but Dalton, certainly not with a woman he'd only known a day, a woman who seemed to take pleasure in pricking him, both his mind and his body. "You're an irritant, Charlie. Now would you like to give me directions or should I try guessing?"

"Go to the corner of Fifth and Elm. You can see my bar from there. It's called the Lucky Goose. There's a big sign hanging out front, painted in lime green."

That description alone was enough to make his stomach queasy. "You must be joking."

"Nope." She sent him an impish smile and added, "Lime is the dominant shade in our decorating scheme. Not too long ago, I had to replace several things, and I found a lot of stuff at an auction, real cheap."

"Whenever something is 'real cheap,' there's usually a viable reason why."

She laughed. "You're right about that. The lime is almost enough to make you toss your breakfast, especially with so much of it. But the men who frequent my bar aren't out for the fashionable ambiance. They're there to drown their supposed woes, and as long as they have a stool to sit on and a glass in front of them, they can forgive anything else. And to be real honest with you, the color's kind of grown on me. I figure if I ever get far enough ahead, I'll add some black accent pieces. That'd look good, don't you think? Sort of classy? Black and lime?"

Harry shuddered with the image. *I'll tell Dalton how witty Charlie is, how spunky, how energetic. I'll simply leave out her appalling lack of taste.* When she continued to stare at him, waiting for his response, Harry forced a smile. "Yes, charming."

She beamed at him.

"Tell me about your sister."

"What about her?"

"I don't know. Anything, everything. Does she help you in the bar, things like that."

Charlie turned to look out the window. "Jillian just turned eighteen. She's beautiful, so intelligent she scares me sometimes, sweet, giving. She's also naive and a worrier." Charlie turned back to face him, her expression earnest. "And no, I would never let her work in the bar. That's why I need the money so she can go to college. She's gotten some partial academic scholarships, but not enough to foot the whole bill. If I left it up to her, she'd put off going for a year and save the difference herself, and even then, she'd have to settle for a less expensive college, and she'd lose the partial scholarships. I don't want her to have to do that. She's worked too hard all these years, keeping her grade average up, excelling in all her classes. She deserves the best, and one way or another, she's going to have it."

It was that *one way or another* that had Harry worried.

They rode the rest of the way in companionable silence. The late moon was partially hidden by clouds, not a star in sight. The near-empty roads were still wet and the tires made a slick hissing sound that could lull a turbulent mind.

And then that damn glaring green sign jumped out at him. Charlie hadn't told him it was framed with a neon green gaslight. The color was so bold, it seemed to throb in nauseating waves through the darkness. Cautiously, surveying the area, Harry pulled up to the curb. He swallowed hard, not wanting to ask but knowing he had to. "So, this is the bar. But where do you live?"

"Upstairs." She unhooked her seat belt. "When I bought the place, the second floor was empty, so I converted it into an apartment. My mother was already sick then, so I needed to work close to her and Jillian. The setup is great, though I wasn't crazy about having Jillian at a bar. But the stairs leading up are just inside the door, so Jillian doesn't have to come all the way into the bar unless she wants to. There's a door at both the bottom and top of the stairs, and they're kept locked. Only Jillian and I have keys. Anybody I see messing around with the door gets tossed out and isn't welcomed back. Since the Lucky Goose is so popular, nobody wants to test me on it."

That strange tenderness swelled in his chest again,

making him warm and fidgety. "You're a real tough guy, aren't you, Charlie?"

He said it softly, working the words out around the lump in his throat, but she took him literally. She shoved the door open and climbed out. "I have to be."

She looked surprised when he turned off the engine, stepped out, and activated his car alarm.

"What do you think you're doing?"

Harry grinned. "A gentleman always sees a lady to her door."

She looked nearly frantic with consternation. "I'll agree you're a gentleman, Harry, but I'm hardly a *lady*. You can save your gallantry for someone who'll appreciate it. I don't need to be seen anywhere."

Her denials made that strange tenderness more acute, almost like a pain. She was so used to taking care of herself, with no help at all. She was a small woman, but she gave the impression of being an amazon with her stubborn, forceful attitude. It hurt to think of all she'd been through before perfecting that attitude.

Shaking off the feeling, Harry took her arm and began ushering her reluctantly forward. "You look more than feminine to me." Especially since he knew she wore his silk boxers beneath the long shirt. His palms itched with the need to smooth that slippery material over her sweetly rounded bottom. *No, no, no. Dalton's daughter, Dalton's daughter...* He mentally repeated that litany until his heart calmed.

As they stepped inside the heavy wooden doorway he was met with dim light and a low hum of noise. He looked around with feigned casual interest, when in truth, he felt appalled. He cleared his throat.

"I'd very much like to get a peek at your establishment, and to meet this paragon sister of yours, if you wouldn't mind."

"You want to meet Jillian?"

"Is that a problem?"

"No, it's just…why?"

He shrugged, trying to fetch forth a logical excuse that wouldn't make her more suspicious. *So I can describe her to Dalton.* "Because she's your sister, and I'm vastly curious."

Charlie looked doubtful, but just then the door to Harry's left burst open and a tall, slender, very young girl bounded into the hallway. "Charlie!"

Harry had already thrust Charlie behind him and taken a fighter's stance. The girl's eyes widened as she stopped dead in her tracks, one hand lifting to her throat. From behind him, Charlie snickered in a most irritating way.

And Harry muttered, "Ah, hell."

Peeking from around him, Charlie said, "Harry, meet my sister, Jillian. Sis, this is Harry Lonnigan. You'll have to ignore his chivalry, but you did bust out like a tornado. You see, Harry has these odd heroic tendencies, and he was trying to protect me, in case you were a threat."

Harry pulled her around to the front of him and growled, "I am not a hero."

"No? Well, Ted or the dogs might disagree. And you saved me from a cell phone today, remember? And now you just protected me from my sister." She snickered again, and the sound grated along his raw nerves. "You're either a hero, or you're nuts. Take your pick."

CHARLIE CONTINUED TO smile as Jillian cautiously stepped forward, her eyes huge, staring at Harry with absolute awe. Charlie knew the feeling. It seemed every time she looked at him, he impressed her anew. He was just so…big. And so manly and hard and solid. Despite the fine clothes, the immaculate haircut, Harry Lonnigan had an aura of savagery about him.

She liked it.

Harry reached out and gently took Jill's hand. "Never mind your rather disputatious sister here. She seems to take immense enjoyment in plaguing me for no evident reason." Jillian stared, and Harry added, "It's a pleasure to meet you, Jillian."

Jillian licked her lips, glanced sideways at Charlie, and whispered, "What did he say?"

Charlie laughed. "Who knows? He always talks funny, but it seems to be getting worse as the night goes on. I think he needs to get some sleep and recharge his wits."

Jillian nodded, then turned back to Harry. She clasped his hand with both of hers. "Thank you so much for bringing my sister home safe and sound. She tends to get herself into trouble awfully easy, but from what she told me, she topped herself tonight."

Harry nodded. "Hmm. Her intentions are good, but she appears to be misguided by too much pride and bravado."

"Yep, that's Charlie. I tried to talk her out of doing something so stupid, but—"

"Jill."

Jill smiled. "Would you like to come up for a drink? I was just making some hot chocolate."

"Jillian…"

"Thank you, I'd love to," Harry said, cutting off Charlie's protest. "Hot chocolate sounds like perfection."

Charlie rubbed her head. "Harry, don't you think it's getting kind of late?"

He glanced at his wristwatch. "Very. What time do you close the bar?"

"At two. And as soon as I change, I have to check on things. So really, it'd be better—"

He gave her his back. "Jillian, if you'd like to lead the way, I'll drink my hot chocolate and then head home. Charlie's absolutely correct that it's been a rather full day."

Jill smiled. "Follow me."

Eyes narrowed, Charlie stomped along behind them up the silent stairwell. When they reached the top, Jill used the key hanging from her wrist to unlock the door. She said over her shoulder to Harry, "The doors automatically lock when they shut."

"Good idea. Are you ever bothered by the noise downstairs?"

"Not at all. I'm used to it."

"And the patrons respect your privacy?"

"Patrons?" Jill giggled as she headed down another hall and into the kitchen, the first room on the left at the top of the landing. Water already boiled in a softly whistling teapot, so Charlie got down three mugs and the tin of chocolate powder. Jillian dug three spoons from the drawer. "I'd hardly call the guys who hang out here 'patrons.'"

"No? Then what would you call them?" Harry seated himself at the Formica table and crossed his long legs. He looked entirely too much at his leisure to suit Charlie, especially when she noted him looking around, surveying their small but tidy kitchen.

Jill shrugged. "I don't know. Regulars? I suppose that's the nicest thing I can come up with. Oh, really, they're not all bad. But as Charlie has always told me, we attract a certain clientele here at the Lucky Goose, and it doesn't include anyone who's too discriminating."

Charlie finished stirring in the chocolate and handed Harry his cup. He sipped, made appropriate sounds of approval, then leaned back in his chair. "Do you ever go into the bar?"

"Are you kidding? Charlie has fits if I even peek in there after four o'clock. Before that, it's pretty tame, just a few guys hanging around, usually getting a sandwich and a beer. She doesn't mind if I'm in there then. But the rowdiest crowds don't start until after seven."

"What time do you open?"

"Charlie opens it up from two in the afternoon to two in the morning. She's got things pretty organized and we get a pretty steady crowd."

Harry made a pretense of drinking his chocolate, but Charlie could easily see the crafty interest in his gaze. "Those are long hours to work. What other employees do you have?"

Waving a hand, Jill commented, "Charlie likes to keep things simple, so she doesn't hire in much help. She does almost everything herself, which means she works much more than she should."

"So it seems."

"The only relaxation she gets is in the tub. I swear,

she'll soak for hours. There've been a few times she's fallen asleep in there—"

"Jill." Charlie could feel the heat pulsing in her face.

Twin dimples showed in her sister's cheeks when she grinned, proving Charlie's warnings did little good.

"We have a bouncer, of course, who also serves as a bartender on occasion. Then there's the regular bartender, and two women who help serve drinks during the busiest hours. Other than them, we have a few part-timers who fill in every now and then."

"Do you have need of the bouncer very often?"

"Nope." Jill leaned forward and dropped her tone to a conspiratorial whisper. "If you saw the guy Charlie hired, you'd know why. He's a real sweetheart, but no one seems to know that, and given his handicap and the way he always—"

Charlie interrupted, thumping her mug of chocolate onto the table and spilling a bit. "That's enough, Jill." She didn't want Harry getting the idea she had an overly soft heart, but if Jill had her way, she'd start telling stories that could give anyone the wrong impression. Her sister had a way of slanting the perspective to always put Charlie in a very rosy light.

She narrowed her gaze at Harry. "Okay, give. Why the third degree?"

After another long drink of his chocolate, Harry pretended confusion. "I have no idea what you're talking about. I was only making idle chitchat."

"Chitchat? Is that what you call it?" She glanced at Jill, who looked horrified by her sister's sudden rudeness, and explained, "Harry's a P.I. Snooping is his business."

Fascinated, Jill stared.

Harry raised a supercilious eyebrow. "Actually, I investigate. I do not snoop."

"Uh-huh. So why snoop here? I'm paying you to check on my father, not to pry into my personal life."

Jill groaned. "Oh, Charlie, you didn't? I thought we agreed! There's no reason—"

"Don't start being dramatic, Jill." In an aside to Harry, she explained, "Jill is prone to melodrama, no doubt because of her age."

Harry made a rude sound to that. "More likely due to her sister's penchant to get into trouble."

"Harry—"

"No, don't berate me. My brain is tired and I really do need to head home." He finished off the chocolate, stood, then took Jill's hand once again. "It's amazing your hair is still brown and not gray. I swear, while I was with her today, I could feel the gray hairs struggling to sprout."

Jill giggled. "She has a way about her."

"Indeed."

"She's also the very best sister in the world."

"I got that impression."

"That's enough out of both of you!" Charlie circled the table and stood toe to toe with Harry. She had to bend her head way back to meet his gaze. "When do you think you'll know something?"

He cocked a brow. "I know an abundance of things, Charlie. Can you be more specific?"

She ground her teeth together. "When, exactly, do you think you'll be able to give me some info on my father? I don't mean to rush you, but I don't want to wait too long, either."

"Patience," Jill muttered as she put Harry's mug in the sink, "is not one of Charlie's strong suits."

She was ready to refute that when Harry touched her cheek with two fingers. "I'll get back to you just as soon as I can. Try not to worry, okay?"

She gulped, feeling that simple touch all the way to her bare toes and back up again. "Can you…maybe give me a ballpark guess?"

He smiled. "I'll tell you what. Give me your phone number and I'll call you tomorrow evening. By then I should be able to have a better idea, okay?"

Charlie hurried to a drawer to pull out a pen and paper. "I'll give you our personal number, for here in the apartment, and the number for the Lucky Goose. You should be able to reach me at one or the other."

Harry slid the slip of paper into his back pocket. "Jill, thank you for the drink."

"Thank you, Harry, for bringing Charlie home in one piece."

"That was my pleasure. Well, at least part of the time. There was the occasional moment when—"

With a shove, Charlie started him on his way. She knew he was laughing, but she didn't mind. She walked him down the stairs and with every step, her heart thumped heavily. She was so acutely aware of him beside her, tall and strong and warm. When they reached the end of the stairwell, Charlie still one step above him, putting her on more even ground, she caught his arm before he could open the door.

He turned to face her, his look questioning.

She cleared her throat. His biceps were large and

thick and she knew even both her hands wouldn't circle him completely. She lightly caressed him and her breathing hitched. She was so damn ignorant about this sort of thing. "Harry, I really do appreciate all you did tonight. Not that I couldn't have handled it on my own—"

"But it was nice to have the company? My sentiments exactly."

She tilted her head, searching for the right words. This entire situation was awkward for her, because she'd never really wanted anyone before. "I know you said you don't want to get involved, and I feel the same way."

His entire expression softened. "Charlie—"

"No, you don't need to explain. I understand. But…"

"But what?"

His voice was low, the words gentle. She could feel him looking down at her, and so she mustered her courage, looked him straight in the eye, and said, "But I want you. There. I said it."

He stared, shock plain on his face, and she took advantage of it, throwing herself against him. She felt his arms automatically catch her, and she kissed him while his mouth was still open in surprise. He was motionless only a moment, then he turned, pinned her to the wall, and with a low deep groan, proceeded to kiss her silly.

CHAPTER SIX

HARRY ENTERED THE hospital with his heart in his throat and his pulse racing. The day, which had begun with no indications of a catastrophe, continued to slide rapidly downhill. Actually, he thought, he was well into a new day. Surely things would begin improving, surely Dalton would be all right.

A nurse directed him to the CCU, or coronary care unit, and the name alone made Harry break out in a sweat. *A heart attack,* Dalton had suffered a heart attack. He felt sick with anxiety and throbbing guilt.

It took him mere seconds to reach the right room, and as soon as he was close enough, he could hear Dalton complaining. He increased his pace, rushed into the room, then came to a standstill.

Dalton, pale and obviously agitated, was in a sterile white bed, oxygen hooked up to his nose, other apparatus connected in various places. He fought to sit up while a nurse struggled to keep him still. Harry drew himself up and said, "What is going on here?"

The nurse looked at him with utter and complete relief, then asked hopefully, "Harry Lonnigan?"

"Yes." He stepped forward and nudged her out of the way, giving Dalton a glare. "Be still."

Dalton rested back with a smile.

The nurse heaved a heartfelt sigh of relief. "He

needs to be resting, but he was insistent on seeing you. I told him we'd left a message for you, but when you couldn't be reached, he wanted to get out of bed and try calling you himself—"

"I'm sorry for the delay. The storm knocked out my answering machine and I didn't receive any message." He frowned at Dalton. "I called your house and the housekeeper told me what happened. I got here as quickly as I could."

Dalton gripped his hand. "She contacted me, Harry."

Harry looked down at the man he loved like a father and winced. Dalton was still good-looking at fifty-nine, tall, lean, with only a smidge of gray mixed in with his dark hair. He'd always looked so vital to Harry, but now, he looked shrunken and frail. "Who contacted you?"

"My daughter."

Everything in Harry jolted. His wits jumped about hither and yon, his heart thumped. He cast a quick glance at the nurse, then squeezed Dalton's hand. To the nurse he asked, "Can I speak with you in just a moment? I'd like to be updated—"

She patted Harry's arm. "Get your father settled, then come out. I'll be at the nurses' station. But please—" and she bent a warning look on Dalton "—he needs to be still and calm."

Harry nodded. "I'll see to it. And thank you."

The nurse went out, closing the door behind her. Harry hadn't bothered explaining to her that Dalton wasn't his father. In all the most important ways, he'd been the only father Harry knew.

The room was silent, with an acoustical ceiling and floor, good lighting, and a variety of electrical, suction, and other outlets. Monitors were hooked up to Dalton, and other assorted machinery sat at the ready. Overall, it should have been a distressing sight, but to Harry, it showed the competent level of emergency care available, giving him a sense of security. Dalton wouldn't die. He was well cared for here.

Harry scooted a narrow chair closer to Dalton's bed and seated himself. He had a feeling a lot had happened that he wasn't aware of.

Dalton gave him a shaky smile. "I got a letter from my daughter today. The oldest one, Charlotte." His smile widened. "She's a gutsy little gal. Do you know what she said? She said I owed her a lot of back child support and she wanted to claim it. She said she *would* claim it. What about that?"

Harry winced, both at the name Dalton called his daughter, and the irony of the situation. So Charlie had sent her father a letter. That was likely her reason for being in the store in the first place. She'd been waiting, Harry remembered, peeking out the window on occasion. And Dalton's jewelry store was directly across the street from the grocery. The little witch. Had she hoped to see her father's reaction?

Would she be happy with the results?

He no sooner thought it than he shook off the disturbing notion. Charlie wanted what she considered her due, but she didn't strike him as the type to wish actual harm on anyone. Well, except maybe Floyd.

Dalton cleared his throat. "The girls…they're alone now. Charlotte told me in the letter that her mother recently passed away."

"I'm sorry, Dalton."

"It was a hell of a shock, reading that letter and

knowing in my gut what my girls have gone through. Rose wasn't much when she was around, but she was still their mother. Damn, if only I could have found them."

Harry wondered where to begin, but before he could finish formulating his thoughts, Dalton actually laughed. "Here I was, watching for a sign from you, then that damn letter arrived. I could hardly believe it—liked to stop my heart."

Oh God. "From what your housekeeper told me, it almost did stop your heart."

"Ha! Now that I know I'm this close to getting my girls back, there's no way I'm going to let a little heart trouble stop me."

Harry stared at Dalton, that *ha!* sounding all too familiar. He wondered if Charlie had inherited the blunt expletive from her father.

"No sir," Dalton continued, full of vehemence. "I'm going to make it up to them, everything they missed out on because I wasn't there. But Harry, I still don't know where they are. The letter didn't say. So I was hoping you could…"

Harry decided before he could say anything, he needed all the details on Dalton's condition. He patted the older man's hand, then slowly stood to pace. "Everything will work out, Dalton, you'll see. As soon as I find out about you, we'll talk about the letter and what to do next, okay?"

"Damn right we'll talk about it. It's all I can think about."

"You need to rest, you know, if you want a chance to meet Charli—Charlotte." He barely caught himself, then shook his head. "Promise me you'll sit there quietly until I get back."

Dalton made a face. "What choice do I have? They've got me connected to so many wires, they know if I'm going to burp before I even do it!"

"Good. I like it that way. Now sit tight and I'll be right back."

It took Harry about ten minutes to find out that Dalton had suffered a mild heart attack, although *mild* wasn't really descriptive of the condition. Dalton had evidently suffered some discomfort through the night, including dizziness, but being the stubborn cuss Harry knew him to be, he'd ignored the problems, determined to be at the shop that day to observe Harry's meeting with Floyd and Ralph.

The nurse didn't know what had upset Dalton, only that a customer had called the paramedics when he'd turned deathly pale and grew nauseous. They took an EKG as soon as he reached the hospital, and then had to insist that Dalton not leave when they found evidence of a heart attack. He kept claiming he had important things to do.

Harry had to shake his head. What rotten timing for Dalton.

The nurse explained that a cardiologist on call had been in to see Dalton, and that they would continue monitoring him throughout the night. He had no prior history of problems and was basically a healthy man. In the morning they'd check his cardiac enzymes and see how his heart rhythm had done through the night, which would tell them more.

Though the nurse was reassuring, Harry still worried. It took him another five minutes to figure out what he wanted to say to Dalton about Charlie, censoring it in his mind so as not to upset him further. Such an awful situation. He could almost be angry at Charlie, except that her life hadn't been an easy one, and she'd obviously been led to believe her father hadn't cared. Under those circumstances, she could hardly be blamed for her actions.

Dalton's face was turned away, staring out a window when Harry returned. He immediately turned to face him, and that damn smile was back on his face. "You need to read the letter, Harry. It's in my pants pocket, over there in the cabinet. Take it home with you for safekeeping."

Harry retrieved the letter and stuck it in his pocket. "I'll take care of the letter, Dalton, don't worry about that. But first I need to tell you something."

Dalton blinked. "Well, damn, I'd forgotten all about Floyd and Ralph and those other idiots. How did it go? You didn't have any trouble with them, did you? I got that damn letter, had the attack and the next thing I knew I was in here and no one would listen to me when I said I had to call you."

"I'm really sorry about that. You know if I'd gotten the message, nothing could have kept me away."

"Of course I know it. That's why I was worried about you when you didn't show up right away."

Harry swallowed hard. "I have to tell you something, Dalton."

"Out with it. I'm not so delicate I'll swoon, you know."

"Well, to come right to the point, I met your daughter today."

Dalton lurched, he was so surprised, and Harry

rushed to soothe him. "Settle down now before they throw me out of here."

"But I don't understand! You met her? Where?"

"In the grocery. She was there, evidently waiting to see your reaction to her letter, though I didn't know she'd sent a letter. I didn't…ah, find out she was your daughter until much later."

"This is incredible!"

"Yes, I know." Harry didn't mean to sound facetious, but the whole situation was too ironic. That last kiss that Charlie had forced on him—forced, ha!—had damn near killed him. He'd forgotten himself, and within a heartbeat he'd had her pressed against the stairwell wall, her small hands clutching him, her hips squirming against his, inciting his lust, making him hard. Damn. Even now he gasped with the pleasure of it. Never in his adult years had he been hit by so much uncontrollable lust. He'd tasted Charlie and wanted to go on tasting her, everywhere, all over her small sweet body. He could have spent hours doing just that.

He shook, remembering.

He'd been a hairsbreadth away from taking her right there in the stairwell, and probably would have if a commotion in the bar hadn't jolted him out of his lust-induced stupor.

After that, he'd all but run from her. And she'd actually had the gall to laugh at his predicament.

He shook his head, wondering how he was ever going to be able to handle this absurd situation. A reluctant smile caught him unawares. "She's something else, Dalton. A little bitty thing, barely reaching my shoulder."

"Everyone just barely reaches your shoulder, Harry. You're what we average people call *tall.*"

"She's shorter than most, though. But you're right about the guts. Ralph and Floyd tried to intimidate her, but she easily got the best of them. Calling her fearless would be a gross understatement."

Dalton shuddered. "Thank God you were there to keep her safe. If those hoodlums had hurt her..."

Harry had a feeling she might have done just fine on her own. Under no circumstances would he tell Dalton that she'd been dressed as a boy—or that he was the one who'd inadvertently blown her cover.

Dalton drew a slow breath. "When I last saw her, she was nine, missing a few teeth, skinny as a twig, and loved football much more than dolls. Her mother kept her hair cut short so she wouldn't have to spend time working the tangles out. If I remember it right, Charlotte begged her to do the cutting. She was the epitome of the American tomboy. Of course, she's a young lady now, so none of that matters.

"I worked too many long days back then, and I missed out on so much. Then I caught her mother cheating, found out it wasn't even the first time, and when I sued for divorce, the witch ran off with my kids."

Harry left the chair to sit on the side of the bed. He clasped Dalton's shoulder. "You can explain it all to her now, Dalton. She'll understand. From the time I spent with her, I can tell she inherited her father's intelligence."

"Did she mention me at all?"

This was the tough part, but Harry didn't see any way around a few truths. "As a matter of fact, she wanted to hire me to find out more about you."

"No fooling?" Dalton seemed pleased by his daughter's curiosity.

Harry nodded. "I didn't say I already knew you. I wanted to give you the chance to tell her everything yourself."

"Did you…you know, get a feel for what she thinks of me? What her mother might have told her about me?"

Harry hesitated, unsure just how far he could stretch the truth.

"Out with it, Harry." He grinned. "From her note, I'm already assuming she has a healthy chip on her shoulder where I'm concerned. And knowing her mother the way I did, I can easily guess at how she probably lied about me."

Helpless, Harry admitted, "I think that's more the case than not. Charlie seemed under the impression you'd abandoned them."

"Charlie?"

"That's the name she goes by."

"Ridiculous! She has a lovely name."

Harry kept his opinion in check. By his way of thinking, *Charlie* suited her much better than the too-reserved *Charlotte.* Of course, Dalton wasn't reacquainted with her, so couldn't yet know that.

"Did she mention Jillian at all?"

Ah, safer ground. "Actually, I met her. It's a long story, and no, get that look out of your eye because I'm not telling it right now. You've had enough excitement for one day."

"Tyrant."

"I promise to fill you in on all the details tomorrow. But as to Jillian, she's a lovely girl. Eighteen now, and the opposite of Charli—Charlotte. Tall, light brown hair. But the same blue eyes."

Dalton's blue eyes crinkled at the corners with a huge smile. "I have an idea, Harry."

Harry rubbed his forehead with a sigh. The past several hours had depleted him sorely. He needed some sleep, he needed something to eat.

He needed Charlie.

His head snapped up with that errant thought, and he coughed. "Dalton, I'm sure if I go to her now and tell her what's happened—"

"No! You can't do that. Why, she might blame herself for my ill health. Finding out the truth, that I didn't leave her, is going to be enough of an adjustment. She'll know her mother lied all along, that she kept us apart out of sheer spite. That'd be tough for any young lady to accept, especially now that Rose is gone and can't admit the truth."

"Dalton, this particular young lady is tougher than shoe leather. Really. I don't think—"

"No. I tell you, it'd be too much. And if she thought she caused my heart attack—which of course she didn't—"

"Of course not," Harry agreed with wry cynicism.

"—she just might run off again. I can't take that chance, now that I'm so close to being reunited with her. She just might leave without giving me time to explain."

From what Harry knew of Charlie, she wasn't going anywhere without enough money to get her sister started in the college of her choice. The woman could vie with a herd of mules and come out ahead on stubbornness.

"No," Dalton continued, thinking out loud, "a better idea will be if you pretend to work for her."

"What?"

He rubbed his hands together. "You can soften her up for me, Harry. Leave little hints about the past, pretend to uncover clues about how much I do care for her, to let her know I wasn't just another neglectful father. Then she can get accustomed to the idea little by little. When she's ready, you can arrange a meeting between us."

"You want me to lie to the girl?"

Dalton managed a supreme look of affront. "Not blatant lying, no. Just little white lies, for the good of all of us. Besides, you've already lied to her by not admitting you know me, so don't get sanctimonious on me now."

"Dalton, you're not in the best of health. You've had a really rough day and you're not thinking straight." Besides, Harry wasn't at all certain he could maintain a facade of indifference to Charlie. He wanted her, and being around her while resisting her would be an undeserved hell, especially as she seemed determined to seduce him—when she wasn't doing her best to irritate him.

Dalton slammed his fist down on the side of the bed. "I'm thinking just fine!"

His actions reminded Harry so much of Charlie, how she'd slammed her own smaller fist down on his table, he almost grinned. Stubbornness definitely ran through the genes. Charlie had come by her obstinate nature legitimately. "Okay, so you're impervious to health concerns, wise beyond your years and immortal to boot. I still don't think it's a good idea."

Dalton fell back against his pillows, and Harry again noticed how pale, how drawn he looked. He frowned in concern. "Dalton—"

"No, never mind," Dalton sighed in a pathetically weak voice. "I shouldn't have been such a bother. You're already working on the extortion case for me, and heaven knows that's more than I should have asked of you. Though those young punks are idiots, it could still be dangerous."

Harry could attest to that.

"And now this, dragging you into the middle of my personal affairs." He sighed again, closed his eyes, and looked forlorn and dejected. Even knowing it to be a ruse, Harry couldn't stand it.

He came to his feet and propped his hands on his hips. "You don't play the martyr worth a damn, Dalton, so spare me the theatrics."

Dalton peeked one eye open. "I know that tone. It means you're ready to relent. Right?"

"Yes," Harry said, then groaned. "I suppose I have no choice, given you're lying there in a sickbed and you're not above using it to make me toe the line."

Dalton beamed at him. "You're a real hero, Harry. I don't know what I'd do without you."

"I am not a damn hero!" He felt mired in conflicting emotions. Regret, because Charlie was now off-limits and he was honor-bound to keep his hands off her delectable little body and his thoughts away from lascivious ventures.

Anticipation, because despite being off-limits, he'd be seeing her again and her spunk and wit never ceased to amaze and amuse him.

He also felt anxiety, because he had no idea how

he'd placate her infatuation with him while still keeping her a discreet arm's length away. She seemed determined to seduce him, given that last scorching kiss, and he'd have to find a way to feign disinterest without hurting her.

It was enough to boggle the mind, and Harry's mind, at present, was already overtaxed and sluggish. "I'm a stooge maybe, but never a hero."

"Yeah, well, right now, you look like an exhausted stooge. Why don't you go on home and get some sleep? My God, it's nearly dawn. And with all this excitement, I'm suddenly pretty tired myself."

Alarmed, Harry started forward, only to have Dalton wave him away. "It's not my heart, son, only my age and the excitement. Honest. We'll talk later and go over what you should tell Charlotte. We need a plan of action."

"You think I might have forgotten all your sterling qualities? You think I might not be able to make you sound a veritable icon among men?" Harry tsked. "You should know better, Dalton. I'll sing your praises until she cries mercy."

Somber, Dalton took Harry's hand and squeezed it. "I can't tell you how many times I've wished you were my own son."

Harry felt a lump in his throat that could strangle an elephant. "In all the ways that matter most, you're the only father I've ever had. And a damn good one to boot."

Dalton wiped his eyes, then said gruffly, "Aw, get the hell out of here. You look worse than I do."

Harry laughed. "That's saying a lot." On impulse, he leaned down and gave Dalton a hug, then straightened and headed for the door. "I'll be back, but in the meantime, I'm giving my home number and cell number to the nurses in case you need me for anything."

"You sure you don't want to leave your social security number, too?"

"If I thought it necessary, I would." He heard Dalton grumble and had to smile. "I mean it, Dalton. If you need me for anything, even conversation, simply call, all right?"

"Don't rush back just to hold my hand. Take care of business instead. I'd rather know you were seeing to my daughters and protecting my friends. Besides, there's a few cute nurses here willing to keep me company. If you hang around, they'll all be looking at you, instead."

Shaking his head, Harry said, "I'll let you know what your daughter thinks of my investigative skills. Even she should be duly impressed, given I'll have found out several remarkable things about you within half a day."

"Make me look real good, son."

"No problem. It'll be a piece of cake."

Or so he wanted Dalton to think. He couldn't abide the idea of causing him undue worry, but he knew from experience that nothing with Charlie would be easy, and she'd be the hardest person in the world to impress, especially where Dalton was concerned.

A reluctant grin curved Harry's mouth as he made his way to the nurses' station. *He would have to spend more time with her.* The decision was out of his hands, his motives altruistic and pure…

It would be a struggle to keep his hands to himself, to keep his thoughts on the straight and narrow.

Charlie was just so damn…*cute,* in a perky, twisted, Annie Hall kind of way. He couldn't remember ever being so intrigued by a woman.

He wondered what she'd look like in regular clothes, how she'd dress, how she'd wear her hair.

He also wondered how anyone in his right mind could possibly call such a unique, independent, headstrong woman *Charlotte.* Absurd. Charlie suited her far better. He only hoped Dalton would realize that, to avoid any disappointments.

CHARLIE KNOCKED, BUT when that didn't bring forth a response, she leaned against the buzzer. Judging by the commotion on the other side of the door, at least the dogs were at home. She really wanted Harry to be in, too, so she could share her news. She needed…

Oh, who was she fooling? She simply wanted to see him again, and when such a good excuse presented itself, she couldn't resist. It was almost noon, so Harry surely was up, despite the late night they'd had. She was amazed she'd managed to wait this long.

Keeping one shoulder on the buzzer, she smoothed her hair, then caught herself and dropped her hand. She was not a prissy person and damn if she'd start acting like one now just because she had the temporary hots for a very urbane gentleman with outlandish diction.

Charlie grinned. Actually, she'd sorta grown used to the way he talked. It was smooth on the ears, certainly not something she was used to when the men at her bar tended to slur and used very crude language.

When the door suddenly opened, she was caught with that outrageous grin still on her face. And Harry, all six feet five inches of him, looked disgruntled. He was—she gulped—wet, and wearing only a towel. The dogs were now quiet, peeking around Harry's bare knees.

His eyes narrowed when he saw her. "Perhaps you're not aware of it, but you're leaning on my doorbell."

Charlie, never to be confused with an idiot, widened her eyes and quickly stepped away from the bell. "Oops! I'm sorry. I didn't realize."

Harry stilled, then slowly looked her over. His gaze lingered on her hair, her breasts, then skimmed down to her feet. She stared back. He stood there blocking his doorway, wearing only a towel, clean shaven. Droplets of water clung to the hair on his chest and trickled through the silky line of hair leading from his navel downward. He smelled of delicious male scents that made heat bloom and curl in her belly. She delicately sniffed the air, breathing him in, then sighed.

His voice was gruff when he said, "You certainly look different out of your male apparel."

Charlie glanced down at her slim-fitting, well-worn jeans, her lace-up brown work boots. Donning a soft, cream-colored sweater was as far as she'd been willing to go to try to impress him with her less than apparent femininity. Anything more, anything as ridiculous as a skirt, would have been too obvious. She wasn't altogether certain she even owned a skirt.

Besides, any efforts to make her look more ladylike would have come across as asinine. She just didn't have the heart for it.

Harry reached out and touched her hair, tugging

one curl through his fingers. His cheekbones flushed and he whispered, "Like silk. Warm silk."

Charlie wanted to melt. Oh, the man had a way of saying things that hit the pit of her stomach and radiated out to make her shaky and hot and… She sighed again. If he'd wanted her to, she'd have stood there all day letting him play with her hair. But then his fingers touched on her bullet earring and he suddenly stiffened and stepped back.

"Good heavens. Come in before someone sees you."

"Me? You're the one who's nearly naked."

She walked in, thoroughly greeted by the dogs who went all out by jumping and shaking and appearing happy to see a new face. Harry, however, was already stalking away. He waved vaguely toward the kitchen. "Go make yourself at home and I'll be right back."

Charlie admired the view of his retreating backside. His shoulders were wide, hard, his spine straight, muscles evident all over the place.

She'd have admired the view even more if he'd dropped the towel. "Don't dress on my account!"

"Brat." He galloped up the steps without looking back. She heard a door slam.

Well, well. He certainly was grouchy this afternoon. Charlie slipped off her lightweight jean jacket, laid it over a chair, and went to investigate the kitchen. The dogs followed on her heels and their nails tapped-tapped on the kitchen tile floor as they danced around her.

She wasn't surprised to find coffee just finished brewing. Remembering how Harry had taken his, she fixed his cup as well as her own. Then she spotted Ted, glaring at her from his seat at the table. She shrugged. "Don't mind me. I'll sit way over here. You won't even know I'm around."

Sooner howled, as if he found that hilariously funny.

Harry returned only seconds later wearing suit pants and buttoning up a blue dress shirt with one hand. In the other hand he carried shoes, socks and a tie.

Charlie raised a brow. "What? You didn't trust me alone in your kitchen? Or did you think Ted and I would be brawling? You had to rush back half-dressed?"

He slanted a frown her way and picked up the coffee cup for a healthy sip. "At least allow the caffeine to penetrate my brain cells before you start sniping. I've had very little sleep, certainly not enough to counteract yesterday's adventures." As if by rote he opened the back door and the dogs darted out.

She hadn't gotten much sleep the night before, either. She'd spent most of the evening staring at the ceiling and thinking of that last kiss. She doubted he'd done the same. Maybe he just slept late when he needed to. She, however, didn't have that luxury, not with the bar to run. "Uh, Harry, are you on your way out?"

"As a matter of fact, yes, so perhaps it would be auspicious for you to explain this unexpected visit?"

"Auspicious, huh? All right, don't get red in the face. I found out some info on our villains."

He froze with the cup to his lips, then slowly lowered it. "I assume you're referring to Floyd and Ralph?"

"Aren't they the only villains we know jointly?"

He frowned, took a large drink as if to fortify himself, and she continued.

"They're going to drop in on Pops again today, so I figured I'd follow them when they leave, just to see where they go, and I wondered if you'd want to tag along to keep me company—"

Coffee spewed across the table, making Charlie jump back a good foot. She growled. "Damn it, Harry, you do seem to have a problem with coffee, don't you?"

He thunked the coffee cup down and took two menacing steps toward her. Ted raced past her with a vicious hissing complaint, but since Harry seemed the bigger threat, she didn't dare look away from him. She widened her stance, braced herself and waited.

Through gritted teeth, he said, "You're not to go anywhere near them, Charlie, is that understood?"

She fetched forth her most direct, intimidating look, and must have succeeded, given his stormy expression. "Uh, Harry. You're not trying to give me orders, are you?"

He stepped closer still, until her neck felt like it might cramp from the drastic angle it took to meet his gaze and his breath hit her face with the force of a puffing bull. "Yes," he said succinctly. "I'm giving you an explicit directive to stay the hell away from anything and anyone that has to do with Ralph and Floyd."

He was so close, she couldn't resist, and leaned just a scant inch closer to smell him, her nose almost touching his chest.

Harry leaped back as if burned. "What do you think you're doing?"

"You smell so good, Harry. If I could bottle you, I'd make a fortune."

He flushed, blustered for a moment, then started in frowning again. "You're trying to distract me, damn it."

Actually, distracting him had never entered her mind. Charlie examined her nails. "They kidnapped me, Harry. They threatened me. You can't expect me to just let them get away with that."

"I told you I'd take care of them."

"Terrific. I'll go along to see that you take care of them right. I haven't forgotten you're the one who was too chicken to push Floyd off the truck."

He looked nearly apoplectic. "You bloodthirsty little…it would have killed him! I do believe I can handle things without resorting to murder."

Charlie sniffed. "He's too mean to die. He'd probably have just gotten his hard head bruised a little."

"Charlie." He clasped her shoulders and shook her lightly. "You don't know what you're playing with."

She wanted to play with him, but he didn't look overly receptive to the idea at the moment. No, he looked like it took all his restraint not to choke her.

"Forget it, Harry. If you're too much a sissy to go with me, I can go alone. No problem."

Choking became a distinct possibility.

After several moments where she held her breath, waiting to see which way the chips would fall, Harry finally released her and stepped away. He picked up his coffee.

She eyed it warily. "Careful. I don't want you to drown yourself."

He drank the rest of the cup in one long swallow, glaring at her over the rim all the while. After he finished the cup, his expression grew crafty. "I have a deal for you, Charlie."

"I'm listening."

"Remove yourself from my business with Floyd and Ralph, and I'll tell you what I've discovered concerning your father."

Her breath left her in a whoosh and she gripped the edge of the table. "You've found out something already?"

He looked down his nose at her. "Quite a few somethings, actually, which is why I didn't get to bed until the early hours of the morning, and why I was just rising when you arrived. Now, do we have a deal or not?"

Charlie weighed her options, decided lying would be the most expedient way to go, and said, "Whatever you say, Harry. Now tell me everything you know."

CHAPTER SEVEN

HARRY STARED AT her hard, but she didn't so much as flinch. Still, he knew without a shadow of a doubt she had no intention of backing away from Ralph and Floyd, despite her rapid agreement.

With a sound of disgust, he dropped into a chair and bent to pull on his socks. "You're lying through your teeth and you aren't even doing it well."

"That's absurd!" She pulled out a chair and sprawled into it. "I'm an *excellent* liar!"

He looked nonplussed for a moment, then laughed. "You're something else, you know that, Charlie?"

He sounded...affectionately exasperated. But then what did she know? She'd never heard honest affection from a man before. And she'd certainly never known a man like Harry. "I like watching you dress, Harry." He glanced up at her, startled, and she smiled. "I think I'd probably like watching you undress, more."

A shoe dropped from his hand, thumping onto the floor. Harry swallowed, made a strangled sound. Charlie eyed him. "Thank God you're not drinking coffee, huh?"

He stared, then jerked his gaze away from her. Furious, he yanked on the rest of his clothes, including a silk tie, then began pacing the kitchen. Glancing at her, he accused, "You've traumatized my cat."

"I'm not the one who can't swallow coffee."

His eyes narrowed. He looked downright harassed, and he kept checking his watch. The dogs scratched to come in, and again he went through the chore of cleaning their feet. Afterward, the dogs cuddled up to him and got thoroughly petted. He even whispered to them, though she couldn't hear what he said.

Charlie loved watching him with the animals. He was so big, so strong, but so incredibly gentle, too. She remembered the way he'd touched her, how he'd kissed her, and she was instantly jealous of the attention he lavished on his pets.

When Harry stood, Sooner and Grace came over to her for a few pats. Harry watched, his brows down, and he warned, "Don't try to ingratiate yourself with my dogs. I already explained to them how conniving you can be."

She gave each dog an extra hug. "Yeah, well, since they know you, they've probably realized you're just being unreasonable." The dogs didn't agree or disagree, they just went off to sleep.

Charlie crossed her legs and waited. He had news to tell her, but she did her best to look indifferent despite the churning in her belly and her anxiety. She couldn't give him the upper hand.

"Okay, are you interested in knowing what I've discovered or not?"

"What a dumb question! Of course I'm interested." Then in the coolest tone she could manage, she asked, "Do you think he has any money? Will he be able to pay what he owes?"

Charlie watched, fascinated, as Harry's lean jaw hardened, as his muscles bunched and flexed. For a second there she thought his eyes turned red, but then he stepped around her and headed out of the kitchen.

"We'll have to discuss this in transit. I'm late already."

Charlie hustled after him. "Late for what?"

The look he gave her wasn't promising. "I was intending to tail Floyd and Ralph."

Grinning, she skipped to keep up with his long-legged stride. "Then you already knew—"

He held her jean jacket while she slipped it back on, causing her thoughts to jumble. It was a first for her, that small courtesy, and it amused her that even while he was so obviously irritated with her, his unrelenting manners came through.

She leaned back against him as he settled the coat over her shoulders, and he jumped away, grumbling, cautioning her "Charlie…".

"Hmm?"

He frowned, blinked at her, then shook his head. "Come on, let's get going."

Charlie had to hide a smile. He fought her, but he was tempted. Maybe she'd be able to work on that.

Looking decidedly perturbed, Harry pulled on a suit coat, then his raincoat. The dogs stirred themselves enough to look up as Harry said goodbye to them, then they went back to sleeping peacefully. He led her out the door, locking it behind him.

"So, Harry, you did know about the visit Ralph and Floyd have planned?"

"Of course I knew. I'm the P.I., if you'll recall."

"Well, I only found out late last night from a regular. When I went in to close the bar, I overheard two guys talking and I recognized part of what they said. I asked a few questions and found out Ralph and Floyd have been trying to drum up some assistance."

Harry led her to his car and opened her door. "You shouldn't be asking questions, Charlie. What if it gets back to Ralph or Floyd and they figure out where you live? Is that what you want?"

"Of course not. I'm not an idiot, I know what to say and not say. I was careful."

"You don't know the meaning of the word *careful.*" He looked at her long and hard, then touched her cheek. "I don't want to have to worry about you."

Contentment bubbled up inside her. "I don't want to worry about you either, Harry. That's why I thought it'd be nice if we did this together. I mean, considering you're so squeamish about actually hurting anyone." And it'd give her a good excuse to spend more time alone with him.

He dropped his hand and sighed. "Get in the car, Charlie."

"I brought my own transportation. Will you drive me back here?" She'd almost taken the bus today, then realized leaving her truck behind would provide a good excuse to return to his apartment. Her plans weren't exactly orthodox, but then, neither was she.

Her life had never been easy, and she'd learned to be hard and brazen and forceful by necessity, to take care of her mother, to protect her sister. Now, for the first time that she could ever remember, she really wanted a man. She didn't know how to deal with that except to give it her best shot.

Harry rubbed the back of his neck, cursed softly, then asked, "I don't suppose you'll go on home and let me take care of things?"

"Ha! Don't be stupid, Harry."

"No, I didn't think so. All right, yes. I'll bring you back here. But Charlie, promise me you'll do as I tell you. I don't want to drag you along only so you can act recklessly again and end up hurt."

She slid into the stupendous car with the butter-soft leather seats and the smell of money. "I'm never reckless. Quit worrying. You're starting to sound like Jill."

He slammed her car door.

They were five minutes on the road before Charlie said, "All right. Are you waiting for me to beg or what?"

He glanced at her, clearly distracted.

"Harry, what did you find out about my father?"

"Oh, sorry. My mind wandered."

"Where did it wander to?"

He stared hard at the road. "Never mind. Besides, you seemed so disinterested, I wasn't sure you even cared."

She scooted closer to him. "Didn't you sleep well, Harry? You're awfully snide today."

"I slept fine for the short time I had in bed."

Very casually, she touched his thigh. It was hard and warm and the muscles flinched under her palm. She smiled. "Now who's lying?"

He growled, gripped the wheel, then blurted, "By all accounts, your father didn't abandon you."

That was *not* what she'd been expecting to hear. She was so surprised, she sat back on her own side of the seat, releasing Harry. The old resentment rose to the surface, and her tone was sharper than she intended when she said, "No? He had amnesia and forgot he had children? He was taken prisoner in a foreign country and only just got free? It's been eighteen years since I've seen him or heard from him, Harry. I'd pretty much call that abandoned."

Harry sighed, then incredibly, reached for her hand. "Honey, he tried to find you. He really did."

He called her *honey.* She felt all warm and mushy inside again. Clearing her throat, she asked, "How do you know that?"

"He's worked at that same jewelry store for some time now, so a lot of the other proprietors are familiar with him. Many of them told me he's spent years looking for his daughters, that even now he hasn't given up hope of finding you."

She tried to pull her hand away, but he held her tight. "Charlie, he cares about you and Jill."

Charlie swallowed down the unfamiliar lump of emotion in her throat. Even if what he said was true, it didn't matter. "Concern and caring from a father back when I… I had to work two jobs and my mother was so sick and Jill got cheated out of Christmas twice would have been real nice. But I don't care anymore about that. All I want from him now is enough money to get Jill through college. Does he have money, Harry?"

Harry sighed, and she snapped, "Oh, stop that! You're forever sighing, like you're so put-upon whenever we're together."

He fought a smile. "I'm sorry. I suppose it's just that I expected that answer from you, and I'll admit I'm disappointed. Charlie, your father can't help it if your mother took off and he couldn't find you."

She snorted. "How hard did he try? True, we moved around a lot. I remember that, mostly because it made it so damn difficult for me to get Jill settled. But even so, a single woman with two children should be easy enough to track down. The school records alone—"

"Did you go to public schools?"

"Yeah, well…come to think of it, we almost always settled in real small towns."

"How small?"

She forced a casual shrug. "Almost nonexistent. The schools were independently run by the townsfolk, since there usually wasn't more than a handful of kids attending." She felt a twinge of doubt, but ruthlessly shoved it aside. She would not be suckered that easily. Dalton Jones had a lot to account for. "We chose small towns because the housing was generally cheaper, not because it was a good way to hide!" She hated her own feelings of defensiveness, and added, "It made finding an after-school job almost impossible. At least, until I got older."

His large thumb brushed over her knuckles, gently, soothing. "Where did you work, Charlie?"

She stared at their linked hands and marvelled that such a simple touch could make her feel so funny. Funny in a very *nice* way. "When I was twelve, I got a job helping out at a market stand. It was seasonal, but I loved it. Being outside, meeting so many people. And I didn't have to dress up. In one town, my mom got me a job helping this old lady out at her boutique. I hated it. She expected me to wear dresses."

Harry laughed. "You're not into female frippery?"

"Can you imagine me in a dress, Harry? It's ridiculous." She stupidly blushed just thinking about it. But whenever she talked about that time of her life, she felt vulnerable. She'd been out of her element, and it had been the first time she'd realized just how different she was, and what a disappointment she was to her mother.

He sobered, then pulled up to a red light. "I think you'd look very nice in a dress, but no more so than you do in those snug jeans."

Her heartbeat tripped. "You…uh, like my jeans?"

He kept his gaze deliberately on the road. "You're very attractive, Charlie, regardless of what you're wearing. Surely men tell you that often?"

She wrinkled her nose. "I work in a bar, Harry. Men tell me a lot of things, but I don't pay much attention to slurred words and suggestive innuendo."

"Will you pay attention to me?"

She felt flushed and drew a slow deep breath. "Since you haven't been drinking all day, and your words are coherent, then sure. I suppose so."

He looked undecided for a moment, then turned to face her. "You're beautiful." Their gazes locked, and Charlie felt drawn in, surrounded by his attention. His hand released hers, but then lifted to her cheek. He smoothed the back of his knuckles over her cheekbone in a very tender gesture, tucked a curl behind her ear. She could get very used to being touched so tenderly. "You don't need any frills to turn a man on, Charlie."

"Really?"

He continued to touch her, small touches that elicited so many feelings. "I think you're one of the sexiest women I've ever met."

"Then…"

"But I'm not going to get involved with you. It has

nothing to do with you, and everything to do with me. Okay?"

"No."

"Charlie—"

She laughed, because he looked so frustrated. She decided a dose of honesty couldn't hurt. "I want you, Harry. That's pretty unique for me, so I can't just forget about it. Besides, I'm used to fighting for what I want." When his eyes nearly crossed, she said, "Go ahead and sigh if you really need to, but it won't change anything. Consider yourself forewarned."

A horn blared, prompting Harry to drive now that the light was green. He shook his head, then chuckled as he stepped on the gas. "Only you, Charlie, could make a seduction sound like a threat."

She lifted her nose and tried for a seductive look. He didn't laugh, so she considered herself more successful than not. "I prefer to think of it as a promise, Harry."

HARRY FELT STRUNG too tight. It was absolute torture, sitting next to Charlie while knowing she was smugly plotting his salacious downfall. He could tell by the way her dark blue eyes slanted in his direction every so often, or the way she looked him over, as if sizing him up for a meal. It was possibly the most erotic thing that had ever happened to him.

And he couldn't do a damn thing about it.

He shouldn't have shored up her confidence by admitting he found her sexy. But he couldn't help himself. The second she started speaking of her past, she'd looked…uncertain, not her normal indomitable self.

Her eyes, usually so forthright, had filled with reserve and he'd wanted nothing more than to reassure her.

Now she knew he was susceptible to her, and he could almost hear the wheels turning in her head.

He needed a distraction, but he was hesitant to pursue the topic of her father. Maybe after she considered things, she'd soften just a bit. She was bull-headed, but not cruel. He decided on the next order of business. "Are you at all nervous about seeing Ralph or Floyd again?"

She gave him a double take. "Nervous?"

"Yes. It would make sense, you know. Yesterday was fairly tempestuous, what with being kidnapped and held at gunpoint."

Strangely enough, her expression softened. "We were shot at, too."

"Yes."

Suddenly she scooted closer and hugged herself up to his right arm. "Harry, I think it's wonderful that you're still determined to protect those old people despite being scared."

"What?"

"It's nothing to be ashamed of. As you said, yesterday wasn't easy. It even rattled me a little."

"Well, gee. That makes me feel so much better."

She patted his shoulder. Then rubbed. Then squeezed. "You have very nice muscles, Harry."

"Stop that!" Her voice had gone all throaty and warm. "Return to your own seat and put on your seat belt."

"Sheesh. I was only trying to—"

"Comfort me? This may come as a shock to you,

Charlie, but I wasn't unduly upset by what happened. I was, in fact, mostly just concerned for you."

"What? Now why would you be worried about me?"

"Why, indeed?"

Her lip curled and she gave him a look fraught with disgust. "Because I'm *female?*"

Hiding a smile, he added, "And small. It's the truth, honey, you're on the…short side."

She stretched out her spine, managing to look an inch taller. "What the hell does that have to do with anything?"

Now she looked more inclined to punch him than kiss him. He felt relief—and other things he didn't even want to ponder. "My wife was a small woman. Not as small as you, but still considered petite. She hated it that I chose to be a P.I. In fact, she flatly refused to have anything to do with it."

"How could she be married to an investigator and not have anything to do with it?"

"Ah. Good question."

"Oh, you're divorced." She winced. "Is that the reason you broke up? Just because of what you do?"

"I had other options. My father had recently passed away and he'd left me a small fortune, as well as the opportunity to get involved in his business ventures. But I had no interest in such things." He lifted one brow. "She was adamant that I toe the line, that I give in to her will, but as it turns out… I didn't. And she couldn't stand it. She said my job was too dangerous, and if I didn't give it up, she'd leave me."

"And she did?"

He nodded. "Without much reluctance, but with a

lot of dissension. She's remarried now, very happily. And she controls her husband with a velvet glove."

"I think your job could be exciting, although so far it's been kind of dull."

"Is that so?"

"And Harry? I don't own any velvet gloves."

He glanced at her, then grinned. "I wasn't drawing a comparison, brat. Well, perhaps I was, in an obscure, peripheral manner. You may not own velvet gloves, but I'll bet you own leather ones—maybe boxing gloves. Or possibly even brass knuckles?"

She blushed, giving herself away. "One of the men at the bar had a pair of those. I confiscated them when he kept causing trouble."

Harry raised a brow, wondering exactly how she'd accomplished that. "You're unlike her in many ways, Charlie. But you're even more controlling." It dawned on him that he could use this argument to turn her away from her seductive course. He truly had no intention of getting involved with any woman who wanted to call the shots.

"Harry, this may come as a shock, but I didn't ask for your hand in marriage. I just want to try out this…um…"

Knowing Charlie and her penchant for boldness, he decided to help her out before she said something too descriptive, too luring, that would push him right over the edge. He cleared his throat and offered, "Chemistry?"

"Yeah!" She beamed at him. "This chemistry we have going. I like it. I've never felt it before."

He gulped and almost swerved off the road. He shouldn't ask, because the less he knew, the better, but he couldn't seem to keep the words contained. He *had* to know. "Never, as in…?"

"As in never. The men I've known weren't the type to inspire illusions of lust. It's the truth, and I hope you won't hold it against me, but I'm pretty much inexperienced in this kind of thing."

He closed his eyes briefly, not enough to wreck his car, but enough to suffer a moment of silence. When he opened them again, he realized nothing had changed. He still could barely breathe. How did she keep doing this to him? "Charlie, when you say inexperienced, do you mean—"

"I'm almost a virgin."

His head throbbed. "How does a woman remain *almost* a virgin?"

She shrugged. "Once when I was nineteen, I felt rebellious and gave in to this total dweeb who lived close to us. What a mistake that was! I ended up punching him in the nose he was so inept. I mean, I *was* a virgin then, and he was twenty-two years old, and supposedly experienced, but even I knew more than he did. And he was so obnoxious about it, blaming me." She snorted in renewed righteous indignation over the slight.

"Good God."

"Then, when I was twenty-three, I got engaged to a guy I thought was nice. And even though I didn't really want him particularly bad, I figured I should know if we were compatible in bed or not before I shackled myself to him."

"And?"

"It's a good thing I didn't marry him." She shuddered in revulsion, then twisted in the seat to face

Harry, full of confidences. In a stage whisper, she said, "He peeled off his clothes, and Harry, he had hickeys that I hadn't given to him in the strangest damn places!"

Harry bit his lip.

"Ooh, it was disgusting." Her voice lowered even more. "And his body wasn't all that great, either. Nothing like yours. He didn't have any hair at all on his chest. Slick as a baby's bottom. Can you imagine?"

Harry, who had a nice covering of chest hair, sighed. Well, hell. "You know, you really could benefit from just a pinch of discretion."

"I shouldn't have told you?"

"I might have suffered less not knowing." Her admiration had the ability to fully arouse him from one heartbeat to the next. He could already envision her fingers tangled in his chest hair, smoothing, stroking…

"Why should you suffer? I'm the one who's had to contend with fools and abstinence."

He choked on a laugh. "Charlie—"

In a mournful tone worthy of the divine, she said, "It really has been rough, you know."

Dalton's daughter, Dalton's daughter, Dalton's…

She peeked up at him, a study of feminine adoration. "If he'd looked anything like you, Harry, I might have been able to ignore the hickeys, even though they weren't mine, and even though I can't imagine anyone putting their mouth on him *there.* But he wasn't you and he'd been with someone else. And if I wasn't going to marry him, and of course, after knowing that, I wasn't, then I didn't think I should have to sleep with him."

Harry didn't think she should have to, either. He didn't particularly want to think of her sleeping with anyone, certainly not a man with a hairless chest, not a man who'd been with someone else and gotten love bites in unlikely places. *What places?* No, he didn't care what places. He didn't want her with any man, except maybe himself, and he was out of bounds.

He pulled up to the curb across the street and a few doors down from where their human targets would be making mischief. "Promise me that no matter what, you'll keep your cute little bottom in my car. I don't want you to start—"

"You think my bottom is cute?"

He bit his tongue. "It's a figure of speech used whenever addressing female bottoms."

"Oh."

"Promise me."

She shrugged. "I don't intend to start a brawl in the middle of the street, if that's what you're worried about."

"You're unpredictable. I worry about a lot of things." He glanced at his wristwatch. "We have some time before our neighborhood psychopaths are due to exit. There's a pattern to their visits, and they have the timing down. It's my hope to do nothing more than follow them today, see where they go, then perhaps I can turn the authorities on them without involving the proprietors."

"Why don't the proprietors want to be involved?"

"They want to be involved. Badly. If it was left up to them, they'd have set a trap already and, like vigilantes, exacted their own sort of justice, which I have a feeling is as bloodthirsty as your own. But my…friend, fears retribution against them if they do so. Being the stubborn cusses they are, they refuse to involve the police. They've called on them a few times, for less serious issues—minor vandalism, loud music, loitering, that sort of thing. And the police were unable to do much more than offer to drive by more frequently. It injured their pride."

"And so they've given up on the police?"

Harry nodded. "I can understand them. They're older, but resistant to the idea of being frail. All their lives they've been independent, able to handle all situations. They're settled and productive and happy. Then a few months ago the extortion began, and they can't tolerate it, but their pride insists they don't need the police now, not when they couldn't help them in the past. My friend is concerned, of course, but he did promise them he wouldn't contact the law. And actually, I'm concerned that if they did, especially without rock solid evidence, things could become worse. Ralph and Floyd are only minions. They answer to Carlyle."

"So it's Carlyle you want?"

"Yes, I want him. Badly." Harry rubbed his hands together, imagining what he'd do to Carlyle. "I detest a bully, but a bully who picks on the elderly ranks right up there with the devil himself. With any luck, once I find out where they gather, I'll be able to link them with more than extortion. They're criminals, and I hope to find them with illegal firearms, drugs, anything that will implicate them with the law, without involving the extortion."

He happened to glance over at Charlie, and caught

her staring—worshipful lust in her big blue eyes. He scowled. "Stop that."

Her smile was almost sappy. "You're incredible, Harry. A real—"

"Don't say it!"

"But don't you see? You are a hero."

He bent a severe, utterly serious look on her, determined to make her back off before his control snapped. "I'm not a damn white knight, Charlie. I'm not the man you've been waiting for, even though I have a hairy chest and no unseemly love bites. I'm doing a job, that's all."

"I saw the way you looked, how eager you are to get hold of Carlyle. You're a good man, Harry. And good men are few and far between. Believe me, I know."

She looked warm and soft and admiring, and he liked it. He responded to it. She was such an enigma, so strong, so outspoken and confident, yet still so very female. She was quirky, rough around the edges, but so brutally honest she took his breath away. And unlike his ex-wife, she seemed to thrive on the excitement of his job. She actually admired him for what he did, rather than disdaining his choices.

Of course, she also thought he was afraid, and as much as that rankled, he supposed allowing her to believe in some flaws would only add to his efforts to push her away.

He clenched his muscles and forced his honor to the forefront of his brain, nudging the lust aside. "Your father is a good man, by all accounts." She stiffened immediately, but he pressed on. "Wouldn't you like to meet him? I could arrange it, you know."

"That's not necessary."

"You should be pleased, Charlie," he said gently, knowing this was difficult for her, glimpsing again that damn vulnerability that squeezed his heart. "He can assist you financially, and he can be a friend, if you'll let him."

He saw it in her eyes before she even moved. The determination, the cunning. He braced himself, both distressed and anxious, and then she was against him, her hands gripping his shoulders, her body as close as she could get it.

"I don't need a friend, Harry. Right now, I need a lover. You." She kissed him.

Harry tried to resist, he really did. But as he kept telling people, he was far from a hero. Mortal men couldn't be expected to withstand such provocation. He made a desperate effort to recite all the reasons he shouldn't kiss her back; it didn't work.

He felt her breath on his jaw, the silkiness of her hair on his temple when she slanted her head. Her tongue stroked tentatively over his closed lips and he groaned.

"Harry, please…"

Before he knew it, his hands were on her body, under her blue-jean jacket, cupping her small, perfect breasts through her sweater, and there was nothing mysterious about them. They were soft and firm and her nipples burned against his palms. *"Damn."*

Charlie panted. She bit his jaw, nuzzled his neck and kissed his throat. Somehow she managed to get one slender thigh up and over his and he helped her, smoothing a hand over that luscious, resilient bottom and cuddling her closer, letting his fingers probe and explore and entice. She straddled his lap and he could feel her feminine heat from the juncture of her thighs against his abdomen, and it made him nearly wild with need. He wanted her naked, in this same position, riding him gently, then not so gently. He groaned.

With her breasts pressed to his chest, her heartbeat mimicked the furious rhythm of his own.

Then he heard a shout.

He opened his eyes, trying to orient himself and his fogged brain. He saw Floyd scurry out of the meat market, his last stop of the day. Harry stiffened.

Ralph had already gotten in on the passenger's side of a blue sedan, and two seconds later, just as Floyd got the driver's door open, the proprietor, Moses, came out swinging a fist.

All hell broke loose.

CHAPTER EIGHT

CHARLIE WAS SHOCKED when Harry suddenly tossed her into her own seat with the growled order to buckle her seat belt. The convertible ripped away from the curb, leaving the smell of burnt rubber in the air and a number of interested folks on the sidewalk. Charlie managed to say, "What the hell—" before Harry grabbed her head and forced it down in the seat.

"Stay down."

Furious and confused, she tried to lift back up, but his hand remained locked in her hair, keeping her immobile. She thought about punching him, but the car was going too fast, swerving, then pulling away again with a vicious squeal of tires. Harry released her, using both hands to turn the wheel sharply, and when she sat up, more than a little ready to commit murder, she found he had a look of grim satisfaction on his face.

Charlie huffed. Her body was still tingling all over, her mind sluggish, her heart beating too fast. As she smoothed her hair out of her eyes, she decided to give him a chance to explain before she extracted revenge for his high-handedness. "You care to tell me what that macho display was about?"

He cast her a quick glance, then brought his gaze

back to the road. "We're distracting Floyd, before he hits Moses and I have to kill him."

"Moses?"

Harry nodded while constantly glancing in the rearview mirror. They were doing about seventy-five and still gaining speed. "A grouchy old relic who's evidently gotten tired of being robbed. His shop is part of the lineup Floyd hits. Moses took a swing at Floyd as they left the store, but when I cut close to him, he leaped out of the way and forgot about retaliating in favor of trying to catch us."

Excitement bubbled up inside her. She whipped around and sure enough, there was a blue sedan trailing right behind them. "Does he know it's us?"

"I have no idea. Not that it matters. Hold on."

She barely had time to grip the door handle before the car took a sharp turn onto a side street, without slowing down much at all. Charlie fetched up against the door, then just as quickly found herself thrown against Harry.

"I told you to hold on!"

"I'm trying!" Readjusting her position, she again looked out back. "I don't see him."

"That was the point. Now that we've lost him, we'll circle back around and still be able to follow him."

"That won't be risky?"

His lips firmed in a calculating smile. "Are you getting nervous on me, Charlie?"

He sounded downright hopeful and she scowled. "No way. I just want to know what we're doing."

"I'm tracking. You're just along for the ride." The car slowed a tiny bit as Harry maneuvered in and out of side streets. “And this is the last time. I work much better alone.”

“Suit yourself. I can work alone, too.”

He growled, surprising her with the suddenness of it. “You’re not going to work on this, Charlie. Promise me, or I’ll pull over right now and toss you out.”

He sounded serious, but she didn’t think he’d actually do it. He’d lose too much time in trying to catch up with the Bumbling Boys. “Go ahead. I can make my own way home, or rather, back to your place. Then I’ll get my truck and start my own surveillance.”

Whatever he said was mumbled low enough that she couldn’t hear, but his inflection was plain enough. He was beyond frustrated and likely wishing a curse on her head. Then his expression sharpened and a slow smile appeared. “There he is.”

Charlie realized with a start that he was enjoying himself. It amazed her that someone so polished could have such an evil smile. Harry pulled into the main flow of traffic, now going a moderate speed that wouldn’t draw attention. Charlie looked around, but didn’t see a single familiar thing. “Where?”

“About twelve cars up, enough that he probably won’t notice us.”

“Probably?”

His look was smug. “Even if he does, my car could outrun his any day.”

Aha. So there was a reason for the expensive wheels, besides great looks and the expression of wealth. “There’s a wild side to you, Harry Lonnigan.”

He didn’t bother to answer, and she used the quiet moment to study his profile. That last kiss had filled her with unfamiliar tension that still throbbed and teased and kept her edgy. When she'd climbed over his lap, being deliberately brazen in her efforts to seduce him, she'd felt his erection and it had thrilled her.

She smiled, then tilted her head and asked, "Did you like kissing me before?"

His jaw flexed, but he didn't look at her. "Any red-blooded male would enjoy kissing you. It didn't mean anything."

"Because I'm too bossy, like your ex-wife?"

"That's part of it. And no, I'm not up to a barrage of questions right now. Let me concentrate, will you?"

A few minutes later they entered a commercial district where old and new warehouses stood together. Harry slowed the car even more, and eventually pulled up behind an abandoned building. He checked his watch, cursed, then turned to look at Charlie. He chewed his upper lip a moment, his expression both weary and considering. Eyes narrowed, he asked, "Do you think you could handle my car?"

It was the kind of question that never failed to rile her because it pricked her pride. Her spine stiffened and she said, "I can drive anything, including a semi."

"I'm sure that accomplishment will look sterling on a résumé." He held up a hand when she would have replied, and only the seriousness in his gaze kept her from being insulted. "I'm going to go take a look at where our thugs are headed. I'd like you to slide behind the wheel. If anything strange happens, if anyone approaches you, just drive away."

She tucked in her chin and stared at him in disbelief. "Without you?"

"I'll be fine. But not if I have to worry about Floyd getting hold of you again. Believe me, honey, he won't take any chances with you the next time. And his interest isn't only in revenge."

She really liked it when he called her honey. "You think because of my disguise, he's as interested in my breasts as you were?"

Harry drew in a quick breath. His gaze darted to her chest, and then quickly away. His hands tightened on the wheel and he looked ready to snap it in two. "It's possible, but I don't think you'll enjoy his interest."

He looked so furious, she decided against baiting him further. Though she had absolutely no intention of going anywhere without him, she nodded agreement. "Fine."

He studied her face, looking for the deception, but as she'd told him, she was a good liar. He spared her one brisk nod. "Lock the doors as soon as I get out. I should be back in a few minutes. If it takes me more than that, leave."

Then he leaned forward and cupped her chin. Charlie held her breath, hoping for a kiss, but all she got was a threat. "No matter what, don't you dare get out of this car. Do you understand me?"

She especially loved it when he touched her. His hands were always hot, a little rough, and it excited her. She probably would have agreed to anything when he was touching her. She forced air into her lungs and whispered, "I understand."

His gaze dropped to her mouth, and with a slight curse, he pushed himself away. He was out of the car in the next instant. She watched him crouch low and race around the building, keeping to the shadows. More than anything, she wanted to follow him, to protect him, but what if they got separated and he came back to the car? What if Floyd chased him, but she wasn't where she was supposed to be? Though he expected her to run like a coward, she knew Harry would never leave without her. He was naturally protective of anyone or anything smaller than himself. He wanted to help the senior proprietors, he'd willingly tried to shield her from Ralph and Floyd before he'd even known her. And just seeing him with his animals, the way he took care of them, even surly Ted the cat, reaffirmed in her own mind how special Harry was. He could deny it all he wanted, but he had the makings of a true hero.

Waiting was one of the hardest things she'd ever done.

It seemed an hour had passed, but she'd checked the car's clock every minute, and knew it had been less than a quarter of that time. When she saw a shadow fall across the pavement, coming from the direction Harry had disappeared, her shoulders started to sag in relief.

Then the man stepped around the brick building and he looked as shocked to see her as she was to see him. He wasn't Harry, no, not even close. This man was shorter, heavier, and he had an aura of menace about him. Even when he smiled, she wasn't encouraged, because there was no comfort in his baring of teeth or the tilt of his thin lips. Charlie felt her senses scream an alert.

Where the hell was Harry?

The car was still idling, so she put it in gear, undecided on what to do. The man approached as if driven by mere curiosity. He tapped on the window, and Charlie, nervous but not wanting him to know it, lowered the window a scant inch.

The man looked her over. "Is everything okay, miss?"

"Fine, thank you."

She started to roll the window back up, and he quickly asked, "Can I help you with something? This isn't a good place for you to be loitering around alone. Or are you alone?"

She tried to think, but her worry for Harry had doubled and she didn't know what to say. "I'm just… lost."

"Where did you want to be?"

"Um…" *Where?* She had no idea. She hadn't even been paying that much attention while Harry drove, choosing instead to look at him.

The man grinned again, one brow lifted. "If you'll just roll this window down a little more so we can talk—"

Of course she had no intention of doing any such thing, but then it became a moot point anyway. The man suddenly swung around, but not in time. Harry, who'd crept up with neither she nor the man knowing it, landed a powerful blow against the man's jaw, driving him hard against the car. Charlie jumped.

But the man didn't stay put. In half a heartbeat, he'd pulled himself together and lunged at Harry. Charlie stuck the car in park and would have gotten out to help, but the two men again fell against the car, blocking her door. She tried to climb over the seat and keep watching at the same time. The shorter man hit Harry in the eye, making him curse and duck, then grabbed up a piece of pipe lying on the ground and swung it at Harry's head.

Frozen in very real fear, Charlie screamed.

She struggled with the door, but she'd forgotten it was locked, and by the time her frantic hands got it unlocked and open, Harry was there, cursing her and shoving her back in. "Damn it, I told you to leave!" he roared, and then he slid in beside her, forcing her to move, to climb over the controls to the passenger side while she tried to assure herself his head was still where it was supposed to be.

"Oh my God, are you hurt?"

Harry pushed her away, jerked the car into reverse and stepped on the gas. The car shot backward, and Harry jerked the wheel, spinning the car in one fluid motion so it faced forward, then speeding out of the lot.

Charlie came to her knees beside him and touched the swelling bruise already visible around his eye. "Harry—"

"Put your seat belt on, damn it."

She ignored him. "What happened? I… I thought he was going to hit you with that pipe and—"

"And you screamed." He looked at her, his injured eye swollen almost closed. "I never thought to hear such a female sound from you."

That gave her pause, but she shook the discomfort off. "You weren't even looking. I thought he was going to split your head open."

Harry grunted. "I kicked it out of his hand. The fellow was a totally pathetic fighter, slow and inept, and I'll thank you to have a little more faith in me, if you please."

Charlie sank back on her heels, nonplussed. He was actually insulted that she'd worried for him? "You, ah, handled that very well."

"You didn't." Without looking at her, he began the same tedious drive in and out of side streets, making it difficult for anyone to follow, though he didn't seem overly concerned with the prospect. "I think I could be happy if even once you'd follow my instructions. What were you waiting for? For him to open the car window with the pipe he tried to use on my head? What would you have done if I hadn't shown up?"

"I don't know. But it was dumb of you to tell me to leave without you. I'd never do that."

In a burst of temper, Harry hit the steering wheel with a fist. "This is exactly why you should have kept your stubborn hide at home instead of dogging my heels!"

His tone was vicious, not loud, yet twice as intimidating for the low tone. Charlie swallowed, more hurt than alarmed by his anger. Guilt gnawed at her because she knew he had a valid point. He'd obviously had everything under control, but for the first time in her life, she'd panicked. The realization was so new, so alien, she couldn't quite fathom it.

Of all the stupid things, she'd fallen in love with Harry Lonnigan.

"That was one of Carlyle's henchmen, you know. He'll tell him we were there. If you hadn't blundered, I could have looked my fill with no one the wiser. But now, they know we know where they're at, and odds are they'll move. Tracking the idiots will be twice as difficult after this!"

She had no idea what to say. They'd been through a

lot together already, and not once had Harry sounded so fed up, or so disgusted with her. Slowly, she sank into her seat and relatched her seat belt. She stared out the window, hoping to collect her thoughts enough to offer an excuse, a reply of some kind. But how could she tell him that she cared, that she was worried about him? Obviously the man was big enough, tough enough, to take care of himself without her questionable assistance, so she surely couldn't use that excuse. And mentioning love, or any type of emotion, was out of the question. Harry had been very clear on his feelings for her. He didn't even want her anymore and did his best to fight her off. She was such an uncouth yokel compared to his sophistication and background. She hadn't thought of it before, but now she had no choice.

The ride home was made in painful silence. Several times Charlie glanced at him, wincing in sympathy over his swollen, bruised eye. But the mulish set to his mouth, the hard glitter in his eyes, kept her from commenting on it.

After Harry had turned the car off in the parking garage he drew a deep breath and faced her. "Where's your truck?"

She shrugged, doing her best to look cavalier. "I parked on the street."

"Charlie…"

That sympathetic tone of his made her spine stiffen. She didn't want his pity, especially when he refused to share anything else.

Various emotions seemed to bombard her, wearing her down, but she was made of pretty stern stuff, not one to wilt when things went sour. So she wanted him? It was in her nature to fight for what she wanted, but this situation was different, wanting a man. She knew he desired her, and that had strengthened her resolve, but it was also obvious he didn't want to desire her, and she could understand his reasonings very easily.

Pride forced her to give in graciously, to salvage what she could of her self-respect. She worked up an icy smile, then opened her car door before looking at him. "I've decided to let you off the hook."

The swelling black eye seemed obscene on his handsome face. He didn't move, just sat there staring at her. "What the hell are you talking about?"

She lifted one shoulder. "I won't pester you anymore. I've decided to quit playing spy and get back to my own business. The bar doesn't run itself and I've neglected it these last few days. If you want to send me a bill for what I owe you—"

His good eye narrowed, giving her pause.

"—for the info on my father, I mean. I'll get the money to you right away."

"I haven't finished telling you what I know of your father."

Though she wasn't a coward, had never been a coward, she wanted to leap out of the car and run away. She didn't want to continue sitting there, chatting like everything was fine when she'd just had the most astounding realization of her life. There were very few people she'd ever loved, and other than Jill, they'd all been mistakes. She hated to think of Harry that way.

"That's all right. You said he hadn't completely abandoned us, so I'm assuming he'll pay what he owes. That's all I really need to know. I can have a lawyer contact him. Or maybe I'll just send him a letter..."

Harry reached for her and she slid quickly out of the car, dodging him. If he touched her, she'd want to touch him back, and she was determined not to make a bigger fool of herself. "Thanks for the help, Harry. I can handle it from here."

He, too, left the car and slowly stood to face her. The slamming of his door echoed around the empty garage. She closed hers more carefully. When Harry started around the car toward her, she began back-stepping to the entrance. She tried an airy wave. "It's been...fun."

His growl reminded her of a rabid animal. He kept coming, his narrowed eyes looking more lethal than ever with the dark bruise and the swelling. He was large and imposing and somehow all his sophistication seemed to have melted away under his basic masculinity. "You're coming inside with me."

Her spine stiffened. "No thanks. I need to get going."

"I'm not asking, Charlie. I'm giving an explicit mandate. We have things to talk about, and I'm fed up with your unaccountable stubbornness and scurrility."

"I don't even know what that word means, Harry." He looked like he might lunge at her any minute, so she kept backing up. Unfortunately she didn't look behind her, and she fetched up against a concrete wall, clunking her head. "Ow."

While she rubbed her head, he closed in on her, using his long muscled arms to cage her in, stepping so close she could feel his warmth and breathe in his hot scent. He stared at her face, at her eyes and her mouth. She felt the gentle touch of his breath, and the blast of his temper, in sharp contrast.

"It means," he said succinctly, "that cutting wit of yours which you dispense with no thought to consequences and without evident remorse."

She forgot she wanted away from him, or even that her head hurt. Her own temper snapped and she leaned closer to taunt, "Oh, poor baby. Have I said something to hurt your feelings?"

His jaw worked. They were so close her nose bumped his chin. Then he took her arm in an unbreakable grip, stepped back, and headed for the town house. She got dragged in his wake. "No, but I do believe you prodded me into hurting yours. And for that, I'm sorry."

"What nonsense! I don't need an apology from you. Really… *Harry,* let me go!"

"No."

He tugged and pulled and coerced her along until they reached his door. Losing a fight really went against the grain, so she doubled her efforts. She didn't want to hurt him, so she was at a distinct disadvantage. She tried going limp, hoping her weight would throw him off-guard, but he managed to control her by the expedient method of wrapping one arm around her and lifting her off her feet. Mortified, Charlie went perfectly still.

He unlocked the door with his free hand and stepped inside to the sounds of excited barking. With a laugh, Harry released her to relock the door, and Charlie, seeing red, gave up on trying to get away from him. Instead, she launched her own attack. She took Harry off-guard and he stumbled and with the dogs flying around their feet and Ted screeching out a raucous complaint, they went down on the floor, hard.

Unfortunately, Charlie was on the bottom.

HARRY DODGED A tight fist aimed for his bruised eye. He'd expected no less of Charlie, especially since he was well aware of her more bloodthirsty tendencies. But for a moment there, she'd seemed too withdrawn, almost sad, and the thought that he might have hurt her feelings with his temper had been a squeezing pain in his heart. When he'd seen that thug leaning on the Jag, talking to her… He never wanted to feel that possessive, that protective or enraged again.

She swung at him again, demanding his immediate attention. Laughing, he captured her hands and pinned them over her head. The dogs were going crazy, taking the struggle as a free-for-all game. Sooner jumped close enough to stick a wet snout in Harry's ear, then dodged away again, howling maniacally. Charlie got a gleeful lap across the temple from Grace, and she struggled even more, cursing Harry and trying to discourage the dogs.

Her wriggling body had a very basic effect on him. He looked down at her, seeing the way her short, glossy black hair tumbled around her head, the way her cheeks flushed with her efforts. She lurched up against him, her head thrown back, her teeth catching her bottom lip, and he nearly groaned. Damn, she looked like a woman in the throes of a climax.

Her legs were caught under his and she tried to kick one free. Harry used his knee to spread her thighs, then settled between them. This time when she lunged upward, there was no way she could mistake his state of arousal. He had a throbbing erection and she froze.

The dogs moved in, taking advantage of the inactivity, whining and barking and nudging the humans. Harry barely noticed. Charlie had opened her eyes and locked her gaze on his, and the emotional connection was so strong, so powerful compared to anything he'd ever felt, he couldn't move. It was like he was inside her already.

She gasped for breath and he raised himself slightly, not enough to let her get away, but enough so she could breathe. She immediately lifted herself to press against him again. She could drive him crazy, he thought, even as he settled his hips against hers, giving in to her silent demand. His pulse raced, his muscles drawing tight. It felt so right to be with her like this.

Her knees bent, and she slowly moved her pelvis against his in an unpracticed, voluptuous sway. Mesmerized, he watched her face, saw the trembling in her lips as she drew in a shaky breath, saw her beautiful blue eyes darken, saw her skin heat.

Sooner howled again and without looking away, Harry commanded, "Go lie down." The dogs complained, but they finally obeyed.

Charlie tried to pull her hands free, but he held tight. "No you don't. I like you like this," he whispered. "You need just a little controlling, someone to keep you in line."

Though her eyes were heavy lidded and filled with sensual need, she lifted her chin. "You have to let me up sometime."

As far as threats went, it held no weight. Harry

leaned down and nuzzled the soft skin beneath that raised chin. "Who says?"

Her eyes drifted shut and she hooked her feet behind his thighs. "You feel so good, Harry. Will you make love to me now?"

Everything righted itself in that instant and his brain cleared. With a vicious curse he released her and sat up. She didn't. She remained sprawled on the floor beside him, offering the most delectable temptation man could imagine. He tried not to look at her, but he couldn't help himself.

"Damn, I'm sorry."

"I'm not," she whispered.

He ran a hand through his hair. "How do you keep doing this to me?"

"I didn't do anything except try to let you off the hook. You're the one who dragged me in here."

After a calming breath, he forced himself to say, "I don't want off the hook. And I'm sorry I yelled at you."

"All things considered, I'd kinda forgotten all about that."

He looked at her, lying there so sweet and submissive—surely a first for Charlie—and his muscles cramped in rebellion of what he knew he had to do. "Honey, this is all wrong. I brought you up here to talk about your father, not to…ravish you on the damn floor."

"I rather liked being ravished on the floor."

He couldn't help but laugh, she was so persistent and candid and honest. There wasn't a single ounce of guile in her expression, and the fact that she was as free, as unreservedly sexual as himself, made him crazy. She hadn't minded their rough play in the least, and wasn't offended at being debauched on a floor. She would be his sexual equal, and knowing it made his arousal even more keen.

But she was Dalton's daughter, and Dalton would be appalled to know just how low Harry had sunk.

He stood, caught her arms, and pulled her to her feet. She stared up at him and he cupped her face. "Tell me you'll at least give your father a chance, okay?"

To his surprise, she seemed to be considering it. "Why is it so important to you, Harry?"

With complete and utter honesty, he said, "Because I think he's a good man and he loves you. I think he deserves a chance to tell his side of the story. And because I was never able to connect with my own father. It's something that bothers me still, something that every so often vexes me because now the man is gone and more often than not I don't even mourn him. I don't want you to ever suffer that, to wonder if only you'd softened a bit you could have had a wonderful relationship. For Jill's sake, for all it will mean to her, why don't you at least try?"

Harry held his breath, praying she'd relent. With any luck at all, Dalton would be getting out of the hospital today. Harry didn't want him under unnecessary stress, and he knew Dalton would stew endlessly about the situation until he was reunited with his daughters. If Charlie would agree, it could be taken care of within a week. That would give her time to prepare and give Dalton time to rebuild his strength.

Also, Harry's control was almost at an end. For his own sanity, he had to tie up loose ends so he could distance himself from her before he made a mistake he'd live to regret. Dalton deserved his loyalty, and Charlie deserved a man who would love her forever.

Unfortunately, the thought of her with another man made his system revolt, so he quickly shoved that thought aside.

Harry had no idea which part of his discourse convinced her, but after several moments of deep thought, she nodded. "All right." She hesitated, then stepped close and embraced him. "Will you…go with me?"

Harry wrapped his arms around her and held her tight, too tight, judging by her laughing, mumbled complaint. He didn't understand the near desperate urge to hold her, but he knew her embrace hadn't been designed to seduce him this time. Rather, it was the need for emotional comfort, and it touched him to his very soul. She willingly showed him her vulnerable side, something she normally kept well hidden, and he'd never felt so gifted in his entire life.

Though he knew it would be incredibly awkward, he kissed her temple and nodded. "Of course I'll be there."

She leaned back with a relieved smile. "When?"

He couldn't make her any promises until he found out how Dalton had fared. He'd called the hospital when he first got up, and the nurse had told him all seemed well. Dalton had been in high spirits, anxious to know what Harry had planned—a tale Harry related with precise discretion, leaving out any reference that might upset Dalton. He hadn't spoken to him again since the doctor's visit, and now he was anxious to do so. He led Charlie to the door, though he was equally reluctant to let her go.

With a last kiss on her forehead, which was a habit he desperately needed to break, he said, "Try not to worry, honey. I'll arrange everything as soon as I can, and then I'll let you know."

She smiled up at him, her eyes big and soft and filled with gratitude. "Thanks, Harry. I know it's stupid, and if you ever tell anyone I'll deny it, but it's kind of a relief that I don't have to do this alone. I owe you."

As she left, his guilt doubled until it nearly consumed him. Damn it, what would she think when she found out he'd known Dalton all along? Would she understand? Or would she likely feel betrayed by the one person she'd started to trust? The worry gnawed at him, making him angry with regret, until the phone rang.

It was Dalton, and he was ready to come home.

CHAPTER NINE

THE SECOND HARRY stepped through the barroom doorway, he could tell Charlie was nervous. He'd spent the past week with her, and her mannerisms and mood were very familiar to him now. He picked up on the small frown, the way she repeatedly swallowed. She was behind the thick, scarred wooden bar, a clipboard clutched tightly in her hand, taking some kind of inventory. Beside him, Dalton looked around in horrified disbelief.

"My God. She can't actually work here?"

Pulling his gaze from Charlie, Harry said, "She does, and she manages quite credibly. I don't think it's been easy for her, but she's the type of woman who once she sets her mind on something, it gets accomplished one way or another." Harry knew there was a wealth of pride in his tone, but he couldn't seem to help himself. He *was* proud, and he wanted Dalton to be, too.

The bar wasn't yet open. Charlie had insisted they meet there, partly, Harry assumed, because she felt it gave her an advantage to be on her own territory and in familiar surroundings. She wouldn't admit it, not even to herself, but she was very uncertain about meeting her father.

Her insecurity, and the need to hide it, endeared her

to Harry all the more. He smiled toward her, though Charlie was still unaware of them. They were early, but keeping Dalton away any longer had proved impossible.

Harry had convinced Dalton to wait a week, to give himself plenty of time to recover. He refused to let Harry tell Charlie about his heart attack, so there was no telling how Charlie would react during the meeting, but Harry thought it a safe bet she'd be antagonistic and stubborn. She had a lot of past grievances to get through before she'd be able to fully accept Dalton.

Harry found himself very ambiguous about the meeting. He worried for Dalton, though the doctor had said he was fine. Other than routine checkups and a warning to take life easier, Dalton was free to do as he pleased.

Harry also worried for Charlie. This wouldn't be easy for her, having the foundation of her resentment pulled out from under her. Today she would find out her mother had been a bitter, vindictive woman, and Harry would have done just about anything to shield her from that.

But he had another motive for putting the reunion off until today.

Over the past week he'd spent nearly every day with her, arguing, doing his best to protect her when she insisted on forcing her way into danger. Whenever he tried to accomplish something without her, she threatened to go off on her own. But despite her interference, he'd learned quite a bit about Carlyle, while keeping Charlie in the dark. She might suspect a few things, but thankfully, she had no solid evidence of his plans. If she had, she wouldn't have agreed to meet her father today.

Harry was counting on the meeting to keep her busy until everything was finally resolved.

Dalton was still looking around, his expression appalled. Harry had been in the bar many times, however, and the bar was empty with the lights turned up. True, the lime green was almost blinding. But the place was tidy, and comforting in a lived in, relaxed sort of way. The wooden floor wasn't highly polished, but it was immaculately clean, and though some of the round, mismatched tables looked less than elegant, they were sturdy and in good repair. The walls were bare except for the occasional unframed poster, curling at the edges.

She'd obviously done the best she could with the bar, and Harry hoped Dalton would see that. Charlie had been given too much responsibility and too few breaks in her young life, and Harry was more than a little relieved to introduce her to her father, knowing Dalton would offer her new opportunities.

"Damn it, I wish Jill was going to be here. Charlotte's just being stubborn."

It was an unending refrain, and Harry sighed. They still hovered in the doorway, preferring to survey the bar and Charlie without notice. With a hand on Dalton's shoulder, Harry reminded him, "She doesn't yet know you, and she's fiercely protective of Jill. Until she's certain you won't disappoint or hurt her, I think you'll just have to be patient. In a way, that should reassure you, because you can tell Charlie's taken excellent care of her sister."

Dalton's hands fisted. "Damn Rose. None of this

was necessary. If only the woman hadn't tried to punish me by running off."

"True, but go easy on what you say today," Harry advised. "Rose is the only parent Charlie knows, and I have a feeling her stubbornness would force her to be defensive even about that. And remember, I'm just a P.I. I don't want her to have to deal with my deception today, on top of everything else."

With that last reminder, Harry determined to get the whole thing going. He wanted to see Charlie and Dalton settled, so he could attend Carlyle's little surprise party.

He stepped forward and cleared his throat.

Charlie jerked her gaze up, then stilled. Harry could see the near panic in her beautiful eyes, and it smote him clear down to his masculine core. He wanted to hold her, but of course, he couldn't. "Hello, Charlie. I'm sorry we're early, but your father was a bit anxious."

Very slowly, her gaze shifted from Harry to her father. She looked like a small animal caught in the headlights of an oncoming car, but only for a moment. Harry saw the resolve stiffen her spine, saw her summon that indomitable courage. He felt emotion expand inside him, and though it scared him spitless, he smiled.

Charlie plunked down the clipboard, skirted the bar, and started toward them with a swanky, confident walk. Her clothes were even more disreputable today, her jeans well worn and a tad frayed at the hem, her boots scuffed. She wore a T-shirt with a suggestive beer logo on the front. It was at least two sizes too big, tucked into her snug jeans, and Harry thought she looked adorable.

Judging by the expression on Dalton's face, he didn't.

All nervousness had disappeared from Charlie's mien. She stood within a few feet of them, hands on her slim hips, feet spaced apart. She could have been facing Floyd and Ralph again for all her arrogant bravado.

"So." She glanced at each of them, then focused on Harry. "I had a delivery this morning I had to deal with. Usually I'm not even up till ten, given the hours I'm open, but the delivery guys always come early. I'd almost forgotten about them after the week we've had."

Harry didn't even want to think about that and cast a quick glance at Dalton to see if he'd caught the insinuation. Dalton had no idea Charlie had involved herself with the embezzlers, and he'd be twice as upset if he found out. But Dalton still stared at Charlie, and thankfully, looked unaware of the conversation.

Harry had tried refusing to let her accompany him as he continued checking into things, partly because he'd feared for her safety, and partly because he didn't trust his dubious control around her. It boggled the mind the way she could push his buttons, but damn if she didn't manage it every time she got near. She laughed and he wanted her. She stuck her stubborn chin in the air and he went hot with lust. And her eyes—when she looked at him with her sultry, bold expressions, it took all he had not to give in to the urge to have her.

Over the past week, he'd twice found her snooping on her own. The urge to put her over his knee had been overwhelming, and had dampened his carnal appetites. Yet when he'd offered that threat, she'd merely laughed, proving she knew he'd never hurt her. To his chagrin, *she* was the one who discovered Carlyle hadn't moved his operation at all. Evidently the man was so cocky he was totally without caution, disregarding Harry's interference as a threat.

After today, Carlyle would have to rethink that.

Harry looked at Dalton, who remained mute, and decided he'd have to get the ball rolling before Charlie disclosed things better left concealed. "Charlie, this is your father, Dalton Jones."

She tilted her head at Dalton, studying him closely. "You don't look as old as I had you pictured."

Dalton smiled nervously. "Did your mother show you any photographs of me?"

"Sure. But they were years ago. Eighteen years ago to be exact."

Dalton's eyes closed briefly and he nodded. "Eighteen years that I regret more than I can ever tell you."

His words and tone were so heartfelt, Charlie wavered. Harry could see her expression shift, the uncertainty come into her eyes. He took her arm and said gently, "Why don't we sit down? You two have a lot to talk about."

Once they were at a round table toward the middle of the floor, Charlie looked at Harry with a slight smile. "Your eye is healing—the bruises are only green now instead of black. But you still look wiped out. If you can keep from strangling on it, I'll go get some coffee from the back and we'll see if that can revive you."

He smiled, too, pleased to see the appearance of her wit. "I promise to only sip, to cut back on the chances of strangulation."

She glanced at Dalton and hesitated before asking, "Would you like some, too?"

He nodded. "Actually, Charlotte, I'd love some. Black, please."

Harry winced at the name, but quickly forestalled the storm he saw brewing on Charlie's face by saying, "Isn't that just how you take yours, Charlie? Black?"

Her smile turned sickly sweet. "Just." She walked away without another word.

When she was out of sight, Harry turned to frown at Dalton. It wasn't his place, but still he said, "She prefers to be called Charlie."

Dalton pulled out a chair and sat down, prompting Harry to do the same. With his back to the kitchen doorway Charlie had gone through, Dalton whispered, "It's a horrid nickname, probably her mother's doing, which is a good reason for me not to follow suit."

"God." Harry rubbed his face, unsure how to convince Dalton he should back off. Charlie definitely wasn't a woman you wanted to push, and especially not when she felt cornered emotionally.

Dalton stared around the bar with a grimace. "Don't you see? She deserves better than this, and it's my duty to see to it. She's wearing grubby clothes and working in a dump, when I want her to be free to be a young lady. I'll worry myself into an early grave if I have to think about her being here every night. I can help her now. She can sell this place and get a respectable diner or something instead. Or she could work for me at the jewelry store." His face brightened with the prospect. "You know I'd love to have her there."

"You're jumping the gun, don't you think?"

"Ha! She deserves a lot better than working in a place like this."

The sudden stillness in the air was palpable and Harry jerked around to see Charlie frozen behind them, a tray with coffee, mugs, cream and sugar in her hands. Her jaw was positively rigid, her face pale. There was such a wounded expression in her eyes, he knew he'd never forget it as long as he lived.

He and Dalton both stood. Dalton, fidgeting nervously, took the tray from her and put it on the table, then held out a chair. As she sat, Harry touched her arm, but she shook him off. Dalton poured coffee while she stared at him.

"You know, Jill looks a lot like you."

Her calm, controlled tone reassured Dalton. But it didn't fool Harry for a single second. She was up to something, and he knew it wouldn't be pleasant. He cleared his throat. "You all have the same blue eyes."

Dalton grinned. "I'm anxious to meet Jill. Though from what Harry has told me, she's lovely and doesn't look a thing like me."

Charlie shook her head. "You've got the same color hair, the same smile. And you both look the same when you feel guilty." She ignored Dalton's searching glance. "I look more like my mother."

"Yes, you do. And she was beautiful."

"Not toward the end she wasn't. She'd led a hard life, always drinking too much, smoking, never getting enough sleep. We found out she had emphysema and she had to go on oxygen. She hated it, because dragging the oxygen around made her feel old, but she was always tired, so she used it when she absolutely had to. One day she got pneumonia and just died."

Charlie recited the facts as if it had been a play, something unreal that had happened to someone else. Without even realizing his intent, Harry took her hand. She clutched at him, but her gaze never left Dalton.

"This *dump* paid for her funeral. It's also kept my sister clothed and fed for the last few years when I had no idea where you were." Charlie tilted her head, and her grin was without an ounce of humor. "And of course, it's given me the opportunity to be free."

Dalton, already looking stricken by what she'd said, asked cautiously, "Free?"

Charlie shrugged. "I'm my mother's daughter. Did you think she hadn't told me? I knew she'd cheated on you and I heard all her excuses for why you should have forgiven her. She blamed you completely, you know, because she said you weren't around often enough. Even if she hadn't told me, her character was pretty plain to see for anyone with eyes, much less a daughter who lived with her. So what makes you think I'm any different?"

Dalton blustered. "Well, I never thought… I mean, that wasn't the indication I was…"

Charlie pulled Harry's arm over and hugged it to her breasts. Harry, taken off-guard, gawked at her.

She laughed. "Harry didn't tell you that? Well, of course he didn't. Harry is a gentleman, and gentlemen never kiss and tell."

She leaned over and lightly kissed Harry on the

jaw, and he stiffened. When he got her alone, he planned to throttle her. "Charlie—"

"I appreciate your efforts on my behalf, Harry. But whether Dalton likes it or not, the bar suits me. I'd go nuts in a nine-to-five atmosphere with rules and restrictions and you know it. Besides, the men here are always so complimentary—when they're not too tanked to get the compliments out."

Harry locked his jaw and struggled to think of a way to get her off-track. He understood her, knew exactly what she was doing, but he didn't like being used.

"Now Harry, he's such a smooth talker, he never runs out of compliments." At Dalton's unblinking stare, she added, "You didn't think he only *worked* for me, did you? No, Harry and I have gotten real close."

Harry cursed when Dalton looked at him, brows raised in question.

At a momentary loss, Dalton swallowed hard. Finally he shook his head. "I understand how difficult your life must have been, Charlotte, believe me. But I'm here now and—"

"And I've been doing as I please too long to start restricting myself at this late date." Her tone was hard, uncompromising. "If you hoped to step in and play father by correcting all my faults, forget it. I happen to revel in my faults."

Dalton directed a commanding look at Harry, then slowly stood. "I… Could you excuse me a moment?"

Charlie nodded, watching him with narrowed eyes. "Sure thing. Boy's room is in the back, down the hallway and to your left."

Harry, having correctly interpreted that look, started to follow, but Charlie didn't let him go.

He turned on her, as furious with the situation as he was with her absurd theatrics. "What the hell are you doing, making him think you're…we're…"

"Lovers?" She made a face and sipped her coffee. "Why not? He obviously thinks I'm lacking and has some harebrained idea of reforming me. This way, he'll know right off it's a lost cause and not start meddling in my life."

Harry sank back into his seat. Dalton could wait for the moment. He turned Charlie's hand so he could lace their fingers together. "He thinks no such thing. He's very proud of you, he just wants to help."

"Ha!"

Harry grimaced. He was getting damn sick and tired of that expression.

"I heard what he said, Harry. He wants to help me get my life straightened out, but it's the truth, I enjoy my life. Other than wishing I could give more to Jill, I wouldn't change a thing."

Harry knew that wasn't merely pride talking. The bar was home to her, and she wouldn't give it up easily. He sighed. "All right, so tell him that, but don't start pretending there's something going on between us—"

"Isn't there? Well, okay, not as much as I suggested, but I was on your floor the other night, Harry, and I enjoyed what you did to me. I'd like us to do it again."

"Damn it, Charlie…."

"You're working for me, right? So consider this a side assignment—with bonus pay."

Harry narrowed his eyes. "You're pushing me."

She leaned toward him with a wicked grin. "I like pushing you." Then the grin was gone, replaced by a stubborn set to her mouth. "But this is important. And since you *are* working for me, I figured you wouldn't mind helping me dupe him just a little bit. I know it pushes the boundaries of reality to think of us actually involved in anything more than a quick fling, but Dalton can't know that. So what's the big deal?"

Harry groaned.

"If he really does care, which I have serious doubts about, it won't matter to him what I do or who I am. And if it does matter, well, then, he can give me the money for Jill's education and get lost for another eighteen years. The money is all I really care about anyway."

Harry stared at her, knowing she lied. He could see it in her eyes, how much her father's apparent disapproval had hurt her, and he decided to give Dalton a piece of his mind.

"I'm going to check on him. Stay put, okay?"

"Did you think I'd run off and hide? Not likely."

Harry found Dalton standing in the tiny gray bathroom. The walls were painted brick and cement, the ceiling light a bare bulb. Dalton looked at Harry with bleak eyes. "She can't really like this place."

Harry crossed his arms over his chest and leaned against the door. "You know, Dalton, I've gotten to know Charlie—and *yes,* she is Charlie whether you like it or not!"

Dalton subsided, biting back his complaint.

"I've gotten to know her beyond what she presents to most of the world."

Dalton quirked a brow. "So she said."

Harry waved that off. "That's just her way of getting even for your censure. She wanted to hurt you, the way you hurt her."

"But I didn't mean to hurt her! I just wanted her to know she has choices now."

"I know that, but she doesn't. She's a wonderful, caring, independent woman who prides herself on those qualities. I have the feeling she's never asked anyone for anything, and coming to you now for money really rubs her the wrong way."

"It shouldn't. I'd gladly give her anything I have."

"But don't you see? She's always been able to get by on her own through gumption and strength of will. She turned this run-down dive into a favored local saloon, and she's supported her sister and ailing mother by doing so. I've watched her working here. From the regulars to the occasional drop-in, Charlie deals with them all in her own special way, protecting herself, but not really offending, being friendly, but never letting any man get too close." *Except for himself.* He shoved that thought aside and continued. "She's rightfully proud of this place and what she's accomplished. When you insult it, you insult her."

Dalton rubbed his face. "It's just so—"

"Not what you'd expected? What you'd want for her? I never thought to say it, but you remind me of my own father, Dalton."

That got his attention, his head snapping up and he frowned.

"She has to lead her own life, not the life you'd choose for her. All you can do now is be there for her. She's twenty-seven years old, a grown woman, and frankly I don't think she needs to change."

Dalton drew back, both brows shooting high. "You sound like you care about her."

Through his teeth, Harry said, "I like her as a friend."

"Hmm."

Harry decided it was time to change the subject. "Dalton, she has this crazy idea of making you think we're lovers. I have to tell her the truth."

"No! I think this might be the perfect opportunity. I screwed up, I admit it, but maybe I can fix things." He began pacing back and forth in front of the sink. "I never meant for her to hear me, it's just that I'm anxious to help. But now I can prove to her that I do care. As long as she's only acting with you, I'll know she's safe. I'll be able to show her that I accept her, that I..." He swallowed hard, his eyes misty. "That I love her no matter what."

Harry's insides cramped. "That's an asinine plan."

"No, don't you see? She's doing this to shock me because she thinks I'll walk away repulsed. But now I can show her I'll never leave her again, no matter what."

Harry muttered a crude curse that had Dalton blinking in surprise.

"All right. But I'm telling you, I don't like it. You'd better prove yourself to her and fast because I can't take too much more."

Harry stomped out of the bathroom without explaining what it was he couldn't take, and almost ran over Charlie, who'd come to see why it was taking them so long. He caught her to keep her from falling, and she landed against his chest with a thud. She saw Dalton behind Harry, and that was all the encouragement she needed. She threw her arms around his neck, plastered her body up against his, and kissed him so thoroughly he thought he was having his own heart attack.

"I just got off the phone," she whispered against his mouth. "I found someone to cover for me so I could have the night off. I guess we've got a date after all."

CHAPTER TEN

CHARLIE ALMOST LAUGHED at the look on Harry's face. He went from heated response, to shock, to chagrin. Luckily her father was still behind him and didn't see that variety of reactions. She kissed him again for good measure, and as he removed her arms with a chastising frown and started around her, she patted his butt.

Harry jumped, looking like a man who'd just been stung, then took her hand and literally dragged her to the table. Dalton came along, smiling like a damn Cheshire cat, though what he had to grin about, Charlie had no idea.

When they reached the table, Harry pulled a chair out for her. She laughed, pushed him into his seat and dropped onto his lap. She was prepared to put on a real show, not only to prove to her father she was beyond redemption, but because this gave her the perfect opportunity to be close to Harry. Very soon now, their time would be over. He'd brought her father to her, and he planned to wrap things up that week with Floyd and Ralph. He wouldn't share his plans in that regard, but she'd come to know Harry very well and knew he was up to something. Just the fact that he'd been hanging out in the Lucky Goose all week told her he wanted to keep an eye on her, to make sure she didn't blunder into whatever plans he had in mind.

It didn't bother her. She was so at ease with Harry, she could enjoy his company while being herself.

To her surprise, Harry didn't try to push her away. He sighed, then looped his arms around her waist. In her ear, he whispered, "There's always retribution to be paid, Charlie. Don't forget that."

She ignored this threat, just as she ignored all his others. Harry wouldn't hurt her and she knew it. She turned to Dalton, to judge his reaction to the scene, and saw him staring toward the doorway. With an inkling of dread, she whipped about and there stood Jillian. She had a shopping bag clutched in her hands and a frozen expression on her face.

"Oh hell." Charlie started to scramble off Harry's lap, but he tightened his hold.

"Ah, ah. Don't turn cowardly on me now."

"Harry, I don't want Jill—"

"To meet her father?" He gave her a gentle hug. "Honey, relax. It'll be okay."

"Not with me on your lap! What will she think?"

"That you're up to mischief again, no doubt."

Dalton came to his feet like a sleepwalker. "Jillian?"

Jillian's smile trembled the tiniest bit, and then she walked forward cautiously. She glanced at Charlie, and her eyes widened when she saw how her sister was seated. Charlie groaned. "It's not what you—"

Laughing, Harry interjected, "I'd stand, but you can see I have a vexatious burden in my lap."

Jill nodded politely. "Is there, ah, any reason why?"

With a smile that was pure wickedness, Harry said, "We're passionately involved, don't you know."

Charlie's elbow came back hard enough to make him grunt, then she smiled at Jill. "I was going to tell you later, after...well, I wanted to make sure everything would be okay..."

Jill glanced at Dalton, then back to her sister. "I understand. Would you like to introduce me now?"

"I suppose I don't really have a choice, do I? Jill, this is our father, Dalton Jones."

Jill caught her breath and dropped her bag. She blinked hard, trying to fend off tears. "I thought... I mean, you look exactly as I imagined, but I just wasn't sure..."

Dalton, his own eyes wet, reached out to her. "I never gave up hope of finding you."

Jill took his hands. "I have so many questions."

"Me, too."

They seemed to be in their own little world and Charlie, disgusted and a tad jealous, shook her head. Her sister was so much more accepting than she could ever be. She leaned back against Harry and whispered, "Don't start looking smug. If he does one thing to insult her or upset her, I'll toss him—and you—out."

Frowning, Harry appeared to consider that. "I don't think you can just toss a lover out. No, a lover gets to stick around through thick and thin."

"You're enjoying yourself, aren't you?"

"I'm beginning to."

Charlie looked at his totally shameful grin and had to smile herself. He did enjoy matching wits with her, that had been apparent from the first. She enjoyed it too, along with a great many other things.

She forgot about provoking Dalton and leaned forward to kiss him. Jill cleared her throat.

"Oh." Charlie straightened, flustered, while Harry looked sublimely unaffected.

"Don't mind us," he said, "she just can't keep her hands off me."

With a smothered laugh, Jill said, "I'm going to run upstairs and put my stuff away, then I'll be right back down."

Dalton stepped forward. "You live upstairs, is that correct?"

"Yes. Would you like me to show you around?"

Charlie stiffened, ready to refuse despite Harry's gentle stroking on her back, when Jill added, a touch of warning in her tone, "Charlie won't mind. She never lets men upstairs—well, except for Harry, but he's different."

"So I understand."

Jill laughed. "Charlie is rigidly uncompromising about how she handles having our home above the bar. She's never wanted any of the men here to get the wrong idea. She won't admit it, but she's something of a mother hen most of the time."

Dalton glanced at Charlie with a smile. "I realize that. And it soothes me to know what a wonderful job she's done handling everything."

Charlie's mouth fell open in surprise at the praise, and Harry started to laugh, tempting Charlie's elbow again. She gave in to temptation, and at the same time prompted her sister with, "I thought you were going to put your things away."

Jill rolled one shoulder. “I don’t know why you’re so shy about being a good sister. It’s not like it’s a bad thing.”

Dalton took Jill’s arm to start them on their way. “Maybe you can tell me more about… Charlie, during our tour?”

“I’d love to!”

As they disappeared through the doorway, Charlie dropped back against Harry with a groan. “Jill and her big mouth.”

Harry smiled against her temple. “If I laugh, will you poke me with that sharp elbow of yours again?”

“Absolutely.”

“Then I’ll content myself with telling you how childish you’re acting.” She started to pull away, but he locked his arms around her, just below her breasts, and held her secure. “Allow your lover just a little leeway, please. It’s my right as such to point these things out.”

“Okay, so pretending we’re involved was a bad idea on my part. You can quit punishing me for it.”

“Is that what I was doing?”

“Yes. You’ve made your point. I’ve acted like a total idiot.”

“I never said any such thing and I’ll thank you not to put words in my mouth.”

She twisted to face him, bracing her hands on his shoulders. “All right, so what would you say?”

He smoothed her hair away from her face and his expression grew serious, his golden-brown eyes intent. “That you’re fighting yourself more than anyone else. Dalton’s reaction wasn’t one of disapproval, but guilt. He doesn’t know you well enough yet to know you wouldn't be taken advantage of. He doesn't know how strong and capable you are."

"But you do?"

His hand cupped her neck, caressing. "You're the strongest person I've ever met."

"Too strong?"

His brows lifted in admission. "Sometimes. You plow your way through life assuming sheer determination will get you what you want."

She wondered if he was talking about himself. True, she'd been coming on strong, but that was the only way she knew. Sheer determination *had* gotten her everything she wanted—with the exception of a responsible mother or an available father.

She looked down at his chest and toyed with a button on his shirt. "Today...well, this was just for show."

"I wasn't talking about us, Charlie. I was talking about this unreasonable assumption you have that you can handle men like Carlyle, or even Floyd and Ralph."

"Oh." She waved that away. "I'm not worried about them, even though you're keeping secrets from me." She slanted him a look. "I know something's going on, and I'll figure it out sooner or later. Now, don't look like that, Harry. You know I will! I'm not dumb, and despite all your warnings, they don't scare me."

His sigh was exaggerated. "I know, and that's what worries me. I have enough appreciation for their malevolent capacities for both of us."

Charlie grinned. "I love it when you talk like that. *Malevolent capacities.* It sounds dirty."

He shook her slightly, but she could see the amusement in his eyes. "I'm serious here, Charlie."

"Yeah, well, I'm seriously starting to wonder what's taking them so long. Our apartment is pretty small. You could walk the whole thing in under two minutes."

"You're incorrigible."

"Tell my father that." Harry grew so solemn, she sighed. "All right, I'm sorry."

He grabbed his head and weaved in the chair, almost toppling Charlie. "I must be delirious. Surely you didn't just apologize? Not Charlie Jones, the toughest—"

"My elbow hasn't gotten any softer you know." She stifled a chuckle as she made the threat, drawing her arm back in warning.

Harry grabbed her close and kissed her mouth, laughing against her lips. It was a ticklish kiss—at least at first. Then his mouth softened, slowed with awareness. She was on his lap, feeling his heat, his strength. At first the closeness was a game, but now it struck her how cozy it could be.

She'd never sat in a man's lap before meeting Harry.

They both remained motionless for a long moment, and Charlie could hear the thundering of her heartbeat in her ears. Her lips parted, and with a groan, Harry tilted her back over his arm. His mouth was suddenly hot, hungry, his tongue stroking past her lips, tasting—

"Maybe we should leave the lovebirds alone."

Harry jerked back so fast he made Charlie lose her balance. She almost slid off his lap. He managed to catch her arms, saving her the disgrace of falling on her behind. To her disgust, she could feel her face heating.

"Ah, Jill, we were just..."

"I'm young, sis, not stupid." Jill shook her head at Harry, then continued. "Father and I have decided to go to dinner. He said you two had a date, so we'll just use the time to get better acquainted."

Charlie felt her temper start to boil, but then Dalton stepped closer and said, "That's if it's okay with you. Harry drove here, but we can catch a cab. I thought after dinner, I could show Jill the jewelry store I own on the other side of town. I'd love for you to see it as well, but of course, I don't want to interfere with your personal time."

Momentarily stuck in her own deception, Charlie said, "Uhhh...."

Harry had no such problem. "That's fine. I'm sure we'll manage without you."

Charlie stood and stared hard at Dalton in warning. "Where are you going to dinner?"

He didn't look the least put off by her tone, or her question. "I thought we'd go to Maria's. It's a nice little Italian restaurant not too far from my store."

It was a restaurant she'd never been to, a very ritzy, expensive place well above her budget. She glanced at her sister and saw that Jill had changed into a dress and looked very excited by the prospect of dining there. Charlie didn't want to let her go. Old protective instincts clamored inside her, reminding her of all the years she'd spent looking out for her sister's well-being. But Jill was eighteen now, a young woman, and it was time to give her some freedom.

It went against her instincts, but Charlie nodded. "All right."

Jill stepped forward and gave Charlie a tight hug. "Thank you."

She waved her off. "Don't thank me. I'm not the one taking you."

"But we both know I wouldn't go if you asked me not to."

Uncomfortable with Dalton and Harry listening in, Charlie made a face. "Yeah, well, I'm assuming Dalton will take good care of you."

Dalton's mouth twitched at the malice in her tone. "Absolutely." Then he, too, stepped forward for a hug, taking Charlie by surprise. In a low voice meant only for her ears, he said, "I can't tell you how pleased I am to finally meet you. Pleased, and so damn proud."

Charlie was still mute after they'd walked out the door. Harry, with a twisted grin, waved a hand in front of her face.

"Are you all right or did Dalton put a trance on you?"

She shook her head as if to clear it, then looked at Harry, but she didn't really see him. A jumbled mix of emotions made her shaky inside. *Her father was proud?* She swallowed hard and tried to digest that information, but every stubborn, fighting instinct she had rebelled against it. Accepting any accolades from him would make her weak, would detract from the foundation she'd built over the past months and alter her goals completely. It was too much to take in all at once, and so she did what came naturally instead.

With a determined look that made Harry draw back, she walked around him and started out of the bar.

He hustled after her. "Where are you off to, brat?"

"I'm going to follow them."

"What?"

"He can visit with my sister all he likes, as long as I'm close enough to take care of her if anything goes wrong." Using her key, she unlocked the bottom door and rushed through it. Harry caught it in time and went up the steps with her. "I'm going to change, then I'm leaving. If you want to come along, fine, but I don't need you there."

He tried to catch her arm, but she shook him off to unlock the door at the top of the stairs.

"Charlie, this is insane."

"Think what you like. I'm still going to do it." She went down the hall to her bedroom, aware of Harry right behind her, and of his shock to her decorating scheme. He'd been upstairs many times, but never in her bedroom.

He stood there with his mouth open, his face blank. "Good God. You have ruffles."

Belligerent, she said, "Yeah, so? It's my room and I can decorate it any way I want." She pulled out a clean pair of newer jeans and a white button-down oxford-cloth shirt. It was the closest thing she had to "dressier."

Harry touched the fluffy white quilt on her bed. "I like it, so don't sound so defensive. It's just that I pictured you with..."

"Barbed wire? A bare mattress?" She snorted. "The quilt is warm and the bed skirt hides all the stuff I stick under my bed."

Harry bent and looked. "There's nothing under your bed."

"Go to hell, Harry."

He laughed, but when she pulled off her T-shirt to change, his humor died a quick death. Sounding strangled, he asked, "What are you doing?"

"Changing. I can't very well go unnoticed if I wear what they've already seen."

"Charlie." With his gaze glued to her upper body, bare except for her bra, he clasped her shoulders. "Don't do this to yourself."

She tried to shrug him off, but his large hands held firm. "I have to hurry."

"You're not going anywhere, sweetheart."

Turmoil exploded inside her, making her hands shake and her stomach pitch. In a voice that was less than steady, she growled, "Don't start with me now, Harry. I *have* to go."

"Shh." Despite her resistance he pulled her close and his big hot hands smoothed up and down her naked spine. "I know, babe, I really do. This is so damn hard. But you need to indulge in a little trust."

"Trust a man I barely know?"

He kissed her ear, still making those "shushing" sounds. "You know me, and I've told you the man is safe. And you should certainly trust your sister. What responsibilities did you have at eighteen?"

The trembling became worse and she leaned into Harry, for the moment letting herself relax, letting his heat seep into her. "None that I want Jill to have."

"You've done an incredible job with her, Charlie. She's an intelligent young lady and an excellent judge of character. She has enough sense to call you if anything should go wrong."

She bit her lip, trying to sort out her thoughts. "Why should I trust you when you don't trust me?"

His hands stilled.

"Something's going on with Carlyle. I can feel it."

A look of alarm passed over his features and his frown turned fierce. "That has nothing to do with you."

Flabbergasted, she leaned back to look at him. "And my personal life has nothing to do with *you,* but I noticed that hasn't slowed you down any!"

Her new posture pushed her pelvis closer to his, while baring her upper body. His gaze again lowered to her breasts, and he remained silent.

Tension radiated off him and she shifted. "What? No answer to that?"

His hand coasted down her spine to her backside, cuddling and stroking. In a near rasp, he said, "We're standing in a bedroom, you're taunting me with these luscious little breasts of yours, and I'm so aroused I can barely think. Did you really expect me to indulge in conversation?"

Her own arousal hit like a tidal wave, stealing her breath and filling her with undulating heat. All her confusion, all her nervousness, magically transformed into sexual awareness. She could barely get a whisper past her constricted throat. "Harry?"

Shaking his head with a denial she didn't understand, he closed his eyes. "I can't do this anymore."

The heat of his hard chest beckoned her, and she braced her palms flat there. "Do what?"

Startling her with his suddenness, he lifted her, walked the two steps to the bed, then dropped with her to the mattress. He caught her hands and lifted them over her head, then groaned as her breasts pressed to his chest.

The weight of his body both appeased and intensified the ache, making her squirm. “I love how you feel, Harry. So hard and hot and strong.”

The low gasping of his breath tickled her ear. “I’m glad you think so, because I’m in no hurry to move.”

“I don’t want you to move. Let my hands go.”

“No.”

“What do you mean ‘no’?” When he didn’t answer, she tried to pull away.

“Not this time, honey. This time we finish it. *My way.*”

Charlie felt both excited and slightly alarmed by his uncompromising tone, uncertain how she should react. Then she realized she really had no choice. Harry wasn’t letting go, and that meant she’d have to accept whatever he had planned.

Her eyes narrowed sensually. She’d wallow in every second of his dominance.

RAISING HIMSELF SLIGHTLY, Harry smiled and transferred both her hands into one of his own, then cupped her jaw. “You’re just filled with demands, aren’t you?”

“I wasn’t…”

“Hmm. Yes, you were. It’s part and parcel of who you are. But I like it. Most of the time. Right now, I like you soft and submissive beneath me.” He kissed her gently, pulling back when she tried to deepen the kiss. “Do you like it too, honey?”

“Yes.”

That soft whisper shook his resolve. Harry closed his mouth over hers, felt her lips part and immediately stroked his tongue inside. Her slender thighs tightened restlessly, her body shifting in subtle, erotic moves. His free hand slid down her side, then to her soft breast. Damn she felt good. Her nipple was already puckered, pressing against her thin cotton bra, and with a low curse, he caught the cup with his fingertips and pulled it down until her firm breast came free.

Harry tore his mouth away from hers to look at her. He leaned back and to the side, keeping her hands firmly clasped, watching in heated appreciation as she strained toward him.

Her breast was so white, the nipple a soft pale pink, and he wanted her. He leaned down with no forewarning and drew her into his mouth.

She gave a stifled scream.

"Hush. Someone downstairs might hear you."

"Harry…it's too much."

"Nonsense," he said, taunting her with his assurance. "You'll like this. Just be still."

She didn't even try. As he licked and gently sucked, she struggled against him, moaning, twisting. She kept trying to pull her hands free, but he didn't think she was even aware of it. She didn't want to be free, it was just in Charlie's nature to fight any type of restriction. He felt provoked by her reactions, and grew all the more determined to control things.

From the day he'd met her, she'd made him crazy with her take-charge ways, even while his admiration for her courage grew. Little by little she'd seduced him, not just sexually, but emotionally as well. He wanted her, and he was tired of denying himself. Unlike his ex-wife, who tried to manipulate with tears, Charlie fought fair, with upfront demands and honest compromises. He enjoyed his battles with her, rather than feeling guilty over them. She excited him on every level, and he couldn't resist any longer.

Later, he'd work through the problems. But now, in this precise moment, all he cared about was making her his own.

He loved the taste of her, her hot reactions, and he wanted more. Coming up to his knees, straddling her hips so she couldn't scoot away, he tugged the bra completely off. Charlie froze for an instant as the heat of embarrassment colored her face and throat. "You're looking at me."

"Yes." With one finger he touched her exposed nipples. "You're wet from my mouth, tight and sweet."

Her eyes closed again and she made soft sounds of desire. Her breasts were plump, offered up by the way she kept straining toward him. The mere sight of her aroused him as much as an hour of foreplay. "You're right, sweetheart. These are very special."

"You're embarrassing me, Harry."

His mouth tipped in a small smile. She didn't sound embarrassed. She sounded excited. Her breasts shimmered with each breath, her diaphragm expanding. Her abdomen was silky smooth, narrow. The waistband of her jeans curled out away from her skin and he deftly flicked the snap free. He could hear her rasping, anxious breaths as he slowly tugged down the zipper. Her belly was taut, her hips straining upward. He dipped one fingertip in her navel, then followed the line of her zipper downward, gradually parting the material until he came to the elastic waistband of her bikini panties. Because he'd already seen her bra, he wasn't surprised that these were also white cotton.

"You have very conservative taste in underclothes," he murmured.

His finger continued to tickle up and down just inside her zipper and her voice shook when she replied. "No one sees them but me."

Her words filled him with satisfaction, and the possessive urges no longer alarmed him. "I think this one is jealous," he said of the breast he hadn't yet tasted.

"Harry..."

Her tone was a whimper in anticipation of what she knew would come. He wanted her to understand that she couldn't always control him, that some things were better left in his hands, especially the sensual things.

With that in mind, he bent and carefully kissed her breast, avoiding the erect, puckered nipple and ignoring her soft cries. Relentlessly he teased, always staying just out of reach no matter how she turned or tried to coax him to take her into his mouth. She cursed him softly, then moaned, her thick lashes drifting down over her eyes, her body going utterly lax, with no fight left at all.

Harry tried to stifle the overwhelming feeling of triumph, but knowing he'd won with this one particular woman—and that she'd enjoyed letting him win—filled him with primitive instincts. He loosened his hold and whispered close to her ear, "Don't move, sweetheart."

"Harry...*please*."

His heart tripped. He'd never thought to hear that word from her mouth. She'd not only given over to him, she trusted him enough to show her full need. Releasing her hands and sitting up, Harry pulled off her boots and socks, then hooked his fingers in the waistband of her jeans and tugged them down to her knees. She helped him by kicking them off the rest of the way.

Charlie watched him through dazed eyes. Her soft mouth was slightly open, her hands resting above her head, the palms up and vulnerable. He shook he wanted her so badly.

Coming down on his elbow beside her, he kissed her hungrily and she groaned in relief. Impatient, he stroked his hand down her belly and below, cupping his fingers over her mound, feeling the heat of her, the dampness of the cotton panties. He could hear the race of his blood in his ears, and the sexy little sounds Charlie made.

She was already so close, and he'd barely begun. He leaned away from her and saw her hands were now fisted tightly, her chest heaving, her pale thighs clenched. He pushed his hand inside her panties and with his middle finger pressed and stroked. "You're so wet, honey. Do you like that?"

"Yes."

She didn't hesitate in answering, though her reply was an almost incoherent hiss. He'd always loved watching a woman climax, but seeing Charlie, her head pressed back, her neck muscles straining, her pretty breasts heaving—it was more than he'd ever expected. More than he likely deserved. Very slowly, he worked one finger inside her. Though she was silky wet and very excited, she clenched his finger tightly. He groaned, imagining how she'd feel squeezing his erection. His heart pounded.

"Ah, Harry, I..."

"Does that hurt?" he whispered. His free arm was beside her head and he smoothed her silky dark hair away from her face.

She shook her head, then said, "A little. But don't stop."

"No, I won't stop." It pained him to smile, he was so aroused, but he felt full to bursting with love and contentment. He kissed her cheek, her nose, then used his thumb to find her small clitoris. He touched it lightly and she jerked, her reaction very telling.

He found a rhythm, using her own wetness to slick the way, to make the friction sweeter. He could tell she held her breath, her entire body tensed in expectation, and when she suddenly lurched and cried out he kissed her, swallowing the sound, taking it into himself. She forgot his instructions and wrapped her arms tightly around him, gripping him as if needing an anchor, as if she needed him as close as possible. Harry continued to kiss her, his tongue stroking in her mouth just as his finger stroked inside her. Her climax was long and full and she held him, her thighs rigid, her inner muscles trembling. She was so explosive, so *real,* he nearly lost control.

Making love to her, actually being inside her, might well kill him. But he was more than willing to take the risk.

As she quieted, he tenderly kissed her trembling lips. "You okay?"

She mumbled something he couldn't hear and burrowed a little closer.

"Should I take that as a yes?" He wanted to tease, but his voice shook and he knew he wouldn't last a minute longer.

For an answer, she bit him. He jumped, then rubbed his chest, though the small nip of her teeth hadn't really hurt. "Your vicious tendencies never cease to amaze me."

She gave him a scorching look and smiled. "My vicious tendencies will explode if you don't get on with it."

"Impatient wench." But he stood beside the bed and began unbuttoning his shirt. Charlie watched, lying on her back at her leisure, unashamed of her nudity or the sensual pose she presented.

Impossible as it seemed, her gaze grew even warmer and she breathed more deeply as he tossed his shirt aside and unbuttoned his slacks. He removed his wallet and pulled a condom from it, tossing it onto the nightstand beside her bed. She smiled.

Holding her gaze, he toed off his shoes, then pulled down his slacks, removing his shorts and socks at the same time. He straightened, then stood there, letting her look her fill.

She took a leisurely perusal of his body, from his shoulders all the way down to his feet. Once that was done, her gaze lifted to focus on his erection. He throbbed painfully, feeling her attention like a tactile touch.

"Well?"

With warm cheeks and hot eyes she nodded. "You'll do."

The laugh emerged as a bark, relieving a bit of his tension. He climbed back into bed with her. "Merely satisfactory, huh?"

"On the contrary." She crawled over him, lying

along his length, propping her elbows on his chest. Her voice turned low and husky as she stared down into his eyes. "You're so incredibly sexy there are no words."

The breathless compliment pushed him right over the edge. "Charlie." He turned her beneath him and kissed her deeply, groaning at the acute sensation of her nakedness beneath him. With her arms free this time, she explored him, her small palms coasting over his shoulders, down his spine to his buttocks. He groaned again, then reared back. "Damn it. I'm sorry, but I can't wait. I wanted to make this last, to glut myself on you—"

"How romantic."

He shook his head, unable to banter with her at this moment when his need was so great. "I'll explode if I don't get inside you right now."

Her smile was pure female satisfaction. "So explode. I'm not stopping you."

Muttering another curse, he leaned over to the nightstand and grabbed the condom. Charlie watched in fascination as he put it on, then squealed when he quickly tucked her beneath him. "Put your legs around me."

She obeyed. He reached between their bodies, touching her, opening her for his thrust. "You're small, honey."

Her eyes were huge, watchful. "And you're not."

"No." He ground his teeth together while his fingers again explored her. Her feminine flesh was swelled, hot. And she was wet from her release. He closed his eyes. "I don't want to hurt you."

"It's all right, Harry. I won't break."

He wanted to laugh. Even now, she was full of bravado, unwilling to show any weakness. He wanted to wait, to ease into her gently, but she kept touching him and her hips squirmed against him. His control snapped. With a harsh curse, he entered her.

She caught her breath, but didn't fight him.

"Easy, sweetheart." He saw her through a red haze of overwhelming lust and tenderness, emotions that when mixed became volatile. She quivered, and her eyes closed, her neck arched. She gave a small moan, of pain or ecstasy, he couldn't tell. Then her legs tightened around his waist and her fingers tangled in his hair, and he was gone.

He rode her as gently as he could considering every muscle in his body strained for release. He felt sweat on his shoulders, felt her uneven breaths on his throat. And he felt Charlie, soft and inquisitive and delicate, despite the impression she liked to give the world.

Sliding one hand beneath her hips, he tilted her pelvis to allow him a deeper penetration, driven to bind their bodies together, to make her a part of him. She cried out, and her inner muscles clamped down on him.

"Come on, sweetheart," he ground out through his teeth, thrusting harder, faster, his control a distant memory. "Come for me again. I want you with me."

He felt the spasms in her legs first, then the way her entire body tensed. She caught and held her breath, her eyes squeezed tight, and she climaxed, holding him, whispering his name. Tears seeped past her lashes and as he joined her, his own release strong enough to steal his strength, the truth hit him. He loved her. Damn, how he loved her.

Now the real trouble would begin.

CHAPTER ELEVEN

"OH HARRY. THAT was...indescribable."

She heard a grunt that could possibly pass for a reply, and grinned. Harry at a loss for words? What a novelty.

Her hands coasted over his slick shoulders and she kissed his throat. He tasted good. He smelled good. She admitted he *was* good. Her body still tingled pleasantly in very interesting places. "I wouldn't mind doing this again."

The grunt turned into a groan. With obvious effort, Harry raised his head. His light brown eyes were soft and sated and filled with some emotion she didn't understand.

He touched her hair, her cheek. "Insatiable, are we?"

"A tribute to your skill."

"Hmm. I suppose I could be convinced—in about an hour."

She laughed, then pushed at his shoulder. "In that case, you need to move. I have things to do."

Obediently, Harry rolled to the side, sprawling on his back like a vanquished warrior. When she started to crawl over him, he made a sound of appreciation and pulled her flat to his chest. "Don't you know lovers are supposed to talk after sex? It's callous to just use mc and then leave the bed without any soft whispering and cuddling."

Toying with the hair on his chest, she laughed. "Callous, huh? I wouldn't want to be accused of that. But maybe we can talk later? I need to get going."

A frown appeared where before he'd been all smiles. "Where is it you think you have to rush off to?"

She tried to get up again, but now he had both hands cupping her bare backside, anchoring her in place. "I told you, I want to go keep an eye on Jill."

Harry closed his eyes with a soft curse. When he opened them again, she was struck by the cold determination there. "You don't need to do that."

"So says a man who doesn't have a little sister. Look, Harry, I know you said you checked up on Dalton. But how much could you have really found out? There could be all kinds of skeletons in his closet, and until I'm assured—"

"There aren't."

"You sound awfully sure of that." She watched him skeptically, knowing that particular tone and look.

With a sigh, Harry lifted her to the side of the bed and sat up. "We need to talk."

Charlie scrambled for the sheet and pulled it over her. "And we will. Later."

Resignation darkened his features as he glanced at her over his shoulder. "I know your father."

A strange foreboding made her stomach pitch. She pressed a fist to it and said logically, "Of course you do. You brought him here."

He waved her logic away. "I knew him before that. I've known him for years." He turned to face her, still naked, his powerful shoulders gleaming in the lamplight, his dusty-brown hair rumpled. His gaze never wavered from hers but tension emanated off him, pelting her with his resolution. "Dalton Jones has been like a father to me."

Feeling unsteady and sick, she moved away from him. She needed distance; she needed to be off the bed where they'd just made love. Backing up until she bumped into the dresser, she watched him. Harry never so much as flinched. "I don't understand."

"Dalton has looked for you for years, honey. He's suffered more than any one man ever should."

"You know him?" That one fact wouldn't quite pene-trate.

Harry stood, too, but when she clutched her sheet tighter, he went still, making no move toward her. "My father was a cold, distant man who barely knew I existed. Dalton stepped in and did all the things for me that a father should do. He supported me in my decisions, and helped me get through my divorce from hell. He encouraged me and—"

"And did all the things for you that he didn't do for me." She felt lost, wounded to her soul.

"Not because he didn't care! He's spent a small fortune trying to locate you and Jill."

Not for anything would Charlie let him see how he'd hurt her, how her heart felt ready to break into pieces. She clutched at the sheet and tried to order her thoughts into some decipherable rationale. "Why didn't you tell me?"

Locking his jaw, Harry paced away, giving her a distracting view of his muscled backside. It angered her that even now she was drawn to him, finding him irresistible.

He turned to face her and propped his hands on his hips. "I didn't know what the hell to do when you asked me to find your father. At the time, I felt my loyalty was to Dalton. It was his responsibility, his *pleasure,* to get to explain that he hadn't abandoned you. But you were so hostile about the whole thing, so…detached. You'd sent him that damn letter—"

"You knew about the letter?"

He gave a small nod. "I knew. Dalton told me that very night at the hospital. And he asked me not to tell you the truth yet, because he wanted a chance with you. He thought if I pretended to investigate him, I could give you a few facts that might soften you toward him."

That word *pretend* felt like a slap, bringing home just how much of her relationship with Harry was based on lies and manipulations. "So you played along?"

"Honey, I didn't know what else to do. I tried to talk him out of it, but he was afraid of losing you again."

"And of course, what he wanted is the only thing that mattered. I mean, you hardly know me really. I'm just…" She stopped in midsentence because she had no idea what she meant to Harry. Obviously not much or he couldn't have deceived her so easily. Needing something to do before she fell apart, she went to the closet and pulled out a T-shirt.

The bed creaked when Harry sat back down. "I'm so sorry, Charlie. I swear I never meant to hurt you."

She pulled clean jeans from the dresser, fighting

off the tears the best she could. "I understand. I don't like it, of course." The laugh, sounding close to hysteria, took her by surprise and she quickly suppressed it. "I feel pretty damn foolish, too. I can just imagine how the two of you must have been snickering. Especially after my stupid display tonight."

"No."

He started to get up, to come to her, but she warned him off with a bleak look. If he touched her, she'd sit down and cry like a baby, and that was something she hadn't done in too many years to count. "Don't even think it, Harry. The pretense is over."

Eyeing her rigid stance, he said carefully, "It wasn't all a pretense."

"No? Well, some day you'll have to tell me which parts came close to the truth. Right now, I'm just not interested. I'd like you to leave."

He swallowed hard, still watching her. "No."

"I need to get dressed!" The panic was real, making her voice too loud, too high. She needed to be alone. Already her hands were shaking and her legs were following suit.

"Charlie." Despite her warnings, he started toward her. She shook her head, but he looked more determined now than ever. "We have to talk about this."

"About how you used me? How you played along so Dalton wouldn't be disappointed?" His hands reached for her and her temper snapped. Without really thinking it through, she slapped him. Hard. The loud crack of her palm striking his handsome face sounded obscene. For an instant, they both froze. Then she covered her mouth, appalled.

Harry fingered his cheek, his brows up in surprise. "I didn't see that coming. Knowing you as I do, I was watching for a fist, or maybe a kick. Not a feminine slap."

"Don't you dare tease me now."

"I'm sorry. But Charlie, there's more I have to tell you."

"Oh?" Her stomach clenched, but she forced herself to be flippant. "Did you maybe just fake what we did in bed?"

Incredulous, he stared at her a moment, then laughed. "Honey, men can't fake a thing like that."

Her teeth ground together. "You know what I mean. And don't call me honey."

He hesitated for the briefest moment. "No, I didn't fake it." His gaze softened, turned intimate, and he whispered, "I love you."

Her chest hurt so much she gasped. She felt raw and exposed, and she almost hated him. *Almost.* "Did Dalton tell you to say that? To do whatever was necessary to appease me?"

"No."

In a burst of temper, she snapped, "Will you at least put some damn clothes on!"

His expression didn't change. "Dalton had a heart attack the day you sent the letter." He caught her before she dropped to the floor, then led her to the bed. He spoke quickly now, rushing his words together. "I was so worried about him, it's part of the reason I let him talk me into this harebrained plan, because I didn't want to see him disappointed again. You've been so hurt, I couldn't guess how you might react to the truth, if you'd even give Dalton a chance. And if you didn't, with his health in danger—"

She was back off the bed in a flash, no longer worried about her sheet or keeping her body covered. She jerked on her jeans and pulled the T-shirt over her head, then stepped into a pair of sneakers.

"Charlie—"

She rounded on him. "You bastard!" Stepping close so she could shake a fist in his face, she yelled, "My father could have died, and you didn't tell me?"

He caught and held her fists. "He's fine now, Charlie. He only needs to be more cautious."

She shoved him away then turned for the door. Harry grabbed her shoulder. "Where are you going?"

"To see him. I want you out of my place." She picked up a key off the dresser and flung it at him. "Let yourself out."

"Wait!" He started rushing into his own clothes. "I'll go with you."

"Ha!"

"It's not safe, Charlie! Damn it, you don't know what's going on!"

But she was already hurrying down the hall. Harry tried to follow after her, and she barely slipped through the door in time. She heard his fist hit it with incredible force, and he yelled her name again. She ignored him. She knew by the time he got the key and unlocked the door, she'd be gone. And if she never saw him again, it was only what she deserved.

CHARLIE CHECKED FIRST at Maria's, the restaurant where they'd planned to eat, but Dalton and her sister weren't there. She assumed they had gone on to Dalton's jewelry store, so she headed in that direction. At the moment, she had no idea what she planned to say to her father, but she needed to reassure herself that he was okay. Whether he cared about her or not, he was her father, and that mattered. It mattered more than she'd ever thought possible, and she now regretted all her plans for revenge. It made her almost sick to think she might have played a part in his ill health with her hurtful letter.

All her concentration was centered on the problem with her father. She couldn't think about Harry. If she did, she might start bawling like a baby. She loved the arrogant, obnoxious jerk, and yet he'd used her. The really sad part was, she could understand his reasons for the deception. In his position, she might have done the same. And if she hadn't pushed so hard, their relationship probably wouldn't have become intimate. She had only herself to blame. She'd been a complete fool—and she'd behaved like her mother. The truth hurt so bad she didn't think she could stand it.

She trudged up the sidewalk to the jewelry store, lost in thought. At first she didn't notice when a car pulled up beside her. Absently, she turned to look, and was stunned to see Floyd in the passenger seat, grinning at her with evil intent. The car stopped and she broke into a dead run, but she'd only gotten a few feet before he caught her arm and jerked her back. She stumbled, going down hard on one knee. She groaned at the jarring pain.

The car pulled alongside and Ralph got out. "Get her in the back seat."

Hearing that cleared the pain from her knee enough to allow her to fight. She started kicking and shouting, doing anything she could to fend them off. Somehow she knew if they got her in the car, she might never get out again.

Floyd managed to drag her as far as the curb, using her arm and her shirt collar for leverage. Even in her struggle, she saw the unfamiliar man in the front seat. She had the brief impression of a polished businessman before shouts sounded behind her. Her blood nearly froze when she recognized Dalton's voice.

"No!" He couldn't get into a skirmish because of her, not with his heart condition. If anything happened to him… She doubled her efforts, and caught Floyd low in the stomach with a fist. He grunted and loosened his hold. She tried to roll away, but Ralph reached for her.

"Let her go!" Dalton leaped onto Ralph's back, knocking him down, all the while cursing so vividly Charlie couldn't help but be impressed. The third man in the car got out and started toward them with a purposeful stride.

Suddenly other men were there, leaving their shops in a rush, leaping into the fray, crowding together on the sidewalk. It became a chaotic free-for-all with the elderly swinging canes and brooms and fists. Vile threats filled the air from both factions. Charlie was tossed aside and landed on her butt, but she was back up in a heartbeat when she saw the man from the car reach inside his jacket. *Oh God, a gun!*

Dalton threw himself in front of her, and no matter how she tried, she couldn't get around him. The brawl ended, no one daring to move. Floyd and Ralph, with a lot of blustering, brushed themselves off and straightened their jackets. Six older men and two gray-haired women stood in a circle, their hands in fists, their faces red.

"What should we do with them all, Carlyle?"

Carlyle. Again, Charlie strained to see around Dalton's shoulder, curious about the man Harry wanted so badly. After being kidnapped and harassed, she owed Carlyle much, and now with him threatening her father her rage grew.

She ducked under Dalton's arm, but before she could take two steps Harry was there. In a flash, he was around the parked car, jerking Carlyle's hand up so the gun fired in the air with a loud crack of sound, and wrapping one long muscled arm around his throat, squeezing tight enough to make Carlyle's eyes bug. Sirens whined in the distance.

Ralph and Floyd started to back up, but they were quickly subdued by the older folk. Floyd screeched like a wet hen when his arm was twisted high, and Moses, with a look of disgust, muttered, "Sissy."

Pops stepped forward and wagged a fist. "Shoot 'em!"

Harry's gaze met Charlie's, and he smiled. "He's as bloodthirsty as you are, brat."

Carlyle lurched, trying to break free, and without a single hesitation, Harry punched him in the jaw. The man went down like a lead balloon. Very slowly, Charlie applauded.

The police showed up in two patrol cars and a plain sedan. The detective in charge appeared to know Harry. With the men subdued in cuffs, the trunk of Carlyle's car was opened and Charlie glimpsed a variety of weapons, rifles and guns and ammunition. There were so many of them, it looked like an arsenal.

One of the officers whistled low.

"They're dealing in illegal and stolen weaponry." Charlie noticed Harry didn't mention the embezzlement, keeping to his promise not to involve the older proprietors. "I can give you an address of an abandoned warehouse where you'll find more of the same, as well as evidence of other illegal activities."

The detective clapped Harry on the shoulder and they spoke quietly for a few minutes. The officers were questioning everyone and to Charlie's surprise, the seniors loved it. They fairly crowed in their excitement. Charlie used the moment to go to Dalton.

"Where's my sister?"

He was still catching his breath, but he looked relieved. "Inside. My assistant is practically sitting on her. She wanted to rush out with me, but seeing you threatened was more than enough." He touched her face and his hand trembled. Charlie took his arm and hustled him to a shop stoop to sit. Even as he did her bidding, he asked, "Are you okay?"

She smiled. At the same time big tears welled in her eyes. "That was my question to you."

"Now that you're safe, I'm fine. But I don't mind telling you, seeing that bastard put his hands on you nearly stopped my—"

"Your heart?" She knelt down in front of him and took his hands. "Are you sure you're all right?"

"You know?"

"That you had a heart attack? Yes. Harry finally came clean."

Dalton sighed heavily. "It wasn't your fault, you know. Your letter didn't distress me. It thrilled me and made me so proud I wanted to dance up and down the street."

"It was a hateful letter."

"It was a letter filled with guts and courage and pride. I knew the moment I read it you were an incredible young woman. I was right."

The tears trickled down her cheeks and she impatiently swiped them away. "That was a dirty trick you played on me, having Harry lie about everything. But under the circumstances I suppose I understand."

"Do you? I couldn't take the chance you'd shut me out. I'd waited too long to get my girls back." His own eyes teared up, breaking Charlie's heart. "I'm so sorry I hurt you earlier today."

She shook her head. "It doesn't matter."

"That's not what Harry said. I've known him since he was a boy, back when his father and I were friends. We've always been as close as two men can be, and that's the first time he ever raised hell with me."

Once again, her temper rose. "Harry yelled at you?"

Scoffing, Dalton shook his head. "Harry never yells. He just gets glib and lectures. He told me what a wonderful woman you were, and he insisted there wasn't a single thing about you that needed to be changed."

Charlie was absorbing that when a voice from behind her said, "What I didn't tell you is that I love her."

She jerked around so fast, she landed on her rump. Since that particular part of her anatomy was already sore from the skirmish, she scowled at Harry. He didn't give her a chance to grumble, reaching down and grabbing her under her arms, then lifting her completely off her feet until she was eye level, dangling in the air.

Charlie gulped, eyeing Harry cautiously. His shirt was untucked and only half-buttoned, and he had on shoes but no socks. He'd obviously dressed in a rush.

Shaking her slightly, he shouted, "You scared the hell out of me, taking off like that!"

Charlie glanced over at Dalton, who sat there grinning, and she said, "I thought he never yelled."

Dalton shrugged.

Harry shook her again, making her feet swing. "In the normal course of things, when not unduly provoked, I *don't* yell! But you have a way of pushing me on everything."

Despite her ignominious position, she lifted her chin. "Good. Because you push me, too."

That vexed him for a moment, and he growled, "Damn right! And I'm going to continue to do so. I love you, damn it. Doesn't that matter at all?"

Pops leaned in to say, "It should matter."

Moses nodded. "Always used to matter in the good ole days." The rest of the seniors offered mumbled agreements.

An elderly woman with gray hair escaping her bun patted Charlie on the arm. "You should listen to him, honey. Harry's a good man, and he packs one helluva punch."

They all nodded, even the officers. Moses stepped forward and he looked sheepish. "Harry convinced us we couldn't handle those punks on our own. We should have trusted the cops. Even outnumberin' 'em two to one, they almost got away from us."

Harry, still holding Charlie off the ground as if her weight were totally negligible, said to the hovering group, "I couldn't have done it without your assistance."

Charlie frowned. "It was a plan?"

"A very sound plan. I knew Carlyle would be with Ralph and Floyd today, and I knew they'd have the guns."

Charlie gasped. "This is the news you refused to share with me! I suspected something was going on, but you wouldn't tell me a damn thing, and you kept sneaking off without me—"

"Which wasn't easy, I'll have you know. You're too nosy for your own good."

Dalton blustered. "*Charlie* was involved in that?"

Harry didn't answer, however his eyes glittered. "After picking up the money, they were going to make a deal—and the police would be ready." He glared at Dalton. "Things would have gone as planned if people didn't throw wrenches into the works, skipping dinner and coming here first."

"I had no idea!" He frowned at Harry, then shrugged. "I needed a reservation, so we were going back in an hour."

"And," Harry added, drawing Charlie so close she could see the fiery specks in his light brown eyes, "if stubborn women would only listen when given a heartfelt declaration of love."

"It really was heartfelt?"

"Haven't you been listening?" He shook her again, then hugged her tight. "It was extremely heartfelt."

Charlie looped her arms around his neck. "I haven't forgiven you yet for lying to me."

Harry pulled her slightly away and he looked at Dalton. "I compromised your daughter."

Dalton started in surprise. "You did?"

"Yes. But I'm willing to do the right thing."

The old people cheered all the more.

Charlie, enjoying herself now that she no longer doubted her father—or Harry—pretended to think things over. "I'm going to keep my bar."

"Fine. As long as you live with me."

"What about Jill?"

"She's more than welcome as long as she doesn't object to Ted, or Grace and Sooner."

Dalton stood. "Or she could live with me!"

Jill appeared, dragging the assistant in her wake. Several of the young officers looked at her with interest as she forged a path to her sister. "I'm going off to college, remember? But it's nice to feel so wanted. Who're Ted and Grace and Sooner?"

Harry brought Charlie close again and kissed her. In a whisper, he said, "I do love you, Charlie. So damn much. Please don't ever scare me like that again."

Those stupid, ridiculous tears threatened, but they were happy tears now. "If I marry you, can I help in all your investigations?"

He pretended to stagger with the mere thought, making her laugh. But that was the thing about Harry. Even from the first, he'd managed to bring fun and laughter back into her life. He'd even given her back her father. And now that she had those things, she couldn't imagine letting them go.

She pressed her face into his throat and said, "Since I love you, I suppose we should get married."

"That's a yes?"

"That's an absolute."

Sirens from the retreating patrol cars mingled with the shouts from the seniors and the happy shrieks from her sister. Dalton just sat there grinning—like a very proud papa.

* * * * *

Also available from
Sarah Morgan
and HQN Books

The O'Neil Brothers

Maybe This Christmas
Suddenly Last Summer
Sleigh Bells in the Snow

Puffin Island

First Time in Forever
Some Kind of Wonderful

For a complete list of books by Sarah Morgan,
please visit sarahmorgan.com.

ONE ENCHANTED MOMENT

Sarah Morgan

To Jill Shalvis,
who is kind, warm, generous and funny
and also writes brilliant books.

CHAPTER ONE

SKYLAR TEMPEST STEPPED out of her hotel and lifted her face to the sky. Soft, thick flakes of snow drifted down from a sky of midnight blue, dusting her hair and blending with the wool of her white coat. It was like standing in a snow globe.

She reached out and caught a snowflake in her palm, watching as it slowly dissolved, its beauty fleeting and ephemeral.

London was experiencing a cold spell and bets were on for the first white Christmas in years. The snow had been falling for a couple of hours and the streets were frosted white. It was easy on the eye and lethal underfoot, which was why she'd decided to take a cab rather than walk the glittering length of Knightsbridge to the gallery.

She didn't want to arrive at the most important night of her life with a black eye.

Smiling at the doorman, she stepped into the waiting cab.

Cocooned in the warmth, she watched as people bustled along the crowded streets. They walked, heads down, snuggled in layers of wool to keep out the cold. Stores with elaborately decorated windows shone bright with fairy lights, beaming shimmering silver across the snow.

Drinking in the light and color, she fought the temptation to reach for the sketch pad she always carried. In a world that often presented its ugly side, Skylar looked for the beauty and captured it in her art. She worked in a variety of mediums, dabbled in ceramics, but her first love was jewelry.

The necklace she'd chosen to wear tonight was an example of her work and the only splash of color in her outfit. She'd designed it as part of her latest collection, but she'd fallen in love with the piece and kept it. The stones were a mixture of blues and greens, Mediterranean hues that added warmth to a cold December evening.

Tonight was her big night, she was in one of her favorite cities at her favorite time of year and Richard was joining her.

They'd been an item for over a year. A year in which his entire focus had been his political career. Since he'd won his senate seat, the pressures had intensified. They'd barely seen each other in the months leading up to the election and the time they had spent together had been marred by his incendiary moods. She'd resigned herself to attending the private showing of her collection alone, so his call from the airport had been a surprise.

Now she was eagerly anticipating the night ahead.

Starting tonight, everything was going to be different. With the stress of the election behind them, they'd finally be able to enjoy quality time together and do all the things they'd talked about doing.

He'd hinted that he had a special Christmas gift for her.

A trip to Florence maybe?

He knew how much she'd always wanted that.

Or Paris, maybe, to visit the Louvre and the Musée d'Orsay.

Her mood lifted.

They'd celebrate her exhibition and later they'd enjoy a more intimate celebration. The two of them, her luxurious hotel suite and a bottle of champagne. Tomorrow, they'd visit the ice rink at Somerset House. She'd walked past it the day before and spent a happy hour people-watching. Her creative brain had soaked up the kaleidoscope of color and smiling faces. She'd absorbed it all; the uncertain, the wobbly and the graceful. Twirling teenagers, parents holding eager children, lovers entwined. After that, they'd visit the London Eye at night. She'd watched the slow, graceful rise of each capsule over the dark ribbon of the Thames and decided she wanted to experience that.

It would be romantic, and she and Richard needed to spend more time on their relationship.

She stared out of the window, thinking about it.

Was this love?

Was this it?

She'd always assumed that when she finally fell in love she'd know. She hadn't been prepared for all the doubts and questions.

"Christmas party, love?" The cab driver glanced in the mirror and Skylar gave him a smile, glad to be distracted from her thoughts.

"Not exactly. A private showing. Jewelry, pots and a few pieces of art." A series of watercolors she'd painted on a trip to Greece to visit Brittany. Having a best friend who was an archaeologist had expanded her horizons. That trip had been the inspiration for her collection. *Ocean Blue.*

"Where are you from?"

"New York, and it's pretty cold there right now." She chatted freely, loving how friendly the cab drivers were in London.

"I hope you brought your credit card. Prices are high in this part of London. Whatever you buy is going to cost you."

"It's mine." Excitement mingled with pride. "My collection."

He glanced at her in his mirror. "I'm impressed. To have your work on display in these parts at any age would be something, but for someone as young as you—well, you're obviously going somewhere. Your family must be really proud."

Her good mood melted away like the snowflake she'd held in her palm.

Her family wasn't proud.

They were exasperated that she persisted with her "hobby."

She'd invited them. Sent them a pretty embossed invitation and a catalog.

There had been no response.

Turning her head, she focused on the snowy scene beyond the windows of the cab. She wasn't going to let that ruin her evening. Nothing was going to ruin the evening.

The cab driver was still talking. "So you'll be flying back home for the holidays? Family Christmas?"

"That's the plan." Although not the reality. "Family Christmas" sounded cozy and warm, like something from a fairy tale. It conjured up images of prettily wrapped gifts stacked beneath a tall tree festooned with twinkling lights and homemade decorations, while excited children fizzed with anticipation.

Christmas at her parents' house felt more like an endurance test than a fairy tale, more corporate than cozy. The "tree" would be an artistic display of bare twigs sprayed silver and studded with tiny lights, part of a larger display planned and executed every year by her mother's interior decorator. Stark, remote and not to be touched at any cost. The "gifts," artfully stacked on various surfaces for effect, would be empty boxes.

Any child hoping to find something magical under her family tree would be disappointed.

Those gifts summed up her family, she thought.

Everything had to be shiny and perfectly wrapped. Appearances mattered.

Leaning her head against the cool glass of the window, she watched as a man and a woman, loaded down with bags, struggled through the snow with two bouncing, excitable young children. She imagined them arriving home and decorating the tree together. They'd write letters to Santa and hang stockings, counting the number of sleeps until Christmas Day.

The most important things in life, she thought wistfully, couldn't be wrapped.

She watched as the family disappeared down a side street and then looked away, impatient with herself.

She was too old for Christmas fantasies and with Richard arriving and her exhibition she had plenty to celebrate.

Her phone rang and she tugged it out of her bag, expecting Richard again.

It was her mother and surprise mingled with warmth.

She remembered.

"Mom? I'm so happy you called."

"I shouldn't have to call—" her mother's crisp, cultured tones came down the phone "—but your father and I need to know when you'll be home."

Bridging the gap between hope and reality gave her whiplash. "You're calling about my schedule?"

"Stephanie sent you an email. You didn't respond."

Stephanie was her mother's assistant and Sky knew the email was probably sitting in her inbox, along with all the others she'd ignored while burning the midnight oil to get ready for this week.

"I've been busy, Mom. It's my private viewing tonight, and—"

"We're all busy, Skylar, and I'd appreciate not having to chase my own daughter for a response. Particularly when you're the only one without a job."

Sky thought of the commissions she had lined up. She had enough work to keep her busy through most of next year. "I have a job."

"I mean a proper job. I'm doing the seating plan for Christmas Eve. We'll be eighty for dinner. Lunch is more intimate—forty. When will you be arriving?"

Sky leaned her head back against the seat, not knowing whether to laugh or cry.

Forty? Intimate?

So much for a cozy family Christmas.

"I haven't decided."

"Then decide."

Skylar imagined her mother seated at her elegant Queen Anne desk, ticking off the items on her to-do list.

Phone dreamy, wayward daughter.

"Christmas Eve." At the last possible moment. "I'll be home Christmas Eve, but I'll make my own arrangements so you can cross me off your list. I'll talk with Richard and see what works for him."

"Richard has already sent through his plans."

Without sharing them with her? "He emailed you? I was assuming we'd travel together."

"You need to stop assuming and take action, Skylar. Richard's career is on the rise, but he still found time to respond to my email personally. Your father is impressed, and we all know he's not easy to impress."

Sky's fingers tightened on the phone.

She knew. She'd been trying to impress her father for years, so far with no success.

Something tugged deep inside her.

In third grade she'd painted him a picture. It had taken days of hard, painstaking effort to produce something she thought he'd like. She'd been excited by the result.

Look at this, Daddy. I painted it for your office.

He'd barely glanced at the picture and the next day she'd noticed it in the trash, buried beneath empty cans and juice cartons.

She never drew anything for him again.

She watched as snowflakes swirled and danced past the windows and tried not to mind that Richard had apparently succeeded where she had failed.

"He's smart," her mother was saying. "Persuasive. Charming."

Except when he was under pressure. Then he was short-tempered and far from charming. But that wasn't a side he showed to the voting public or her family.

She stirred in her seat, feeling guilty for not being more understanding.

This was his dream, and she knew how it felt to have a dream.

Richard Everson had nurtured ambitions of running for office since childhood. The occasional burst of irritability at this point was understandable.

Her mother was still talking. "You're lucky to have found a man like him, but you won't hang on to him if you're dreamy and romantic. Relationships require application and hard work."

And that, Skylar thought, was exactly how her parents' marriage had always seemed to her. Work. More corporate merger than loving union.

Was that really what love was?

She hoped not.

"When is he arriving?"

"Christmas Eve, in time for lunch. He'll be excellent at this sort of event."

Event? "It's Christmas, Mom."

"I thought you would finally have grown out of romanticizing the holidays." Her mother sounded impatient. "Your father has given a great deal of thought to the guest list. There are influential people attending. People who will be useful to Richard's career."

Not friends or family. People of influence.

"Anyone I know?"

"The list was attached to the email Stephanie sent. I hope you take time to prepare."

"Preparing" involved absorbing and memorizing pages of notes on each individual. Likes, dislikes, topics to be avoided at all costs.

Even at Christmas it was all about networking.

A wild idea flitted into her mind. Christmas in a cottage on Puffin Island. Log fire, good wine and the company of her friends. She and Richard together without the pressures of the outside world.

It was a dreamy idea.

It was also heresy and it was never going to happen.

"I'm sorry you couldn't be here, Mom."

"You couldn't have picked a worse time. You're putting a great deal of pressure on Richard. As your father said when he spoke to him earlier, expecting him to fly to London right now is unreasonable."

"Richard spoke to Dad?"

"He called this morning." Her mother paused. "Choosing that man is the one thing in your life you've done right. Don't make a mistake tonight, Skylar."

Make a mistake about what?

"Wait a minute—what are you talking about?"

"I've said enough. The rest is up to you. Make good choices." Her mother ended the call and Skylar sat for a moment, staring out of the window.

Make good choices.

Her family had never understood that, for her, art and the process of creating something tangible and beautiful, whether a pot or a necklace, wasn't a choice. It was a need, maybe even an obsession. It came from deep inside. She had images clamoring in her head, ideas crowding her brain. Inspiration was everywhere, there were days where she was dizzy and dazzled by possibilities.

Choice wasn't part of it.

She could no more have given up what she did

than she could have given up breathing, but her family had never understood that. Their approach to life was analytical. Their appreciation of art was limited to its cultural significance or financial value.

Growing up, there had been days when she'd wondered if her parents had brought the wrong baby home from the hospital. They were good people, but she felt as if she was in the wrong house.

The phone rang again. This time it was Brittany and Emily, her friends who were both back on Puffin Island, in Maine.

"Tell us what you're wearing." Brittany's voice came down the phone and Skylar grinned.

No doubt about it, without her friends she'd go insane.

Friends were like solar power, bringing warmth and light to dark corners.

"The silver dress with the white coat. Totally impractical."

"No burgers, no ketchup and stay away from red wine. I bet you look like a snow queen. We rang to wish you luck because after tonight you'll be too famous to talk to us. Are you excited?"

Skylar tried to forget the conversation with her mother. "I think so."

"You *think*?" This time it was Emily. "Sky, this is huge. You should be so proud. We are."

"Drink champagne, take photos and we'll celebrate when you're home." Brittany's voice echoed down the phone. "Wish we could be there with you. You shouldn't be alone."

Skylar hesitated, not sure whether to tell them or not. "I won't be alone. Richard is coming."

There was a brief silence and then Emily spoke. “That’s great.” Her voice was just a little too bright. “We thought he wasn’t going to make it.”

“Last-minute decision.”

“Why the change of heart?”

Sky wondered why the question should make her uncomfortable when she’d asked herself the same question. “He shifted his schedule. I guess that’s a sign that he cares.”

“Right. Well, we’re glad he came through for you.” Brittany’s tone was warm. “I hope having him there makes tonight even more special.”

They didn’t say anything more. They didn’t have to.

She knew they worried about her relationship with Richard.

Now that he’d won his senate seat, she needed to persuade him to spend more time with her friends. She was sure that if he knew them better, he’d love them as she did.

“I have to go.”

“Call us later! And if you see Lily and Nik, give them my love.”

The call left her smiling and she was still smiling as she stepped out of the cab.

The gallery was nestled between an antiques store and an exclusive boutique. Taking pride of place in the window of the gallery was one of her favorite pieces, a vase modeled on an ancient Greek amphora, the birds twisting sinuously against luminous blue glass.

Tempest Designs.

Maybe it had started as a hobby, but now it was a business. She had a small but exclusive international clientele and this was her first show in London. To be able to support herself doing something she loved had made the dream a reality.

So why were her mother's words the loudest thing in her head?

You're the only one without a job.

She paid the driver, reminding herself that Richard believed in her. He'd chosen to fly over for the weekend, which had to be the ultimate in romantic gestures and proof he was taking her choice of career seriously.

It didn't matter what her parents thought.

This was her big night and nothing was going to spoil it.

ALEC HUNTER LEFT the National Maritime Museum in Greenwich, shoulders hunched against the sharp bite of the wind and the falling snow. He'd planned a late-afternoon stroll along the river but the lecture he'd delivered had ended later than planned and afternoon had blended into evening.

In front of him the River Thames wound, ribbon-like, toward the bright lights of the city. He turned up the collar of his coat, pulled his phone out of his pocket and walked upriver.

He had four messages.

One from the BBC following up on the meeting they'd had earlier in the week to discuss his possible involvement with a documentary on Antarctica, one from his mother asking him to buy extra champagne, one from his younger sister telling him he'd better have bought her a great present or he needn't bother coming home.

That one made him smile.

He texted her back and received a flurry of emoticons in return.

The final text was from his friends back in the United States, reminding him that tonight was the VIP night for Skylar's exhibition.

He could imagine them, gathered together in Harbor House on Puffin Island, sharing a bottle of wine and laughing while they sent a joint text.

You need to be there, Alec. The rat boyfriend has decided to show up and Skylar needs the support of her friends.

Rat boyfriend?

Several thoughts flitted through his mind. The first was that he and Skylar could hardly be described as "friends." On a good day they tolerated each other for the sake of their wider friendship group; on a bad day they barely managed to be civil. His second thought was that Skylar's choices in her relationships appeared to be no better than his own, and the third was that Brittany clearly had no idea how far Greenwich was from Knightsbridge.

He checked the time and calculated that by the time he got across town in the traffic, her VIP night would be over. But if he didn't at least show his face, his life wouldn't be worth living.

Brittany and Emily would both kill him and Ryan would cut off his supply of free beer at the Ocean Club bar.

With a faint smile he texted a reply promising to go and pocketed his phone.

He doubted Skylar would be pleased to see him,

but he would have done his duty and with any luck would still be invited to spend Christmas at Harbor House.

Skylar, he knew, would be going home to her family in Long Island.

Walking away from the river to the street, he hailed a cab.

It was going to take a lifetime to cross London but hopefully he'd make it before the evening was over.

He'd congratulate her, she'd smile politely, he'd leave.

Duty done.

THE ROOM WAS BUZZING.

"The turnout is amazing." Judy, the owner of the gallery, was on her second glass of champagne. "Do you see who is over there? Cristiano Ferrara. He owns an exclusive hotel chain. Sicilian." She lowered her voice. "Very sexy."

"And very married. He commissioned a piece of jewelry for his wife, Laurel. She's pregnant." And that, Sky thought, was romantic. Not a stark piece of paper that declared you husband and wife, but thoughtful, loving gestures that showed how much you cared.

It was her favorite type of commission.

A gift designed as an expression of love.

And there was no doubt how much Cristiano loved his beautiful wife. When people approached him he was polite, but it was obvious that tonight was a treat for his wife and she was the focus of his attention. He looked at Laurel as if she were the sun, the moon and the stars all in one perfect package.

Sky watched them wistfully.

She wanted that. She wanted that intense passion, but most of all she wanted someone who thought she was the best thing on the planet.

Confused, Sky glanced across at Richard, who was working the room.

Did he feel that way about her?

And could she feel that for him? Did she feel enough? Was this all it was? Her head was full of questions she couldn't answer.

She'd always believed that if she ever fell in love, she'd recognize the feeling instantly, but maybe it wasn't that simple.

Richard had been the last to arrive and had barely paused to greet her before vanishing into the crowd. Now he was talking to Nik Zervakis, the wealthy Greek-American owner of ZervaCo, who had flown in with his fiancée, Lily, an archaeology friend of Brittany's who had helped Sky with ideas for her new collection.

"Nik has given me free rein to buy anything I like," Lily confided. "So far I've bought those gorgeous starfish earrings and that pot in the corner. It's similar to one he already has at his home in Greece."

"Your home, too."

"Yes, my home! Unbelievable, isn't it? I still want to pinch myself every day."

"How did you know?" Sky's mouth was dry. "How did you know he was the right one? That this really was love?"

"That's a difficult question." Lily pondered, her eyes on Nik. "I can't describe it. But sometimes it feels as if my heart is too big for my chest." She gave a half smile and walked over to the pot. "I really do love this."

"I should be giving you that, no charge. None of this would have happened without your help. You're the Greek ceramics expert."

"Not anymore. I'm turning into a corporate wife. My choice." Lily glanced at Nik again, her eyes sparkling like the lights on a Christmas tree. "Give my love to Brittany when you see her. Will you be spending Christmas on Puffin Island?"

"No. I'll be spending the holidays with my family."

Her family and a hundred and twenty strangers.

People of influence.

It would be as much fun as a trip to the dentist.

Trying not to think about that, she hugged Lily and then mixed and mingled, accepting compliments and answering questions about her work.

It occurred to her that the only person who hadn't congratulated her was Richard.

Even after the two wealthiest people in the room had left to go on to another Christmas event, he continued to network, pumping fists and slapping backs as he made his way round the room.

Sky was starting to wonder why he'd bothered coming when she saw him speak to the gallery owner, clear his throat and get ready to make a speech.

Her heart sank. Was he going to congratulate her publicly?

She would have preferred a more intimate exchange, a few personal words that showed he was proud of her, but she understood that this was the way Richard did things. He was all about reaching the widest audience possible. Why charm one person if you could charm ten?

He lifted a hand to silence the hum of conversation. "I want to thank you all for being here tonight." He delivered his most engaging smile, the one that had carried him all the way to Capitol Hill just weeks earlier. "We're all busy people, but like you I couldn't miss Skylar's little party. I want to thank you on her behalf."

There were a few "ahhs" but Skylar frowned.

Little party?

He made her feel as if she was back in kindergarten. And she didn't need him to thank people on her behalf. She'd already thanked them, as he would have known if he'd arrived earlier. He'd blamed traffic and she'd felt churlish for thinking that he should have allowed more time.

There was a rush of cold air as the door to the gallery opened and she swiveled to see if she recognized the latecomer.

She caught a glimpse of ebony hair, a long black coat and powerful shoulders dusted in silvery snow.

Several women glanced toward the handsome stranger, and then he turned and Skylar saw that it wasn't a stranger.

It was Alec Hunter.

A friend of Brittany's, he was a maritime historian and his expertise and on-screen charisma had combined to give him a lucrative career that straddled academia and media. They called him the Shipwreck Hunter and he'd been credited with single-handedly making history sexy. Thanks to his adventurous exploits in front of the camera, he had droves of female admirers.

Skylar wasn't one of them.

What was he doing here?

Yes, they occasionally socialized, but the truth was they tolerated each other for the sake of their mutual friends. He didn't hide the fact he thought she was decorative and shallow. What had he called her back in the summer? A fairy princess.

If she'd been a dog, she would have been growling deep in her throat.

Telling herself that she didn't care what he thought of her, she looked away.

It was one thing to try to please her parents for the sake of family harmony, but she'd be damned if she'd go out of her way to win the approval of a hardened cynic like Alec.

She knew he was a casualty of a bitter divorce and it didn't surprise her. For her, the surprise was that someone had married him in the first place.

There was no way he would have chosen to come to her exhibition voluntarily, which meant that Brittany must have threatened or bribed him.

She stood still, making mental promises to kill her friend, and then realized that Richard was speaking directly to her.

"Skylar—" his voice carried across the room "—come up here and join me, honey. There's something I want to say to you."

Honey? *Honey?*

When did he ever call her honey?

Not wanting to make a public scene, Skylar walked forward.

Out of the corner of her eye she was conscious of Alec, his stillness setting him apart from the rest of the crowd. There was something remote and inaccessible about him. She knew that those perfect masculine features masked a sharp intellect and an equally sharp and sarcastic tongue. Most women found him insanely attractive. She found him superior and patronizing.

Leave, she thought. *Go home. I don't want you here ruining my night with your brooding scowl.*

But he didn't leave. Instead, he watched her with that intense, focused gaze that made her dress feel too tight.

Her skin prickled and heat whispered across her skin.

She nodded her head briefly in acknowledgment and then forgot about him because Richard took her hand.

Remembering Lily's words, Sky looked into his eyes and tried to work out if her heart felt too big for her chest.

It didn't.

As far as she could tell it was behaving as it should. Normal rhythm. Normal size.

Richard smiled. "A few weeks ago, I achieved a life goal. That achievement meant all the more to me because you were right there by my side."

Forgetting about her heart, Skylar blinked in confusion.

This was her special night and he was talking about himself?

"Richard—"

"I promised myself that when I reached a certain

point in my professional life, I'd turn my attention to my personal life. That moment has come. There's something I want to say to you, and there is no better time than right now in front of our friends."

Her only friends here had been Lily and Nik, and they'd left already.

The rest were acquaintances, high-profile clients and the press.

And Alec.

It niggled that he was here.

Good manners dictated that she speak with him, but what was she going to say?

Go home and stop ruining my fun.

No wonder you're divorced...

All the options that came into her head were socially unacceptable and she knew that when the moment came she'd thank him for showing up. She'd offer him a glass of champagne and they'd make polite conversation about their friends.

Fake, fake, fake.

She wouldn't mention the fact she knew he was here under sufferance, and no doubt he wouldn't mention it, either. On the surface they'd be civil, even though neither of them felt remotely civil in one another's company. She could keep up appearances. After all, she'd been trained by experts. She could talk about nothing for hours.

Richard lifted her hand to his lips. "I've been waiting for the right moment to ask you."

Trying to forget Alec, Sky forced herself to pay attention. "Ask me what?"

"I want you to marry me." He'd had voice coaching and training in public speaking and it showed in the way he addressed the room. "I want you by my side for the rest of my life. From now on, we'll be pursuing goals together."

Sky gaped at him, wondering if she'd misheard.

She opened her mouth. No sound emerged.

"You're in shock." He was confident. Sure of himself. A man dazzled by the light of his own rising star. He was an only child, the sole focus of his parents' ambitions. Unlike her, he'd exceeded their expectations. "I didn't buy a ring. I thought you could make your own and give me a discount." He included the crowd in the joke and there was a ripple of appreciative laughter.

Skylar wasn't laughing. Nor was she appreciative.

Marriage?

She thought about the conversations they'd had over the past year. Intimate exchanges where she'd revealed her dreams.

Had he not listened to a word she'd said?

Apparently not, or he'd know that marriage didn't interest her.

Love? Now, that was a different matter. She wanted love. What she didn't want was a flamboyant public proposal. He was paying more attention to the guests than her, to the point that she wanted to wave her arms in the air and yell, *Hello, I'm over here!*

Beyond Richard's shoulder she could see Alec Hunter and discovered he wasn't laughing, either. He was standing in the same place, the collar of his black coat brushing against the dark shadow of his jaw. She would have drawn him as a vampire or a wraith, she thought. A creature of the night. Even still and silent he had presence, a quality that had no doubt contributed to his success as a TV presenter and his large female fan base.

Had he proposed to his ex-wife in public?

No, because despite his public persona, she knew he was intensely private.

“Skylar?” Richard’s smile was a little tense around the edges. “We’re all waiting for a response.”

All? She wondered at what point a proposal had become a group activity.

Her real response was, *You have to be kidding me*, but she didn’t want that to feature in the press reports of her event the following day.

Grateful for the years of practice in producing fake smiles, she gave one.

“This is a surprise.” Keeping the smile in place, she turned to the guests. “I hope you’ll excuse us. Richard and I need a little time alone.” She turned and walked through the gallery and into the storeroom that was next to an office.

Her heels tapped on the wooden floor. Her knees shook.

She hoped he was going to follow her because she didn’t want to say what needed to be said in public.

There was a click as he closed the door behind them. “Sky? What the hell are you doing?”

“No, Richard, the question is what are *you* doing?”

“I was proposing. All you had to do was say yes and you would have had great media coverage for your little party. Instead you have to go for drama.” He shot her an exasperated look. “Always with you, it’s drama.”

“I—” She was speechless. “I honestly don’t know what to say.”

"The word you were looking for was *yes*, but you missed your cue." He spoke through his teeth and then inhaled deeply and smiled the smile that had first attracted her attention. "You were in shock. This is a big night for you, I understand that."

She relaxed a little. Reminded herself they'd been together a long time, and that no one was perfect. "Good, because for a moment I wasn't sure you did."

His phone rang. "Excuse me one second, this could be important."

She stood, her arms wrapped round her waist, wondering what could be more important than talking about their future.

She glanced around her, trying to stay calm. The room was an Aladdin's cave of creative endeavor. Paintings were stacked against the wall, there were several bronze figurines on a shelf and a rolled-up carpet stood next to a table stacked high with boxes.

Not the most romantic setting.

Richard checked the number and silenced the phone. "It can wait." Sliding the phone back into his pocket, he glanced at her blankly. "Where were we?"

"You were working out whether your phone call was a higher priority than a conversation about our future," she said flatly, "and telling me you understood that tonight was a big moment in my life."

"Of course I understand. A marriage proposal is a big moment in every woman's life."

There was a ringing in her ears. "Excuse me? That's what you consider to be my big moment?"

"Getting engaged is a big deal."

"We're not engaged, Richard."

"We will be when you've answered my question."

He gave her his most winning smile but she felt nothing but frustration.

He wasn't listening to her.

Apparently he'd never listened to her. He steamrollered over her in pursuit of his own goals.

He had a five-year plan and apparently she was part of it.

"I don't remember a question. You said 'I want you to marry me.' Much the same way a child might say 'I want that candy.'" Too stressed to stand still, she paced the length of the room. "In the last year, how much time do you think we've spent together?"

"It's been a crazy year, I'm not denying that. Of course, we would have spent more time together if you hadn't insisted on spending so much time in your studio and on that island. But all that's going to change when we're married."

"I thought I'd made it clear that marriage isn't on my wish list. Didn't you hear me?"

"I heard you, but we both know you didn't mean it. Why wouldn't you want to get married?" There was a hint of impatience in his voice. "Your parents have been married thirty-five years and never share a cross word."

And never a loving one, either.

Never, not once, had she seen her parents show affection.

They didn't hold hands.

They didn't kiss.

There were no lingering glances, no suggestion of a bond of togetherness.

She wanted so much more.

"What are you doing here? I mean, what are you *really* doing here?"

His smile lost some of its warmth. "I came to support you, although given the mood you're in I'm starting to wonder why I bothered. I'm still finding my way around Capitol Hill. Coming here was the last thing I needed right now."

"Thank you."

"I didn't mean—" He dragged his hand over the back of his neck. "You're determined to misunderstand everything I say."

"Maybe that's because I don't understand. You told me you weren't coming tonight, so what changed?" When he didn't answer, she answered for him. "You saw the guest list and thought there might be people here who could be useful to you. Be honest. Tonight was never about me." But she'd wanted it to be. And her creative brain had spun the facts into a scenario that she could live with.

Her mother was right.

She was a stupid dreamer.

Richard met her gaze head-on. "I'm not ashamed to admit the value of networking. You want honest? I'll give you honest. This hobby of yours is fine, but you are wasting your life. You paint pictures and make jewelry and that wouldn't matter except that you're smart and there are so many other more useful things you could be doing. Things that would make me proud."

She felt dizzy. "You're not proud of me?"

"You're not exactly saving the planet, Sky. Even you can't pretend that what you do is important." With a few words he'd dismissed what she did, tossing her dreams into the trash as her father had done with her first painting all those years before.

She felt as if she had emerged from a deep sleep.

"The last necklace I made was taken from a broach left to a client by her grandmother. It had been sitting in a drawer for a decade and she wanted it made into something contemporary that she could wear. Something relevant to her life that would remind her of someone she'd loved very much. It was important to her. Emotions are important." But she knew he wouldn't understand that.

To him, money, power and influence were the important things.

He was like her parents. Which was why they got along so well.

He made a conciliatory gesture. "This is a pointless conversation. We need to move on."

"My work is not 'pointless,' and by 'move on' I assume you're saying that your ambitions take precedence over mine."

He frowned. "No, but you can't argue with the fact that I'm serving a lot of people."

"Are you? Or are you serving yourself? Because sometimes, Richard, I wonder if your career is about your ambition, not a selfless desire to dedicate your life to public service."

His features hardened. "You want to talk about being selfish? What do you think your actions are doing to your parents? It's time you stopped thinking of yourself and made them proud."

"Since when do my parents have anything to do with our relationship?" A disturbing thought slid into her brain. "Why did you call my father?"

"I told him I was going to ask you to marry me. He and your mother were thrilled and they're looking forward to celebrating when we join them on Christmas Eve."

Was it really all about her parents?

Desperately wanting to be wrong about that, she took a step forward. "What if I said that this year I don't want to spend Christmas with my parents? We could have Christmas by ourselves, just the two of us. Rent a little cottage on Puffin Island and spend our time playing games and chatting. Log fire, a real fir tree from the forest, walks in the snow, making love in the warm." She'd said it to test him, but the more she thought about it, the more she wanted it. "Let's do it, Richard. Forget proposals, forget goals and careers—for once let it be the two of us and our friends. We'll make a pact not to talk about work. Emily and Ryan are hosting Christmas at Harbor House and making it extra special for little Lizzy. Zach and Brittany will be there, too, and I'd love for us to spend more time with them. It will be perfect."

"Perfect?" He looked appalled. "I can't think of anything worse than Christmas on Puffin Island. What would be the point? Your parents have invited people who will be useful."

"The point is it's Christmas, Richard. It isn't a business opportunity or an excuse to network, it's Christmas." How could she have been so deluded? They'd spent over a year together. She'd believed they had a future. "If not Puffin Island, how about Europe? We've always talked about going to Paris or Florence. Let's do it!"

"This isn't a good time."

"It's never a good time." And she realized in a flash of painful clarity that she really had been fooling herself. When she cleared away the creative clouds of her imagination, the truth was right there, forming a stark picture. "When we first met I couldn't believe how much we had in common. That first night—we stayed up until four in the morning planning a trip to Florence. Do you remember?"

He shifted. "Sky—"

"It seemed almost too good to be true, to meet someone who shared your dreams so exactly. There were so many things we were going to do, and we never did any of them. It seemed too good to be true, because it was." She swallowed, finding it hard to look the truth in the eye because the truth made a fool of her. "My parents told you about me, didn't they? You studied my interests so that you'd know exactly how to gain my attention."

"There is nothing wrong with wanting to know someone."

"What's wrong," she said slowly, "is that it wasn't genuine. Love isn't a business deal, Richard, it's an emotion. It isn't about convenience or ambition, it's about feeling. Genuine feeling, not something manufactured for the purposes of manipulation."

"There you go again. You expect a fairy tale and when you get reality, you're disappointed. It's the same with your attitude toward Christmas. You've always romanticized Christmas and it's just one day."

They were the same words her mother had used, and she knew it wasn't coincidence.

The thought that they'd discussed her was horrible.

Almost as horrible as realizing what a mistake she'd made.

She felt humiliated and betrayed, foolish and a little embarrassed, but at least she had her answer.

She wasn't the sun, moon and stars to him. She wasn't even a speck of cosmic dust on the bottom of his shoe.

"Maybe it is just one day, but it's an important day and this year I'd like to spend it with my friends."

"Precisely, they're *your* friends. They're no use to me."

"Friends aren't supposed to be of use." She heard her voice rise and tried to control it. "That isn't what friendship is. It's about giving, not taking."

"What can they possibly give you? Your situation is nothing like theirs. You have family, they don't. Emily had an alcoholic mother, Brittany's mother clearly knew nothing about responsibility and don't even get me started on Zachary Flynn. I don't want to risk my reputation by being in the same place as him. Can you imagine what the media could do with that story?"

It was like looking at a stranger and she realized that up until now, he'd carefully shown the side of himself he'd wanted her to see. Even with her, he'd controlled his image. The only times it had slipped were the occasions when he'd lost his temper.

"If you're forcing me to make a choice between you and my friends, there's no contest."

He relaxed slightly. "That's good to know. Obviously you'd pick me."

"No! I'd pick them. I love my friends." And she was incensed by what he'd said. Incensed, deeply hurt and furious with herself for being so deluded. "And a friend would never do what you just did."

She knew now there was no going back. No fixing.

"I know you love your friends, and that love makes you blind. It's thanks to them you've lost sight of what's important in life. We're going to your parents' for Christmas. They want the best for you. And so do I."

She felt numb. Disconnected.

How could she have possibly thought this might be love? "I'm the one who will decide what's best for me."

"That's the theory, but you always make the wrong choices."

Anger flickered to life inside her. "Thank you for making it easy for me to say no to the question you didn't ask."

"Oh, for—" He bit off the word and inhaled deeply. "Skylar Tempest, *will you marry me*?"

"Again, no!" Her voice sounded strangely flat. "And I can't believe you're still asking after the conversation we've just had. You wanted me to choose. I've chosen. Now get out."

He swore under his breath. "My flight leaves tomorrow and I have to be back in DC on Monday. I don't have time to play games. I want to spend the next few hours celebrating, not fighting. All I want to hear is two words, that's all. *Yes, Richard.*"

"I'm not playing games. We don't want the same things. Apparently we never did, but I'm only now realizing that. And even if we did have a single thing in common, I can't be with someone who is so rude about the friends I love. They're too important to me. It's over, Richard."

Her words fell into a simmering silence.

She saw the change in him and her heart kicked hard against her chest. She'd been with him long enough to be familiar with every shift in his mood. It was like watching the sky darken over Puffin Island, heralding an approaching storm.

His temper was the thing she'd liked least about him.

"I propose to you in public and your response is to break up with me? That's not happening." His tone was thickened. "You will not humiliate me. Next time we step out there it will be together and you'll be smiling. This time you are going to make the *right* decision."

"If you really knew me, you'd know that being proposed to in public would be the last thing I'd ever want. I don't believe in fairy tales, Richard, but I do believe two people should be together because they love each other, not because it suits their career ambitions or because it's part of a five-year plan." She saw him take a step forward but she stood her ground, refusing to be intimidated. "You need to go now. If you're worried about being seen then you can use the rear exit."

"I'm virtually a member of your family." His voice was an ugly growl. "Your father loves me."

"Then marry my father and I hope you'll be very happy." She was calm, trying to diffuse a situation that was threatening to explode, but it was too late and she saw the moment his anger snapped the leash and bolted.

In the past she'd handled every incendiary moment with care, never allowing it to reach this point. She'd soothed, placated and occasionally walked out, putting distance between them.

But it was too late for any of those options now.

The pin was out of the grenade.

His shoulders hunched. His features were contorted and ugly and in that single split second she wondered how she ever could have thought him handsome. On the outside he was perfectly wrapped, but on the inside…

"Richard, you need to get control of yourself." Her voice was sharp. "Take some breaths."

"You are a spoiled bitch."

She flinched as if he'd hit her and then realized in a moment of suspended disbelief that he actually *was* going to hit her.

His hand came up and instinctively she sidestepped to evade the blow. Her heel caught on the edge of a box and she fell heavily, smacking her head on the corner of the table.

Pain exploded in her skull. Her vision went dark and there was a distant humming in her head. Something warm and wet trickled down her face and she opened her eyes dizzily, trying to see through the pain.

He stood over her, hands raised to ward off the accusation he was clearly afraid she might make. "I didn't touch you." There was a hint of panic in his voice. "I didn't touch you."

He made no move to help her.

Showed no concern for her well-being, only his own.

Her sense of betrayal deepened.

"Get out, or I swear I will damage more than your career." Her voice sounded strange and distant. The world around her had blurred edges.

Oh, God, she was going to pass out. Just when she needed to be strong and kick his ass, she was going to faint.

"It was an accident, Sky, a stupid accident because you didn't look where you were going. You know how dreamy you are…"

"You wanted two words? I've got two perfect words for you. Fuck off." She lifted her fingers to her head and they came away sticky. "Go. Now."

Crap. Forget ketchup—she was going to get blood on her new dress.

"The press are out there." He growled the words, his eyes wild as his brain computed the potential PR nightmare. "They're supposed to be reporting our engagement. Instead you give them this? Damn you, Skylar. You did this, you deal with it. Maybe a blow to the head will wake you up. When you come to your senses, call me. I'll think about whether or not you're really what I want."

Without looking back he strode out of the side entrance and into the night, leaving Skylar lying in her own blood.

WHAT THE HELL were they doing in that room?

Alec prowled round the exhibition, ignoring the other guests. The crowd was thinning out, people melting away, some speculating on the romantic scene that was going on behind closed doors.

The public proposal had taken him by surprise.

Brittany had described him as the "rat boyfriend,"

which hadn't sounded to him like a relationship on the edge of happy-ever-after.

He'd found the proposal uncomfortable to witness, but judging from the oohs and ahhs from the women in the audience, he was alone with that feeling. That was probably why he was single. What did he know about romance? According to his ex-wife, nothing. She'd wanted sweeping gestures and frequent public demonstrations of his love.

Her insecurities and endless demands had made him feel as if he'd been given a life sentence for a crime he'd never committed.

Trying to delete toxic thoughts, he grabbed a glass of champagne and calculated how soon he could make his escape.

As soon as they reappeared, he'd offer his congratulations and leave.

He needed to remember to say what was expected of him—*Congratulations, so pleased for you, I hope you'll be happy*—and not what he was instinctively driven to say: *Are you both insane?*

He paused, his eye caught by a display of jewelry, intricate silver artfully placed on silk the color of a Mediterranean sky. The design was eye-catching and original and the historian in him recognized the nod to shapes and styles used in Bronze Age Greece.

A woman approached and sent him a smile, her intention unmistakable.

Alec turned away without returning the smile.

He didn't care if she thought him rude. Better to be rude now than have to extract himself later.

Another legacy of his marriage was his aversion to overpolished, high-maintenance women. His relationship with Selina had been six months of sex, followed by an elaborate wedding and two years of bitter arguments that had culminated in an acrimonious divorce.

At her insistence he'd attended two sessions of marriage guidance counseling, ostensibly to "learn about himself." What he'd learned was that he didn't like his wife any more than she liked him.

He'd also learned that he was better off alone.

He was too selfish to make a commitment to a woman.

He liked his life too much to sacrifice it for a relationship.

He glanced across the gallery again. The door remained closed, so he moved on. No doubt Skylar and her boyfriend were locked in a romantic moment, promising to love each other forever.

With time to kill, he prowled around the gallery. He knew Skylar worked in a variety of mediums, and it was only as he studied the pieces on exhibit that he reluctantly began to appreciate the range and extent of her talent.

He paused by a large painting, recognizing the rocky coastline of Puffin Island. He was no expert, but even he could see the composition was good. She'd captured the feel of the island perfectly, the sweep of a sandy bay, the movement of the sea and the threatening hint of a storm in the sky. Looking at it, he could feel the salty spray on his face and hear the plaintive call of the gulls.

He felt a pang of longing for his cottage on the wild north coast of Puffin Island. In a few days he'd be going back there and he'd be staying for a month.

Long enough, he hoped, to finish a draft of his book. He was looking forward to the solitude.

The painting had a red sticker, which meant that someone had bought it.

Good choice, he thought, and then saw the tall, elegant pot in a dazzling shade of cerulean blue placed under a spotlight against a whitewashed wall.

Instantly he was transported to Greece. He could almost feel the heat, and smell the scent of wild thyme and jasmine.

Of all the pieces in the room, this was the one he would have chosen to take home. He could see at a glance that her inspiration had been a combination of Greek mythology and early Minoan ceramics. She'd artfully combined the old with the new and created a piece of startling beauty.

The crowd thinned a little more, but there was still no sign of Skylar.

A movement in the street caught his eye and he saw a tall, dark-haired man stepping into a waiting car.

Recognizing him, Alec frowned. Why would Richard Everson be leaving alone?

He waited for Skylar to come running after him, wearing that skintight silver dress and a megawatt smile, but the car pulled away with only one passenger.

Ignoring the voice inside him that reminded him it was none of his business, he moved silently across the gallery toward the door he'd seen her enter.

He tapped lightly, received no answer and opened it anyway.

The room was empty.

It was clearly a storeroom. There were paintings against the wall, a table stacked with boxes and—

A body.

Shit.

"Skylar?" In two strides he was by her side. "What the hell happened here? Speak to me. Are you—?"

He tilted her face and his hand came away sticky with her blood.

Her beautiful white-blond hair was streaked with it, her lips bloodless in a face drained of color.

His heart pounded. Whatever he'd expected to find, it hadn't been this.

"Sky? Open your eyes." He tried to scoop her up and then dodged as she swung her fist toward his face.

"Touch me and I swear the next thing you feel will be my stiletto in your balls." She slurred her words and Alec swore under his breath and captured her wrist in his hand before she could do him serious damage.

"You might want to work on that pickup line, princess."

Her eyes fixed on him and focused. Confusion changed to recognition. "What are you doing here? Did you come to gloat?"

"I saw Richard getting into a car and came to check on you. Good thing I did. I'm taking you to hospital." Questions rose in his mind. What had happened? And why had Richard Everson walked out leaving her like this? He delved in his pocket for his phone. "I'm calling an ambulance. And the police. Did he do this?"

"No. I fell. And I don't want you to call anyone." She struggled to sit up, her efforts giving him a glimpse of long legs and silk underwear.

Her body is the biggest work of art in the place, he thought, and averted his eyes.

It irritated him that he found her attractive.

"You had a nasty blow to the head. You need to stay where you are."

"People have to stop telling me what I need. I know what I need. Crap."

He turned back to look at her and saw she'd closed her eyes. "What's wrong?"

"Do you have a twin? I'm seeing two of you."

"That's not good."

"You're not kidding. One Alec Hunter is bad enough. Two is my worst nightmare."

He took it as a good sign that she recognized him. "I'm relieved you're still able to make a joke."

"It's not a joke."

He gave a grim laugh. "I know I'm not your first choice of rescuer, but unfortunately I'm all there is."

"Then it's a good thing I don't need rescuing."

He wondered if she had any idea how badly she was hurt. "Let me take a look at your head before you stand up." Leaning her back against the leg of the table, he gently moved her hair back so that he could take a closer look at her injury. He'd been on expeditions to some of the wildest parts of the world and his first-aid skills were more than competent. "You don't need stitches, but you have one hell of a bruise and you might have a concussion. I'm taking you to hospital."

"I'm not going to the hospital. I don't want anyone to see me like this. They might take a photo."

He felt a rush of impatience. "Don't worry, you

still look beautiful and I'll make sure they only get your good side."

The look she gave him should have fried him to a crisp. "I don't care how I look, dumbass. I care about what questions the press might ask. And I care even more about seeing their theories expounded in public. But it's always good to know I'm the fortunate beneficiary of your good opinion. You can leave now. I appreciate you checking on me. I hope you break your nose on the way out."

He breathed deeply. "It was a stupid comment. I apologize."

She gave a weak laugh. "Wow. Now I *am* worried. I'm hallucinating, or hearing voices or something, because for a moment there I thought I heard you apologize. I don't suppose you'd do it again? This time on your knees?" She gave a weak laugh. "Just kidding. Go, Alec. You're done here. Off the hook."

"I'm not going anywhere."

"Why? You think I'm a vain waste of space. Why would you care what happens to me?" She closed her eyes again. "News flash. When a girl hits a crappy part of her life she needs friends around her, not someone who is going to make her feel more crappy."

He ignored that. "Do you feel sick?"

"Yeah, but it will pass as soon as you've left. Don't take it personally. You're just not my type."

It was a relief that she could still take a swipe at him. "Good to know. Come on, princess, let's get out of here."

"Princess? Did you seriously just call me princess again?" She cracked open one eye. "Are you trying to wind me up?"

"Yes. If you're spitting mad, at least I know you don't have brain damage."

"You don't think I have a brain. How can I have brain damage when I don't have a brain?" Her muttered retort was so much in character that his concern eased slightly.

"In case you *do* have a brain, we need to get you checked out. If you don't want an ambulance, we can take a taxi."

"Why are you helping me? You hate me. Hence the reason you call me princess."

"I seem to remember that last time we met you called me an asshole, so you're not exactly complimentary."

"Asshat, not asshole."

"I think the exact phrase you used was 'Professor Asshat.'" He rose to his feet. "Don't move. I'm going to get a taxi by the back entrance. I'll make sure no one sees you."

He wondered who she was protecting. Richard Everson or herself?

He stepped out into the snowy street. For once luck was on his side and he hailed a taxi almost immediately. Instructing the driver to wait, he walked back through the rear entrance of the gallery and was surprised to find Skylar standing up and clutching the table for support.

He couldn't believe she was on her feet. "I told you to stay where you were. I'm going to help you."

"I don't need you to help me. But my dress is covered in blood. It's ruined." She was shivering and Alec removed his coat and covered her up.

"Your dress is the least of your worries."

"Not true. We princesses are very particular about how we look. We never know when a handsome prince might come riding by."

Ignoring the dig, he eyed her bruise. "Right now you look more like a heroine from a Hitchcock movie than a princess." Her hair was the glistening white gold of a Caribbean beach in the sunlight. Even streaked with blood, it was her most striking feature.

"Am I scary?" She gave a faint smile and let go of the table. She swayed and he scooped her into his arms and carried her to the waiting taxi without pausing to ask for permission. "Oh, for— Put me down! I can walk."

"You'll fall, and that will draw more attention." He tried to ignore the scent of her and the feel of her slender curves.

"Whatever. If it validates your manhood, go right ahead and sweep me up, but if you slip on black ice and put your back out, don't blame me." But she stopped wriggling. "This is the point where you tell me I don't weigh anything."

He waited a beat. "If I had to guess, I'd say you weigh the same as a small hippo."

"You have no idea how much I hate you."

"I know exactly how much you hate me." He lowered her gently onto the seat of the cab. "Wait there."

She eased herself into a more comfortable position. "Where are you going? To find a chiropractor?"

He didn't bother holding back the smile. "I'm going to tell a few lies about where you are."

Alec strode back into the gallery, found the owner, made up something that he hoped sounded plausible, picked up Skylar's coat and bag and joined her in the taxi.

The driver looked at him expectantly. "Where to, mate?"

It was a question he hadn't considered until now.

Alec looked at Sky. Her eyes were closed, the livid bruising darkening before his eyes.

"Sky?"

She didn't move.

His instinct was to ask the driver to deliver them to the nearest emergency department but she'd begged him not to, and he understood now it was because she didn't want to risk the publicity.

He didn't even know where she was staying. Was she checked into a hotel somewhere with Richard Everson?

"Sky." He nudged her and her eyes opened slowly, as if she had lead weights attached to her eyelids.

"Go away. I'm going to sleep, probably for a hundred years, and if you kiss me to wake me up I'll kill you." Her eyes drifted shut again and Alec leaned his head back against the seat, wondering what he'd done to deserve this. He was kind to old ladies and tried never to forget his mother's birthday but apparently someone still thought he needed to be punished.

Unable to come up with a viable alternative, he reluctantly gave the address of the hotel where he was staying.

The cab driver did a U-turn and Skylar's head flopped against his shoulder. Alec tried to shift her away, but her body settled against his as if it had been custom designed to fit.

The only way to stop her sliding off the seat was to

put his arm round her and he did that with the same degree of enthusiasm he displayed when completing his tax return.

The coat he'd lent her was open at the front and he saw that the silver fabric of her incredible dress clung to her curves like a body stocking. *A perfectly wrapped Christmas parcel.*

She had the face and body of a Victoria's Secret model.

He imagined unzipping that dress and revealing those curves and quickly averted his eyes.

No way.

Not only was she injured and involved with someone else, but their relationship bordered on adversarial.

Who was he kidding? They didn't *have* a relationship.

So why did he suddenly want to strip her naked and bone her into next week?

What the hell was wrong with him?

Given the circumstances his response bordered on the depraved, but knowing that seemed to make no difference. His body was a throbbing ache and he tried again to ease away from her, but she nestled closer. Immediately he was engulfed by the light, fresh scent of flowers.

He glanced down again, to the shimmer of her nails and the elaborate silver cuff on her narrow wrist that was obviously one of her own unique designs, forcing himself to admit the truth—he was turned on by a woman who set off every alarm in his body. The type of high-maintenance female he went out of his way to avoid.

And he was taking her back to his hotel room.

Last time he'd helped a woman in trouble it had ended badly.

He hoped the minibar was well stocked because he was going to need every bottle in the fridge to get through the next few hours.

Merry Christmas, Alec.

CHAPTER TWO

SKYLAR'S HEAD POUNDED, as if a thousand elves from Santa's workshop were hammering on her skull. There was a tickling feeling on her face and she kept her eyes closed, drifting in and out of sleep, lulled by the hum of the engine and the low murmur of male voices.

Alec's voice. Alec Hunter.

She lay against his shoulder, the strength of his arm keeping her locked against a chest that was solid muscle.

He was an academic. A man who spent at least half the year delivering lectures and studying papers. He wasn't supposed to have the body of a fighter.

She knew she should pull away but she didn't have the energy.

Had she been in a better state she would have laughed.

Of all the people who disapproved of her, her parents and Richard included, Alec Hunter led them all. He made no secret of the fact he thought she was shallow and frivolous.

Princess.

It was the cruelest irony that he'd been the one to be by her side at her lowest moment.

At some point during the journey she felt him

move. She assumed he was about to push her onto her own side of the seat, but then she felt him applying a soft pad to her head and realized that the tickling feeling was blood coming from the wound.

He'd given her his coat, she remembered, which meant that her head was rubbing up against the pristine white of his shirt.

Pristine no longer.

Even knowing that didn't motivate her to move.

She would happily have stayed in the cab forever, all her problems suspended.

Eventually they came to a standstill.

Alec eased her away from him and pushed her hair back from her face.

"Sky? We're here."

She was surprised by how gentle his fingers were.

She opened her mouth to ask where "here" was, but he was already leaning forward to pay the driver and then there was the sound of the door opening followed by a rush of cold air that made her gasp.

She was about to tell him she could walk but he scooped her up without asking and carried her into what was obviously a hotel.

Bright lights dazzled and she screwed up her eyes against the light, thinking not for the first time that Alec Hunter had a touch of caveman about him.

She was treated to a close-up view of the stubble that shadowed his jaw.

He smelled dizzyingly good, a mixture of lemons, winter forest and delicious man.

He didn't pause at the reception, spoke to no one, simply strode through a marble-clad lobby and into the elevator with the same cool authority he seemed to show in everything he did.

"I can't believe they didn't challenge you," she muttered. "You could have drugged me, or kidnapped me for your pleasure."

"They probably took one look at you and knew that no man in his right mind would take you on." He paused outside a door, shifted his hold on her so that he could slide the card into the lock and carried her into the room.

"You're so wrong about me." Her stomach was rolling ominously. "I'm adorable when you get to know me."

"I won't be getting to know you."

"Your loss."

With an exasperated sound, he lowered her carefully to the bed and adjusted the dressing on her head. "It's bleeding again. Remind me why I didn't take you to the hospital?"

"Because I asked you not to and you listened." It felt as if thunder and lightening were exploding in her head. "Do you have any painkillers?"

He disappeared into the bathroom and returned a few moments later holding some tablets. "Paracetamol." Instead of giving them to her, he put them down next to the bed. "Look over my shoulder." He pulled his phone out of his pocket and switched on the flashlight function. He flashed the light over her eyes, checking her pupils. "How many of me are there?"

"One. But that's more than enough so don't go cloning yourself anytime soon."

He didn't smile. "Were you knocked out? Did you lose consciousness?"

"I don't think so." She winced as he took a photograph. "Are you going to post that to Instagram?"

"I'm not posting it anywhere. I'm keeping it in case we need it as evidence."

"Evidence for what? That I look stunning with a black eye?"

"Evidence against your boyfriend." His tone was hard. "Can you remember everything that happened?"

Her stomach roiled.

She thought about Richard. About the things he'd said and the expression on his face when he'd said them. "Yes, unfortunately. I'd give a lot for amnesia right now."

She felt humiliated and irritatingly fragile.

The truth was she'd been completed deluded.

For once her creative brain had worked against her.

Alec hesitated. "Do you want to talk about it?"

He was obviously hoping she'd say no and she was touched that he'd even asked.

"No." She decided to give him a break on that one. "I want to clean up and shut my eyes for a while. I'm sorry to have troubled you."

"It's no trouble."

"Liar."

He shone the phone's flashlight at her head. "That bruise isn't looking good. Do you know who you are? What day it is?"

"I'm the non-prodigal daughter and today is the day I ruined my favorite dress, realized I was in a relationship with a dumbass and ended up in the hotel room of a man who hates me. I'm telling myself things can only get better."

She bit back a hysterical laugh. At least now she knew it wasn't love. No more doubts on that score.

Alec handed her the pills. "If you're going to be sick, I want to know."

Despite their less than perfect history, she almost felt sorry for him.

She knew what Richard was like with anyone who was ill. Instead of sympathy, his mind ran to vaccinations and quarantine. "It's fine. Go check into another room. I'll pay."

"What's the point in that? I brought you here to keep an eye on you."

"But you want a sick warning."

"Because it's a bad sign with a head injury," he said patiently, "and if that happens I'm taking you to hospital."

"Oh. I thought—" She didn't tell him what she'd thought. She was starting to wonder if her time with Richard had twisted her view on the world. "I don't need to go to the hospital, but thank you." She lifted her palm to her mouth but her hand was shaking and one of the pills slid onto the floor and vanished under the bed. "Sorry."

He said nothing. Simply disappeared for a moment and returned to face her. This time he put a fresh pill in her palm and guided her hand to her mouth. Then he handed her the water. "What happened, Sky? Why did he leave you there like this?"

"Because he's a jerk. Because he cares more about the media and his public image than he does about me. Because I didn't do and say what he wanted me to do and say. Because he's in love with my father." It was all so ridiculous she started to laugh.

Alec looked bemused. "Your father?"

"Never mind. It's complicated. You have *no idea* how complicated." Even she couldn't unravel what was real and what wasn't. How many of their conversations had been false? If their relationship had been a movie, she would have watched it again with subtitles to see what she'd missed. "Do we have to talk about this?"

"No. Stay there. I'm going to clean up your head."

She closed her eyes, heard the sound of running water from the bathroom, and then he was back with a washcloth and a towel.

"I'll try not to hurt you."

She didn't tell him that most of the hurt was on the inside. Trying not to wince, she sat still as he gently cleaned her forehead. "I bet I look good. Black and red are my colors, and so is blue."

He smiled. "Scalps are extremely vascular. They always produce more blood than they should and it looks worse than it is."

It was rare to see him smile and she found it hard to look away. It was like catching a glimpse of the sun on a dark, stormy day.

"You should smile more. You look less intimidating when you smile."

The smile vanished. "You have dried blood in your hair, but I can't do anything about that. If we wash it, it will open the wound."

The awkwardness was back.

She wanted a shower, but she wasn't sure she could manage that without help and there was no way she was stripping naked in front of Alec Hunter. She'd suffered all the humiliation she could handle for one day. “Do you have my purse? I’ll call a cab and get out of your way.”

“Where are you going?”

“Back to my fancy hotel room. There’s a bottle of champagne waiting for me. Shame to waste it.”

“Champagne?” His voice sharpened. “He’s staying with you?”

“That was the plan, but I’m guessing I’ll be drinking it alone.” She thought about her plan to make the most of London at Christmas. Ice-skating alone. The London Eye alone. Yay. Fun times ahead.

“You can’t go back to your room. There’s a chance he might show up, and if he doesn’t it would mean you being on your own and you can’t be on your own. Not after a head injury. Someone needs to be with you.” He removed his tie and loosened a few buttons of his shirt.

She noticed the hint of dark chest hair through the gap in his buttons and averted her eyes quickly.

She didn’t need to know more about Alec Hunter than she already did.

“Relax. That ‘someone’ isn’t going to be you so don’t change your plans for me.”

“I don’t have plans.”

“You’re wearing a tie. I assume you had a date.”

“I gave a lecture earlier today.”

The reminder of his standing in the academic world did nothing to rescue her flagging spirits.

Here was someone else with a “proper job.”

She was the joker in the pack.

Feeling truly horrible, she flopped back on the bed and covered her eyes with her forearm. The pain in her head and the tiredness threatened to overwhelm her. She knew she should leave, but she couldn't bring herself to move. "As soon as these painkillers have worked, I'm going back to my hotel."

Somewhere in the distance she heard a phone ring and then the sound of a deep, male voice—Alec.

Whatever his faults, there was no denying his voice was almost hypnotically sexy.

She lay there, eyes closed, thinking she could happily listen to his British accent forever.

"Yes, I made it… No, not really. There were complications." And then a pause. "Yes. Well, you were right." Another pause. "She's here with me now… My hotel room… No, she's sleeping." Another pause. "No, don't do that… I know how close you are but you don't need to come. I've got this… Yes, I promise I won't leave her on her own. I'll call you, Brittany." His voice grew distant and she realized that he'd moved into the bathroom so that he didn't disturb her.

And now she knew who he was talking to.

Brittany and Emily, no doubt calling to see how her exhibition had gone. Judging from the half conversation she'd overheard, they now wanted to fly over, which is what she would have done if it had been one of them in trouble. Only this time it wasn't necessary.

I've got this.

Funny how people could surprise you.

The last person she would have expected to bail her out of a mess was Alec Hunter.

With that thought in her head, she drifted off to sleep and woke to the sound of heavy rain.

It took her a few seconds to realize it was the shower, not rain, and a few seconds more to realize her stomach was churning. She was going to be sick.

Hoping Alec hadn't locked the door, she staggered off the bed, groggy and dizzy.

Shrugging off the coat he'd draped around her, she swayed into the bathroom just as he stepped out of the shower, gloriously naked.

"Holy crap." For a moment she stared, distracted by his tough, muscular build and the shadow of hair on his chest. Through the haze of pain she registered that Alec Hunter might be a hardened cynic, but he had a seriously hot body. Her eyes followed the dusky trail lower and her eyes widened. He was fully, impressively erect. She heard him swear under his breath and then he reached for a towel just as her own body reminded her who was in charge.

She made it to the toilet and threw up, her humiliation complete.

If she'd lived through a worse day in her life, she couldn't remember it.

EXASPERATED AND CONCERNED, Alec knotted the towel firmly round his waist and hunkered down next to her. He tried to forget those few pulsing seconds when her bleary gaze had fastened on his face and then drifted lower to other, more intimate parts of his anatomy. Parts that seemed keen to independently express just how attractive he found her.

"Sky?" Keeping his voice and his hands gentle, he drew her hair back from her face and muttered what he hoped were reassuring words. "I'm going to call a doctor."

She shook her head and then moaned as she retched again. "Go away. Please go away. Just leave me."

He'd never seen a more pitiful sight in his life.

It didn't take a genius to guess how much she hated being ill in front of him.

But what alternative was there? He couldn't leave her on her own in this state.

He rubbed her back, held her, and then when it finally seemed there was nothing left in her stomach, he stood up and left the bathroom long enough to fetch the water from the bedside table.

In those few seconds she had eased herself back against the tiled wall of the bathroom. Now she sat, eyes closed, knees bent, her silver hair flowing over her bloodstained silver dress.

Alec wetted a washcloth and crouched down next to her.

"Here." He handed her the water and put the cool cloth against her forehead.

She sipped slowly and then lifted her hand and took the cloth from him.

"Stop being nice. I hate you and it's hard to remember I hate you when you're nice."

"Don't worry, I'll keep reminding you. You need to go back to bed. You'll feel better." He rose to his feet and held out his hand but she ignored it.

"I can manage." She straightened those long legs and staggered unsteadily to her feet, like a newborn foal trying to work out how to stand. "I bet this is the best date you've had in a long time. Taking care of a semiconscious, vomiting woman must be right at the top of your list of favorite ways to spend a Friday night." Despite her light tone, she kept her head dipped and Alec slid his fingers under her chin and forced her to look at him.

"I know you don't want to go to hospital, but I'm

going to call a friend of mine. He's a doctor. He works in the emergency department near here."

"I don't need a doctor."

"That's the choice, Sky. Either you see my friend, or I take you to hospital."

"Bully."

Alec looked at her, now dressed only in the tight silver dress. Her feet were bare, her hair loose around her shoulders.

With a bruise already turning all colors of the rainbow and her hair streaked with dried blood, she shouldn't have looked good but she did.

She intercepted his gaze. "Bet I don't look like a fairy princess now, hey, Shipwreck Hunter?"

"You look like one of the seven dwarfs."

A tiny spark lit her eyes. "Which one?"

"The really ugly one."

She gave a weak laugh. "Can I take a shower before I go back to my hotel? I don't want to draw attention to myself."

He doubted it was possible for Sky to go anywhere without drawing attention. Even bruised, she was the most beautiful woman he'd ever seen. And that, he reminded himself, was another reason he was never going to lay a finger on her. In his experience very beautiful women were hard work. "You're not going anywhere. And you're not in a state to take a shower. You might pass out."

"I won't, but if you don't hear me singing you can come in and rescue me."

She'd be naked and wet.

He'd probably drown. "Sky—"

"I've already seen you naked. Nice body by the

way." She managed a smile. "Not bad for a puny academic. I guess that comes from wrestling alligators or whatever it is you do to impress your fan club of adoring women. Call me fussy, but I hate having blood in my hair. We both know you and I have nothing in common and anyway, you loathe me so we're perfectly safe even if you do have to barge in and rescue me."

He'd assumed their encounter earlier had confirmed that certain parts of him didn't loathe her.

"Fine. Take a shower. I'll be outside." Leaving the door open, he removed himself from the bathroom, trying not to think of her naked and wet.

He pulled on jeans and a shirt and called his friend.

He'd always intended to make the call, just not under these circumstances.

As he put his phone down, he heard Skylar's voice.

"Alec?" Her words were muffled. "I'm stuck."

Swearing under his breath, he walked back into the bathroom and found her with her arms up, the dress covering her head and leaving the whole of her lower body exposed apart from a thin wisp of silver silk that covered the most vulnerable part of her.

Alec averted his eyes. "What are you doing?"

"Trying to take my dress off like you told me to." She wriggled, her hips moving. "My arms are trapped and I can't see what I'm doing. I'm feeling dizzy and I don't want to throw up in my dress. It's taken enough punishment."

"Stand still." Teeth clenched, he reached for the dress, the movement bringing him into contact with warm, bare skin. She smelled like roses and summer rain. "Doesn't this thing have a zip?"

"No, it's stretchy. It pulls on and off."

He felt as if he was being boiled alive. "You should have pulled it down, not up."

"I know that now, but it's the first time I've worn it and I didn't have a head injury when I tried it on."

The situation would have been comical if he hadn't been so tense.

Alec took hold of the dress, tugged gently and the fabric slid over her head. Which would have been a cause for celebration, except that she wasn't wearing a bra.

He caught a full on eyeful of lush, creamy breasts tipped with pink and then she grabbed a towel and covered herself.

"That makes us equal."

He backed off, searing his skin on the heated towel rail. "My friend is on the way over here now. As luck would have it, he just finished a shift." And the sooner he arrived the better. He didn't want to be alone with Skylar a moment longer than he had to be. "I'll give you some privacy."

He walked toward the door, keeping his back to her.

"Good. That's thoughtful of you." The shower hissed and then she cried out. "Ow! Crap, that hurts. How do you turn this thing off? Alec, you have to help me. I'm drowning."

Wondering what the hell he'd done to deserve this sort of punishment, Alec stopped in the doorway and turned.

She was naked in the shower, her hands over her head to protect it. "Alec?"

"Yeah, I'm here." His voice sounded as if he had a bad dose of the flu.

"You sound weird."

"That's because you have water in your ears. Stand still. I don't want to soak my clothes. My luggage on this trip is ninety percent Christmas gifts. Close your eyes." He picked up the shampoo, reduced the power of the jet and lathered her hair as quickly as possible. "This is your fault for having fairy-princess hair. You should have dyed it a different color and cut it short."

"I never dye my hair."

He rinsed her hair, careful to protect her wound, watching as the water slid down her body. It flowed over the curve of her hips to the shadow and light that nestled in the secret places between her thighs. The brief glimpse was enough to confirm she was indeed a natural blonde.

Heat flashed across his skin. He fought the urge to lower his mouth to her neck and breathe her in. He wanted to trace every delicate curve with his tongue, taste every inch of her.

"Alec?" Her eyes were shut, her lashes clumped with droplets of water. "Are you still there?"

He stood, trying to work out how he could be dizzy when he wasn't the one who had banged his head.

"Yeah." His voice emerged from his dry throat, rough and rasping. "I'm here."

And it was killing him.

"Could you hand me a towel?"

In the grip of a brutal desire, he groped for the controls of the shower and then for the towels he'd left within reach beyond the shower screen. She took one from him and tied it around her like a sarong. He used the other to dry her hair, avoiding her injury.

"I've often wondered if people would take me more seriously if I dyed it black." Her voice was muffled by the towel. "There have been studies, you know."

"Don't dye it black."

"The weird thing is, my brothers all have dark hair. When I was little, I decided that a wicked witch had probably kidnapped me from my proper family and dropped me in the wrong house by accident. I assumed my parents would have given me back if they'd had a return address. They think I'm wasting my life doing arty things. So does Richard. What do you think?"

His brain had ceased to work from the moment he'd walked into the bathroom, but if he'd been capable of rational thought he would have been thinking that he didn't want to know more about her.

As far as he was concerned, the more superficial his knowledge of her was, the better.

"What do I think?" He dried the ends of her hair and then stepped back out of the danger zone. "I think you charge ridiculous prices."

"Really?"

No, not really, but the way she was looking at him, her luminous blue eyes wistful and vulnerable, hardened his resolve.

"Yes, really." He slung the towel over the rail and struggled for words that would ensure she continued to think he was the big bad wolf. It was safer for both of them that way. Safer if he didn't follow his instincts, which suggested he carry her back to the bed and this time join her in it. "Your nod to Greek mythology might be charming to someone with no depth of knowledge, but that doesn't change the fact that there are significant inaccuracies." Droplets of water clung to her cheek. Without thinking, he lifted his hand and wiped them away with his thumb. Her skin was as soft and smooth as the petals of a rose and he felt her still under his touch.

"You took the time to look round my exhibition."

He let his hand drop. "I was killing time until I could get to speak to you."

"Of course you were. You planned to leave the first moment you could." Her cheeks were flushed. "Don't be embarrassed. I was hoping you'd leave quickly. Now I'm glad you didn't."

He wasn't sure how he felt about it.

They stared at each other for a moment and then he heard a tap on the door and stepped away from her, relieved to have an excuse to walk away.

"That will be Michael." He grabbed a robe from the back of the door, thrust it toward her and escaped from the steamy bathroom.

The sleeves of his shirt were wet from the shower and he rolled them up on his way to the door. At least with someone else in the room he was less likely to commit an act of gross indecency.

Despite the circumstances, he was genuinely pleased to see his friend and they chatted for a few moments, catching up on the main events of their lives, before Michael walked over to the bed to take a look at Skylar.

Alec wished he were somewhere else. This whole situation was wrong on every level.

It was too intimate, too *personal.*

He and Skylar barely knew each other.

What if Michael asked her a question Alec didn't want to hear?

As far as he was concerned the bar for "too much information" was set low.

He prowled to the window and stood with his back to the room while his friend examined her. He could see the reflection of her body in the glass, so he pressed his forehead against the window and focused on the street below.

Snow was still falling and far beneath him people and cars moved slowly.

He heard Michael ask Skylar what had happened and heard her dismiss it as a silly accident.

Was that true? Maybe, but something told him that Richard Everson had played a part in that "accident."

And even if he hadn't, the one undisputable fact that stood out above all others was that the guy hadn't stayed to help her.

"Just sick the once?" Michael stood up and pulled a sheet of paper out of his bag. "Alec?"

Bracing himself, Alec turned. "Yes?"

Michael handed over the paper. "Instructions for head-injured patients. You probably know it all, but read it anyway. If you're worried, the next step is to bring her into the department for a scan. I'm in tomorrow, so call my mobile and I'll arrange it."

"Thanks." Alec stared down at the paper in his hand.

Tomorrow he was supposed to be traveling deep into the English countryside to celebrate Christmas early with his family. It had made sense to combine a trip with his other commitments because he needed to be back in Maine in order to meet his deadline.

His friend snapped his bag closed. "She can't be left on her own, of course, but given that she has you, that's not a problem."

Alec realized that Michael had misunderstood their relationship. He opened his mouth to put him right, but his friend was already walking to the door.

"I have to dash. I'm supposed to be having a late dinner with the in-laws. May will kill me if I don't show up. Next time you're over here, email me and you must come for dinner. Bring Skylar." He opened the door and lowered his voice. "Can't tell you how relieved I am to see you getting back out there. We were worried that after everything that happened with Selina you wouldn't take the risk again. And I can see why you were finally tempted back into the scary world of relationships. Skylar is a stunner. Nice smile. Taking her home for Christmas?"

Alec frowned. "No! I—"

"Next time give me more notice. We'll grab a beer. Give my love to your family. May and I are going over there for New Year's Eve. Looking forward to your mother's cooking—wish she'd give mine a few lessons." He slapped Alec on the shoulder and was out the door before Alec had time to correct the misconceptions that were piling up.

He stood in the doorway, digesting the fact that his friends and family were still speculating on his divorce and love life.

He'd carefully laid down ground rules for that.

As far as he was concerned the subject was closed and he'd moved on.

He tried to spend as little time as possible thinking about his marriage. He certainly didn't want others thinking about it.

Aware that there was silence from the bedroom, Alec locked the door and walked back into the room.

Skylar had fallen asleep.

Her hair, clean again, lay in a pool around her shoulders, as if someone had knocked over a jar of pale creamy honey.

Alec stared down at her and felt a flicker of concern.

He found himself wishing she'd wake up and return to her chatty, energetic self. Being with Skylar was like being outdoors without sunglasses on a day when the sun was just a little too bright. Usually he wanted to turn down the wattage, but maybe that was because his own world had been dark and gray for the past few years.

Sleeping Beauty, he thought and gently pulled the cover over her.

There was no question of her going back to her own hotel, at least not tonight.

He dimmed the lights, wondering what to do about his family gathering.

His mother was working on Christmas Day and he'd be back on Puffin Island, so this date for their annual "early Christmas" had been in his calendar for months.

It was the one time of year everyone made an effort to be together.

There was no way he could cancel.

Which left him with the problem of what to do about Skylar.

Through the window he could see the snow falling layer upon layer, leaving an ever-deepening carpet of white on the streets below.

If it didn't stop soon, his journey home the next day would be hazardous. Negotiating English country roads in the middle of a snowstorm was not for the fainthearted.

He opened his laptop, scanned the news and found a photograph of Richard Everson. The caption said that he'd been in London for the exhibition of his girlfriend, jewelry designer Skylar Tempest. There was nothing about the proposal.

Alec closed his laptop and strolled over to the bed to check on Skylar again.

She was still sleeping, her breathing even, the bruising on her head dark against the swathe of pale hair.

The bed was huge, plenty big enough for two people to spend the night and not come into contact, but he lifted the bags from the sofa and piled them on the floor. He'd slept in places where most people wouldn't venture, so the prospect of a night on a sofa didn't bother him.

What bothered him was the woman lying in the bed.

CHAPTER THREE

SKYLAR WOKE TO find her head still pounding. This time it felt as if someone was having a fireworks display inside her skull.

It was still dark in the room and it took her a moment to remember what had happened.

Her relationship with Richard was over.

Over, over, over.

She relived the evening in fast-forward, from the moment he'd taken the microphone to the moment she'd had to sprint to the bathroom.

She'd been ill, and in front of Alec Hunter of all people.

Why, oh why, couldn't she have lost her memory?

She rolled over and buried her face in the pillow to muffle the groan, and then a horrible thought occurred to her and she lifted her head and checked the bed next to her.

It was empty.

Well, that was something to be grateful for. She might have crashed in the wrong bed, but at least she hadn't slept with the enemy.

Feeling wobbly and thoroughly irritated with herself, she slid out of bed and saw Alec asleep on the sofa. He was too tall and broad for it and she suspected he'd had a very uncomfortable night. Strands of dark hair flopped over his handsome face, signposting a bone structure that made the artist in her want to reach for a pencil.

Sleep softened his hard features and made him seem more approachable.

And of course last night she'd seen a different side of him.

He'd been cool, competent and…kind.

Alec being kind was the last thing she would have expected.

Unlike the man she'd been dating, who had behaved like an unprincipled rat, Alec had refused to abandon her. He'd brought her back here, mopped up the blood and held her head while she'd been sick.

That, in her mind, had earned him enough points that he could pretty much do anything and she'd never be able to criticize him again.

Later, she knew that would irritate her, but for now she was grateful.

Grabbing her bag, she dragged herself to the bathroom and recoiled from her reflection.

No wonder he'd wanted to take her to hospital.

She could have starred in *A Christmas Carol* as one of the ghosts.

Lifting her hair, she studied her face. The corner of the table had caught her above the eye, lacerating the skin, but not badly enough for her to require stitches. Worse, was the bruising. She pulled her hair forward, experimenting as she tried to cover the damage.

Another wave of dizziness hit her and she closed her eyes.

When she opened them again she saw her silver

dress rinsed and folded on a towel along with his white shirt.

Only one person could have done that.

Alec.

Rinsing would have ruined the dress, but it was ruined anyway and she was touched that he'd bothered.

Maybe she did have a serious head injury. She was getting soft thoughts about a man who thought she was a waste of space.

She'd go back to her hotel and lie down for a while. That should cure her.

Would Richard be there or had he already flown home?

She stared at herself in the mirror, the question she'd been ignoring looming in her mind.

If she hadn't stepped back, would he have hit her?

The question went round and round in her mind as she splashed cold water on her face.

Then she tiptoed back into the bedroom intending to find her shoes. Instead, she walked straight into the solid wall of muscle that was Alec Hunter.

His hands gripped her arms and there was a fierce frown on his handsome face. "Where are you going?"

"Back to my hotel. Thank you for your hospitality."

His grip on her didn't ease. "You can't be on your own."

"I'm fine. I haven't been sick again and I'll take those instructions your doctor friend left. If I feel worse, I'll take a cab to the hospital."

"It's December and it's snowing. Not easy to get a cab."

"I'll find one." Last night she'd been too ill to feel anything other than annoyance and embarrassment but now, in daylight, the whole incident felt sordid. "Look, I'm really grateful for everything you've done. I owe you, and part of my repayment is getting out of your way. You have a life to live, Alec. I heard you telling your friend that you were going home to your family." She paused, distracted by the stack of gifts by the door. "Is there anything in those parcels?"

"Of course. You think I wrapped up empty boxes?" His gaze was curious and she felt the slow burn of embarrassment stain her cheeks.

He was probably wondering if her strange question was a symptom of her head injury.

"Ignore me. Looks like you're in for a few days of fun."

A normal Christmas.

The sort she'd never experienced.

"It's an early family Christmas. We do this every year." He dismissed it. "You can't stay on your own, Sky."

"You're forgetting I have a bottle of champagne waiting for me at the hotel. I'm going to take a ride on the London Eye at night and go skating at Somerset House. Or maybe I'll try the rink at the Natural History Museum. What do you think?"

"I think," he said slowly, "that you've damaged yourself enough for one weekend."

"I'll have you know I'm a very competent skater. You don't need to worry about me."

"So you're going to go skating by yourself and then drink all the champagne by yourself. That sounds like a lonely way to spend a weekend."

"I might also order up a ton of cookies and comfort eat while watching holiday movies back-to-back. I'll be fine, Alec. Go do whatever it is you were planning on doing today before you peeled me off the floor."

"Will he be there?" He was blunt and direct and she sighed.

"At my hotel? I doubt it, but if he is then I'm sure we'll have a few things to say to each other."

"I'm not leaving you on your own with him."

She was caught in a swirling tide of emotion. Exasperation, frustration that this had happened and something else. Something softer and more dangerous. She was touched. Really touched that he'd helped her and was still helping her.

"You don't have to be all caveman around me." Standing this close, she could see the masculine lines of his face and the stubble that shadowed his jaw. He was strikingly handsome and she now knew he was also strong and decent. For some reason she'd found it easier when she hadn't known that about him. "I can handle Richard."

"The way you handled him last night?"

"I handled him just fine until I fell."

"And if you hadn't fallen?" He spoke softly. "What then?"

She knew what he was asking because she'd been asking herself the same thing. "I don't know," she said finally. "And it doesn't matter now. I appreciate your concern, but this is my problem and I'll deal with it."

"You're not in a fit state to deal with anything. If he walked into the room now, what would you do? You don't have the strength to defend yourself from anyone. You're vulnerable."

And yet hadn't she been a thousand times more vulnerable the night before, with Alec?

He'd seen her stripped down, bare, both literally and figuratively.

And she'd seen him.

Her brief glimpse of his powerful frame was welded into her brain.

Heat poured over her and she tried to make a joke.

"I could vomit on him. That would send him running, believe me."

He didn't smile. Instead he crossed the room, picked up her purse and found her phone. "Check your messages. I want to know if he called."

"I forgot to switch it on. It's an annoying habit of mine." Hands shaking, she took the phone. "He won't have called. I don't think you know Richard very well. I damaged his ego." But that was the least of her problems. She switched her phone on and saw four missed calls. "Two calls from Brittany, one from Emily and one message from my mother." Even though she could guess what it would be about, a faint thread of hope made her press the button to listen. Because her fingers were shaky and she wasn't concentrating she played it back on speaker.

"Skylar? Richard landed at JFK a few hours ago and called to update us, which was good of him under the circumstances. I had hoped that the time had come when I could stop having to make excuses for you. That this once you'd make the right decision. But it seems not. I confess that of all the difficult conversations I've had in my life, that was one of the most awkward and embarrassing. You'd better call him back fast and hope he'll reconsider."

Awkward and embarrassing was having played that back on speaker.

Without looking at Alec she ended the call, digesting the fact that while she'd been bleeding and throwing up in Alec's bathroom, Richard had been flying first-class across the Atlantic.

Feeling as energetic as roadkill, she sank onto the sofa Alec had recently vacated.

"Well, I guess you have the answer to your question. No one is looking for me, so you can safely leave me unprotected."

And alone.

Totally alone.

London no longer felt exciting and full of possibilities. It felt big and impersonal.

"That was your mother?"

Hearing the undercurrent of shock in his voice, Sky kept her head down and sent a quick text to Brittany. "Yeah, she's always pretty formal on the phone. Of course it doesn't help that she's probably gone nuclear over this thing with Richard." Without elaborating, she dropped the phone in her bag. "I have one more favor to ask. Could I borrow a shirt? I'll return it next time I see you."

"I'm not leaving you alone in an impersonal hotel room when you're vulnerable. You're coming home with me."

It was the last thing she'd expected him to say and she glanced up at him, shocked. "You're kidding. Alec, we're not even friends."

"You need to stop being a drama queen. It's too early in the morning." A smile touched the corners of his mouth, distracting her.

She was usually too busy being irritated to notice the detail of his features but this close she could see that his eyelashes were thick and dark. He hadn't shaved and the line of his lower cheek and jaw was dark with stubble.

In that single moment she could understand why he had an army of female fans.

Alec Hunter might be insanely irritating, but he was also insanely hot.

And now she knew what he was hiding away under the smart suits and rugged outdoor wear.

Unsettled, she looked away. Maybe she *was* vulnerable. Something had to explain the way her brain was working.

"Usually you accuse me of being a fairy princess." She tried to lighten the atmosphere. "I'm trying to work out if drama queen is a promotion or not."

"It's a sideways move. Where are you staying? We need to collect your things and settle your bill."

"Alec, you can't just—"

"Either you disappoint my family by making me stay here with you, or you come with me. Your choice."

She gave a choked laugh. "You heard my mom—I don't make good choices."

"You mean you don't make the choices other people want you to make," he said drily. "If you really want to stuff yourself with cookies you can do it at my house. My mother loves to bake. She'll be delighted to have someone with your appetite to feed. There will be enough carbohydrate and sugar on offer to comfort an entire sorority."

"You're British. What do you know about sororities?"

"My father is American."

"I didn't know that about you." She was starting to realize there was plenty she didn't know about him, including the fact that caring for a sick woman didn't put the smallest dent in his calm demeanor.

And he was decent.

Moody, irritating, insanely hot, but decent.

He could have made an excuse and left her alone. Instead, he'd stayed with her.

"What's it to be, Sky? Are we spending the next few days in a hotel room or with my family?"

"I can't just show up at your family's home and join in a private gathering." But the alternative was spending a week alone in a hotel room steaming mad about Richard and that was about as appealing as pulling her hair out at the roots. "Your mother won't want me. I'll ruin her numbers for the catering and mess up her seating plan."

"Seating plan?" His brows rose. "People sit wherever there is room. If we run out of chairs, we use the piano stool. My family is very easygoing and my mother never quite knows who is coming until the day. And as for catering, she always cooks enough to feed half the village."

Skylar tried not to compare that with her own experience of family occasions. Guests were expected to confirm. Last-minute extras were strongly discouraged. "This is your special time with your family and you and I aren't exactly intimate."

His eyes gleamed. "You've seen me naked and I've seen you naked. We're a lot more intimate than we were this time yesterday. Do you need to go back to the gallery?" He moved around the room with stark efficiency, packing things into one small suitcase.

"No. I can call Judy." She chose to ignore his comment about having seen her naked. She really didn't want to think about how she'd ended up naked in a shower with a man who, until yesterday, she'd actively disliked. "Last night was the important bit. Fortunately it was almost over when this happened. She must be wondering what happened to me."

"She isn't. I talked to her before we left. She was the one who gave me your bag and coat."

"What did you say to her?"

"That you weren't feeling well. She obviously isn't a fan of public proposals, so you had her sympathy. She told me to tell you that the exhibition was a huge success and to call her when you're ready." He gave her a long, searching look. "You're pale. Still feeling ill?"

"No." She was careful not to move her head. "But I could use some more of those pills you gave me."

He walked into the bathroom and returned with the packet and a glass of water. "Take two."

She swallowed them and drank the water. "About last night—"

"Forget it."

"I won't forget it, Alec. I'm sorry you had to sleep on the sofa. It looks horribly uncomfortable. Are you aching all over?"

"No, and you need to stop apologizing. It's starting to irritate me. I'm used to you arguing with me."

Struck by another wave of dizziness, she closed her eyes. "I'll start arguing with you as soon as those pills work."

"You're not going to look your best in the Christmas photos this year."

He lifted his hand and smoothed her hair back, taking a closer look at her head. The brush of his fingers sent a rush of tingly heat across her skin.

"My family doesn't do photos. Christmas is a very formal affair. Everything is scripted and planned." The thought of Christmas made her want to curl up under the bedcovers and never come out.

He took the glass from her hand. "I need to call my mother and warn her that we'll be one extra so she can make up the spare room. Then I'm going to find you some clothes. I have a pair of track pants that might do until we can fetch your things. You can roll up the legs and belt the waist."

She was grateful to him for not pursuing the topic of Christmas.

"Great. If my unique seduction tricks of bleeding on you and throwing up on you haven't worked, hopefully wearing baggy clothes will nail the deal."

There was a brief pause and she saw a faint flicker of a smile touch his mouth.

"You'd look good in anything." With that surprising comment, he walked to the phone by the bed. "I need breakfast before we hit the road."

She stared at him, the air trapped in her lungs and her tummy doing acrobatics.

He didn't pay her compliments. Ever. If anything, he went out of his way to make sure she knew she wasn't his type.

True, there had been the moment in the bathroom, but he was a guy, wasn't he? It hadn't meant anything. Healthy, virile, sexually active hot guy meets half-naked girl in the bathroom. It was a moment she'd already forgotten—well, maybe not *forgotten* exactly, but she certainly wasn't reading anything into it.

Half an hour later a tray arrived, heaped with fresh fruit, organic yogurt, pastries and scalding-hot coffee.

They ate while watching the sun rise over a frozen winter morning.

She noticed a stack of notes and his laptop on the desk. "Did you work last night?"

"For a while. I wanted to keep an eye on you."

He'd stayed awake for her? She pulled the corner off a croissant. It flaked in her fingers, buttery and warm. "This is only my second trip to London. I was hoping to see some of the sights before I left."

"When is your flight? You might still have time for that."

"A week on Sunday. Then I'll be back in New York for a couple of weeks before Christmas."

The croissant was too rich for her stomach so she left the rest and picked at a few berries.

Alec, she noticed, drank lots of coffee.

It felt strange having breakfast with him in his hotel suite, wearing his shirt under a hotel robe. It felt—*intimate.* If housekeeping had walked in, they would have assumed they were lovers.

"How are we getting to your parents' house? You have a car here?"

"I hire a car when I'm in London."

"How long will it take us to get to your home?"

"Around two hours, depending on the weather."

"You British are obsessed with your weather."

"When you've seen the roads around Honeysuckle Cottage, you'll understand why."

He packed up his laptop while she dressed, then

picked up the bags of gifts and the rest of his luggage and opened the door to their room.

"Honeysuckle Cottage? Such a cute name." She walked past him, careful not to brush against him. "By the way, I'm not a drama queen."

His eyes gleamed. "Fairy princess crossed with drama queen."

"So what does that make me? A fairy queen or a drama princess?"

"I don't know. I'll let you know after we've spent a few days together."

A few days.

Yesterday she'd been getting ready for her exhibition and now here she was with a bruised head and a bruised heart, going home with a man with whom she'd always had a difficult relationship.

Which all went to prove that whenever you were anticipating a happy ending, life was guaranteed to mess it up.

CHAPTER FOUR

THEY CRAWLED OUT of London and gradually the congestion eased and the roads opened up. It was still snowing heavily and Alec knew the country lanes around his parents' house would be difficult to navigate.

In the seat next to him Skylar slept, her hair a halo of silver-gold around a face almost as pale as the snow.

Concerned by the long silences from someone who usually talked enough for six people, Alec glanced at her from time to time. In daylight the bruising looked worse and her sleepiness worried him. He contemplated calling Michael again, but reassured himself with the knowledge that she'd had a disrupted sleep the night before and was probably just tired.

Maybe her pallor was the result of stress.

He didn't know what had shocked him most, the absence of any evidence of concern on the part of Richard Everson or the cold, unemotional message from her mother.

He couldn't help comparing it to those months after the breakdown of his own marriage when his family had been in constant contact. At the time he'd been exasperated by their refusal to leave him alone, but now he felt grateful that they'd cared enough to bother.

Skylar had close friends, but they were far away on Puffin Island.

Here, she was alone.

Alone, except for him, and he knew without her having pointed it out that he was the last person with whom she would have chosen to spend her lowest moment.

He turned off the main road, driving through untouched countryside, past woodland and fields coated in a thick layer of snow.

The closer he got to home, the more uneasy he felt.

What the hell had he done?

The only woman he'd ever brought home was his ex-wife and the memory of how that had played out was permanently embedded in his brain.

Sweat cooled his skin.

He didn't want to be trapped with Sky. He didn't want to be trapped with any woman who was emotionally vulnerable.

He wasn't fooled by her constant quips and cheery humor.

She was hurting and he didn't want to be within a million miles of a woman who was hurting.

He drove in silence, brooding on the weekend ahead.

Somehow he had to find a way of keeping his distance.

Finally, as he approached the market town near his parents' house, she woke.

She stirred and turned her head, absorbing her surroundings.

Tiny lights glowed in shop windows, illuminating honey-colored stone. Glossy green wreaths studded with plump red berries decorated the doors and a large Christmas tree dominated the village square.

"It's the prettiest place I've ever seen." She stifled a yawn. "Where are we?"

"The Cotswolds. We're about two hours from London. This is the village of Brockburn-on-the-Water. My parents live about five minutes from here, although it might as well be a million miles if they haven't cleared the road."

He waited for Skylar to flip down the mirror and start applying makeup but instead she shifted in her seat and gave him her full attention.

"Tell me about your family. What does your father do?"

"He's a GP. A family doctor. He came over to England straight after medical school, met my mother and never went back. He's senior partner in the village practice. My mother works in the renal unit in the hospital."

"Are you an only child?"

"Two sisters. One older, married with twins, the other younger. Olivia is sixteen."

"Sixteen? That's a big age gap. I bet you freaked out when you discovered your mom was pregnant."

"Why would you think that?"

He'd been completely freaked out.

Her insight was unnerving.

"Because when she was born you would have been—what? Sixteen? Seventeen? No teenager wants to be faced with tangible evidence that their parents still have sex. So you're an uncle and a big brother. I have older brothers, too. They spend the whole time telling me what I should be doing. Are you like that?"

"There would be no point because Liv wouldn't listen." He drove down the lane toward his parents' house, past trees laden with soft snow and fields dotted with animal footprints. The winter sun was low in the sky, sending light shimmering over fields of white.

"So both your parents are in medicine, but you didn't want to be a doctor?"

"No. When I was five I wanted to be an Arctic explorer. My uncle gave me an explorer's kit for Christmas and I remember taking it down the garden and camping out in the shed. Took them two hours to find me and by then I'd almost frozen to death." Mindful of the icy surface, he eased the car round the last bend and turned into his parents' drive. "We're here. This is it."

Honeysuckle Cottage stood as it had for several centuries, its stone walls glowing a soft gold in the sunshine. A large evergreen wreath studded with berries hung in the center of the door and two large bay trees placed on either side of the stone steps sparkled with tiny lights.

"This is your home?" Sky stared at the house. "It's the most idyllic cottage I've ever seen, apart from Brittany's. It reminds me of the house in that movie *The Holiday*. You've probably never seen it."

"I've seen it. Liv tortured me with it a few years ago. I'm still scarred. My revenge was to force her to sit through a turgid documentary on Napoleon."

She laughed. "One of yours?"

"I aim for several steps up from turgid." Before he could even switch off the engine the front door opened and he saw his family crowding into the doorway to welcome them. His mother snatched her apron over her head, evidence that she'd been in the kitchen when she'd heard the car. Behind her was his father with the phone in his hand and next to him his uncle, wearing a pair of flashing reindeer antlers. Alec felt a rush of affection for them and then remembered Sky. He could imagine what she was thinking. "I probably should have warned you that my family loves Christmas. Most of the year they're relatively sane, but there's something about this time of year that sends them over the top. Even my father, although for him the mulled wine probably has something to do with it." He slid out of the car, tense, knowing that this place wasn't going to suit glitzy Skylar.

His ex-wife had hated the rustic country life his parents led. An invitation to join them for the village pub quiz had been met with disdain and a stony refusal, as had all activities that involved the wearing of sturdy boots. Everything had been wrong. The weather too cold, the people too loud and tactile, the food too full of carbohydrates and fat. The final straw had been the animals. On the last occasion they'd visited, Alec had been forced to shut the dogs out of the house and had felt so guilty looking at their mournful faces he'd made their excuses and left early. He and Selina had separated just days later, after an incident he preferred to forget.

As always, just thinking about her elevated his stress levels.

It didn't help that he was, once again, accompanied by a woman who looked as if she'd stepped straight out of the pages of a glossy magazine. Even with her bruised face and no makeup, Skylar was stunning.

What had he been thinking?

He shouldn't have brought her here. His family didn't deserve another Christmas like the one they'd had three years before. He should have found another way.

He slammed the car door, his mood darkening with each passing second.

No way was he shutting the dogs out this time. If she wanted to avoid them, she could spend time in her room. And her reluctance to get her feet muddy, or her fingers frozen by snow, would give him the opportunity to spend time alone with his family.

He was still working out how to best manage the situation when his sister flew out of the door, her booted feet making indentations in the snow.

She was wearing an oversize sweater with a sparkly star in the middle and her hair tumbled in chocolate-brown waves around her shoulders. "Alec!"

Ignoring Skylar, Alec strode to meet her and caught her in a hug. "Is that the Christmas jumper?"

"Yes, Granny saw a picture in *Cosmo* and copied it for me. I am the envy of my friends. Karen was given one with a truly gross reindeer. She's wearing it inside out." She eased away and he saw her eyes widen as she noticed Skylar. "Oh, my— Who—? She's— *Wow*, Alec. How did a geeky guy like you get someone as gorgeous as her?"

Aware that his sister's whisper was louder than most people's normal conversational tone, Alec clenched his jaw. "Could you maybe speak a little louder? Embarrass me a little more?"

Grinning, she rose on tiptoe and kissed his cheek. "I could probably manage that. Embarrassing you is my favorite pastime."

"Skylar, this is my sister Olivia." Anything he might have added was interrupted by barking as the dogs heard his voice and tumbled in an excited frenzy out of the house.

Nelson was first, his glossy black coat a startling contrast against the white of the snow, but close on his heels was Churchill, who hated being left behind.

Cursing under his breath, Alec made a grab for them but they sprang toward Skylar, tails wagging.

Why was it that dogs made a beeline for the person least interested in them?

He waited for her to recoil and take refuge in the car, but instead she dropped into a crouch and embraced both dogs, laughing as they licked and jumped all over her with clumsy enthusiasm and a blur of wagging tails.

It wasn't the reaction he'd expected. "They'll ruin your coat."

She didn't seem to be listening. Her hands were all over the dogs, and she rubbed Nelson behind his ears until he whined in ecstasy and rolled in the snow.

"When I asked you to tell me about your family, you didn't mention these beautiful, *beautiful* dogs."

"But I hope he mentioned his beautiful, beautiful sister," Liv said happily, letting go of Alec and joining Sky. "The black Lab belongs to Alec. His name is Nelson. He's pretty old now but young at heart."

Hearing his name, Nelson rolled over and shook himself, showering Sky with snow.

"Thank you, I needed that." Laughing, she wiped snow out of her eyes. "And who is the beautiful chocolate Lab?"

"He's mine. He's called Churchill, but we call him

Church. He's only two. We hoped he'd be wise and statesmanlike, but so far it's not looking good. I'm trying to train him but neither of us is very disciplined so that hasn't turned out so well." She dragged him away from Skylar and then saw the damage. Her smile melted into panic. "They've made a horrible mess of your lovely coat. I'm so sorry. I'll have it cleaned."

Alec tensed, understanding the reason for the stammered apology. Selina had made a song and dance about having her clothes cleaned after the dogs had jumped on her and Liv had taken the brunt of her displeasure.

"I don't care about the coat." Sky kissed Nelson on the head and stood up. "It was a stupid color to buy but I was having a low moment and felt like treating myself."

Alec wondered why she'd been having a low moment. She would have bought the coat before her relationship had crashed and burned, surely?

Livy looked at it longingly. "I've always wanted a white coat."

Sky looked wistfully at the dogs. "I always wanted dogs." She'd braided her hair into a loose plait and it fell casually over one shoulder. The beam of the sun highlighted shades of wheat and pale gold that almost dazzled in the light. If Alec didn't already have evidence to the contrary, he would have assumed the color couldn't be natural.

Recalling exactly how he knew she was a natural blonde made his body heat. Irritated, he scowled. "You don't seem like a dog person."

His sister sent him a curious look and Sky smiled. "How does a dog person look? Any relation to a princess person?" There was a spark of fire in her eyes that told him that however battered she was by the events of the past twenty-four hours, she was still perfectly capable of holding her own with him. "You have a habit of thinking you have me all figured out. People with blond hair wearing a white coat can't own dogs, is that it?"

Liv gave a snort of laughter. "That's my brother. Thinks he knows best about everyone. It's infuriating. Drives me crazy." Sky turned to say something to her and Liv gasped in consternation. "What happened to your *head*?"

"She fell," Alec said shortly, "and she should probably be sitting down so let's get indoors."

"Good idea." Incurably friendly, Liv slid her arm through Sky's. "Come inside. You need to meet Mum, Dad and Uncle Harry. And Granny is here. She can't wait to meet you."

Alec watched as Skylar was swallowed up by the embrace of his enthusiastic family. The dogs were barking, everyone was talking at once and he was left on his own to unload the luggage.

Nelson nudged his leg and he gave a grunt.

"It's your lucky day, pal. She likes dogs. Looks like you won't be spending the weekend shut in the garden after all."

By the time he'd transferred everything to the hall, everyone was in the kitchen and Sky was standing by the range cooker holding a glass of mulled wine and looking slightly dazed.

"I've never had mulled wine before."

"It's red wine, spices, a few slices of citrus fruit. Delicious. I think it counts as one of your five a day, but Simon disagrees." His mother opened the oven and removed a tray of golden-brown, flaky pastry snacks. "Fetch the cooling rack please, Liv."

"And a touch of brandy. Don't forget the brandy." Uncle Harry winked and then crossed the room and embraced Alec. "The wanderer returns. We've killed the fatted calf in your honor."

"It's a turkey. Calves don't have wings, Uncle Harry." Liv pulled the wire rack out of the cupboard and set it down on the center of the table. "And we're eating it tomorrow. Tonight is game casserole. I helped make it. The meat has been marinating in wine for the past two days. Mum used one of Dad's precious bottles and he threw a fit so you'd better say how delicious it is."

Alec shrugged off his coat. "Where is Dad?"

"He's on the phone as usual. He's not even supposed to be working this weekend but the practice has been decimated by a flu bug. You know how it is at this time of year." His mother arranged the pastries on the rack while Skylar sipped the wine and closed her eyes.

"I don't know what I was expecting, but it wasn't this. It's—"

"You probably shouldn't be drinking alcohol anyway." Alec interrupted her before she could deliver a caustic remark that might upset his mother. "Leave it and I'll find you something else."

Skylar opened her eyes. "No way. It's delicious. I was going to say it tastes like Christmas." She ran her tongue over her lips. "It tastes like Christmas in a glass."

"I always think the same thing." Alec's mother

handed her a plate and gestured to the rack of cooling pastries. "This end is mushroom, garlic and chestnut. The far end is feta and spinach. You need to relax, Alec. You're very tense."

Of course he was tense.

He'd brought a stranger into his home at a time of year that was reserved for family, although so far he couldn't fault her manners.

"You should sit down," he said to Skylar, his voice gruff.

His mother nodded. "Yes, you should. That bruise of yours is nasty, dear, and you do look very pale."

"I always look pale without makeup." Skylar licked her fingers. "These are delicious. The only thing I can produce in the kitchen is soup. You're a wonderful cook."

Alec saw his mother melt like ice cream left in the sun.

"Settle yourself there and rest," she said. "Simon will take a look at your head as soon as he's off the phone. Maybe we should give you something nonalcoholic. After all, you have to save yourself for the champagne later. We don't want you falling asleep in the middle of the celebrations." She glanced up as Alec's father walked back into the room. "Well?"

"It was Mary from the village. She needed reassurance, that's all."

"So you don't have to go out? That's good."

"Celebrations?" Alec helped himself to a pasty. "What are we celebrating?"

"You really need to ask?" His mother exchanged looks with his father. "It's been three years since you brought anyone home, Alec. We'd almost given up and now here you are with Skylar. I know you won't want to talk about it, but—well, we're just so happy for you both."

CHAPTER FIVE

ALEC STARED AT his mother in appalled silence. "You—*What?* Mum, Skylar and I aren't a couple."

Not for a moment had it occurred to him that his family might misinterpret his relationship with Sky.

"You don't have to pretend, dear. Liv is old enough now. Half her class seem to be sleeping with their boyfriends, although frankly I don't—"

"Mum!" Alec's tone was sharp as he cut across her. "Skylar and I aren't together. Not like that. Why would you think that?"

"Well, because Maggie Poynter called me last night." His mother wiped her hands on her apron, a puzzled look on her face. "Michael phoned her the moment he left your hotel suite. He thought we'd want to know. He was being reassuring. We've all been worried about you since—since—" Her voice trailed off as she caught her husband's eye and she cleared her throat and mumbled something indistinct. "Sorry. I know I'm not supposed to mention it."

Alec closed his eyes.

He should have known Michael would call. Their families were close.

"What did he say, exactly?"

"That we could all finally relax because you were with the most stunning woman he'd ever met—" she beamed at Sky "—and that you were gentle and caring toward her and that you seemed more like yourself than you've been for a while, since—well, you know."

Torn between exasperation and irritation, Alec pressed his fingers to the bridge of his nose and then heard a choking sound from the end of the table. He let his hand drop and saw Skylar laughing behind her hand.

"Sorry." She sent him a look of mute apology. "It's just that the thought of Alec and I being together in that way is beyond hilarious. Most of the time he and I—" She broke off and he suspected she'd been about to say *can't stand each other* but instead she gave a limp smile. "We don't agree on much. We drive each other a little crazy." If she'd thought that admission would support her denial she was wrong.

Alec saw his mother's expression brighten.

"And that's exactly what he needs! Someone to stimulate his mind. Alec is very clever. His professor at Cambridge said that he was the brightest student he'd ever taught. But I say he needs to be challenged and not have life all his own way."

"You're embarrassing him, Mum—" Liv bit into a crumbling pastry "—which is totally brilliant by the way. Time to get out the naked baby photos."

Knowing that Sky had a more updated image of him naked, Alec breathed deeply. "Enough." He spoke through his teeth. "The subject is closed."

"Of course it is, if that's what you want. But Sky, you're the first woman he has brought home since the divorce, and you are so, *so* welcome, dear."

It was information he would never have chosen to share. "Sky and I are friends. That's the end of it."

"Of course you are. Now sit down by Skylar, Alec, and Liv can sit on your right." Sending Alec a soothing look, his mother removed her apron and started placing plates of food on the table. "We didn't know what time you'd be here because of the traffic, so lunch is simple. Honey-roasted ham, some lovely cheese from the Baxters' farm and a loaf your father made this morning. I'm not sure buying that bread maker was a good idea if I'm honest. And I have potatoes baking in the oven. Liv, fetch some of the chutney from the cupboard and then go and tell Granny lunch is ready and Alec is here with his new girlfriend. Friend," she said quickly. "I mean friend. I make the chutney myself with the apples from our tree, Sky. At the time they all complain about the smell of vinegar but when Christmas comes they're all pleased enough to be eating it." She broke off as the phone rang. "I don't believe it. That's the fourth time in an hour."

"I'll get it." Liv walked across the room and grabbed the phone. "It's the medical center, for Dad."

Her mother looked up at Alec's father. "Simon, your son is home for the first time in months. Unless someone has chest pain or a limb hanging off there is nothing that can't wait until after we've eaten. If you must play doctor, you can examine Sky's head. That bruise looks nasty. If you need to lie down, just say so, dear. Alec, sit. You're in the way."

Sliding into the seat next to Sky, Alec decided that he was the one who needed to lie down.

Why had he thought this was a good idea?

SHE WAS THE first woman he'd brought home since his divorce?

Sky sat quietly at the table, digesting the information, letting the conversation flow around her. It hadn't occurred to her that Alec's family might think they were an item and it was only after seeing their delightfully clumsy attempts to dig for information while still vaguely respecting his boundaries that she realized just how bad his divorce must have been.

Clumsy or not, it was obvious they were worried about him and equally obvious from his prickly demeanor that he found their concern about as welcome as a computer virus.

So she wasn't the only one whose family interfered with their love life, she thought.

Alec was seated next to her and she could feel the tension simmering from his powerful frame.

With so many people round the table, seating was tight and every now and then her leg brushed against the solid power of his.

Heat rushed through her body, stealing her breath.

She kept her eyes on her plate, wondering whether the blow to her head had done more damage than she'd thought.

Yesterday, she'd been dating Richard. Today she was insanely attracted to a man who, up until the events of last night, she hadn't even liked.

And now, here she was, seeing him at his most vulnerable because no situation, as she knew from her own experience, exposed a person's vulnerabilities more than being with family.

This was a million times more uncomfortable than seeing him naked.

She suspected he would rather have died than share details of his damaged marriage with her. No doubt he was already deeply regretting the impulse that had driven him to invite her to join them.

Part of her wanted to leave the room, but another part, a curious part, wanted to know more.

She wanted to know what had happened.

Over the past twenty-four hours she'd seen glimpses of a different person. The person Alec might have been before divorce had chewed him up and spit him out.

Relationships, she thought, had a lot to answer for.

The pain in her head had receded to a dull throb and the sickness had gone, but she felt bruised all over, and simmering beneath the pain was the knowledge that her relationship had been fake all along.

And yet her parents were still hoping she'd find a way to fix it.

As she listened to the conversation around her, it was impossible not to make comparisons. Whereas Alec's parents' interference was clearly driven by love and concern for him, her parents just thought she was a screw-up.

Not once had they asked how she was.

And neither had Richard.

She stabbed her fork into a slice of ham.

She wanted to pretend that their relationship had meant something, but it was hard to pretend when the cold hard truth was pressed in your face.

She was relieved to be here, away from it all.

Alec's sister took the chair on the other side of him and his parents, uncle and grandmother sat opposite.

They questioned him in detail, wanting to know everything he'd done since they'd last seen him.

"My street cred has rocketed since your series on the Amazon aired. My friends watched it." Liv slipped food to the dogs under the table. "Gloria thinks you're hot. I'm supposed to introduce you."

"Well, of course he would be hot." Alec's grandmother spoke in a loud voice. "The Amazon is a jungle and jungles are hot."

Liv grinned and put a dollop of butter in the center of her baked potato. "Not that sort of hot, Granny. Sexy hot. They think our Alec has a luscious bod."

Skylar kept her eyes on her plate.

She still had a clear image of that body, streaming with water, powerfully erect.

Next to her, Alec was still.

Nelson nudged her knee with his nose and she lowered her hand to his silky head, only to find Alec's hand already there. For a few pulsing seconds she was tangled up with long, strong fingers and then she snatched her hand away, knocking her fork onto the floor along with the slice of ham.

Nelson wolfed it down and sat gazing hopefully up at her.

"You'd think he was starving." Oblivious to the tension, Alec's mother rose to her feet and fetched Sky a clean fork. Then she tried to tempt the dogs out of the kitchen. "This is your fault, Olivia. How many times do I need to tell you not to feed the dogs at the table? They'll never leave us alone."

"We don't want them to leave us alone. They're part of the family. They should be part of the celebration. I'm making Nelson a tinsel collar for tonight and I've hung his stocking next to the fire."

Her mother gave up trying to assert control and sat down again. "For the next few days, let's try to pretend we're a normal family, otherwise Sky won't want to visit us again."

Alec put his fork down. "Mum—"

"I was being polite, Alec, that's all. So Skylar, Alec tells us you're very talented."

He'd said that?

Remembering how he'd been careful not to say a single word in praise of her, Sky turned her head to look at him, but he was busy trying to stop a very superior looking cat from torturing the overexcited dogs.

"You need to leave her alone." He pulled Church back. "She is going to unsheathe those claws and take a swipe at you."

Skylar wondered if that was what his ex-wife had done.

Something had to be responsible for the fact he was so guarded and she doubted it was his upbringing. His family was frank and open.

Alec's father helped himself to more ham. "Tell us about your work, Skylar."

She knew they were being polite and she described what she did in a few short sentences.

"So you've built a career out of your passion?"

"Obviously it's not a very traditional path, and—"

"I think it's wonderful. Bold, exciting—you followed a dream." He added a hunk of bread to his plate. "I wish I'd been that brave."

"What are you talking about?" Suzanne glanced

across at him. "You're a wonderful doctor. And you love it."

"I enjoy my job and I find it worthwhile, but the truth is I chose medicine because it was a logical, sensible step and I always had good grades in science. It was never a passion. I never woke up in the night thinking, 'God, let me be a doctor.' In fact half the time when I'm woken in the night I think, 'God, why did I choose to be a doctor?'" He reached for his glass. "Sky is doing what she really wants. I admire that."

It wasn't the reaction she'd expected. "You do?"

"Of course. Most of us aren't given the talent to do what you're doing. You're using a gift. It must have been hard at the beginning, though. Did your parents help you out?"

"No. They wanted me to do something more conventional. Law." Her mouth was dry. "They wanted me to be a lawyer."

"Well, as a parent I can understand that. Probably worried about job security and your future. I expect they wanted you to take the safe option. But there are millions of people who have what it takes to be a lawyer, and only a handful of people who have the talent to do what you do and make it work. Must have been a slog to get where you are today."

Sky thought about the long hours in the studio. "It was. My parents thought I was wasting my time." And that had been the slog, not the work. Trying to show them that this was what she wanted, trying to please them while at the same time trying desperately to follow her dream.

"They must be extremely proud of you now. Tell us about the exhibition."

Proud? Her parents weren't proud. They were exasperated.

Alec was silent and she wondered if he was thinking of the phone message from her mother. Remembering that agonizing moment made her feel fragile and exposed.

Maybe he wished she didn't know so much about him, but he knew an equal amount about her.

It felt strange, she thought, knowing that your secrets were in the hands of someone you'd never had reason to trust.

But there was no denying that whatever she might have thought of him in the past, Alec had been a good friend to her over the past twenty-four hours.

"I would have liked to have made it up to London to see your exhibition but the clinic has been decimated by this flu bug so I won't be able to take the time off." Alec's father sat back in his chair. "I paint a little myself. Mostly watercolors, although I occasionally dabble in oils. We have an artist's group in the village. Next time Alec brings you home we'll have to time your visit to coincide with one of our meetings and you can join us. We meet in the church hall, so not particularly exciting as a venue—not Knightsbridge—but we're a friendly, enthusiastic bunch."

They talked about her "next visit" as if it was inevitable. She would have been touched had it not been for Alec's darkening mood.

"That isn't going to happen, Dad." He spoke through his teeth. "I've told you—"

"You paint?" Feeling sorry for his parents, Sky interrupted. None of this was their fault, was it? If anything it was her fault. "I'd love to see some of your work."

"His paintings are all around the house." Suzanne pushed a cheese platter toward her. "We swap them sometimes and of course he sells a few from time to time. Not that it's profitable. The framing is expensive. I expect you sell a lot."

"My sales are growing but it's always nerve-wracking."

"She's being modest. She sold everything in her exhibition on the first night." Alec's tone was gruff and Sky turned to him in surprise.

"How do you know that?"

"I saw the red stickers." He reached for his drink. "You deserved to sell everything."

"You said my work was overpriced."

"If your exhibition was in Knightsbridge I wouldn't think price is an issue. Were there journalists there? Will there be reviews in any of the papers?" Simon glanced at the clock on the wall. "I need to take the dogs out. I could go via Village Stores and pick up *The Times*."

Sky realized she'd given no thought to reviews. Nor had she checked her emails.

Her exhibition had taken a backseat to everything else going on in her life.

"I'm not sure I want to look." What if the reviews mentioned Richard?

"I can check online." Liv pulled her phone out of her pocket and searched. "How do you spell your surname? Oh, I've found you! Listen to this—'Exciting new talent, Skylar Tempest…' Wow, you're an exciting talent. And here's another one, 'Blah, blah—

innovative, creative and startlingly original.' They love you. And this one has a photo and you look like a model or something. That silver dress you were wearing is incredible. This is *so* cool. Now I know two famous people."

"That's it?" Sky's voice was a croak. "They haven't said anything else?"

Alec's sister shook her head as she scrolled down the search results.

"This really is exciting. We had no idea." Suzanne looked impressed. "If someone had paid money for something I'd made, I'd be boasting about it from the rafters. Simon, you must track down a newspaper, then Sky can keep it as a souvenir for her parents. They'll want to see it."

Sky knew they wouldn't and to her horror felt her throat thicken. "That's kind of you."

Oh, God, she was going to cry.

She was going to sob over her plate of food and make a fool of herself in front of these lovely people.

Under the table, she dug her nails into her palm and then felt a warm, strong hand close over hers.

"I had an interesting meeting with the BBC." Alec calmly took over the conversation, while with his right hand he coaxed her fist to relax. "They were sounding me out about filming in Antarctica. A documentary on Shackleton. Someone let them down."

His uncle grunted. "Antarctica has been at the top of your list for a long time. Do it."

"I will if I can. I'm waiting to hear." His thumb stroked Skylar's fingers gently. "It might not happen. I'm not counting my chickens."

"It's Christmas," Liv said, "you should probably count turkeys."

"How's the boat?" Harry's eyes were bright. "Any good sailing lately?"

"She's in storage. Which is the only way to keep a boat like her safe through a Maine winter. And I don't have time to sail until this book is done."

His father put his knife and fork down. "How's that going?"

"Slow. I'm planning on shutting myself away and working on it over Christmas."

"Oh, Alec," his mother murmured, "I can't bear to think of you alone on that snowy island with only the sea for company—" She subsided as her husband gave her a look. "What?"

"He's a grown man, Suz."

"I know that. I want him to know he's welcome at home, that's all."

"Well, of course he knows he's welcome at home," Alec's grandmother said, "that's why it's called home."

"I'm home now," Alec said mildly, "so maybe we could all just enjoy that. And the island has a permanent population and a decent number of winter visitors. I'm not a hermit."

Sky sat there, listening to the conversation flow round her, focusing on the firm pressure of his hand.

Gradually the urge to cry faded, the unexpected wash of emotion receding like the tide.

She knew she should pull her hand away, but she didn't want to.

Right now Alec felt like the one solid, sure thing in her life.

And perhaps he knew, because what other reason was there for him to keep his hand firmly over hers?

How could a man who'd always shown himself to be thoroughly insensitive suddenly be so sensitive? Or maybe he just didn't want her to make a fool of herself in front of his parents.

His mother was still fretting. "What if the power goes out like it did last year?"

"I have a generator."

Sky watched in silent admiration as he handled their concerns. He showed love and respect, but not once did he waver in his decisions or compromise on what he wanted to do.

She'd thought it was annoying that he didn't try to please anyone but himself, but now she was starting to admire him for it.

He controlled the conversation, talking eloquently and fluently about his current projects.

Sky relaxed slightly and finally felt him withdraw his hand.

She wanted to grab it back, which was ridiculous of course.

Even though his family interfered, too, Sky decided she'd never met a nicer, warmer group of people in her life. Even when they were arguing, the Hunter family was a unit, spokes of the same wheel, moving in the same direction. Watching their interaction intensified the feeling of isolation and loneliness that had been part of her since Richard had walked out the day before.

By the time they'd eaten their main course and enjoyed dessert, a homemade pavlova with whipped cream and raspberries, the throbbing in her head was worse.

Suzanne stood up, her chair scraping on the floor. "Sky, you're looking very pale, dear. You should lie down for a few hours. This family is many things but restful isn't one of them." She fetched a glass of water. "Your room is all made up, Alec. Clean sheets and fresh towels. There are shelves and shelves of books, Sky, so you won't be short of reading. If you need anything else let me know. I'll let Alec show you the way."

Alec put his glass down. "You've put her in my room?"

His mother sighed. "I'm willing to respect your wish not to talk about your relationships, but I'm not going through that farce of putting you in different rooms. For a start we're short of space because Uncle Harry wasn't supposed to be arriving this week, and I don't see the point of putting people in a position where they have to creep out of their rooms in the middle of the night. It's unnecessary and at your age frankly ridiculous. I brought you up to make your own decisions and you make good ones. Who you're sleeping with is your business."

"All right, that's enough." Alec's authoritative tone cut through the hum of conversation and everyone fell silent. "Sky and I are *not* together."

"We know," his mother soothed. "You're not involved, we get the message. You're just—what do they call it, Olivia? Friends with extras."

"Benefits." Liv fed Nelson the last of the ham. "It's benefits, Mum."

"That's it. Friends with benefits."

Skylar didn't dare look at Alec.

He'd been so kind to her and she'd put him in a horribly, hideously awkward position with his family.

Before last night she never would have described themselves as friends and she was willing to bet that right now he couldn't see a single benefit to having helped her.

Friends without benefits.

CHAPTER SIX

ALEC CARRIED SKYLAR's case up the stairs, and gestured to the door in the corner.

"That one." He tried to sound like a gracious host but knew he was failing dismally.

None of this was her fault.

He was the one who had invited her here and in doing so had unwittingly given his family the best Christmas gift ever.

They thought he was serious about a woman.

And now he had to unravel that.

She paused for a moment in the doorway and then turned to him. All her usual bounce had drained away. She looked pale and exhausted. "Thank you."

"For what?"

"For what you did in the kitchen. If you hadn't—I was feeling—"

"I know what you were feeling." He'd sensed her mounting distress and her battle to hold back her emotions as his parents had innocently provided the enthusiastic support and encouragement that her own parents had withheld.

Having been a reluctant witness to the message from her mother, it wasn't hard to understand why she'd been upset. What must life have been like for her, growing up in such a barren, sterile environment?

He pushed the question away. He already knew far more than he'd ever wanted to about her life. He didn't need to know more.

"You keep helping me. Why?" Her eyes were huge and he tensed, instinctively withdrawing from anything remotely suggestive of vulnerability.

He didn't want her leaning on him.

"Because I thought the last thing you needed after everything that has happened was to fall apart in front of a bunch of strangers. That's all it was."

He was no one's idea of a white knight and it was important that she knew that.

He opened the door and ushered her into the room, hoping she didn't read anything into his behavior.

He'd averted a potentially emotional situation, nothing more.

And now he had another situation to deal with—the fact that his mother had put them in the same room.

A fire crackled and blazed in the hearth and ropes of lights had been twisted around the wooden beams, adding a warm festive glow to the room.

By the corner window was a small Christmas tree, complete with the star Liv had made for him when she was in nursery school. His mother stored it and each year it reappeared, slightly more battered than the previous year.

Until his marriage, this room had been somewhere he'd always been able to relax.

Now, mixing with the smell of logs and pine needles was the light floral smell of Skylar's perfume.

He watched, tense, as she walked over to the large windows that overlooked fields and farmland.

"This is your room?" Her voice was wistful. "What a stunning view. So peaceful."

Desolate, his ex-wife had called it, before sinking into another of those long awkward silences that had peppered their marriage.

"I'll take the sofa. You can sleep in the bed." He knew he sounded terse, but he couldn't help it.

Why hadn't it occurred to him that his family might think there was something more to their relationship? They were so desperate to see him with someone again, they didn't care who it was. Apparently any woman, even a stranger, was better than seeing him alone, even though being alone was his preferred choice.

He made a mental note to kill Michael next time they met.

"If my family embarrassed you, then I apologize."

She gave a choked laugh and wrapped her arms round her middle. "We both know that in a contest to find the most embarrassing family, I'd win, Alec. You don't need to apologize. Your family are wonderful. They love you."

"They interfere."

"But you don't let them. They respect your opinion."

"Occasionally. When it suits them. There's a bathroom through the door on the right." He dumped her case on the floor and she turned, eyebrows raised. Instantly he felt churlish and the associated guilt did nothing to improve his mood. "Make yourself at home."

She eased away from the window. "You're mad because they think we're an item. This is all my fault.

You were planning a wonderful family weekend and I've ruined it. I shouldn't have come. I really am sorry for everything."

Her sweet apology cut him off at the knees. He preferred arguing with her and getting irritated to feeling the way he was right now. He was used to her being ballsy and combative. Even a little prickly.

This version of her made him feel uncomfortable.

It made him feel—

Protective.

Dragging his hand over the back of his neck, he tried to keep his tone neutral.

"You're not the one making false assumptions. It's not your fault."

"It is. You brought me home, and it's obviously a big deal for you to bring a woman home. They've been worried about you. I guess that's why they want to see you with someone."

"And you know how that feels. Seems my parents are like yours."

"We both know your parents are nothing like mine." She gave a wan smile. "I'll talk to your mother later and tell her the truth. I should have tried harder over lunch but they all seemed so happy and I wasn't really sure how to handle it." Pale as a fresh fall of snow, she sank onto the edge of the bed and Alec frowned.

"You're feeling terrible. Why the hell didn't you excuse yourself sooner?"

"I'm feeling just fine. But I'll lie down here for a while and that will give you a chance to be alone with them." She slid off her shoes, crawled onto the bed and curled up like an injured kitten.

Concerned, he took a step toward her and then stopped. Whatever she said to the contrary, he knew she was vulnerable. The last thing he needed was for her to see him as some sort of rescuer or hero figure.

He already knew how that ended.

"Do you need more pills? You should have said that you were feeling this bad."

"I'm not feeling bad."

"You must have been stressed by it all. The questions. The talking."

"Envious," she murmured, her eyes drifting shut. "I was envious."

He stood there, locked in a mental battle between instinct and common sense as he tried to decide how to handle this.

And then he realized there was no decision to make because she was already asleep.

He waited a moment and when she didn't stir he walked over to her, reached for the thick, dark green throw from the bottom of his bed and covered her gently, careful not to wake her.

When she didn't stir he leaned over and moved her hair gently, studying the livid bruise on her head.

He thought again about that sterile, emotionless message from her mother. It was likely that she hadn't known about Sky's injury, but she knew about the breakup and not once had she asked her daughter how she was feeling.

Her friends were thousands of miles away.

All she had was him.

Ice filled his veins.

He didn't want that responsibility.

The door opened and Nelson plodded into the

room. Without looking at Alec, he sank down in front of the fire.

Alec sighed. "You shouldn't be in here."

Nelson yawned, stretched and ignored him.

Alec glanced toward the bed and then back at the dog. Why not? "You're on guard. If she moves, come and get me."

Nelson settled his head on his paws and Alec went in search of his family intending to lay down some ground rules.

And while he was at it, he thought, he needed to make a few for himself.

SKY WOKE UNABLE to move. Something heavy and hot was pressing on her legs.

She opened her eyes drowsily. The only light in the room came from the fire. Outside there was nothing but darkness.

Wondering what time it was, she tried to sit up and realized that the weight on her legs was the dog.

He grunted but didn't move and she was about to lie down and go back to sleep when there was a tap on the door, and Alec's mother walked into the room carrying a tray.

"I didn't want you to sleep too long, in case it stops you sleeping tonight. You're probably jet-lagged. Alec is always the same for the first few days after he comes home. I've brought you tea and one of Granny's scones. It's the only thing she makes since her eyesight has failed and she does them by hand." She put the tray down and flicked on the light, smiling when she saw Nelson. "That's where you are! You do know Alec isn't the one in the bed? Come on, move. Sky doesn't want you there."

"Yes, I do." Sky pulled the dog closer. "I like him. He's like a comforter."

"He loves this room. When we first brought him back here as a puppy, he wouldn't leave Alec's side. He slept by his bed and howled every night for a week. Not once did Alec complain. He got up, soothed him, went back to sleep. I couldn't believe the way he took care of that dog."

He'd done the same with her, Sky thought. He'd taken care of her when she'd needed help.

And because of his generosity his family now assumed they were involved.

And it was up to her to fix it.

She took the tea Suzanne offered her with a smile of thanks. She had no idea what a scone was, but it looked and smelled delicious. "About Alec—"

"He's just a friend. I know. He's told us the whole story while you were asleep." Suzanne sat down on the side of the bed. "I apologize if we embarrassed you. The thing is, we didn't think he'd ever bring a woman here again. His relationship with Selina was such a disaster. You've never seen two people more wrong for each other."

"That would be the two of us." Sky sipped her tea, deciding that honesty was the only way to convince them of the truth. "Alec and I kind of wind each other up. I irritate him and he annoys the hell out of me. I hope that doesn't offend you."

"Not at all. He annoys the hell out of all of us quite frequently," Suzanne said calmly. "He's my only son and I adore him, but he can be very stubborn and one of his biggest flaws is thinking he's right all the time. Simon is the same. When the two of them argue, it's like two stags clashing antlers. It often takes Alec a while to climb down from a stance he's taken, but he gets there eventually."

"He came to my exhibition because our friends forced him to. We barely even know each other, and then—well, things happened and— I don't know why he helped me."

It was a question she'd asked herself repeatedly.

He could have walked away and she wouldn't have given it a second thought. He owed her nothing.

"If you don't know the answer to that one then I believe you when you say you don't know him. He couldn't not help you. Alec would never walk past a person in trouble. That's how he first met Selina. She was in trouble and he went to her rescue. What he didn't know was that she was always in trouble. It was the way she lived her life. She'd had a very unsettled childhood, poor thing, and she couldn't live without the attention." Suzanne looked tired. "She exploited the kindness in him, drained every last drop of goodness until he was so empty and bitter there were days when I barely recognized my own son. He became hard, and my Alec was never hard. And I've said too much." She gave an apologetic smile and Sky frowned.

If she'd had questions before she had a million more now.

"He rescued her?"

"He hasn't told you how they met?"

"He's told me nothing. We barely know each other."

Suzanne looked at her thoughtfully. "And yet he

brought you here, and is very protective of you. He was adamant that no one was to come up here and wake you."

Sky felt a strange fluttering in her chest. "Yeah, well, from what you've been telling me, that's the way he is. It's not personal." She wasn't going to pretend for one moment that it was. And she didn't want it to be. She had enough complications in her life. "He thinks I'm a brainless blonde. When he wants to wind me up, which is often, he calls me princess."

Alec's mother laughed. "Wonderful."

"Is it? I confess I didn't take it as a compliment."

"He's clearly more affected by you than he'd like to admit, even to himself." Suzanne picked up her tea and sat down on the sofa. "And he certainly doesn't think you're brainless. How could he? You're very intelligent and he has made no secret of the fact he admires your work greatly."

"I've never heard him admire it before today. Mostly, he's pretty hostile toward me. We mix socially from time to time because we have mutual friends, but we don't know each other. We're not…intimate." *Apart from seeing each other naked and knowing all the embarrassing details of one another's families.* "He only came to my exhibition because our friend Brittany asked him to. Then I found myself in trouble and he helped me."

And because she wanted to be clear about everything, because she owed it to Alec, she told his mother the whole truth, including details of the proposal and the fall.

Suzanne listened without interrupting. "So this Richard cared enough to propose, but then he walked out? That's shocking. You poor thing. You not only have a bruised head, you have a bruised heart." Suzanne reached out and covered her hand with hers. "How are you feeling about it all?"

It was the one question her own mother hadn't asked.

She'd asked why Sky had broken up with a man who was perfect for her, when she was going to start making good choices and when she'd be home for Christmas.

She hadn't once asked how her daughter was feeling.

Sky looked at Suzanne. She didn't even know this woman, but something in the gentle warmth of her gaze unlocked something inside her. "I don't know. Part of me is mad with him, but I'm even madder with myself. I keep going back over all the time we spent together trying to work out if any of it was real. I'm probably supposed to feel heartbroken, but instead I feel—"

"Betrayed?"

"Yes." It helped that she understood. "And so foolish for not seeing it. I thought we were close and it turns out I didn't know him at all."

"Knowing someone isn't just a question of spending time with that person. They have to let you in. Opening up must be difficult for someone who believes his career relies on him projecting a certain image."

"He wasn't interested in the real me."

"Then he is the wrong man for you." Suzanne straightened the covers. "Life is a big, exciting, sometimes scary adventure, and you have to choose the person you take that adventure with very carefully. You need someone who is going to cheer you on when you succeed and pick you up when you fall. Would he have done those things?"

Sky stared into her tea. She didn't bother trying to drink. She knew she wouldn't be able to force the liquid past the lump in her throat. "No. I did fall. Literally. And I honestly don't know if he would have hit me or not if I hadn't moved. I hope he wouldn't. But he didn't even stay to check that I was all right."

"You're not my daughter, but if you were I'd be telling you to run, not walk, from a man who stepped over you when you were injured, whether or not he was responsible for that injury." Suzanne reached out and took the cup from her. "Don't think about it now, dear. Just rest, recover and then see how you feel later on."

It was the type of conversation she would have loved to have had with her own mother.

"I don't know what would have happened if Alec hadn't come to check on me. He was—" she swallowed "—he was so calm. I bled on him and I was horribly ill and he didn't leave my side. The only reason he brought me here was because he didn't want to leave me on my own in London."

"I'm glad he did. Because it shows that deep down my Alec is still there. I was worried he might have changed forever after what happened, but I see now he's just buried that caring side of himself. And I suppose no one can blame him for that." Suzanne handed her the scone. "Try this. It's delicious."

Skylar nibbled the corner of the scone. It was warm and buttery and crumbled in her mouth. "It's good."

"I hope I didn't embarrass you by putting you in this room. It was a misunderstanding. Michael is an old family friend and he called his mother and she called me and—well, Alec is furious of course, but we're full at the inn so I can't give you your own room even if I wanted to. Alec can sleep on the sofa. It's perfectly comfortable."

He'd already spent one night on a rock-hard sofa because of her.

"I could sleep in the living room, or share with Olivia—"

"The living room will be noisy with people coming and going and Liv has a tiny room in the eaves of the attic. On top of that, she sleepwalks. You need your rest and so does Alec. You'll both be fine in here." She picked up the tray. "Come down when you're ready. We're going to open champagne."

"Champagne? But now that you know that Alec and I—"

"We have plenty of other things to celebrate. Alec being home for a start, and your success!"

"Mine?"

"Yes, your exhibition. Simon picked up a stack of papers and most of them have mentioned you. I know you're feeling all mixed up about everything, but that mustn't stop you feeling proud or enjoying your moment. It's important never to walk past an excuse to celebrate. I'm sure your family feel the same."

No, Sky thought. *No, they don't.*

Alec's family had been more supportive in a few hours than her parents had been in a lifetime.

"Do you have many guests coming tonight?"

"No guests, just family, and you've already met all

of them. It will be very informal." Suzanne left the room and Sky flopped back against the pillows and stared at the flickering fire.

"No guests, just family," she murmured to herself. "Informal. I can't even imagine how that looks."

"It usually looks pretty untidy. Why? What happens in your house?" Alec's voice came from the doorway and she sat up again, startled.

"I didn't see you there."

"I know. Because you were talking to yourself." He closed the door and sat down on the edge of the bed. "How is your head?"

It felt strangely intimate, being alone in the bedroom with him.

Remembering what his mother had said about him being unable to walk past someone in trouble, she produced her brightest smile. "Great. The sleep really helped." Her head throbbed, but there was no way she wanted him to feel responsible for her. He'd already done more than enough.

"Did my mother wake you?"

"No. I was awake, and it was great talking with her."

He gave her a long look. "So tell me what Christmas looks like in your house."

Nelson whined and she leaned forward and stroked his head. There didn't seem any reason not to tell him. "My parents entertain a lot, so Christmas is a busy time. Christmas Eve lunch is an intimate gathering of forty people."

"That's a big family."

"It's not family. It's mostly colleagues of my father's, a few of my mother's, people they consider useful and interesting. Movers and shakers. They like introducing people to other people. Networking is an obsession for both of them." She stroked Nelson's soft ears, wondering how much to say. "When I was young, I had to memorize a file on everyone coming and my mother would test me."

His brows rose. "You mean they'd test you on how much you knew?"

"Yes, she'd say, 'John Brighton Junior'—and I'd have to summarize what he did and his interests. Then I was expected to do enough research to be sure that when we were talking I could hold a conversation."

"You did that for forty people?"

"Forty is lunch. In the evening they have a bigger party and the numbers are closer to eighty. It's the invite everyone in Manhattan hopes for."

"And you had to study the background of eighty guests?"

"Pretty much. She divided the list into *A* and *B*. We all had to know all the A-list guests, but my brothers and I were allowed to divide the B-list guests between us."

"Because they were less important?"

"Right." Christmas was something she didn't want to think about. Thank goodness it was still a few weeks away. "What did you do while I was asleep?"

"Shoveled snow. I helped my dad clear the path and the drive outside the garage."

The sleeves of his thick black sweater were pushed back, revealing powerful forearms. The dusting of dark hair made her think of the moment she'd seen him naked.

He smelled of the outdoors, of fresh crisp air tinged with a hint of wood smoke, of lemon and spice and man.

Something stirred inside her.

I could draw him like this, she thought, *standing with the light behind him looking brooding and dangerous.*

"I told your mom the truth about us."

He rose to his feet. "Did she pay attention?"

"I think so. I mean, I told her Richard proposed to me last night so that's pretty good evidence that you and I couldn't have anything serious going on."

"Not necessarily." He stood with his back to her, his wide shoulders blocking her view out of the window. "Not everyone waits to end a relationship before they start another."

She wondered if he was talking from experience, but decided it was none of her business.

"I do. Relationships are hard enough without having two at the same time. This dinner tonight—what should I wear?"

"Wear anything. It's just family. Tomorrow my older sister, Cathy, is joining us with her husband and the twins, Rosie and Tom. They live in the next village."

"Uncle Alec." She slid off the bed, relieved to discover her head felt a little better. "I bet you're good at that. Snowball fights and snowmen?"

His eyes gleamed. "Occasionally."

"Then it's only fair to warn you, you'd better get outside and practice. If there was a sport called snowballing, I'd win the gold medal."

"I wouldn't have thought you were the type to enjoy getting cold and wet."

"Yeah, I prefer to stay indoors and file my nails." She kept her tone light but felt a flicker of frustration. "I thought we'd got past this, but you're still treating me like a delicate fairy princess, Alec."

"I know you're not delicate." His gaze dropped from the bruise on her head to her mouth and lingered there. "The past twenty-four hours have been tough on you."

Her heart bumped a little harder. "Tough on you, too, being stuck with me."

He didn't comment on that. "Do you think you'll get back together?"

"With Richard? No."

"He asked you to marry him."

"But when I needed him, he stepped over me." It was still the thing that shocked her the most and she agreed with Suzanne; you ran from a man like that. "Who does that? I wouldn't step over a stranger if they were injured and in need of help, but to do it to someone you supposedly cared about enough to propose to—"

"And your parents wanted you to marry this guy?"

"They introduced us. They were hoping—" She shrugged. "Let's just say they have ambitions for me."

"You can have ambitions about relationships?"

"I've failed at the career ambitions," she said, "so relationship ambitions are about all that's left."

"I'm sure they just want you to be happy."

"No. That's your parents, not mine. Let's not pretend you didn't hear that phone message. If we're going to be utterly humiliated by our respective families, the least we can do is laugh about it." She walked to the windows and stared across the fields. The snow was luminous, bathing the countryside in a ghostly glow. "Both our families interfere, the difference is that mine do it because they have ambitions for me that I refuse to fulfill. They don't care whether I'm happy or not as long as I make them proud. That's the only thing that interests them. It's all about achievement. Christmas is my least favorite time of year because it's when they put the most pressure on." It depressed her to think about it.

"So don't go home."

"I have to. They're my family. It's tradition." She swallowed. "I guess I'm not alone in dreading it. Plenty of people find Christmas stressful. For once I'm almost glad I'll be sharing it with dozens of strangers. My parents will want to talk about Richard. I don't know what I'm going to say."

"You could start with 'he scares me.' That should be the only explanation they need."

Skylar stilled. For some reason she didn't understand her eyes filled. "Yeah, that should do it." Oh, God, she was going to cry. "Excuse me." She turned to walk to the bathroom but Alec stepped toward her and closed his hands over her arms.

"Wait." His tone was raw. "You're upset."

His chest was right there, broad and powerful and she had a crazy urge to lean her head against all that hard muscle. Holy crap, she was turning into the type of woman she usually wanted to strangle. Maybe the blow to her head had been worse than she thought. She stood still, fighting the impulse. His mother was right. He wasn't the sort of man who could walk past someone in trouble, even if he wanted to. And she didn't want that to be their relationship dynamic. She didn't want him to have to keep throwing her a life preserver. "On reflection, I think I'll stay up here with Nelson tonight."

"I'm not leaving you up here on your own."

"Alec—"

"That's not going to happen so you can forget it."

"Don't be nice to me." She could feel the strength of his hands, holding her steady. She sensed something had changed between them and wasn't sure it was a good thing. "It was easier when I hated you."

"If it would help, I'll try harder to be a—what do you call me? Asshole."

She gave a choked laugh. "Asshat. Dumbass." Worried she might howl, she eased away from him. "Fine, I'll come down if that's really what you want but you'd better do something stupid fast, or I'll start to think you're a good guy. Then where would we be?"

He gave her a long, disturbing look. "We'd be in trouble."

CHAPTER SEVEN

"AREN'T YOU A little old to be poking presents?" Alec watched as his sister crawled under the tree, covering herself with pine needles as she shook and prodded the prettily wrapped parcels under the tree.

His mother had left the curtains open and snow glided past the window like silvery tears, dissolving against the glass. A fire crackled in the hearth and a basket of logs stood ready to keep the flames topped up.

Skylar was still upstairs in the shower. He hoped she wasn't upset. The thought made him shift uncomfortably in his chair. She was obviously determined not to lean on him and he should have been relieved about that.

He *was* relieved.

"You're never too old to poke a present." Liv held one up to her nose and sniffed. "Smells good. What have you bought Skylar?"

"I haven't bought her anything. Why would I? I've told you repeatedly—"

"You're not together. I know, but I wish you were. She's a million times nicer than anyone you've brought home before. And she is sooooo beautiful, Alec. Her hair could be in a shampoo ad."

He thought about the silken flow of Skylar's hair and the way it had felt in his hands. "I hadn't noticed."

Liv retied a bow that had come loose on one of the parcels. "For two people who supposedly don't like each other, the pair of you are like an experiment in a science lab. Not that science is exactly my thing, but I'd say the two of you are one small spark away from a serious chemical explosion."

"You're imagining things."

"Don't treat me like an idiot, Alec."

"You're my little sister, and we're not having this conversation."

"I'm a teenager. I think about boys a lot, or didn't you get that memo? I'm old enough to recognize sexual tension."

"Evidently not. Skylar and I have mutual friends. She was in trouble, but I would have helped no matter who she was."

"You brought her home, Alec. You haven't brought a woman home for three years."

He wondered if somewhere in the house there was a calendar marked with the highlights of his love life. "I brought Skylar home because she has a concussion and I didn't want to leave her on her own in London."

"So you were rescuing a damsel in distress? I don't believe it. No way. Not after—" She broke off guiltily. "Sorry, Al. I have a big mouth."

And a big heart.

He chose to ignore the damsel-in-distress reference.

"There is nothing going on. She isn't my type. I don't even find her attractive—" The words jammed in his throat as the woman in question walked into the room.

Her red dress hugged the curve of her narrow waist and ended at midthigh. She'd teamed it with black tights and black boots, displaying legs long enough to make a gazelle die of envy. Her hair gleamed pale gold and two jagged twists of silver, like lightening bolts, hung from her ears.

She looked as far from a damsel in distress as it was possible to be.

The intimacy between them, that moment of vulnerability that he'd witnessed firsthand, might never have happened.

"Not attractive at all," his sister murmured under her breath. "Close your mouth, Alec. It's rude to stare." All guilt apparently forgotten, she scrambled to her feet. "Sky, that dress is incredible."

It *was* incredible.

So were her powers of recovery. Or her willpower. He couldn't work out which was responsible for the fact she was on her feet and looking better than most people looked after a week at a spa.

He looked closer and saw a hint of blush on her cheeks.

Underneath, she was pale.

Which meant it was willpower keeping her on her feet.

Willpower and those gleaming black leather boots.

It didn't seem to matter what she wore, he kept seeing her undressed. Every time he looked at her.

Naked.

It was as if the internet had crashed in the middle of a movie.

The image was frozen and nothing he did could delete it from his brain.

Naked, naked, naked.

Alec could imagine her, blue eyes laughing, straddling some very lucky man.

Judging from the look she sent him, he wasn't going to be that man and it seemed he'd just sent himself right back into the "asshat" category.

Which was probably the best thing for both of them.

Ignoring him, she flashed a smile at his sister. "Thank you."

Alec ran a hand over the back of his neck and hunted for the right thing to say. He knew he should pay her a compliment, but he didn't want to go there. "Look, I—" Usually words came easily to him, but today they'd all crashed in his brain. "You're—I'm—"

In trouble, he thought. *In a whole lot of trouble.*

"Ignore him," Liv advised. "It's the best way. You look truly *amazing*."

She did look amazing, Alec thought. And she looked even more amazing naked.

Why the hell had he gone to help her in the shower?

If he hadn't gone to help, he wouldn't be in this position.

The last thing he needed in his life was a woman like Sky, but in a race between intellect and libido, libido was heading to the finish line in first position.

Fortunately all her attention was on his sister. "You look amazing, too! I love what you've done with your hair and that dress is super cute."

Alec watched his sister turn pink with pleasure.

"Do you like it? It's new." It was obvious that Sky's opinion really mattered to her and Sky seemed to know that.

"Great choice. Do you know what would make it perfect? This." She pulled a stylish twisted silver bracelet from her wrist and handed it to Olivia. "Merry Christmas."

"No!" Liv's eyes almost popped out of her head. "You can't lend me that—it's yours."

"I'm not lending, I'm giving. If you'd like it."

Having seen the prices people were willing to pay for Skylar's work, Alec knew it wasn't a small gift. "You can't do that."

"I made it. I can do what I like with it."

"It's stunning." Liv stroked her fingers over it in awe. "I've never owned anything this beautiful before."

"I'm glad you like it! I always want my jewelry to go to a happy home and live a fun life." She paused. "A fun, exciting, fearless, frivolous life, worthy of a princess." She was looking at Liv but he knew her words were directed toward him.

"Thank you! I need to show Mum." Liv shot out of the room, tripped over Nelson, who had taken advantage of the open door to investigate the fuss. She vanished in the direction of the kitchen, leaving Alec alone with Skylar.

He braced himself for a comment on his rudeness. He knew he deserved it. Instead she smiled at him.

"Your sister is adorable. You're so lucky."

"It was generous of you to give her that." He breathed deeply. "Look—"

"It's fine, Alec. You don't have to say a thing."

"I owe you an apology. I was rude and—"

"I'm really grateful for that, because you reminded me why I can't stand you ninety percent of the time."

Something in the way she said it made him smile. "For the record I think your dress is great." More than great. Looking at her he felt as if he'd been dragged naked through the molten core of a volcano.

"I really don't care whether you like my dress or not, Alec. I didn't dress for you, I dressed for myself. I don't need you to tell me I look good."

He stared at her. Selina had needed to hear it. She'd needed to hear it a thousand different ways, a thousand times a day and no matter what he'd said or how he'd said it, it had never been enough. Her insecurity had been the most exhausting thing about their relationship.

Sky's gaze met his and he saw something that looked like sympathy in her eyes, but she didn't say anything. Instead she strolled over to the Christmas tree.

"I always wanted a sister."

He grabbed hold of the change of subject as a drowning man might grab a floating branch. "You have brothers?"

"Yes. All lawyers. It's part of our DNA although somehow it missed me. Mealtimes are like a day in court. Growing up, if I didn't want vegetables I used to say 'objection.' Of course my mother would say 'overruled' and drop them on my plate anyway." She examined the ornaments. "A tree like this would be part of my dream Christmas."

He opened his mouth to ask about her dream Christmas and then closed it again. Information, particularly personal information, was a prelude to intimacy, and that wasn't a word he wanted anywhere near his relationship with Skylar. Circumstances had thrown them together, but that didn't mean he was interested in getting to know her on a deeper level. He already knew more than enough.

"My mother insists on a real tree."

"My mother can't deal with the fact she can't control the activities of each individual pine needle. Where did this one come from?"

"Local farm. Going to choose the tree is part of our family tradition." The more she revealed about her family, the more he wondered how they'd produced someone as creative and free-spirited as Skylar. A different person would have been crushed, or at least taken the path of least resistance.

She examined everything in detail and then reached out and touched an uneven snowman. "Who made this? It's cute."

"Me. My mother refuses to throw it away. That is yet another embarrassing detail you now know about me."

"She doesn't throw it away because it has meaning. I love that." She examined every decoration, asked about each one. "Your whole family history is right here on this tree."

"The handmade decorations you made as a child were probably elegant and perfect."

"My parents have always employed an interior designer to decorate the house for the holidays."

Alec looked at the misshapen snowman that his mother insisted on hanging on the tree every year. "You never made your own decorations?"

"Oh, I made them a few times but they always ended up in the trash."

"Why?"

She ran her finger over a glittering angel. "Whatever I made was the wrong look for the tree."

Her tone was matter-of-fact, but dappled with hints of wistful sadness. It tugged at him, drawing him in a direction he didn't want to go.

He could only see her profile, but he was aware of her with every one of his senses. Apart from the livid bruise at her temple, her skin was creamy white, her hair falling in a sheet over one shoulder. He wanted to lift that hair and discover the skin beneath. He wanted to seduce her mouth and coax a smile from her.

She turned her head to look at him and he wondered if the burn of his gaze had triggered some internal alarm system. Maybe she had a built-in heat sensor.

Their eyes met and held.

The only noise in the room was the crackle of the fire.

He could hear the sound of muffled laughter and the clatter of crockery from the kitchen, but here they were completely alone.

She shook her head slowly. "Unbelievable."

"What is unbelievable?"

"Here I am, spilling my guts to you again, and there you are taking it like a man instead of telling me to shut up." She spoke a little faster than usual. "You're treating me as if I'm made of glass, Alec, and you don't need to. Say what's on your mind. A bit of the old brutal Hunter sarcasm would probably be good for both of us right now."

He was spared having to answer because at that moment Liv came back into the room and the rest of the family piled in behind her.

His father had several newspapers tucked under his arm and was carrying a tray with glasses. His mother was carrying two bottles of champagne and Alec stood up to help her.

"Two?"

"One to welcome you home and one to congratulate Skylar. You should read what the papers are saying about her. We had no idea this was so big! It's like having royalty in the house."

Liv curled up on the sofa. "It would be horrid having royalty in the house. There would be cameras outside and it would be impossible to get Church to curtsey. He never does as he's told."

Alec noticed that his sister hadn't stopped playing with the bangle on her wrist.

"I bought two copies of everything." His father put the tray down and passed Sky the newspapers. "One for you, one for your parents."

Alec winced inwardly, but Sky's smile didn't slip.

"That was kind. Thank you." She took the newspapers and put them on the table next to her.

"The piece is toward the back in all of them. Aren't you going to take a look?"

"I'll take a look later."

Alec drew attention away from the newspapers. "That bracelet you gave Liv is pretty. How long does it take you to make something like that?"

"That particular piece?" She talked a little about the creative process and Alec realized that, far from being dreamy, she was sharp and focused. He was surprised to discover that all of her work now was bespoke. He wondered why her parents weren't more supportive. From the little he'd seen, she'd managed to channel her vivid imagination into a lucrative business.

Liv was fascinated. "So someone tells you what they want and you make it? Cool. Do you use diamonds?"

"Yes, but I usc other precious stones, too—emeralds, rubies and sapphires—they can be as rare and expensive. And I love working with silver."

Liv touched the bangle on her wrist. "How do you make different shapes?"

"Hammering, soldering—"

"Soldering?" Alec stared at her. "You solder?"

"For making hot connections, although technically it's called silver brazing. You're joining metals using an alloy that has been heated to melting point. The molten solder interacts with the metal and when it's cooled you have an invisible seam. It's basic physics."

"Hot connections aren't confined to jewelry," Liv murmured, and Alec sent his sister a look that should have welded her to the chair without the use of a blowtorch.

"So people come to you and ask for something specific?" His mother picked up a plate of canapés. "It must be very satisfying making something personal."

"And a little scary. All I have is the brief from the person buying it. My fear is always that they won't like the end result."

"Has that ever happened?"

"No," she admitted. "But that doesn't stop me being afraid that it might. I do what I can to avoid that happening. Get as much information as possible about the person. Their likes and dislikes. How they wear their jewelry."

Alec raised his eyebrows. "There is a way to wear jewelry?" It was news to him.

"Of course." She took a glass of champagne from his father with a smile of thanks. "Some people keep it in a drawer and bring it out for special occasions. Other people like something they can wear all the time. And jewelry can evoke different feelings depending on the sentiment with which it was given. It can make you feel warm and loved, it can make you smile, it can make you feel glamorous. Either way, I make sure it's individual. I never make the same piece twice."

Liv touched her bracelet reverentially. "So there isn't another one like this anywhere in the world?"

"Actually, that's an exception. There's another one exactly like that upstairs in my suitcase. It's one of a pair. One for each wrist."

"So now we have one each. I love that. You didn't make this for anyone special?"

"I originally intended it to be part of the collection showing in London, but I liked it so I kept it."

"At least you have one gift then, Liv," Alec drawled, "in case Santa hears the rumors that you've been naughty and doesn't show up on Christmas Eve."

"He wouldn't do that to me." Liv grinned at her dad. "Would you, Dad?"

"No jokes about Santa tomorrow when the twins are here." His mother handed round the plate of canapés. "They still believe he exists."

"So do I." Liv sneaked Nelson some ham. "And

Boris is hoping for a blind date with one of the reindeer so I'm going to brush him and make him look his best."

Skylar looked at her. "Who is Boris?"

"Our donkey. He lives in the field behind the house. The family next door own horses and he keeps them company so they don't get lonely and jump out of the field. I'll take you to see him tomorrow if you like. We can lend you some boots and a warm coat."

Alec was trying not to look at Sky's endless legs. "She'd probably rather stay indoors."

"Indoors? No way. I'm building a snowman as soon as it's light. We can see Boris at the same time."

"Do the twins really believe Santa still exists?" Alec's father looked vague. "Haven't they grown out of that?"

"They're only four years old! And generally it isn't something you grow out of," Liv said. "It all depends on who breaks the bad news to you. I heard it on the radio when Mum was picking me up from school. There was a phone-in about what age you should tell your kids. I was in shock for a week."

Suzanne gave a sympathetic murmur. "You never said anything. All those years we carried on leaving sweets for him and making dusty footprints on the hearth."

"That's why I didn't say anything. The footprints were cute and I ate the sweets." Liv stroked Nelson. "What age did you stop believing in Santa, Granny?"

"Eight. Your great-grandfather tripped over the end of my bed while creeping around in the dark trying to stuff my stocking. I screamed and he ended up in hospital with a broken ankle."

Liv laughed. "What about you, Sky?"

"I never believed in him." Sky took a sip of her champagne. "My parents believed in the truth, the whole truth and nothing but the truth. At least, that's what they told me." She gave Liv a conspiratorial wink. "I figured it was because my father would have looked terrible in a Santa suit."

Liv looked appalled. "So no tooth fairy?"

"No tooth fairy and no Easter Bunny or any of his cute furry relations. I was raised in an atmosphere of uncensored reality. No dreaming allowed." Sky raised her glass and smiled. "To the power of imagination."

It was a testament to her resilience that her creativity had survived.

It was like planting a sunflower in the desert and expecting it to thrive.

Alec finished his champagne, reminding himself that her background was none of his business. He'd offered her a roof over her head. He didn't need to provide psychological support and he certainly wasn't looking to deepen their relationship.

"The twins are going to love you," his mother said, topping up her glass. "The rest of us display a distinct lack of imagination when it comes to making pasta necklaces. There's only so much I can do with a bag of rigatoni."

Skylar grinned. "Pasta necklaces are my specialty. I'm already looking forward to it. No soldering required."

"Such a good sport." Alec's grandmother reached across and patted her hand. "You're a lovely girl. I'm so happy Alec found you."

"Sky isn't his girlfriend, Mum. I already explained

that." Suzanne sent them both a look of apology and his grandmother adjusted her glasses so that she could take a closer look at him.

"He's brought her to our family gathering. If Skylar isn't Alec's girlfriend, then who is she?"

Alec considered abandoning champagne in favor of neat Scotch. "She's a friend."

Twenty-four hours ago he would not have described her even as a friend, but a lot had happened in a short space of time.

"But you brought her home for Christmas. It's years since you brought anyone home. And she's sleeping in your room. In my day that meant something."

"Well, today it just means we're short on space," his mother said quickly. "We have both you and Harry staying and I'm assuming you don't want to share with him. Alec's room is large. That's all it is. He isn't in a relationship right now, Mum."

"Well, he should be. It's time he found a woman."

Alec's father winked at him and reached across to top up his glass. "Merry Christmas," he muttered under his breath and Alec gave a half laugh.

"I'm not interested in finding a woman. I don't want a woman."

His grandmother turned to his mother with a puzzled look. "What did he say?"

Suzanne Hunter raised her voice and spoke clearly. "He said he doesn't want a woman."

"That's what I thought he said, but it doesn't make sense. Why wouldn't he want a woman? Is he saying he's gay? Has he come out?"

"He's not gay, Mum."

"Are you sure? Because Skylar is a beautiful girl. The only reason a healthy, vigorous, single man wouldn't be interested in her would be if he were gay. And that would be fine. I want him to know we'll love him whoever he is."

Alec clenched his jaw. "I am not gay." He was aware of Skylar, sitting across from him. Her head was bent over Nelson so he couldn't see her expression but he was fairly sure she was laughing.

Liv was definitely laughing. "Don't post anything about being gay on Twitter, you'll break a hundred thousand female hearts."

"If he isn't gay, why isn't he seeing someone?"

"He's not in a hurry to get involved again," his mother said briskly. "And we've talked enough about Alec's private life. You know he doesn't like discussing it with people."

"We're not people, we're family. Family care about these things. If this is about the divorce, well, it's been several years since Selina, and picking badly once doesn't mean he's going to do it a second time. Just because you bite into one rotten apple, doesn't mean you have to chop down the whole tree. He needs to get back on the horse."

Liv sent Alec a look of sibling solidarity. "You're mixing your metaphors, Granny."

"He should be dating again. Skylar is single and the dogs love her. They're a very good judge of character."

Alec wondered what it was going to take to get them to leave his love life alone. "I'm grateful for your concern, but I can manage my love life by myself. If and when I choose to start seeing someone, I can do it without the help of my family. And that includes the dogs."

"Nelson and Church could set up a dating agency," Liv suggested helpfully. "I've got the perfect slogan. 'Don't let your relationship go to the dogs.'"

His mother finished her drink and stood up. "Mum, come and help me in the kitchen," she said firmly. "I need to deal with the food. Dinner is game casserole."

"Made with a bottle of my best burgundy," his father murmured as he stood up, giving Alec a sympathetic look over the top of his glasses. "Let's hope not all the alcohol has evaporated. I have a feeling we're going to need it. By the way, did I tell you all that Lydia Taylor is pregnant?"

Attention shifted away from Alec and his parents and grandmother walked into the kitchen together, catching up on village news. Church took advantage of the open door and bounded into the room, his wagging tail sending decorations flying.

Liv grabbed him. "You have to start behaving now you're running a dating agency. You're CEO. Canine Executive Officer." She hauled him out of the room, leaving Alec with Skylar.

He was the one who broke the silence. "I apologize for my grandmother. I hope she didn't embarrass you."

"Not at all. But I'm guessing she embarrassed the hell out of you." Her eyes were alive with laughter. "Oh, Alec—" She gave up containing it, laughing so hard the tears poured down her cheeks. "I love your grandmother. She is a wonderful, priceless, *darling* person. I want to pick her up and take her home with me."

Right then he wouldn't have stopped her.

Much as he loved his grandmother, he would have packed her bags and stuck her on the plane himself. "She doesn't know the meaning of the word *tact*."

"But that's what's so perfect. She's honest. She's speaking from the heart. She cares about you." Wiping her eyes, she sat up. "Sorry. I don't mean to laugh, but your family is so—so—"

"Exasperating? Interfering? Certifiable?"

"Special. If I were a writer, not an artist, I would have got a movie script out of tonight." Her smile sent desire marauding through his body. She held nothing back. When she was angry she showed it. When she was amused, she laughed. She wore her emotions on the surface without apology or restraint. With Skylar there was no guessing. What she felt was right there for everyone to see. She lived life with the brakes off.

He wondered if she was as open and unrestrained in the bedroom.

His palms ached with the desire to reach out and haul her against him. He wanted to rip her clothes off and screw her right there on the couch, an urge he intended to resist at all costs no matter how much it would delight his grandmother.

"What would you have called your movie? *The Twelve Humiliations of Christmas*?"

Her smile dimmed. "You're really upset. I'm sorry."

"Why are you sorry? You weren't the one trying to manipulate my love life."

"But I know how that feels. And I'm sorry because although I know you hate talking about your marriage under any circumstances, the real reason you're upset is because your grandmother talked about it in front of me. Not only am I pretty much a stranger, but you don't even like me. Revealing deep feelings to someone you don't know is an uncomfortable experience. It makes you feel vulnerable. I know, because that's how I felt yesterday."

The only sound in the room was the crackle of the log fire.

"You didn't seem vulnerable."

"Are you kidding? First I bled on you, then I threw up in front of you. That, believe me, is a low point for anyone, so don't talk to me about being emotionally vulnerable because where you are concerned I have been naked in every possible sense of the word. I have a clear recollection of thinking 'kill me now' at several points last night." She gave a crooked smile that told him that no matter how bouncy she seemed, the past twenty-four hours had wounded more than her head.

"Out of all that, the worst part was throwing up?"

"No. The very worst part," she said slowly, "was needing your help in the first place. If I'd made a list of all the guys in the world I would not have wanted to see me at my lowest point, you would have been right there at the top. In the summer you made it clear you thought I was hopeless, and I actually enjoyed our moments of unarmed combat where I proved you wrong and then suddenly, *wham*, I'm in a situation where I prove you right." Her surprisingly honest admission unlocked something inside him.

"That's not how I see you."

"I know exactly how you see me, Alec. To you I'm this ditzy, useless, princess blonde who can't get through a meal without having her hand held and the annoying thing is that I can't even prove you wrong right now." There was an edge to her tone and she rubbed her fingers over her forehead and gave a helpless shrug. "Ignore me. It's not a contest."

"That's not how I see you," he repeated. "I know I'm the last person you would have chosen to have by your side through this, and yet despite everything, despite the fact that your life has been shredded in front of someone you hate, you have been gutsy, good-humored and dignified."

Her throat moved and she stared hard into the fire. "I don't hate you. And that's probably the nicest thing you've ever said to me."

"Probably the only nice thing I've ever said to you." And he felt a flash of guilt because he knew that the reason for that had nothing to do with her. "I think you're the strongest woman I've ever met, but you're right that I'm not good at disclosing personal details in front of people. Anyone. It makes me feel—"

"Naked? Alec, I *was* naked in front of you. Literally. So I think I'm winning in the battle of personal humiliation."

He wished she hadn't brought that up.

"I hate it when my family talk about me. It's like walking into the supermarket and discovering I've forgotten to put on my trousers."

"That happens often?"

"Never. But it was a recurring nightmare of mine when I was eight. It stayed with me."

Her smile was back, warm and generous. "Mine was discovering I was wearing odd shoes."

"It worked out well for Cinderella."

"That was one shoe, not odd shoes. I don't think

Prince Charming would have looked twice at her if she'd been wearing one red Prada and one silver Jimmy Choo." She started clearing up the glasses. "Why do you hate talking about your marriage?"

"I'm not good at admitting failure."

"Is it failure or is it life?"

"It definitely feels like failure. I tried to make it work, but I couldn't give Selina what she wanted." Why the hell was he telling her this? "I hurt her. Badly."

Sky gave him a long look. "And she hurt you."

"Most of it wasn't her fault."

"You really believe that? Is that why you don't date? Because you think you're this bad guy who is going to hurt women? That's bullshit, Alec."

"You don't know me."

"I've learned a thing or two since yesterday. I never would have guessed this in the summer, but it turns out that buried underneath that badass, moody exterior is a real chivalrous streak. I know that because nothing less than a chivalrous streak would have driven you to take me back to your hotel room and then bring me here. And I suspect that is what prevents you from placing the blame for your divorce where it should surely lie. On the shoulders of your ex-wife." She walked to the door and paused while he opened it. "I think your grandmother is right. You should start dating again, Alec."

He clenched his jaw, thinking that he felt more naked now than he had when he'd stepped out of the shower. If the weekend carried on like this, they'd have no secrets left by the end of it. "That isn't going to happen."

"It should. It's true that you border on the arrogant and your communication tends to veer toward sarcasm, but you have great biceps, and there are plenty of women who find brooding and cynical to be attractive traits. If you kept your mouth shut, I'm sure you could attract one of them." Flashing a smile, she walked past him, leaving him drugged by a light cloud of perfume and a lethal dose of lust.

CHAPTER EIGHT

It was the nicest evening Sky could remember.

Dinner was delicious, the conversation lively and afterward they all gathered in the living room. With its exposed beams and blazing log fire, it was warm and cozy.

There were books everywhere, she noticed. Not just crammed into the floor-to-ceiling bookcases, but stacked on tables, markers in the pages. Books that weren't there for display, but to be read and talked about. Part of life, not an artful piece of decoration.

Suzanne was obviously enjoying having a house full of people. "Charades, Sky?"

She turned. "Sure. I love charades."

They split into teams. She, Liv and Alec's mother on one team versus Alec and his father and uncle. She threw herself into it, acting, miming and indulging her dramatic side.

They won easily, but not before Sky found herself laughing so hard she couldn't breathe.

Why didn't they play this at home?

She dismissed the thought instantly. Not even after a few glasses of champagne could she imagine her parents, or even her brothers, suspending dignity long enough to play charades.

Alec was sprawled in front of the fire, long legs

stretched out in front of him, watching her from under those thick, dark lashes.

His scrutiny made her uncomfortable.

She was well aware that their relationship had altered in subtle ways. They were locked in a strange, indefinable intimacy while at the same time being virtual strangers.

Whenever they'd met in the past, he'd left her feeling like a cat whose fur had been stroked the wrong way. She'd felt judged and feeling that way had stoked her resentment, but she knew she'd been guilty of judging him, too. She'd dismissed him as a hardened cynic but after twenty-four hours in his company, she knew differently.

She also had more questions than she had answers.

There was no doubt that his divorce had been bitter and acrimonious and that the experience had sharpened the edges of his cynicism.

There were plenty of family photographs placed around the warm, friendly living room, but none of Alec's wife. With the exception of his grandmother, the family tiptoed round the subject, as if they were dealing with a grenade with the pin removed.

Glancing at the photo on the mantelpiece, she saw a boy of about twelve wearing a determined expression as he hauled himself up a rock face.

"That was taken in Wengen, Switzerland, near the Eiger." Intercepting her glance, Alec's father lifted it from the shelf. "Do you remember that trip, Alec?"

"Of course. It's not easy to forget a trip where we both nearly died. That was one of my earliest lessons in survival."

Suzanne put her hands over her ears. "I'm not listening. I'm better off not knowing."

"The weather changed," Simon murmured. "I had to make a decision about whether to descend or bivouac overnight. I decided we'd be safer staying put until morning."

Alec held out his hand for the photo. "The snow was so heavy we had to dig our way out of the tent in the morning."

"And there was a perfect blue sky." Simon handed him the photo. "We went on climbing expeditions every summer until Harry seduced you over to the dark side."

Sky glanced between them. "The dark side?"

"The sea." Suzanne poured coffee and passed round the cups. "Harry was a marine. Whenever he was home on leave, he'd take Alec sailing and diving. You'd think that would have given me less to worry about, but instead of scaling mountains in snowstorms they were exploring wrecks in the deep, dark ocean."

Harry grinned, unrepentant. "I take full responsibility for Alec's chosen career path. Forget Oxford and Harvard—the outdoors is the best classroom in the world."

It was like watching a team sport being played.

Family life.

They passed the ball and worked together.

They painted a picture of a boy who was bold and adventurous. He wasn't remote, she thought, he was self-contained. He'd learned to care for himself.

A survivor down to the bone.

He'd been raised in a family who had encouraged him to explore and push himself to his limits.

She thought about her own childhood, regimented and tightly scheduled. She'd gone from piano lessons, to French classes, to dance classes, every moment of her day planned out. Her parents believed in expanding the mind and keeping busy. Sometimes all she'd longed to do was lie on her back in a field and look at the sky but inactivity was actively discouraged in her family.

There had been no time to relax and let her imagination run free.

She sat, nestled on the large sofa in front of the fire, wishing she could freeze time. Here, in this cottage, the outside world had ceased to exist. Here, for a while, she could forget about Richard, her parents and all the difficult decisions that needed to be made.

She delayed the moment when she went to bed, but in the end they agreed that with two energetic four-year-olds arriving the following morning they all needed their rest.

Sky didn't look at Alec. She didn't need to. The tension was flowing from him in waves and it was obvious that sharing a room with her for another night was yet another intimacy he would rather have been spared.

She went up to the room first and stood watching snowflakes fall onto frozen fields. The landscape glowed ghostly pale in the moonlight. Instinctively she reached for her pad and drew several swift sketches. Moon, stars, snowflakes—she played with different shapes and ideas knowing that most of them would never leave her sketch pad.

But some of them—

She stared at the sketches. Some of them could turn into something.

Maybe…maybe…

An idea floated just out of reach and before she could grasp it the door opened behind her.

She closed the pad quickly as Alec walked in.

"You can sleep in the bed. I'll take the couch." His tone was brusque as he closed the door firmly between them and the rest of the house.

Even though his family was on the other side of the door, here they were alone.

The contrast between the rigid set of his shoulders and the intimacy of the room didn't escape her.

"This is awkward, and you're mad at me."

"I'm not mad at you." He undid a couple of buttons on his shirt and then paused, as if trying to reconcile the reality of their relationship with their current situation.

"Do you think your mom kept me in here on purpose?"

"Probably. She's hoping we're going to succumb to temptation." He rolled back the sleeves of his shirt and dropped to his haunches in front of the fire.

"We know each other better than either of us ever thought we would, that's for sure."

And the really complicated thing was that the more she knew, the more she liked.

Alec added another log to the flames. Then he stood up, his powerful frame almost blocking the flickering light. He seemed about to say something else but at that moment her phone rang and she picked it up and froze.

It was her father.

It didn't matter how many years passed, she felt the same way she had at the age of eight when she'd been told that he wanted to see her in his study.

"I—I need to take this."

Alec gave a curt nod and walked toward the door as Sky gritted her teeth and turned her back to answer the call.

"Hi—"

He called her maybe twice a year, and never for a chat.

She listened while he told her in blunt terms what he thought about her refusal to marry Richard.

It couldn't have been any further removed from the sympathetic talk she'd had with Suzanne.

"I don't love him—" She wasn't even allowed to finish her sentence and half way through the painful hammer of harsh words, she realized that Alec hadn't left the room. He was standing still, his hand on the door, clearly uncertain whether to leave her or not.

It was like playing emotional strip poker, she thought numbly.

Another layer removed. Another layer revealed.

Her father's words smashed into her like pebbles caught in the tide. *Selfish. A disappointment. Dreamy.*

She waited until he finished talking, added something bland and noncommittal and dropped the phone onto the bed.

Alec was scowling. "Who the hell was that?"

She swallowed. "The Judge."

"The Judge?"

"My father."

"You call your father the Judge?"

"Yes, because you always feel as if you're on trial.

Even my brothers call him that. He listens to the evidence and then gives his ruling and it's never in my favor." She tried to keep her tone light. "Forget *The Good Wife*, I could write a script called *The Bad Daughter*."

Alec released the door handle and walked toward her. "You're upset. More upset than you were about Richard."

"Richard was a mistake. The Judge is…family. It's never easy falling out with family."

"Did you know he was going to say all those things?" Alec's tone was harsh and she nodded, wondering how much he'd heard.

"I pretty much could have scripted it word for word."

"Then why the hell did you answer the phone?"

"Because not answering simply postpones the inevitable conversation until later. I'd rather get it over with."

"But that puts him in control."

"He is in control."

"Of your life?" He walked back toward her and she shook her head.

"Not the decisions I make, but he controls the approval ratings and the mood of the household. I'll be blamed if we have an ice storm at Christmas."

"I assume you're not talking about the weather."

She gave a humorless laugh. "When we were young, my brothers and I used to issue weather warnings to each other as shorthand for his mood. 'Stormy today' or 'cloudy with a chance of sunshine.' Although there wasn't much sunshine. My father is a very serious man."

"Why didn't you tell him the truth about Richard?"

"Which part should I tell him? That I don't even know who he really is? That he might have hit me if I hadn't moved? What sort of story is that? My father hears solid evidence every day. He would accuse me of being dramatic. A victim of my own creative brain." And in a way she had been, because she'd imagined that given time things might work out with Richard.

"Next time, don't pick up the phone."

"That would make the conversation twice as lively when it eventually happens."

He was standing right in front of her, legs spread, arms folded. Solid. Strong.

"So they're not supporters of independent thought and decision making. What happens if you stand up to him?"

"I did. I didn't marry Richard, did I? And they support independent thought as long as those thoughts and decisions align precisely with theirs. If not—" she shrugged "—they have various methods at their disposal for trying to secure the outcome they want."

"But you studied art at college, so clearly there have been times in your life where you followed your dreams."

"That was one of them." Turning away from him, she leaned her cheek against the cool of the window and stared out across the winter sky. "My parents were so angry they refused to take me to my halls. They sent me with a driver. Took me a while to live that one down with Brittany and Emily. They thought I was a spoiled princess." Remembering that he felt that way about her, too, she gave a short laugh. "I guess you can identify with that. You think the same thing."

"Not anymore." Something in his voice made her turn her head.

She met his gaze and the look they exchanged was infused with a strange, thickened intimacy.

Trapped by the burning heat of his dark eyes she felt her heart rate steadily increase. "Turns out we were both wrong about a lot of things."

Most of all, this. The deep, dangerous attraction that seeped through her skin, sending luxurious waves of arousal through her body.

She'd always acknowledged that he was handsome. She was an artist, and she could appreciate a perfect bone structure and a strong masculine jaw as well as the next woman.

Still, whenever they'd been together the simmering anger had burned off any temptation she might have had to find him attractive.

But now…

Something had shifted. Maybe it was the numerous times he'd come to her aid over the past twenty-four hours, or the kindness he'd shown her, but all she could think about was how it would feel to go to bed with him. To slide her hands over those powerful shoulders and press her lips to his skin.

He had more sex appeal than should have been allowed in one man.

The moment he'd stepped out of the shower naked was embedded in her brain. It was as if her brain had turned into a Pinterest board, covered with images of Alec. Her mouth felt dry. The only place she wanted to pin him was to the bed.

Shaken by the power of her feelings, she broke the connection, scooped up her bag and strolled toward the bathroom.

"Thanks for listening, Alec."

As she opened the door, she decided it didn't really matter where she spent the night. After the look they'd just exchanged, she rated her chances of getting any sleep a big fat zero.

ALEC ROSE AT seven after a night without sleep.

He contemplated a cold shower and decided he didn't want to be in the room with Skylar any longer than was necessary.

Keeping his eyes averted from the tangle of blond hair, long limbs and bedding strewn across his bed, he dressed quickly and went downstairs.

It didn't help that she'd had a restless night, too.

He wondered if it was the conversation with her father that had kept her shifting in the bed until the early hours. That conversation had played on his mind, adding yet another piece to the picture he was forming of her. A picture that looked nothing like the image he'd had before.

He'd found it easier when he didn't know anything about her.

Easier to consign her to a box in his head labeled Do Not Touch.

The rest of the house was still asleep and he walked into the kitchen and stared blankly at the coffee machine. Good coffee was one of his father's enduring passions, and the trusty old machine had been replaced by a fancy Italian machine that appeared to have been designed to the same specifications as a Ferrari.

"All I want is a damn cup of coffee," Alec muttered as he stared at the bank of levers and gleaming chrome.

"Can I help? I speak fluent coffee machine." Skylar's voice came from behind him and her slightly husky, morning tone triggered another rush of the same hormones that had kept him awake for most of the night.

Having spent sleepless hours listing all the reasons why joining her in the bed was a bad idea, he was in a foul mood.

He'd been counting on having a few quiet hours to regain his equilibrium.

He'd thought he had the place to himself.

He certainly wasn't ready to be polite and sociable.

Selina had rarely emerged before lunchtime, which had given him half a day of peace.

Sky, it appeared, wasn't prepared to extend him the same courtesy.

She was wide-awake and dressed and even though he knew none of this was her fault, he felt a rush of resentment. "I didn't expect you to be an early riser."

"I'm a morning person." She eyed him cautiously. "You, on the other hand, clearly are not."

"I love mornings." Just not this particular morning. He reached for his father's prized coffee beans and gave the machine a savage look.

"I don't think glaring at it will help," she said mildly. "Turning it on might."

Alec braced his hands on the work surface and closed his eyes. He didn't want to think about being turned on. He was so damn turned on he wasn't sure he could walk across the kitchen.

"I'm probably better off left alone until I wake up properly."

She didn't take the hint. "You're not likely to wake up until you've had coffee. Here, let me." She nudged him to one side and reached for the coffee beans. "Are you sure you're a morning person? Because from where I'm standing it doesn't seem that way."

She was standing close to him.

Far too close.

The soft, feminine scent of her engulfed him in dizzying waves. He struggled against the impulse to grab her and wake them both up in the most primitive way known to man.

Instead he gripped the granite counter until his knuckles were white, feeling a rush of frustration that he couldn't control his feelings.

"You're perky for someone with a head injury and jet lag."

"I love mornings. Every new day starts full of possibilities. You never know what could happen."

He knew exactly what could happen, and he was trying his damnedest to stop it. "You sound like one of those quotes they put on a poster."

"Judging from the snarl in your voice, it wasn't one you would have hung on your wall in college." Her tone light, she turned to look at him. "If you really are a morning person, then something else is wrong. Did I do something? Say something?"

The fact that he knew he was being unreasonable did nothing to improve his mood. "It's not you. It's me."

"Alec, your teeth are clenched."

"I'm tired. I didn't have a great night."

"Me, neither." There was a pause while she did something to the coffee machine. "I was lying there wondering whether we should both get naked and make the most of the moment and that lovely big bed. Were you suffering from the same problem?"

He turned his head slowly. She was still standing close to him and her mouth was curved into a smile of impish amusement. He dragged his gaze upward and saw laughter in her wicked blue eyes.

His libido punched his intellect unconscious.

He was doomed.

"No." His voice sounded robotic. "I wasn't."

She gave him a long, speculative look and then turned her attention back to the coffee machine. "Right. My mistake. Good job I didn't jump on you in the night. You probably would have screamed and struggled, and that would have shocked the hell out of your grandmother."

Part of him was tempted to confess it hadn't been a mistake. That she wasn't wrong. But that would mean taking the first step on a path he had no intention of walking.

Since Selina, he kept his relationships simple. Some would call it superficial.

He intended to keep it that way.

Blood rushed through his body, proving that some parts of him were more awake than others. Still, at least he hadn't wandered down in his pajamas. He was grateful for that.

"Jet lag." His mouth was dry. "The reason I couldn't sleep was jet lag. How is your head?"

"The color has changed, but I think it suits me.

What do you think?" She lifted her hair and showed him her bruised temple. "Very impressionist. A touch of Monet's water lilies. Generally one has to be careful with shades of blue and yellow, but this works."

On her, everything worked.

He wondered if it was possible for her to look bad.

"So you think you can persuade this thing to produce a cup of coffee? It's new. My father is an enthusiast."

"I can see that. This is a great machine. Todd has the same one."

"Who is Todd?" He spoke without thinking and saw her eyebrows lift. "Ignore me. None of my business."

"Todd is a friend," she said mildly. "A glass artist. We share studio space." She turned her attention back to the coffee while he watched. "I'm guessing strong and black."

"You guessed right."

Her spine was straight, her movements a little less smooth and relaxed than they'd been a moment before.

He knew he owed her an apology but decided it was safer if she disliked him.

Safer for him, and definitely safer for her.

If his rudeness kept her at a distance, then he would have done them both a favor.

He was terrible at relationships and after what she'd just been through she didn't need more pain from him.

He breathed deeply, acknowledging that his strategy wasn't driven entirely by selfless motives.

He didn't need the pain, either. Not the pain, not the guilt, nor the lingering sense of failure that tainted everything that came after.

It was about self-protection. Self-preservation.

The coffee machine purred under her expert touch and moments later she put a cup in his hands.

"Here. I hope this helps."

So did he.

After a night without sleep, a night during which his libido had been wide-awake and having a party all by itself, he needed the caffeine. Sexual arousal appeared to have fried his brain.

The first cup barely touched the sides of his throat and she made him a second one without being asked.

"So you're practical as well as artistic."

"I'd argue that making truly excellent coffee is art." She turned her attention back to the machine and repeated the process for herself.

Tasting what she'd produced, he wasn't about to disagree.

By the time he'd finished the second cup he was feeling more human.

All he needed now was a bracing walk in the cold air and hopefully he'd be able to make it through the day.

"You should go back to bed. Relax for a while. I'll be back in about an hour."

"Where are you going?"

To try freezing his hormones. "The dogs need a walk."

"Can I come?" She curved her hands round the mug, breathing in the aroma of fresh coffee. "I promise not to talk or be—what did you call it? 'Perky.' But I'd love a walk."

"You wouldn't enjoy it. Have you looked out of the window? It's been snowing most of the night.

It's freezing out there. Slippery underfoot. The windchill is—"

"Alec, it's fine." She finished her coffee and put the mug down. "I get it. You'd rather go on your own. Not a problem. You don't have to entertain me. I'll stay here and maybe go exploring later. Have fun." She turned to walk away and he reached out and caught her arm.

He knew he should let her go. *Why the hell wasn't he letting her go?* "How long would it take you to get dressed?"

"I'm dressed." She glanced down at herself, as if to check she wasn't missing something obvious. "All I need is socks."

He glanced down, too. Her feet were bare and he caught a shimmer of pink nail polish on her toes. And that single glance was all it took for him to start seeing her naked again.

He snatched his hand away as if she were radioactive.

"Jeans will be useless in the snow. If you slip, they'll get wet and cling."

She was looking at him as if he was a crazy person. "Then I'll change into something else."

"I'm leaving in five minutes. I want to be back to lend a hand in the kitchen before Cathy arrives." He half hoped she'd tell him there was no way she could be ready that quickly, but she simply put her mug in the dishwasher and headed for the stairs.

"I can be ready in four."

She was as good as her word and before he'd put on his coat and boots she was standing next to him wearing layers of wool and a beaming smile.

He sighed.

At least there was no sign of yesterday's vulnerability.

"You need boots."

"I bumped into your mom a moment ago and she said I could borrow hers. We're about the same size."

He found the boots and greeted Church and Nelson, who were crazy with anticipation, their tails wagging wildly as Skylar zipped up her weatherproof jacket.

Alec made no comment, but he was surprised to see she'd packed something so practical.

"What happened to the white coat?"

"That was for show. This is for warmth."

"I expected you to spend ages on your makeup."

"You think Nelson and Church are going to have a problem with the way I look?"

No one could possibly have a problem with the way she looked.

She radiated so much warmth and energy she virtually glowed. It was like standing in a beam of sunshine. And his sister was right. Sky could have starred in a shampoo ad. Her hair flowed over her shoulders like buttermilk blended with honey.

"I assumed—"

"Yeah, you do that a lot." She patted him on the arm. "Don't feel bad about it. For the record, I don't tend to wear much makeup unless I'm going to a glitzy event or trying to attract a guy. Since we've established you'd rather have sex with a two-headed lizard than climb into bed with me, there doesn't seem much point in bothering. Shall we go?"

He shifted with discomfort. "Sky—"

"What? You don't have to feel awkward, Alec. I'm not one of those women who thinks every man on the planet has to find her attractive. I rub you the wrong way for some reason. I'm trying my hardest not to, but I seem to manage to annoy you just by being alive. Why don't we start again? You're not that into me. No problem. My ego can take it."

Nelson bounded over to her and she bent down to kiss him, while Alec thought that if he was any more into her he'd have her naked underneath him on the nearest flat surface.

"You don't annoy me." It was the best he could do in the circumstances. Like giving a little more rein to a bolting horse in the hope it might somehow slow it down.

"Good to know. Who's a gorgeous boy? I don't drive you crazy, do I?" She crooned, stroked and fussed and Nelson threw himself on the floor and rolled over in total ecstasy.

Nelson, it seemed, was totally into her.

Alec rolled his eyes. "Nelson, show a little control."

Her gaze lifted to his, those incredible blue eyes faintly mocking. "Control can be overrated. Let's go, Professor." She turned up the collar of her jacket. "What time will your sister arrive?"

"Midmorning. The routine is that we'll open presents, then have lunch and go for a walk."

"Sounds like fun."

He opened the door and they were engulfed by a rush of freezing air.

He wondered if the bitter cold might make her change her mind, but she tugged on gloves and stepped out of the door.

The countryside stretched in front of them, gentle undulating hills interspersed with hedges and areas of woodland covered in a thick layer of winter white. The air was still, the sounds muffled by snow, and they trudged up the lane through the soft snow and smothered silence, past frostbitten trees and the silvery shimmer of icy tracks. The dogs bounded ahead, tails wagging, excited to be outdoors.

The sun shone brightly, as if to overcompensate for the icy chill of winter.

Skylar strode out, sure-footed and confident, her boots leaving footprints in the untouched snow. “Where are we going?”

“The footpath runs through the fields all the way to the beech wood at the bottom of the hill, but we don’t have to go that far.”

She squinted against the sun. “It doesn’t look far.”

“It’s a cold day. You might change your mind when you’ve been out in this for five minutes.”

Whistling to the dogs, they walked along the road, past cottages with walls of warm honey stone.

She paused in front of one of them. “Beautiful house. It looks like a Christmas card.”

“It’s the original manor house, built at the same time as the parish church.”

“I love the colors. Honey stone peeping through snowy creeper. Shades of white. I’ve been looking for a theme for my next collection. I wish I’d brought my camera.” She pulled out her phone and took a photo with that instead.

“You always have a theme?”

“Yes. My first one was called ‘Mediterranean Sky’ and my latest one is ‘Ocean Blue,’ but next time I want to get away from the beach and do something a little different. I'm thinking of winter." She took a few more photographs and then gave him a smile of apology. "Sorry."

"For what?"

"For making you wait while I take photographs. It's an irritating habit of mine. Don't wait for me."

He wished he found it irritating.

He wished he found anything about her irritating.

They crossed the road and he paused by the gate. "This gate doesn't open. Can you climb?"

Giving him a disparaging look, she all but vaulted the gate. "Alec, you need to stop treating me as if I've never walked in snow before. My best friend lives in Maine. That's the equivalent of an intensive course in managing winter weather. Maine winters are hardcore." She stopped, her breath clouding the air as she studied the holly growing at the edge of the field. "Berries. Why didn't I think of that before?"

He climbed the gate and joined her. "Think of what?"

"Holly. Mistletoe. Winter jewel colors, reds, greens and maybe pearls. The shimmer of pearl on silver." She was talking to herself, lost in her own thoughts. "Lots of silver. Snowflakes, an elaborate set of jeweled mistletoe. Earrings and a necklace. Snow Queen. I love it." She delved into her pocket, pulled out a notebook and drew a few quick sketches.

Her pencil flew over the page, shaping and shading while he stood there. He knew she'd forgotten his existence.

The cold had whipped a pink glow to her cheeks

and her eyes were a splash of intense color in a world that was white.

Alec was engulfed by a wave of lust so powerful and all-consuming that he actually lifted his hand toward her.

He was moments from sliding his fingers into her hair when Church bounded up, barking madly and breaking the spell.

Alec dropped his hand a second before Sky glanced up and smiled.

"Someone is excited."

Yes, he thought. *Someone is.*

The dogs bounded ahead, leaving footprints in the snow.

"Why jewelry? What do you love about it?" He hadn't intended to ask the question. Hadn't intended to do anything that might deepen his knowledge of her, but he couldn't help it.

She slipped the notebook back in her pocket and snuggled deeper inside her coat. "I'm shallow and I love sparkly things."

He should have taken that flippant response and used it to reinforce the belief that she was exactly like Selina.

But he knew she was nothing like Selina.

And that was his problem.

He was grateful to the dogs for constantly coming between them because otherwise he might have been tempted to push her up against the nearest snowy tree.

"What was the first piece of jewelry you made?"

"Apart from a pasta necklace for my mother?" She stooped to make a fuss of Nelson, who was circling round her legs. "A wedding ring. It was my first commission."

"How many commissions do you take on a year?"

"It depends on how big they are. Some take longer than others. I try not to book myself too far ahead. It crowds my brain and stifles creativity. Some commissions are more complicated than others, depending on the purpose." She saw his curious glance and smiled. "Jewelry can be a statement, like a wedding ring. It can have meaning, it can be a bribe, a thank-you, an expression of love, or it can simply be pretty. The use of jewelry as an adornment dates back to prehistoric times. Gold was a status symbol to the early Egyptians, and they buried it with the dead to go with them to the afterlife. In Bronze Age Greece they used it as a symbol of power, to celebrate the gods and to ward off evil. But of course you probably know all this."

"It isn't my area of expertise." But it was obviously hers. And the more time he spent with her, the more he realized how grossly he'd misjudged her. It frustrated him not to have a clear picture of who she was. It was like looking through a camera lens and constantly having to adjust the focus.

"Speaking of expertise, it's your turn. Tell me about you, Shipwreck Hunter."

"What do you want to know?"

She pushed her hands into her pockets, her breath clouding the freezing air. "Was Selina the love of your life?"

He tensed.

Most people skirted around the topic, treated it cautiously, but he was fast discovering that Skylar was nothing like other people.

"Why are you asking me that?"

She gave a faint smile. "I guess having seen each other naked, I figured we might as well go all the way. This is the psychological equivalent of second base. So was she the love of your life?"

"Is there any such thing?"

"Oh, yes." A tiny smile touched her mouth. "I think so. I hope so."

"That's your romantic side playing tricks on your rational brain."

"We're making progress—a couple of days ago you didn't think I had a brain at all."

"You still believe in true love and all that even after Richard?"

"What I had with Richard wasn't love. I wanted it to be love and for a while I wondered if it might be, but it wasn't."

"How do you know?" He wondered why he was having this conversation with her when all his instincts were screaming at him to kill it dead.

"Because love is honest and unselfish. And it isn't demanding." She spoke softly, her words the only sound in the stillness of the winter day. "It's a cup of tea in bed on a cold day, it's a foot rub when you've walked for hours, it's a listening ear and an encouraging word. It's encouraging, accepting, tolerating, not trying to change. It's give, not take. Action, not words."

Tension rippled across his shoulders.

You don't love me, Alec. I know you don't love me. Tell me. Say the words.

"Are you saying you don't want to hear those words?"

"Of course, every woman does, but I'd rather have

a man show me he loves me than tell me because words mean nothing by themselves."

They'd reached the beech wood, and the trees clustered together, snowy sentinels guarding the inner sanctum.

"How do you know?" He paused at the edge of the wood. "How do you ever know if it's love?"

There was a long silence. "I asked Lily that question the other night. She said her heart felt too big for her chest."

"She should see a cardiologist."

She laughed. "Maybe, but I guess if you don't know if it's love, then it isn't."

The dogs circled happily, excited to be outdoors.

"So why did you stick it out with Richard if it wasn't love?"

"I persuaded myself that it might be." There was a long silence. "Dating Richard was the first thing I'd ever done that pleased my parents. Finally I had their approval and it felt good. I know it's crazy for an independent woman to need, or ever want, the approval of their parents, but I did. I do."

"It sounds like a human response to me. And it might have worked between you."

"We would have been miserable." She frowned. "I should have realized that before but relationships aren't that clear, are they? It's not like buying a food item that comes with a list of ingredients you can check in case there's something that you're allergic to. People are complicated. And Richard had a tendency to present only the ingredients he knew people wanted."

"You're saying he turned himself into organic red velvet cake to appeal to your palate?"

She laughed. "In my case it would be chocolate brownie." Her smile faded. "Honestly? It wasn't just about pleasing my parents. I wanted to be in love. Really in love. I tell everyone I believe in it, but the truth is I've never actually felt it. I've never been in love. Not the sort of love I want."

He could walk away now. He could make some comment about how they needed to get back. But something, some invisible thread, kept his feet welded to the snowy ground.

"What sort of love do you want?"

"I want to feel like Lily, as if my heart is too big for my chest. My feelings for Richard—and his for me—were like being on a low-carb diet. I was permanently starving and craving something more substantial. When it comes to love I want a feast. How about you? Do you think you'll fall in love again?"

"I hope not. I intend to do everything in my power to avoid it."

Her eyes widened. "You don't want love in the future?"

"No. I enjoy the life I lead too much to give it up for love."

"Why would you have to give it up?" She sounded puzzled. "You make it sound as if you have to choose between them."

He thought back to the prison of his marriage. "My lifestyle isn't compatible with a relationship."

"Surely that depends on the relationship."

"No. Relationships require compromise. Two people with different goals, struggling to find some areas of common ground. In practice, that means giving up the things you love or only doing them some of the time." Accounting for every minute of his time. Falling short of expectations. *Failing.*

"Wow, Professor, you make it sound as much fun as root-canal treatment. Carry on talking like that and you could even put *me* off romance. It sounds selfish and like a whole lot of hard work. Why would anyone want that?"

He didn't. He didn't want that. "You probably see a lot of different versions of love. Men probably come to you for Christmas, birthdays and Valentine's Day to buy shiny jewelry that will save their relationships."

"All the shiny jewelry in the world can't save a relationship that isn't working. The best I can do is design something that is a permanent expression of the emotion one of the partners feels."

"What would you design to evoke exasperation?"

She laughed. "I'm going to have to get back to you on that. Generally jewelry is positive. So far I haven't made the 'root canal' collection. I'm not sure it would be a big seller."

"But you believe in the fairy tale. That's what you want." It was a relief to discover he'd been right about something where she was concerned. "A huge diamond, a white wedding, two children, a dog and a house in the Hamptons."

"I don't think love is a fairy tale. And I don't believe love is a diamond, a white wedding, two children, a dog and a house in the Hamptons. That's a lifestyle, not love. You can have those things without love and you can love without those things. I don't have any ambition to get married." She glanced at him, amused. "You don't believe me, do you? You think I'm one of those women who says 'I don't want to get married' while secretly choosing dresses on the internet. Honestly, that isn't me. If marriage happens, great. But it isn't marriage I want, it's love. I grew up in a stable home with parents who were legally committed to each other. But I didn't see love. I wanted love."

"Of course. You're an artist. You probably lay on your back in a field of sunflowers dreaming of it."

Her laugh was infectious and he found himself smiling, too. There was something about her that lifted the mood of every room she entered.

"The dream was to find someone who loves me. The *real* me. Not a different improved version, but the one standing in front of him, flaws and all. Someone I never have to pretend with, never have to put on an act with." Her voice was serious, and all traces of laughter had gone. "Someone who thinks my dreams are brilliant and possible, not ridiculous and impossible. Honest and simple love."

It didn't sound simple to him. It sounded as statistically likely as winning the lottery.

"What if someone thinks they know who you are and you know they're wrong?" His mouth was dry. "What if you spend your time trying to live up to something when you know you can only fail?"

"Then it isn't love." A frown creased her forehead. "And you can't fail at love, Alec. It isn't an exam, it's a feeling. You either have it or you don't and if you don't that might be sad, but it isn't failure."

It felt like failure to him.

The constant simmering knowledge that he was falling short of every expectation.

Nelson darted into the trees then turned and barked.

Sky tucked her chin inside her scarf and they followed him into the woods. Snow clung to the trees and carpeted the ground and the dogs bounded ahead, kicking up a shower of white as they paused to dig and explore. "Being with Richard always made me feel bad about myself. It was nothing major, just small criticisms, but the result is a slow erosion of who you are, like filing the edges of someone to try to change their shape. Be more of this and less of that. With him, I tried to be less me."

He gave a humorless laugh. "Whereas I refused to be anything but me. And both of us ended up in the same place. How did you meet him?"

"My parents introduced us and we bonded instantly. He was fun, handsome—we liked the same things. Or I thought we did." She brushed snow from her sleeve. "We talked all night. It was a meeting of souls. Like me, he wanted to travel. We both loved the Impressionists and he told me that flying to Paris to see Monet's collection was high on his wish list. He wanted to visit Florence and eat gelato. He wanted to tour the Greek islands. I couldn't believe I'd met someone so like me. It was the most romantic evening I'd ever had and I thought that was it. I saw a fabulous future for us."

"This is like reading a book where I already know the ending."

She was silent for a moment. "I still haven't got my head round the ending. I can't accept that he didn't really want to do any of those things, even though the evidence was right there in front of me. In the year we were together, we never went to Paris to see Monet and we never took a trip to Florence. I bought tickets to concerts he was too busy to attend and went to galleries on my own. I did go to Greece, but that was to visit Brittany and Lily. I made excuses, the way people so often do when you know instinctively that things aren't right but you don't want to give up on them. I told myself we were both busy, that coordinating our schedules was a nightmare, that it would get better. It didn't."

"So everything he said to you—"

"Lies." She picked up a pinecone and slipped it into her pocket. "Richard is the consummate politician. He knows exactly what to say to get the result he wants. He studied me, in the same way my parents made me study all those people who came in and out of our house."

"But how would he have even known those things about you in advance?"

She stooped to pick up the end of a branch that had snapped under the weight of snow, her hair sliding forward in a shiny curtain. "Because my parents briefed him."

"They—" He was shocked. His parents meddled a little and worried, but… "You're saying they orchestrated the whole thing?"

"Right down to the finale. Richard talked to them about proposing to me."

Alec ran his hand over his jaw. "I'm starting to understand why you threatened to stab a certain part of me that night."

"I was angry. Mostly with myself. I should have seen it. It was a campaign. A campaign to win me because he thought, and my family thought, I'd make a good wife. Another business contract. I was his goal, except that I had my own goals and they didn't match his. I worked it out the other night, when he revealed a few things he probably didn't intend to." She turned the branch in her hands. "I like the shape of this. It would make a wonderful table decoration."

Alec looked at the gnarled, misshapen piece of wood and decided it was one of those situations where it was best not to comment. "You must be furious with your parents for interfering."

"I am. It's manipulative, isn't it? Controlling. And insulting, to think that I'm not capable of making those decisions for myself. It's proof that they still don't accept who I really am, and keep trying to mold me into the daughter they would like to have." She tugged a hat out of her pocket and slid it onto her head. "I hate that I was so deluded. I feel foolish."

The sweet, honest admission tugged at his heart.

He watched as she gathered up a few more branches and twists of greenery, wondering what she was going to do with them.

"Will you call him?"

"No. We don't have anything to say to each other. I'm moving on." She glanced around, scanning the snow-covered hedges. "Do you have mistletoe in your garden?"

He tensed, wondering exactly what she meant by "moving on." "Why?"

She gave him a long look followed by a sympathetic smile. "Wow. She really did do a number on you, didn't she?"

"What do you mean?"

"You know what I mean. And giving me that look and using that chilly tone you use to silence your poor family isn't going to work on me. I won't walk on eggshells around my friends. Friends are always honest with each other. That's how this goes. So don't freeze me out."

"Are we friends?"

"Well, we've seen each other naked." Her eyes gleamed with humor. "And you stroked my back when I was ill. Any person who does that is a friend. You know a bunch of embarrassing facts about my parents, and I know about yours. I've just shared a hell of a lot I don't normally share, and I'm guessing you're the same. So tell me the truth. Have you dated anyone since your divorce? Had wild sex with anyone?"

He inhaled sharply. "Sky—"

"Oh, come on, Alec. You're a sexy, physical guy. A million women will have put the moves on you. Are you telling me that iron self-control hasn't been tested once?"

He wondered what she'd say if he confessed that the biggest test had been with her. "I haven't dated much. I don't want the complication."

She lifted her eyebrows. "Sex isn't complicated."

"Sex is never just sex. There's always an agenda."

"You think so?" Her gaze slid to his mouth and lingered there for a long moment. Then she stepped forward and slid her hand round the back of his neck. Before he had time to react, she rose up on her toes, drew his head down to hers and kissed him.

A shock wave of heat burned through him.

Her lips were warm and sweet, her mouth moving over his in a slow, thorough exploration, as if answering a question he had no memory of asking.

He stood still, hands clenched by his sides, heart pounding, desire engulfing him in brutal waves.

Her hand moved from his neck to his cheek and he felt the warmth of her palm as she cupped his face. He opened his mouth to ask her what the hell she thought she was doing and felt the tip of her tongue trace his lower lip and glide lightly against his, smooth silk and dizzying seduction.

He should have pulled away, but he didn't. Instead he brushed his mouth over hers, allowing himself a single, tantalizing taste of what she was offering. That brief, intimate touch was all it took. Engulfed by a savage, sexual heat, he dragged her against him and plundered her mouth as if her kiss was an antidote he needed to survive.

All around them was snowy silence and the raw cold of winter, but his whole world was her mouth, the jagged rhythm of his heart and the slow, relentless pumping of his blood.

The few fleeting relationships he'd had since parting with his ex-wife hadn't left the tiniest scratch on his emotional defenses, but if there was one thing he'd learned over the past couple of days it was how badly he'd underestimated Skylar. Or maybe he'd always sensed that she was a threat, and that was the reason he'd kept her at a distance. Either way, he knew she had the power to break down every barrier he'd ever built.

His fists unclenched and he was about to push her away, when she eased away and stepped back.

Her smile finished the job her mouth had started.

Alec's head spun. He felt as if he'd banged it on a low beam, or drunk an entire bottle of whisky in one session.

He tried to make sense of it and failed. "What the hell was that for?"

"That, Alec, was a kiss with no agenda. You're welcome." Smiling, she stooped to pick up the branches she'd piled on the ground, and walked back down toward the cottage.

CHAPTER NINE

So that might not have gone *exactly* the way she'd planned, Sky conceded, trying to calm the crazy rhythm of her heart. It had been intended as a bit of fun, to prove a point, to ease some of the tension she sensed in him and to indulge a restless, reckless part of her that wanted to crush caution under the toe of her boot. Instead it had felt as if she'd lit a fuse under a sexual time bomb. It was as if every one of her sensory receptors had connected perfectly with every one of his. And he hadn't even kissed her back, not really. Just a brief brush of his mouth, a hint of something repressed, a suggestion of something dark and erotic that had sent heat spearing through her from head to toe.

Kissing him might have been a mistake, she decided, not only because she couldn't walk without concentrating, but because now he wasn't speaking to her. Far from encouraging him to open up and relax, it had had the opposite effect.

He'd closed down, as if she'd triggered an alarm protecting him from intruders.

After the unexpected exchange of confidences, she'd thought their relationship was comfortable enough to take a little fun. He was so bitter and damaged after his divorce, she'd thought he needed to be reminded that a kiss could be fun and flirty and his expression when she'd said the word *mistletoe* had made her wonder if he even remembered what fun was.

But fun and flirty had fast turned into something else.

Deciding that the wise move was to give him space, for her sake as well as his, she walked ahead of him into the house.

The delicious smell of turkey filled the hallway. Keeping her head down, she gave a sigh of appreciation as she removed her boots.

"I'd cross a continent for your mother's cooking." *And your kiss, but let's not talk about that right now.*

"Your mother doesn't cook?"

She took it as a positive that at least he was still speaking to her. "She doesn't cook warm, cozy family meals where everyone pitches in and talks about their day." She watched as he unzipped his jacket, keeping a safe distance from her. "Alec—"

"I'll take your coat."

His gaze met hers briefly, but long enough for her to see the raw heat in his eyes a fraction of a second before he masked it.

Her insides melted.

What exactly had she unleashed?

And did he really think that not mentioning it was going to make it go away?

She was pondering the implications of that as they walked into the kitchen. Liv was still wearing her pajamas and her feet were tucked into slippers that looked like a bear's feet.

"I'm a teenager. I shouldn't have to wake up at this hour," she grumbled. "It's inhuman."

"The twins will be here soon and I want breakfast out of the way." Suzanne Hunter bustled around the kitchen. "Thank you for taking the dogs out, Alec. Did the two of you have a nice walk?"

Alec kept his back to his mother as he dealt with the dogs and it was left to Sky to respond.

"It was wonderful. I picked a few things to make a table decoration." *And I kissed your son.*

She felt as if the evidence should be emblazoned on her forehead.

Liv stared through the door at the pile of greenery on the flagstones of the hallway. "You're going to make something with that?"

"It will be pretty. I was going to use holly and mistletoe but then I thought maybe you wouldn't want berries around the twins." And she was no longer sure that having mistletoe anywhere near Alec was entirely safe. Sky smiled her thanks as Suzanne put a cup of coffee in front of her. "I'll improvise and use red ribbon instead."

After breakfast and a quick change of clothes she spread the greenery over the scrubbed kitchen table. Then she took the twisted piece of wood she'd found and used it as the central feature, selecting different pieces of foliage, snipping, twisting, threading and using the ribbon while Suzanne and Liv started on the food for lunch.

As usual the process of creating something distracted her.

There was no sign of Alec and she wondered if

he was intentionally avoiding her or whether he was caught up with his father.

She'd just finished the table centerpiece when her phone rang.

This time it was Brittany, and she excused herself and took the call into the living room.

"What's going on, Sky? Where are you?"

Sky stared out of the window across a landscape of snowy white and then looked back at the Christmas tree. It had slightly uneven branches, was thinner on one side and leaned slightly to the right. The less than geometric perfection warmed her. She could happily stay here forever. "I'm at Alec's house in the Cotswolds."

"He has a house in the Cotswolds?"

"It's his parents' house. His family home."

"Wait a minute—you're telling me Alec took you home with him?"

"He didn't want to leave me in a hotel room on my own with a head injury. He's chivalrous." And he was a lot of other things, too.

Things she didn't trust herself to think about.

"Alec? We are talking about the same Alec? Shipwreck Hunter, proof-that-it's-possible-to-be-smart-as-well-as-sexy Alec? Mr. Dark, Brooding and Silent Alec."

"Yes."

"He took you home with him. Well, that's—" Brittany cleared her throat. "Good for him. So you're with his family? What are they like?"

"Adorable. You know that dream family Christmas I always wanted? This is it." She glanced at the tree with the gifts stacked haphazardly beneath it. "They're just so *normal*."

"Where are you sleeping?"

"His granny and his uncle are here so they're short on space." Skylar hesitated. "I'm sleeping in his room."

"And he's downstairs on the sofa, right?"

"No. He's in the room, too."

"Holy crap."

"Yeah, it's been kind of tense, particularly as his family assumed we were romantically involved."

"You two?" Brittany was laughing. "Sorry, but the thought of the two of you—"

"Yeah, I know. Crazy." Except that after the past couple of days it didn't seem so crazy anymore. And it certainly hadn't seemed crazy when she'd kissed him. "Are you about done laughing?"

"Nowhere near. So are you keeping each other warm at night?"

"No. And if you can't at least pretend to listen, this will be the last time I call you."

"I called you." Brittany chortled and then cleared her throat. "Okay, I'm under control. And you know I'd love to see you having a rebound relationship, I just hadn't thought about Alec when I was drawing up a list of suitable candidates."

She hadn't thought about Alec, either, but since that moment he'd walked out of the shower, she'd thought about nothing else.

"He wouldn't be interested. He's very guarded."

"Yeah, well, from what I can gather the divorce wasn't a whole load of fun. Ryan's the only one who knows the details."

You didn't need details, Sky thought, *you only needed to see the result.*

"So how is everything with you and Zach?"

"It's good. How is your poor head? When are you coming home?"

Brittany's choice of words warmed her. It was true that Puffin Island was the place that felt most like home. "I don't know. My flight to New York is next Sunday. I'll try to squeeze in a visit to the island before Christmas." She hadn't thought that far ahead.

She knew she had things to think about, decisions to make, but they could wait.

"You shouldn't be on your own in the city. Come straight here. You can stay at Castaway Cottage with us, or at Harbor House with Em and Ryan if you prefer."

It was tempting. "I don't want to cramp your style."

"Oh, please—you didn't just say that."

She smiled. "You're a good friend, Brittany Forrest. Even when you laugh at me."

"I'm not laughing. Come to Puffin Island. We miss you."

Feeling a hundred times better, Sky hung up and was still smiling as she walked back into the kitchen.

Her table decoration sat as she'd left it. Looking at it critically she could see that it needed a little more height, and added a few more leaves and pinecones, twisting them together with florists' wire and spritzing them with water.

"That's truly beautiful." Suzanne watched her in astonishment. "Is there anything you can't do?"

"Plenty of things."

Liv vanished from the room and returned with a

big photo album under her arm. "Where's Alec?" she asked her mom.

"Talking to your father and Harry, why?"

"Because I wanted to show Skylar these and I want to live to eat my turkey." Grinning, Liv opened the book.

"Oh, look at that—" Suzanne put down the knife she was using to peel sprouts and studied the photo. "That was his first and last day at scout camp. I should have known it wouldn't work out for him. He hated being regimented. Whatever he did, he wanted to do it by himself."

Liv turned the page. "This is the best one. He played the rear end of a camel in the school production of *Joseph and the Amazing Technicolor Dreamcoat.* Whenever I see him on TV looking authoritative and a little bit intimidating, I pull this one out."

The contrast between serious grown-up Alec and young Alec made her smile. "So he was a camel's butt. I'll remember that."

Liv flipped through the book, pointing out other photos and then one slid from the back and fell on the floor.

Skylar stooped to pick it up and her breath jammed in her throat.

It was Alec, looking like James Bond in a dinner jacket. Clinging to his arm like a piece of bindweed was the most delicate, fragile-looking girl Sky had ever seen. She looked as if a strong breeze was all it would take to snap her in two.

"Who's this?"

Suzanne glanced at the photo and made a sound in her throat. "How did that get in there? I thought we'd got rid of all of them. For goodness' sake, don't let Alec see that." Flustered, she took the photo from Sky. "All the others are safely locked in a drawer in Simon's study. I don't know how this one escaped the net."

"That," Liv said slowly, "is the reason Alec hasn't brought a woman home for three years."

Skylar stared at the photo. "That's his wife?"

"Ex-wife." Suzanne lowered her voice and glanced toward the door. "You probably think we're ridiculous to be dancing around the topic, but it was such a horrible time and he's seemed a little more himself lately so none of us want to risk opening that wound again. We don't want to say the wrong thing. She wasn't the right woman for him."

"She was unhinged," Liv said. "She chased him. She'd ring here, sometimes twenty times a day. I was glad we didn't have rabbits or we might have had a bunny boiler moment. Thank goodness Boris the donkey was too big to go in the pot."

"She wasn't very happy, poor thing," Suzanne said quietly. "Her parents divorced when she was young and she was desperate to find a sense of security."

Skylar could see what someone like that might see in Alec, especially if he'd stepped in and rescued her. "She was drawn to his strength."

"And his public profile." Liv tipped cranberries into a saucepan. "She wanted to be invited to premieres and lots of glittering events. But Alec hates all that. He'd rather be alone in a dark corner of a dusty library or shivering in a tent in the Arctic eating whale blubber."

Suzanne glanced guiltily toward the door. "We

shouldn't be talking about this. But it's good for you to understand why he's the way he is. Selina wasn't the easiest to deal with."

"She was a bitch."

"Liv!"

"I'm sorry, but it's true. She hurt him," Liv said flatly. "It's fine for me to hurt him, that's my role as sister, but no one outside the family can."

"You can't meddle in someone's marriage. Add some fresh orange juice to those cranberries. And then have a look outside. I heard a car. Your sister and the twins must be here. For goodness sake put those knives out of reach."

"I'm allowed to meddle when she screws my brother up." Liv reached across and grabbed an orange from the fruit bowl in the center of the table. "And she tried to kill Nelson by feeding him a chicken bone."

"I'm sure that was an accident. She didn't understand dogs."

"Didn't understand Alec, either." Liv shot to the door to greet her sister and Suzanne sighed.

"I'd have to agree with that."

Sky made the finishing touches to her table decoration, her fingers not quite steady.

She'd often wondered what she'd done to make Alec behave with such hostility toward her.

And now she knew.

She'd done nothing except bear a striking resemblance to his ex-wife.

THE KISS HAD meant nothing, so why the hell hadn't he been able to stop thinking about it all day?

He felt as if he'd been wired to a generator, with power pumping through him.

"I had so much fun today." Sky strolled into the bedroom ahead of him. "Tom is going to be a real heartbreaker. Only four years old, but those *eye-lashes*—" She stopped as she noticed Alec standing just inside the door. "What's wrong?"

"Nothing is wrong." Nothing except that he didn't trust himself to be in a room alone with her.

"Alec, you're so tense I could snap you in two."

And she was the reason for that. "Family gatherings are stressful."

"Some family gatherings." She gave him a long look. "Not yours. Yours are fun, warm, supportive, occasionally a little intrusive but overall friendly and loving. No stress. If anyone is stressed it's them, by tiptoeing round you and trying not to mention she-who-must-not-be-named."

He inhaled sharply. "Enough." But the tone he adopted that worked like a stop sign with everyone else didn't work with her.

"Yeah, you know what? It *is* enough. You're divorced. It happened and it's done. You don't have to talk about it if you don't want to, but you do have to live your life. Are you really going to do that looking backward?"

He wondered what she'd say if he confessed that right now he wasn't thinking about his divorce. "How I live my life is no business of yours."

"I'm making it my business. I'm doing you a favor, Alec. You helped me, so now I'm helping you."

She was the sort of woman who would double any trouble a man was already in.

"I don't want your help. What I want," he said slowly, "is for you to leave this alone."

"Are you sure?" She strolled over to him, thumbs tucked into the pockets of her jeans, eyes sparkling. "Because I was thinking of taking a different approach. More 'hands-on.'"

The thought of how it would feel to have her hands on him sent a hot, torturous ache through his body.

"I don't think that's a good idea."

"Then maybe you need to change your thinking. Take a little help from a friend."

He noticed that her eyes were a deeper blue in firelight than sunlight and that her hair kinked slightly when she came in from outdoors.

"You're offering me friendship?"

"I'm offering you a little bit more than that." She gave a slow, wicked smile. "Friends with benefits."

"I seem to recall that last night you called me brooding, cynical, sarcastic and arrogant."

Her smile widened. "I think I might also have mentioned your biceps." She lifted her hand and hooked the front of his shirt with her fingers. "With a body like yours, I'm willing to ignore the flaws in your personality. This may have escaped your notice, Shipwreck Hunter, but I find you very sexy."

His blood was pounding. The atmosphere in the room was meltingly hot and heavy.

"Perhaps you're not my type."

Her smile faded but her fingers stayed locked in his shirt. "I saw a photo, Alec," she said softly. "I look like her. She's more delicate, of course, thinner, but overall there is a strong resemblance. That's why you've always been so angry around me, isn't it? You look at me and you think of her."

Right now he wasn't thinking of anything much. She was standing so close to him, his brain had virtually shut down.

"Someone showed you a photograph of Selina?"

"No. It fell out of a book I was flicking through. I'm like her."

"You're nothing like her." *And that*, he thought, *is the most dangerous aspect of the attraction.*

"You mean because she'd never threaten to put her stiletto through your balls?"

"She wouldn't be so direct."

"Is that why you're so wary?" She looked at him thoughtfully, head tilted, her gaze frank. "You never quite knew what demands she'd make, is that right?"

He sighed. "How many different ways do I have to tell you that I don't want to talk about her?"

She didn't seem to hear him. "That's why you made that comment about feeling as if you couldn't live up to her expectations. She was full of demands that you just couldn't meet. You couldn't please her, could you?"

"Are you finished?"

"No." She let go of his shirt and paced across the room and when she turned there was a frown on her face. "Being with her totally put you off relationships and, worse than that, now you never take anything at face value. A kiss can't be just a kiss. You're always looking for hidden meaning." She tapped her finger to her mouth, thinking. "She twisted you inside out, made you dance through hoops. She kept you off balance. Being with her was never soothing, or fun, it was like navigating an assault course. There were always obstacles, tasks to perform."

Her insight was unsettling. "Leave it."

"Will you answer me one question? Are you still in love with her?"

His mouth was dry. He felt more naked than he ever had with his clothes off. "I was never in love with her."

There was a long, pulsing silence.

"And that eats you up, right?" She spoke slowly. "You feel guilty about that, because you're a decent guy and you couldn't ever give her what she wanted. Be what she wanted. But no one could, Alec. You got involved with blender woman."

"Blender woman?"

"Yeah—chops you up, spins you round, makes a total mess of you until you come out completely changed from how you were when you went into the relationship. And because of that, now when you meet a woman you find attractive the first thing you wonder is whether it's worth the risk. What if you give her your number and she uses it to call you a hundred times a day? Maybe it's just sex, but what if it isn't and sleeping together gives her unrealistic expectations? You start thinking like that and pretty soon all those what-ifs act like contraception. It's not worth it."

"You're right. It's not worth it."

"Not all relationships have to be complicated, Alec. Sometimes they can be fun. Sometimes people are who they seem to be and want what they say they want. Not all women are like Selina, any more than all men are like Richard. Are you really going to live life with one eye always on the past, because I don't think you're that type of guy."

"It's called learning from your mistakes."

"It's called being a dumbass." But she was smiling and that smile snapped something inside him.

He could no longer remember why he was holding back and he crossed the room in two strides and hauled her against him. He saw her eyes grow wide and then he buried his hands in her glorious hair, and brought his mouth down on hers in an aggressive kiss. She melted into him and he felt her arms wind round his neck, dragging him closer. Her mouth opened under the fierce pressure of his and he tasted the delicious, sugar-coated flavor of her, the addictive fusion of sweetness and heat, the warmth of her breath and the erotic slide of her tongue. Desire jolted through him and she purred deep in her throat.

"I'm so glad you agree with me."

"I don't agree with you." Without lifting his mouth from hers, he yanked her shirt out of her jeans and undid the buttons. He couldn't remember ever wanting anything or anyone as badly as he wanted her. He told himself that it was because he hadn't let himself give in to the feeling, but deep down he knew it was more than that.

There was something about her—

Something—

"If you don't agree, then why are you kissing me?" She was breathless, unbalanced, her hand clamped hard on his biceps to steady herself as he stripped her shirt from her shoulders, exposing skin the color of whipped cream and dips and curves half-concealed by a lace bra.

"It's the only way I know to stop you talking." A single move of his fingers sent the bra to the same place as the shirt and he heard her gasp turn to a soft moan as he kissed her throat, her shoulder and then the swell of her breast. He lingered, teased and then drew the tip of her breast into the heat of his mouth. Her nipple hardened beneath the slow flick of his tongue and he felt her fingers lock in his hair.

"Alec—"

He transferred his mouth to her other breast, while his fingers dealt with the snap of her jeans. He eased them down over smooth skin and soft curves, feeling her shiver under the slow stroke of his hands. The elastic of her panties provided no barrier and he dispensed with those, too. The desire to bury himself deep into her perfect body was tempered by the knowledge that it would be a criminal waste to rush anything this perfect. Now that he had her naked under his hands, he wanted to savor every taste and every touch.

"Every time I look at you I see you naked. Doesn't matter if you're wearing a dress or a coat, I still see you naked. That night in the shower scarred me."

"Scarred?" Her breaths were coming in tiny pants. "Scars are bad."

"Scars are permanent. I can't get that image out of my head. I may need surgery."

They were whispering, their words as intimate as each touch and kiss they stole.

Cupping her face in his hands, he lowered his mouth to hers again, but this time his kiss was slow and gentle. He absorbed her, drank her in, demanded more, deepening the intimacy of the connection until all his senses were screaming.

His hand was on her breast and he felt the tiny tremors that affected every inch of her delicious body.

She gave a sob and he silenced it with his mouth.

"Shh." He spoke softly against her lips and eased her hair back with his hand, giving him access to her neck and throat. He kissed his way across her jaw and lower, feeling her heart in his palm.

Its frantic beat reminded him that he had to be careful.

"I don't want to hurt you."

"You won't hurt me. Your responsibility is to give me an orgasm I'll never forget. That's it. It ends there."

He tried to respond but her words had blown all the circuits in his brain.

He was so focused on her he'd forgotten that he was still fully clothed until he felt her hands fumbling with the buttons of his shirt, tugging in a feverish attempt to gain access. He brought his mouth back to hers, kissing her deeply as he covered her hands with his and helped her finish the job.

And then he was naked, too, just as he'd been in the shower that night, only this time there was no distance between them. She wound herself closer, pressing against the rigid thickness of his erection, her thigh sliding against his.

"You're beautiful." He nudged her back to the bed until she lost her balance and would have fallen if he hadn't been holding her.

He lowered her onto the soft throw, covering her

with his body, his muscles bunching as he shifted to protect her from taking his full weight.

She moaned and he transferred his mouth back to hers, silencing her with a kiss.

"You can't make a sound. If my parents hear us, they'll be booking the church." He felt her nails dig into his shoulders.

"I—"

"Silent sex. Can you do that?" He wasn't sure he could do that but she looked at him, eyes huge and a little unfocused. Then she nodded.

"Yes." She murmured the word against his mouth. "Yes. Anything. Alec, I want— I need you to—"

"Not yet. If we're doing this, then we're doing it my way." He slid his hand down her body, between her thighs and felt her lift and push against his fingers in desperate pleading. She was silken and soft and now he was the one struggling not to make a sound. Sliding his fingers deep, he felt her clamp down on him and muffled his own groan in her neck.

Then he slid lower, kissing his way down her body, hearing her breathing go shallow as he parted her and used his mouth in an intimate exploration that left her shivering. He stroked, licked, tortured and tormented, keeping her pinned there with his hands while he took what he wanted. She writhed against his firm grip but still she made no sound, not even when he brought her close to the edge. He knew she was close, could feel those telltale tremors with his mouth and fingers, and kept her there, poised for the fall, denying her the release she wanted.

She squirmed and twisted in the grip of delicious

agony. "Alec—" She whispered his name softly in the semidarkness. "Alec—"

"Yeah, I know." His voice sounded disembodied in the darkness and he eased up her body, reached into the nightstand and found what he wanted.

She wound her legs round him in pure invitation and he entered her with a series of slow, rhythmic thrusts that brought a cry to her lips.

He smothered it with his hand, then his lips, their mouths welded together as he drove himself deep. He was surrounded by her, engulfed, and he stilled, overwhelmed by the feel of her, unable to move or think.

She was soft, tight, and thick waves of syrupy pleasure washed over him, drowning him.

His mind blanked.

"Alec?" She eased her mouth from his and whispered his name, her hand on his face, tracing his jaw as if she was discovering him for the first time. "Alec—"

He dragged himself back from the edge of oblivion and heard her soft gasp as he rocked deeper inside her.

"Am I hurting you?"

"No." She wrapped her legs around him and licked at his lips. "Don't stop."

Her hips urged him to move and he withdrew slightly and surged into her again, driving the breath from his lungs.

If sex had ever felt like this before then he couldn't remember it.

She closed her eyes and he paused, even though it cost him.

"Look at me."

Her eyes opened and she stared at him without focus. "Alec—"

"Maybe this is just sex—maybe simple does exist—" he breathed the words against her mouth "—but I want you to know who you're with."

"I know who I'm with." Her gaze was locked on his, her eyes fierce. "Do you really think I don't know who I'm with?"

Without breaking the connection, he surged into her and felt her breathing change.

Dimly he heard the sound of a footstep outside the door and he slammed his hand on her mouth and stilled, his body buried deep inside hers.

Her eyes were wide, her body trembling with need and he replaced his hand with his mouth and muffled every breath and every gasp. It took all his control but he kept his rhythm slow and easy, even though there was nothing slow and easy about the feelings that went with it. They ripped through him, tearing at his flesh and his control. He felt her body move under his and knew she was feeling it, too.

And still they kept the connection. Eyes locked. Mouths together. Joined in every possible way.

Pleasure built, expanded and he felt her breathing change as she finally reached that peak. This time he did nothing to suspend the pleasure. He felt her ripple around him, the sensuous pulses of her body gripping his shaft and sending him over the edge. They kissed all the way through it, through every pulsing wave, every slick thrust, locked intimately together, so that he felt every part of her, experienced every bit of what she was experiencing. And she gave everything. Held nothing back, drawing him in with her mouth, her hands, her body.

Emerging from the most ferocious, blinding climax of his life, he knew that whatever this was, it sure as hell wasn't uncomplicated sex.

CHAPTER TEN

"THANK YOU FOR a wonderful weekend." Sky leaned forward and hugged Suzanne tightly, wondering why leaving felt so hard when she'd only met Alec's family a few days earlier. "I can't remember ever having a better time." She felt Suzanne hug her back, sensed the strength of her arms and breathed in the scent of baking. She felt a pang knowing that she probably wouldn't see Suzanne and the rest of the family again.

"Come back and visit us again soon." Suzanne cleared her throat and stepped back. "Alec, you must bring her—we always love seeing your friends."

Knowing that the chances of Alec ever bringing her to his home again were about as likely as a white Christmas in the Caribbean, Sky stepped forward and hugged Olivia.

"Come and visit me in New York."

"Are you serious?" Liv looked as if she'd been handed Christmas and birthday in one package. "When?"

Alec sighed. "Liv—"

"You're welcome anytime." She and Alec finished their goodbyes, patted the dogs for the last time and then climbed into the car for the drive back to London.

The doors closed and his arm brushed against hers. Heat rushed across her skin and her breath caught.

That was all it took.

A simple touch.

The brush of his arm.

When they'd driven here from London the car had felt spacious and roomy, but now it felt small.

And it shouldn't. She'd promised him a night of simple sex. No complications. No hidden anything.

Things shouldn't feel different.

That wasn't supposed to happen.

But for some reason last night had brought a new intimacy, a heavy awareness that thickened the air and altered the dynamic between them.

And suddenly she didn't want the visit to end.

She wanted to stay here with him. She wanted to go for long walks with the dogs, talk to him and make love in front of the fire and she felt a rush of panic because she wasn't supposed to want any of those things.

He glanced toward her. "Are we going to talk about it?" His low, rich tone was thickened by words that hadn't been spoken.

"No. Last night was all about action, not words."

There was nothing she could say that wouldn't freak him out.

She stared straight ahead, trying to get her thoughts under control, telling herself that her feelings were natural. Alec had helped her at the lowest point in her life. Over the past few days she'd escaped from the real world, taken time out, and now she was going to have to face it all again. Richard, her parents—

It was hardly surprising she felt this way.

It didn't mean anything.

They had nothing in common except sexual chemistry, and that would die a death soon enough.

"I know that's what we said." His voice was quiet. Patient. *Kind.* "But are you sure you're all right?"

She felt her heart expand in her chest.

She was 100 percent sure the last thing he wanted was to talk about what had happened, but being Alec he would still ask.

And there was no way she would take advantage of that.

It was important, no, *crucial*, that he didn't know how she was feeling.

"I'm tired. I'm wondering if your mother put two and two together and got sixty-nine." The joke came easily and she saw him shake his head.

"You're shameless. How did I not know that about you?" But he was smiling and she was smiling, too, because being with him felt so good even if it wasn't supposed to.

There was an easy intimacy that hadn't been there before.

Maybe that was what having sex in a multitude of different positions did for you.

"Your mom wants happy-ever-after for you badly. I don't want to make things worse for you by giving her false hope. I don't want to break her heart by telling her I'm just using her little boy for sex."

That's all it was, she reminded herself. Sex. She was on the rebound, and in a way he was, too. Two wounded souls finding comfort.

"*Little* boy?"

She settled back in her seat, smiling. "Thank you, Alec."

"You're welcome. Although I seem to remember it was your idea."

She gave a gurgle of laughter. "Not that. I wasn't thanking you for sex."

"What then?"

"All of it. For not leaving me on my own in London, for staying with me when I was vulnerable, for bringing me here. You were there for me at my lowest point and I'll never forget that." She paused, her wicked streak rising to the surface. "And thank you also for the best sex I've ever had in my life. I won't forget that, either." She gripped the seat as the car swerved across the road. Fortunately they were the only ones on it. "Black ice?"

"No—" his teeth were clenched "—you, in the front seat, talking dirty."

"I wasn't talking dirty exactly. I just wanted to tell you it was the best sex I've ever had."

"Well, don't."

She glanced at Alec's profile and saw that his jaw was clenched. "You're very tense. Are *you* all right?"

"I was fine until we started talking about sex."

"We're not allowed to talk about sex? Is that a British thing? We can do it, but we can't discuss it?"

"No, it's an I'm-turned-on-and-if-you-don't-want-me-to-crash-the-car-you'd-better-shut-up thing."

"You're turned on?" She heard his sharply indrawn breath.

"Sky—"

"How turned on?"

"Enough that I'm going to dump you in the snow any moment."

"Alone, or will you be coming, too?"

He overtook a tractor, his hands tight on the wheel. "You find this amusing, don't you?"

"A little, but mostly I find it flattering."

"You're flattered that I want to dump you in the snow?"

"I'm flattered because you want me and you don't want to want me. I've unsettled you. And it takes a lot to unsettle you because you're pretty controlled, Shipwreck Hunter." On impulse she leaned across and kissed his cheek, feeling the roughness of his jaw under her lips. "Thank you for the compliment."

"It wasn't—"

"Yes, it was. Don't spoil it. Now shut up and drive." Smiling, she settled back in her seat. "I'll be back on Puffin Island at some point over the next couple of weeks. If you feel like indulging your voracious sexual appetite in another no-strings-attached naked workout at any point, let me know. I'm your woman. On a temporary basis, obviously."

Oh, shut up, Sky!

She should have just let it go. Allowed it to turn into their secret, something they never discussed again. He was going to think she was pushing for something more.

"You're coming to Puffin Island?"

"Of course. My friends live there, remember? I visit all the time. This time I think I'm staying with Brittany. Relax. I promise not to send you loving looks or tell them we used up a whole box of condoms in one night."

"You'll tell them. You tell each other everything, but maybe you could skip over the condom part."

"Why? You don't want them to know you scored straight As for stamina?"

He swore under his breath. "Sky—"

"Calm down, Alec. I'm teasing you. And I don't know if, or what, I'll tell them but it's irrelevant really because they are going to know within two minutes of meeting me from the plane."

"You're planning on engraving 'I had sex with Alec in multiple positions' on your forehead?"

"You took me home with you. If you think they're going to let that gesture pass without comment, you don't know them. Don't worry, if it comes to it I'll give them top-line info but I won't tell them the really intimate stuff."

"Well, that's good to know." His dry tone made her smile.

"I wouldn't mention—you know—"

"I do not know."

"Yes, you do. That thing you do—that thing that made me—"

He sighed. "I used to think I wanted honesty, now I'm not so sure."

Her smile faded as she saw the tension in his shoulders. "Do you regret what we did?"

"No, but I'd rather the details of our encounter didn't become the topic of conversation in Harbor Stores."

She laughed. "I can just imagine Hilda saying, 'Seems like our resident professor has been studying more than dusty books.' And Zach and Ryan will tease you in that cute guy way."

"That cute guy way that ends in me giving them both black eyes and throwing them off the dock?"

"Yes, that way." She settled deeper in her seat. "I love the whole bromance thing."

"Bromance?"

"Yes, male bonding. Richard didn't really have that. It should have been an alarm bell for me. I like people who care about their friends. You, Zach and Ryan have a great bond."

Alec rolled his eyes. "There is no bonding."

"And that's part of it, pretending there's no bonding. Pretending that you don't give a damn about each other. Cute."

"It's not cute, it's manly." But there was a smile in his voice and she smiled, too.

"So when we get back to London, you're dropping me at my hotel—and then what?"

"I go back to my hotel." He kept his eyes fixed on the road but she saw his hands tighten on the wheel.

Her heart thudded a little harder. "So each of us goes to bed separately."

"That's the idea."

"I'll be naked. And alone. I hope I don't get cold."

"For—" He pulled off the road into a gateway by a field and yanked on the hand brake. Then he put his hand behind her head and pulled her mouth to his.

Whatever she'd expected it hadn't been this.

Nothing prepared her for the scalding heat of his kiss or the power of her response.

"Oh, God, Alec—"

She'd been kissed plenty of times before and she'd assumed that over the years she'd experienced the whole range from playful to passionate. But this was something different, and she knew that what they'd shared had ripped away some of the insulation he'd used to protect himself from the world. From women.

Alec unleashed, she thought and melted into it.

He licked deep into her mouth, the erotic stroke of

his tongue creating an electrifying, intoxicating rush of sensation that swept over her in waves. He kissed her until her limbs weakened and she knew that if she'd been standing, she would have fallen.

Unbalanced, she closed her hand over his biceps and felt the solid swell of muscle under the soft wool of his clothing.

She was so desperate to touch him that she slid her other hand under his sweater, yanking his shirt out of his jeans. Then her hand was running down the smooth skin of his stomach, and she felt the ripple of muscle and tendon against her burning palm, before she lowered her hand to the thick ridge pressing through the fabric. As she closed her hand around him, he groaned and dragged his mouth from hers.

"We're not supposed to be doing this."

Dizzy with longing she tried to focus. "What?"

"One night, you said." He growled the words, his gaze on her mouth. "This wasn't supposed to happen."

"It hasn't happened. It's still just the one time. Or five times. Six if you count—"

"Shut up." He released her and gave her a searing look. "If you don't stop talking I'll—"

"You'll what?"

"I'll do something that is going to get us both arrested. Do you want to spend Christmas in a police cell?"

"That depends." She loved talking with him, the banter, the fun. It was something she'd never been able to do with Richard. "Would you be there? Would they make us wear clothes?"

His eyes gleamed and he twisted the rope of her

hair into his hand and pulled her face back to his. "Are you going to stop talking anytime soon?"

"I can try, but I don't want to make promises I may not be able to keep. Talking is one of my favorite things. You'd better just drop me off at my hotel room and leave me there. Then I can talk to myself and sing while I'm naked in the shower and I won't be bothering anyone."

"Do you want to swap seats and drive back to London?"

"Sit on the wrong side of the car and drive on the wrong side of the road in snow? I don't think so."

"Then sit still, keep your eyes forward and your hands in your lap, do *not* speak or interact with me in any way and I will try to drive us there without incident." He eased away from her and shook his head slightly.

His self-discipline fascinated her. "Define 'interact'—"

"You're interacting right now."

"Sorry." She decided that "interacting" with Alec could easily become one of her favorite pastimes. "You're very tense."

"That tends to happen when a woman tries to seduce me when I'm driving in snow and ice."

"Er, you were the one who pulled off the road and kissed me. I was minding my own business—"

"You were telling me you'd be naked."

"Well, you've already seen me naked, Alec, from pretty much every angle, so that really shouldn't be enough for you to risk blowing out a tire and having to call a tow truck."

"I said 'no talking.'"

"I'm silent. Not a word. I'm taking a vow of silence until we reach London."

"Good. You can start right after you cancel your hotel room."

It took a moment for the words to sink in and when they did she assumed she'd misheard him. "What?"

"You heard me."

"Where will I sleep?"

"You won't be sleeping. You'll be in a state of active wakefulness. Make the call."

Her chest felt tight and her breathing was shallow.

There were a thousand reasons why what he was suggesting was a bad idea.

She ignored them all and pulled out her phone. Hands shaking, she canceled the hotel room she'd booked for the night. She was desperately aware of him, of the hard jut of his thigh close to hers, the power of his arms as he gripped the wheel and guided them back toward the road.

Intimacy, she thought, was a strange thing.

Not once, in all the time she'd spent with Richard, had she felt as close to him as she did now to Alec.

"So we're going for another night." She kept her voice casual. "Just as long as you know this is just sex. You don't want to go falling in love with me, because I'm a real heartbreaker in case you hadn't heard. And whatever you do don't try to propose to me because you could easily end up with a stiletto in your balls and you wouldn't want *that*."

She risked a glance at him and saw the corners of his mouth flicker as he struggled not to smile.

She wondered how she could ever have thought him humorless.

"We both know you're not a heartbreaker. You believe in one true love and happy endings. You're my nightmare."

"No, I'm not, because while I'm waiting for that to come along I believe in hot sex." She beamed at him. "Lots of it. Which in fact makes me your daydream, not your nightmare."

His jaw tightened. "You should stop talking now."

"You don't really think I'd fall in love with a moody, brooding guy like you, do you? Please. Give me *some* credit. I'll read about Heathcliff but I don't want to have to look at his scowling face while I'm eating my breakfast cereal every morning. I'm now going to sleep so that I conserve my energy, so when you stop to buy condoms make sure you buy a bumper pack. If we've only got one more night together we have to cram as much sex in as possible."

Sex, she reminded herself.

That's what this was about.

Simple, straightforward, scorching sex.

What could possibly go wrong?

ALEC MADE A call and pulled some strings, telling himself that his decision was more to do with practicalities than a desire to fulfill one of Sky's wishes. If they stayed in the hotel room there was a strong chance they'd both be rushed to the emergency department with exhaustion and no doubt Michael would be on duty and would find a way to relay the happy news to his family.

"Where are we going?"

"You'll find out when we get there."

"It's a surprise? Will I like it? I love surprises.

I mean, not the 'public proposal' type of surprise, but pretty much any other sort works for me." Skylar snuggled in the back of the taxi they'd just hailed down, her cheeks glowing. "Do you need to blindfold me or anything?"

He pushed aside the images her words created in his head. "I don't need to blindfold you, and if I told you where we were going, it wouldn't be a surprise."

"Should I close my eyes? Would that make it more exciting?" She was laughing, teasing him, and her fizz and bounce revved up every one of his senses.

"Keep your eyes open."

"Give me a clue. Is it somewhere I've been before? Somewhere I've mentioned?"

"Maybe."

"The London Eye?" She leaned forward, craning her neck to look upward, as the taxi pulled up close to the river. "Wow. You did this for me?"

Seeing the delight on her face, he wondered if he'd done the wrong thing.

Was this an over-the-top gesture? What sort of night out was right for two people who were having simple sex?

She leaned across and gave him a spontaneous hug. "Thanks, Alec. When you're not being a dumbass, you're the best."

"You just managed to insult me and praise me in the same sentence."

"This has been on my wish list for a long time. You listened, paid attention and arranged something you knew I'd like. That's thoughtful."

"For a dumbass. We had to do something, so I thought it might as well be this." He played it down as he leaned forward to pay the driver, then took her hand and ignored the line of people waiting.

"We're line jumping?"

"I know someone." And he'd paid a small fortune, but he didn't tell her that. But it was worth it to see her face when she discovered that they had the capsule to themselves.

"Just us? And champagne?" The doors closed and she turned to look at him, a strange look on her face. "Alec Hunter, you are the king of surprises. This is easily the best Christmas I've ever had."

He handed her a glass of champagne. "And technically it isn't even Christmas yet."

"I'm pretending it is, because real Christmas is going to be a total crapfest." She strolled round the capsule. "Where do I stand for the best view?"

"It doesn't matter. The view is different from all angles. Experiment."

"On my own?" She turned her head, and threw him a smile. "Are you going to experiment with me? Has anyone ever had sex in one of these?"

"Only you would ask that question." He wondered what it was about her that made him contemplate something that would undoubtedly get them both arrested. "I don't know. And don't take that as a challenge."

She lifted her glass. "Happy holidays. You have no idea how envious I am of you spending Christmas on Puffin Island with our friends. Spare a thought for me making small talk with the upper echelons of New York society."

"You could refuse to go."

She stared into the glass, watching the bubbles

rise. "I can't even imagine how that would look. My parents would probably never speak to me again. They're my family. And they're not perfect, but—" she shrugged and drank her champagne "—in their own very controlling way they do love me. I know it's not going to be anyone's idea of a perfect Christmas but it's the one I've got, so it's best not to think about it. Suck it up, that's what I tell myself. And now let's forget it. I want to enjoy this moment, not worry about that one."

He didn't want to forget it. "What is your idea of a perfect Christmas?"

She turned her head and stared through the glass at the carpet of lights beneath them. "A Christmas where I can be myself, around people I already know and love. I want laughter and conversation, not serious faces and polite small talk. I want—" She tilted her head back and smiled. "I want surprises, adventure, small, thoughtful gestures, no agenda, no reason to be gathering, except to enjoy each other's company. I want a Christmas where duty isn't allowed in the room, and yes, I want gifts, not empty boxes. Not expensive but thoughtful. Perfect gifts that show someone has thought about who I am and what I'd love."

There was a pause.

"So you don't want much then."

She laughed, as he'd known she would, and focused on the view. "This is incredible."

"It's just a giant Ferris wheel."

"That's like saying Hawaii is just a bunch of islands."

"Hawaii is a bunch of islands."

All the time they were talking Alec was imagining her surrounded by perfectly wrapped empty boxes, making small talk in a crowd of people she didn't know.

She was dreading it, but still she had that smile on her face.

She was the most resilient person he'd ever met.

He guided her to the front of the capsule and stood behind her, caging her as she gazed through the glass at the city below. "This is my favorite view. Are you warm enough?"

"Not really, but that's because I went for silk and lace rather than thermal. But you already know that of course. Having peeled off my underwear piece by piece a few hours ago."

"I remember the underwear." But most of all he remembered the woman. He eased her against him and wrapped her in the folds of his coat.

"You don't have to cuddle me. That's not part of our deal."

"I'm protecting my investment. I don't mind being adventurous in bed but I draw the line at having sex with a frozen object."

"When I'm trapped making small talk with some boring banker from Manhattan, I'm going to remember tonight."

He was fairly sure the banker wouldn't be bored and the thought elevated his tension levels a few more notches. "Because tonight was the night you developed frostbite?" He felt her curves mold against him as she drew closer.

"It's worth a little frostbite to have this view." She pulled the folds of his coat around her, snuggling closer. "I love your coat. You wore it the night of my show and when you walked in I thought you looked like a highwayman."

He wondered what she'd say if he confessed he was considering stealing her away from bankers and any other men her parents might consider suitable replacements for Richard. "You're saying I look like a criminal."

"I'm saying you look sexy and badass in all that black." She gazed out across the city. Beneath them the River Thames wound like a lazy serpent through decades of history, hiding a thousand secrets in its murky depths. "This is awesome. I feel like Aladdin on his magic carpet."

He breathed deeply and eased away from her slightly. "Just as long as you know that the thing you're rubbing isn't a lamp. Do you always spin reality into fantasy?"

"Who says it's fantasy? Maybe it's just a different way of looking at things." She leaned her head against the glass. "Some people might look out of this window and see a city at night, but half close your eyes and tell me what you see, Alec."

Right now he couldn't see anything through the red mist of raw lust.

He could smell the scent of her and feel her slender form pressed against him. "I see buildings. Lights people haven't bothered to turn off. I see an eco nightmare and an oasis of global warming."

She gave a gurgle of laughter. "No, you're telling me what you know is there. Look again and tell me what you *see*."

Her laugh was like the rest of her. Unrestrained and honest.

Dragging his eyes from her hair, he looked across darkness and shimmering light.

"I see thousands of years of history. Romans, Vikings, William the Conqueror. I see rape, pillage and plunder."

"Ugh. You're warped." She shuddered. "Trust you to spoil a lovely view with grisly facts."

He rested his chin on the top of her head. "Now it's your turn. Tell me what you see. You're the artist."

"I see diamonds and pearls, onyx and obsidian. I see secrets and wild affairs, a beautiful woman dancing at a masked ball—"

"Presumably not with her husband."

"Why not her husband?"

"Because she's disguising herself. If she was dancing with her husband, she wouldn't wear a mask. She doesn't want to be recognized."

"Or maybe she's adding some excitement to their lives. She's loyal, she loves him, but they're pretending they're strangers." She presented the alternate scenario then turned her head and looked in a different direction. "I love this so much. I'm so glad you brought me—that I didn't miss this—"

He didn't want to be charmed but he was, and looking up, he realized that so were a group of men in suits in the capsule above them who seemed more taken with Skylar than London.

Frowning, Alec shifted his position so that he obstructed their view.

Her infectious enthusiasm combined with her ravishing beauty made her the object of attention from every unattached male who passed within range of her sunbeam smile.

She didn't seem to notice. "Thank you, Alec." She turned that sunbeam smile on him. "This was a brilliant idea."

He pulled her against him. "Come back with me." He hadn't planned to say it. Hadn't even acknowledged that he was thinking it. It was a crazy idea.

"To the hotel? Of course. I don't have anywhere else to stay since you made me cancel my room."

"Not to the hotel. To Puffin Island. Forget New York."

She eased away from him. "I am coming back to Puffin Island. I already told you—"

"Not next week, tomorrow. I'll book you on my flight to Boston. We'll travel together."

"Brittany isn't expecting me until next week."

"You won't be staying with Brittany."

Her beautiful eyes widened. "Just to be clear, you're suggesting—"

"Yes."

There was a long, pulsing silence and she curled her hand into the front of his coat. "You're inviting me to stay with you? That's…big. I've never even been to your house on the island. You never invited me before."

He'd never invited anyone apart from his friend Ryan. It was a safe, protected space where he could work undisturbed.

"I'm inviting you now." He stroked his fingers over her hair. It fascinated him, shades of platinum and white gold, like the precious metals she used to make her jewelry. "Can I tempt you back to my lair?"

There was a light in her eyes, a brightness that hadn't been there before. "Why?"

The question froze him.

"Because I don't think you should go back to New York on your own. What if Richard shows up?"

"So you're doing this to protect me from Richard?" Her voice was gentle, her eyebrows raised in question. "Thank you, but I don't need you to make that sacrifice. I'll handle Richard."

"Sky—"

"If there's another reason you'd like me to come back with you, like sex for example, or because I make you laugh, then obviously I'd consider it, but I won't come with you just because you want to protect me."

"Sex is another reason." His mouth was dry. "It's the main reason. And you do make me laugh."

Since when did he have trouble speaking? He spoke fluently to the camera on a regular basis but with Sky's blue eyes fixed on his he wasn't sure he could voice his own name without multiple takes.

"So—Richard isn't the reason, sex is the reason?"

"Yes. I want more simple, uncomplicated sex. I don't want anything else. And if that sounds selfish it's because I *am* selfish. I won't change. I want to be clear about that. I could break your heart."

"Or I could break yours." She looked at him and smiled. "Alternatively, we might part physically exhausted but completely intact. You don't need to spell out terms and conditions, but you want me to know that you're thinking with your penis?"

He felt heat break over his skin and was relieved he'd arranged to have the capsule to themselves. "Possibly. Probably."

"That's good. Your penis makes good, honest decisions. I'll vote for it in the next election."

Smiling, he lowered his head so that his mouth was next to her ear. "What the hell are we doing, Sky?"

She didn't answer for a moment and then she rose on tiptoe, turned her head and kissed him gently on the mouth. "I think it's called 'having fun.' Merry Christmas, Alec."

CHAPTER ELEVEN

AFTER A COUPLE of long flights, Alec and Skylar landed at Logan Airport and took a private plane to Puffin Island.

The pilot was Zachary Flynn. He eyed the pair of them cautiously as they walked across the tarmac, as if he couldn't quite believe he was seeing them together.

Sky couldn't quite believe it, either.

She kept expecting Alec to tell her he'd changed his mind.

"Hurry up," Zach growled, "there's bad weather coming our way. Unless you want to be stranded on the wrong side of the water, we need to leave now."

"There's always bad weather. This is Maine in December. And you can pretty much fly in anything, so stop being a grouch. Good to see you." Sky reached up and kissed his cheek. "Thank you for meeting us, Zach. You're the best."

He took her face in his hands and angled it, examining the bruise. His eyes darkened. "If I ever meet him—"

"It wasn't him, it was me," she said hastily, "and I'm good, thanks. Really good."

To her surprise, Zach, rarely demonstrative, pulled her into a tight hug. "I never would have voted for him. You were right to dump his sorry ass." He muttered the words into her ear and she smiled into his shoulder and eased away.

She loved her friends. "I think so."

Zach nodded to Alec. "I hear you rescued her. Nice work."

Sky hoisted her bag onto her shoulder. "Excuse *me*, he did not rescue me, I rescued mys—"

"She rescued herself." Alec finished her sentence and hefted their cases into the plane. "I provided backup. Let's do this before we ditch in the frozen ocean."

They strapped themselves in for the short flight over the bay to Puffin Island.

The bay, always crowded with boats in the summer months, was mostly empty. She knew that only the hardiest of fishermen worked their lobster traps in the winter. Ahead of her the ocean stretched forever into the horizon.

Home, she thought. It felt like home. So many of her favorite memories featured this island. Long, happy days on the beach searching for sea glass, relaxed, cozy evenings talking around the kitchen table while Brittany's grandmother cooked at the stove.

Beneath her she saw the forest, now white with snow, saw tiny inlets and rocky shores.

Puffin Island.

Zach executed a perfect landing and moments later Sky was standing on the tarmac, shivering in the bitter wind.

"Holy crap, this is so much colder than London."

Zach handed Alec a set of keys. "Your car is in the car park, delivered as requested. Are you going to drop Sky at the cottage or do you want me to give her a ride? Brittany is out choosing paint with Emily but she won't be long. They're fixing up Doug Mitchell's old place on Main Street so Emily can start setting up her shop."

Alec raised his eyebrows. "I bet he's charging her a small fortune in rent."

"Don't you believe it." Sky swung her bag over her shoulder. "Emily looks sweet, but she negotiates so hard you're lucky if you don't lose layers of skin along with the clothes on your back. She'll leave Doug bleeding. And thanks for the offer, Zach, but I'm not staying at the cottage. I'll call Brit later. If there is decorating to be done, I want to be there."

And this time she needn't worry about Richard phoning, making her feel guilty for being there.

Zach's eyes narrowed. "I assumed you'd be staying with us."

"Not this time."

Alec picked up his suitcase. "She's staying with me."

"Right." Zach absorbed that without comment. "In that case, you can both join us for dinner. That's if they've cleared the roads enough for you to make it over to us without landing in a ditch."

Skylar loved hearing the "us." Zach had lived his life alone for so long that hearing him use the word so naturally warmed her. "Dinner sounds good. Thank you."

They parted company and Alec took the coast road that wound along the west side of the island.

"It's a different place in the winter. Every bit as beautiful, but different." Sky huddled in her seat, looking at the landscape. The familiar now seemed unfamiliar, snow altered shapes and blurred edges, softening the sharp and obliterating dips and curves. Landmarks disappeared, as if winter was playing an elaborate game of hide-and-seek. "Is your house warm?"

"Yes, but I'm sure we'll find ways of generating heat, don't worry."

She felt her skin prickle with awareness. "Do you mind having dinner with Brittany? I should have checked with you."

"You mean because she's going to take you to one side and demand every detail? That's your problem." He slowed as they approached a bend. "I'm not the one answering the questions."

"Do you think it will feel awkward, because we've all been friends a long time?" Except for her and Alec. And that was the irony. Out of the six of them, theirs had been the most difficult relationship. "I wouldn't want to damage that."

"It won't be awkward."

The road crested and beneath her in the distance she could see the familiar curve of Shell Bay, with Castaway Cottage nestled just beyond the beach.

Winter, summer, spring or fall, it was a special place.

Instead of continuing down, Alec took a sharp left. The road narrowed and steepened and on the headland she could see the lighthouse that had guarded this part of the island for centuries. To the right of it, sheltered by a dip in the coastline, were two fishermen's cottages that had weathered the wild Atlantic weather.

"What an amazing position. How did you find this place?"

"The owners moved back to the mainland and Brittany mentioned that it was empty. She knew I was looking for somewhere around here."

"It's remote."

"That's the idea." He sent her a look. "Is that going to be a problem?"

"No. With any luck we'll be snowed in. We'd have to stay in bed and rub our naked bodies together to keep warm." She leaned forward and looked at the cottage, intrigued. "You converted it?"

"I did some of the work, not all of it." He pulled up. "I'm glad they cleared the snow, otherwise we would have been facing a few hours of hard labor before we could reach the front door."

She looked at the banks of snow and the steep narrow road behind them. "This place is perfect for tobogganing."

He switched off the engine. "I'd never thought of it."

"Seriously? You are surrounded by slopes, and you don't immediately want to slide down them? Now I know what I'm buying you for Christmas."

"I own cross-country skis and a snowmobile."

"I've never been on a snowmobile. Let's do that. But first I need to buy a thicker jacket." She slid out of the car, her teeth chattering against the bitter cold. "Better unlock that door fast, Hunter, or it's going to be like having sex with a icicle."

He hauled their cases out of the car and paused to empty the mailbox. "Do you ever think about anything other than sex?"

"Hey, that's what you brought me here for, remember? I'm simply sticking to the job description. Think of me as an eco-friendly heat source."

He tucked a wedge of envelopes under his arm and gave a faint smile. "I'm starting to hope we're going to get snowed in."

"Yeah, me, too. We should have dropped in to Harbor Stores and stocked up on emergency supplies."

"I keep a good stock of emergency supplies, keep the car filled with gas and have studded snow tires." He carried the cases to the cottage and then delved in his pocket for the keys. "There's backup power and I always have at least one cell phone on charge. It pays to be prepared. Learned that lesson after my first winter here."

"What about condoms?"

He dropped the keys in the snow. "Sorry?"

"Do you have emergency supplies of condoms? If we're snowed in for several days, demand would be high." She watched with a grin as he found the keys. "I hope we're not going to disturb your neighbors."

"My nearest neighbor is a mile away." He opened the door. "She's eighty."

"So we can abandon the whole silent sex thing?" She stepped onto the flagstone floor of the entryway and paused. "It's not two cottages, it's one."

"It was two. The person before me knocked two of them together. I made a few changes to let in more light."

She walked around, enchanted. "It's wonderful, Alec. It's original and beautiful and the view—" She explored without being invited and almost drooled when she walked into the garden room. Floor-to-ceiling glass flooded the room with light and beyond the windows there was nothing but the sea and the sky. "North light. It's north light. I might never leave." She spoke without thinking and winced, wishing that her mouth didn't run away from her. "It's perfect for painting. Don't be freaked out. I'm in love with your house, not you."

Was he freaked out? It was impossible to tell because his handsome face revealed nothing.

"Most people find it too isolated."

"By 'most people' do you mean your ex-wife?"

"No. She never came here. I bought it after the divorce."

To escape from the world. "It *is* isolated. But that's part of its charm. I can't wait to get out there and explore. Shall we do that right now before we unpack? It would be fun! You can show me around. We can build a snowman. Maybe toboggan—"

"If we're going over to Castaway Cottage later we should probably unpack first." He strolled back through to the kitchen and put the mail down on the counter. "The bedroom is upstairs. And the bathroom. Make yourself at home."

She watched as he flung his coat over the back of a chair and thought absently that Richard never would have done that. He would have reached for a hanger to preserve the shape of the coat. The irony was that Richard, who gave so much thought to what he was going to wear and the impact of his appearance on those around him, didn't come close to having Alec's physical presence or charisma. He worked hard on something that to Alec came naturally.

She picked up her bag and carried it up the narrow

staircase. The first door she opened led to a study. Three of the walls were covered in floor-to-ceiling bookshelves, crammed with books of all shapes and sizes. Biographies as thick as her arm, novels with their spines creased, travel guides, books on history and archaeology. The floor acted as an overflow, with books stacked to hip height. In all she guessed there were enough books to fill a small library.

Under the window, facing out over the sea, was a desk strewn with papers, more books and pens. A pair of glasses lay abandoned on a thick pad of paper.

Here, in this space, she remembered how smart Alec was and felt a flicker of insecurity.

He was seriously academic, like her parents.

Alec walked in behind her. “I should have warned you not to come in here. It’s a mess. When I’m working on a book or a paper I don’t throw anything away until it’s done.”

“I’m the same. I like to keep all my ideas, even the terrible ones, until the final designs are approved. Then I have a ritual throwing-out session.”

He stared at her for a moment. “The garden room is yours while you’re staying with me. I rarely go in there.”

There was a tension about him that hadn’t been there earlier and she wondered if she’d said something wrong.

His phone rang and she smiled.

“Answer that. I’ll just nose around.” She moved toward the window, trying not to listen, although it was quickly obvious he was talking to his mother.

“I was going to call you… Yes, home safely. Just now. We have power although I doubt that will last long, looking at the forecast… Yes, the generator will still be working—" He paused, listening. "Yes, I'm sure she had a safe journey, too… Speak to you soon."

Sky put down a biography she'd picked up. "You didn't tell them I was coming here with you?"

"No. If I told them you were here, my mother's hopes would be soaring into the stratosphere only to plummet down to earth when she realizes this isn't going anywhere. I call it a selective exchange of information."

"I need to try that." But it made her feel a little strange that he hadn't mentioned to his mother that she was here. It was a reminder that this was very temporary. "Are those glasses yours?"

"I wear them when I'm working."

"Put them on."

He raised an eyebrow. "Why?"

Smiling, she picked them up and strolled toward him. "Because I want you to be able to see what you're about to do to me."

"WHAT DO WOMEN talk about when they close the door?" Ryan loaded plates into the dishwasher. "Press your ear to the keyhole, Alec. I want to know."

"I don't. What I want to know is how we ended up doing all the clearing up." Alec sprawled at the kitchen table. "Aren't you supposed to wash the food off those before you load the dishwasher?"

"If you think you can do it better, come and do it." Ryan shoved the last of the plates into the dishwasher. "And where's the 'we' in this? I don't see you clearing up."

"I don't need to barter chores for sex."

"Excuse me?" Ryan closed the dishwasher with a crash. "You think the only way I get sex is by doing the dishes?"

"It's a proven fact that women are more receptive in the bedroom when men help in the kitchen," Alec drawled and Ryan threw him a dark look.

"Then get off your butt and help."

"Why? I don't want to havc sex with you. You're not my type."

"And to think I was looking forward to you being back on the island." Muttering under his breath, Ryan continued clearing up. "I'll have you know it takes an average of five minutes in my magnetic presence for a woman to want to strip naked."

"Spare us the details." Alec stood up and finished clearing the table, trying not to think about Skylar in the next room.

You didn't need to be a genius to guess the topic of conversation.

Dinner had been fun, the conversation light-hearted, and there had been plenty of laughter, much of it from Sky. She had an irreverent sense of humor, a wicked streak that she didn't hold back, and she laughed the way she did everything else, with her whole self.

There had been no tension, and yet he felt tense.

Alec cleared away the empty wine bottles and Ryan glanced at him.

"So Sky has moved in with you. Didn't see that one coming."

The words jarred. "She hasn't moved in with me."

Zach raised his eyebrows. "Are you sure? Because

that was a pretty big suitcase I hauled off the plane into your car."

Tension spread across Alec's shoulders and down his spine. "She's staying awhile, that's all."

And he was starting to regret the impulse that had driven him to invite her.

How did he control what a "while" looked like?

When he'd started dating Selina she'd moved her things into his London apartment without asking him.

One day he'd been living his life, and the next he'd been sharing it with another person. Gradually everything had been eroded. Space, freedom, happiness.

Ryan gave him a long look. "A while being until you've worn each other out."

"Something like that." How could he have thought this could ever be simple? The sex was spectacular, but what would they do when they weren't in bed together? One of the things he loved about Puffin Island was the peace and isolation. He was used to working late into the night, getting up when it suited him and spending time outdoors. Explaining himself to no one. Apologizing to no one.

Now Sky would be under his feet, wanting to know what they were doing, expecting him to keep regular hours, needing to be entertained…

The moment they'd walked through the door she'd started suggesting things they could do together. Build a snowman, try tobogganing—

What the hell had he been thinking?

One of the advantages of being in snowy Maine was that you were frequently cut off. He wanted to be cut off. He needed to be cut off. He had a deadline. He didn't need company.

Heat broke out on his skin.

He just had to hope she'd want to spend time with her friends.

"Why do they use so many pans when they cook?" Zach grumbled as he piled the pans in the sink. "What's wrong with using one pot for everything? Can't these go in the dishwasher?"

"It's full." Ryan picked up an apron hanging on one of the doors. "Is this yours? Brittany really has tamed you this time. Never thought I'd see you looking all domestic."

Zach swore under his breath and threw the apron over the chair.

"It's not mine. And unless you want your head dunked in a sink full of greasy water, you'd better back off."

"I'll back off if you make the coffee." Ryan opened three different cupboards in the hunt for mugs. "When Emily was staying here in the summer I knew my way around this kitchen. You've moved everything."

"Brittany had a clear out last time we were snowed in."

"Is it driving you crazy?" Alec's mouth was dry. "Being on top of each other all the time?"

Zach's eyebrows rose. "You're asking about our preferred sexual positions?"

"No!" Alec ran his hand over the back of his neck. "I'm asking whether the two of you are finding it claustrophobic living together during the winter months."

Ryan frowned. "Did you buy a seat on the plane for your bad mood, or did it come along with the baggage?"

He felt a flash of guilt. “Sorry. Work pressure.”

Ryan gave him a long look. “Yeah? You’re sure your ‘work pressure’ doesn’t have long blond hair, a loud laugh and a fantastic pair of legs?”

Alec gritted his teeth. “I’m sure.”

“Because I can see how having that around might distract a man from his job.” Ryan opened the last cupboard. “Hallelujah. Mugs.” He pulled out mugs while Alec watched, getting more stressed by the second.

“It’s not going to distract me.”

He wasn’t going to let it distract him.

“WELL, CRAP, IT WAS supposed to be your big night and that bastard Richard spoiled it.” Brittany was curled up on the sofa, a glass of wine in her hand. Her hair, oak brown, was caught in a casual ponytail. With her athletic body showcased in skinny jeans and a black sweater, she looked ready for anything the great outdoors threw at her. “It would have been better if he hadn’t shown up at all.”

“No, it wouldn’t because I finally saw things as they really were.” Sky sat on the floor in front of the flickering fire, enjoying the warmth of Castaway Cottage. How many times had she, Brittany and Emily sat here, talking through their problems? This cottage had witnessed most of the highs and lows of their lives. “I should have broken it off before.”

“Yes—” Brittany sent her a stern look “—you should. He was wrong for you.”

“You shouldn’t be passing an opinion.” Emily was quieter, less emphatic. The summer had brought huge changes to her life, but underneath she was still the same, measured person she'd always been. "What if they get back together?"

"He hit her," Brit said flatly and Sky rubbed her face with her fingers.

"He didn't hit me. But we won't be getting back together." She thought about Alec and wondered what he was doing.

He'd been quiet on the drive over.

"At least your bruise is healing." Brittany was still talking. "But if you get back together with him, we'll be forced to do an intervention. We almost did, back in the summer when he made you go home early from the beach."

Emily sighed. "Brit—"

"What? It's true. You were worried, too!"

"I know, but—"

"There is no 'but.' He tried to shrink her. Make her less than the person she is. How is that a good thing? The person you're with is supposed to support your dreams, not kill them dead." She turned back to Sky, ponytail swinging. "Did you bring chocolate? Because if you did, now would be a good time to hand it over. You know I love British chocolate and if we eventually get our coffee—" She turned her head to look at the closed door. "What are they doing in there? How long does it take to load a dishwasher?"

The person you're with is supposed to support your dreams, not kill them dead.

Sky stared at her friend. "If you felt that way, why didn't you say something?"

"I did. I texted you. I said 'Bring chocolate. Urgent.'"

"I meant why didn't you say something about Richard?" It was always the same when they were together. Parallel conversations. Comforted by the familiarity of the exchange, Sky opened her bag and pulled out the chocolate she'd bought at the airport.

"Yum, thank you." Brittany reached for it, the ring on her finger glinting in the firelight. "Your love life was none of my business."

Emily raised an eyebrow. "Since when did you develop boundaries?"

"I'm commenting on her decision retrospectively. It's different. Hey—there are some decisions you have to make by yourself. Who you get naked with is one of them. Sky was the one dating him, not me." She tore the wrapper off a bar of chocolate. "And although the relationship looked pretty toxic from the outside, no one can ever know what the inside looks like. For all I knew he might have had a magic wizarding wand or something."

Skylar snorted. "He didn't have a magic wizarding wand."

"Then there was no reason to stay with him as long as you did. Only truly memorable sex could have justified staying with a controlling shit like Richard. Coffee would go well with this chocolate. It would also wake me up. Seriously, what can they possibly be doing in there?"

Emily blinked. "Did you really just say 'magic wizarding wand'?"

"I did. And you don't need to play the prude given that you and Ryan have been tearing each other's clothes to pieces for the entire summer."

Emily turned scarlet. "There are times when I wonder how you and I ever became friends."

"And then you thank your lucky stars. Without me, you wouldn't have met Ryan. And don't tell me he isn't the best thing that has ever happened to you because I know he is. You walk round glowing." Brittany grinned. "And talking of sex, come on, Sky, spill. You and Alec are having lots of angry sex, yes?"

"Why would we be having angry sex?"

"Because over the summer the two of you were attacking each other like two rabid dogs. He was awful to you. Rude. I would have said that the two of you together would be a hot mess of disaster."

"A moment ago her love life was none of your business," Emily murmured and Brittany ate another piece of chocolate.

"That was her past love life. Her present love life is definitely my business."

"Alec was coming out of a bad divorce. Ryan told us that." And she'd never given much thought to the detail, but now she thought about it all the time.

She wanted to know why he took so much responsibility for the breakdown of his marriage.

Brittany licked her fingers. "He's pretty damaged. I don't want to see you get hurt a second time. I love him and he's definitely hot, but I'm not sure moody Alec is the best person to help you heal."

Sky thought about the past several days. "He isn't always moody."

Emily cleared up the chocolate wrapper. "He helped her when she was in trouble. That's what counts. And so what if he has a bad relationship in his past?" She defended him. "He's not the first person to make a mistake."

"And you would know, because before Ryan there

was boring Neil." Brittany shot her a look and then turned back to Sky. "What I want to know is how you went from breaking up with Richard and knocking yourself half- unconscious to getting into bed with Alec. It didn't sound like a romantic situation from here."

"It wasn't romantic. First I bled all over him, then I threw up."

Brittany gave a laugh. "What wouldn't I have given to see that. I bet he made a rapid exit."

"He didn't." Sky stared into her glass. "He sat with me."

There was silence.

Emily exchanged looks with Brittany.

"Well, damn. He sat with you while you were ill?" Brittany stared at her. "You're kidding."

"I'm not kidding."

"You mean he sat on the edge of the bath and watched you from the opposite corner of the room?"

"No, I mean he sat next to me and held me."

"Okay, this isn't just sex." The chocolate lay abandoned in her lap. "Any man who doesn't run for cover when you're ill is a keeper."

Sky sighed. "He isn't a keeper, but he *was* kind."

"And he took you home to his family."

"Because he didn't want to leave me alone in London with a head injury."

"So he took you home to his family and—what then?"

"They thought we were together. It was—" Sky sighed "—awkward. Why are you laughing?"

"Because then you *did* get together, which is kind of ironic, don't you think?"

"They don't know that. It wasn't— His family want him to have a serious relationship again and that's not what's going on here." Sky shrugged. "We're just having fun, that's all."

Except she was fairly sure that at some point between opening the door of Fisherman's Cottage and walking upstairs, something had changed.

"You wanted a big, overwhelming passion."

"I still want that, but I'm not going to sit at home alone while I'm waiting for it to come along."

"Good point." Brittany snapped another piece of chocolate. "You need to audition people."

"Just as long as she doesn't fall for Alec." Emily walked to the door. "I need to tell them to make me decaf or I'm going to be awake all night. Anyone else? Brit?"

"I don't want decaf. In fact I need double strength. And of course she isn't going to fall for Alec. The two of them are so different I'm amazed they made it to the bedroom in the first place."

"Why do you need strong coffee? Aren't you sleeping? Is something wrong?" Emily asked.

"She's being kept awake by Zach's magic wizarding wand." Sky leaned across and helped herself to some of the chocolate. She didn't contradict Brittany. Why would she? She was right. There was no way she'd fall for Alec. "Go and look for them, Em."

What were they talking about in the kitchen?

Were Zach and Ryan grilling Alec? No, Zach wouldn't be interested in the details, but Ryan had an almost pathological need to uncover facts.

Brittany curled her legs under her. "You still

haven't told us how the two of you got from angry vertical to passionate horizontal."

Emily paused with her hand on the door. "Perhaps she doesn't want to talk about it."

"Well, she's going to talk about it. We made that promise, remember? We're here for each other, no matter what. That means I get to hear the juicy bits."

"We had sex, that's all."

"And he invited you back here. So either the sex is really, really good," Brittany said slowly, "or the Shipwreck Hunter really, really likes you."

Sky thought about how withdrawn and remote he'd been earlier. "Or maybe he issued the invitation on impulse—"

"Thinking with his magic—"

"Yes, that."

And she wondered if they'd been hasty. "If this doesn't work out—if something goes wrong, can I stay with you?"

"You don't even need to ask." Brittany frowned. "Of course you can stay with us. No biggie. And talking of biggies..."

Emily rolled her eyes and left the room.

CHAPTER TWELVE

ALEC WOKE TO find himself lying in a wash of winter sunshine.

He didn't need to check his watch to know it was late. That was the price he paid for pulling a night shift.

He'd waited until Sky had fallen asleep, then gently disentangled himself from the strands of her hair that wound themselves round him like silken threads and retreated to his study where he'd worked until 4:00 a.m. He hadn't made the progress he'd been hoping for and all he wanted was a whole day uninterrupted at his computer with nothing for company but a giant flask of strong coffee.

Unfortunately there was no chance of that.

Sky had no doubt been up for hours already and was probably bored out of her mind.

He took a quick shower, pulled on some clothes and went in search of her, weighed down by a sense of obligation.

What had seemed like a good idea in London now seemed like the worst idea he'd ever had.

Except for marriage.

That one topped the list and always would.

A glance through the window showed him a menacing gray sky and a sea that bounced and danced in the freezing wind, like a puppet being manipulated by a higher force.

Normally the weather would have been the only encouragement he needed to dive into a long working day, but today that wasn't an option.

Today, thanks to a collision between impulse and an overactive libido, he wouldn't be working.

Sky would want to build a snowman, explore the forest or try tobogganing down the slope behind the house.

By inviting her here, he'd sacrificed his freedom.

The best he could do was barter for time, he decided. If they did something together this morning, then maybe he could sneak a few hours to work this afternoon.

His deadline loomed, but there was little hope in addressing it today.

Thanks to a hormonal surge, he now had something he'd never had before in this cottage—

A houseguest.

This, he thought grimly, was why he'd chosen not to dive into another relationship.

That and the fact that parts of him still hadn't healed from the wounds of the last one.

At first he thought she'd left because the cottage seemed empty, but then he saw her through the kitchen window, sitting on the snowy deck, wrapped in his down jacket. It swamped her, but she didn't seem to notice. She'd brushed the snow off one of his chairs and was sketching.

Alec grabbed a spare jacket, stamped on his boots and joined her outside. "What are you doing out here? You're going to freeze to death."

"I'm well wrapped up and I'm only staying a few minutes. It's so beautiful. Incredibly peaceful. Bitter cold and winter sun. The perfect combination." She glanced up at the sky. "If we're going to be snowed in soon, I want to make the most of being outdoors."

Normally the thought of being snowed in didn't bother him. Snow was an excuse to work.

Knowing that was off the agenda elevated his stress levels.

"I'll make us breakfast and then we can talk about what you want to do today." The sooner they started, the sooner they could finish.

"I helped myself to breakfast, but I could use more coffee if it's on offer."

"Do you want me to drive you over to Harbor House to see Emily? Up to the Ocean Club?" He knew he was being short with her but he couldn't help it. "We should make a plan."

"Why? Do we have to make a plan? I'm happy just sitting here."

He needed a plan.

He needed to allocate time to work.

"I'll make more coffee."

Ignoring the question in her eyes, he stomped back inside and made coffee.

He should never have invited her back.

He should never—

There was a blast of cold air as Skylar opened the door and walked back into the kitchen.

"My fingers are so cold I can't hold the pencil." She was laughing as she closed the door and somehow her smile increased his irritation.

She looked relaxed and happy while all he could

think of was the work he wasn't going to be able to finish.

"Black or white?" He dragged mugs out of the cupboard and slammed it shut.

"Black." Her smile faded. "What's wrong?"

"Nothing is wrong." He knew he was being irritable and irrational but he couldn't help it. He poured the coffee and handed it to her. "There isn't a lot in the way of entertainment round here, as you can see, so—"

"I'm going to ask you again, Alec. What's wrong?" She slid her hands round the mug to warm them. "Did my hair strangle you in the night? Did I leave my wet towel on the floor? Did I sleepwalk? Sometimes I sleepwalk."

"No." He didn't want to think about the silk of her hair sliding over his skin. The way it felt or the scent of it. "Nothing like that."

"Well, something has freaked you out. Did I propose to you in my sleep? Sometimes I talk in my sleep, too."

"It's not you."

She glanced around. "Well, unless you're hiding someone in the attic, I'm the only person here."

"You're my guest. I'm trying to be a good host and find out what you want to do, that's all."

And whenever he looked at her there was only one thing on his mind.

Even dressed in sweats and layers of wool, she was stunning.

Her cheeks were pink from the cold and her eyes were a deeper blue than usual. "What would you be doing if I wasn't here?"

"That's irrelevant because you *are* here."

"And I'm sensing that you wish I wasn't. You've changed your mind about this." She put her coffee down. "That's fine, Alec. There's no commitment between us. No promises, just the truth, remember? You're allowed to change your mind." She walked to the kitchen door.

"Where are you going?"

"To pack my things. I'll stay with Em for a few days. Not a problem. We can meet up at the Ocean Club for a drink at some point."

"No!" A few moments earlier he would have been willing to pay her to do just that, but now he discovered he didn't want her to. "I don't want you to leave."

"But a moment ago—"

"I don't want you to leave."

"I don't understand."

He didn't understand, either. He knew he was behaving like a jerk. "I have a deadline, that's all. I need to work."

"So what are you doing talking to me? Go and work."

"I can't."

"Why?" She shook her head, confused. "Writer's block? Jet lag?"

"I need to entertain you."

Her brows rose. "That's what this is about? Alec, I'm not a six-year-old on a playdate. You're not a performing clown and I don't need anyone to 'entertain' me. I can entertain myself. If you need to work, work. I'll see you when you're done, whenever that might be."

His mouth was dry. It couldn't be that easy. "I don't want you to be bored."

"Are you kidding me? I'm never bored." She paused. "This isn't about me, is it? It's about your ex-wife. You're standing there wondering what you've done, inviting someone into your space. Well, today's news flash, Alec, is that I won't be bored. I don't need anyone else to occupy me, so you go do whatever it is you need to do and I'll see you for steaming hot sex later. Or not."

If the words hadn't done it, the look in her eyes would have.

He was swamped with desire, dizzy with it. "What will you do?"

He knew what he wanted to do now and it had nothing to do with the books waiting for him upstairs in his study.

"I don't know. I might do some work myself—I have a commission from the Ferraras so I'll need to do some designs. Or I might read, or go for a walk. I haven't decided yet, but you don't need to be part of it." She strolled across the kitchen, rose on tiptoe and kissed his cheek. "You're grouchy because you think I have a hidden agenda—I don't. Also because you worked half the night. Drink more coffee."

He stared at her. "You knew I was working?"

"You weren't in the bed. I was worried my hair might have driven you to sleep in the spare room or something. I came looking for you and saw you in your study, head down."

"Why would your hair have driven me to the spare room?"

She gave a rueful smile and lifted the ends with

her fingers. "Because it gets everywhere. That's the downside of long hair." She gave a self-conscious shrug. "Richard wanted me to cut it."

"I'm starting to think he could have been neurologically impaired. I didn't know you came to the study. I didn't hear you."

"You were working. I didn't want to disturb your concentration." She scooped her hair back from her face. "You're longing to dive into your work, so go do that and I'll see you later. Hope the words flow."

She'd offered him exactly what he wanted. Space.

So why did he feel like locking the door with her on the inside?

SKY WORKED IN the garden room for a few hours, then borrowed Alec's down jacket, which was warmer than hers, slung her Nikon over her shoulder and went for a walk, reasoning that if she wasn't in the house he wouldn't feel the need to entertain her.

At least now she understood the reason for the change in him.

She wondered if he realized just how much his response had revealed about his relationship with his ex-wife.

Clearly Selina had expected to be entertained all the time and for someone like Alec, adventurous, independent and self-reliant, that must have created an almost unmanageable pressure.

Why did he blame himself for something that was so obviously at best only 50 percent his responsibility?

As usual she had more questions than answers and she pondered them as she strolled up the road that wound round the west coast of the island and down to the harbor, pausing to take photos on the way.

It was a perfect winter's day.

The roads had been cleared and she followed the main road back into town, knowing that if she took a detour she'd end up in deep snow.

As she snuggled inside Alec's jacket and felt the cold numb her cheeks she realized she felt freer than she had in ages. Over the past year visits to the island had been accompanied by a low level of background stress brought on by Richard's undisguised impatience with her for choosing to spend her time "in the middle of nowhere." She hadn't let his views stop her coming but she'd be lying to herself if she pretended his disapproval hadn't lessened her enjoyment.

Disapproval.

He'd tried to control her with disapproval, just as her parents did.

Why hadn't she seen that?

It felt almost decadent to be here alone, with no one to answer to but herself. No one to hurry back to. No one complaining if she didn't answer her phone within two rings. For once she wasn't juggling Richard's needs with her own.

Was this how Alec had felt in his marriage? Had it been a constant tug-of-war between what Selina needed and what he wanted?

The cold air cleared her brain and lifted her spirits and by the time she dropped down past the Ocean Club she was smiling.

She heard the blare of the horn as the ferry left for the mainland and stood for a moment, comparing winter to summer.

Main Street, bustling with tourists in the summer, was transformed by snow and decorations. Lights twinkled in windows and wreaths of greenery decorated the doors.

She strolled past Harbor Stores, its windows full of festive food and gift ideas, and on impulse went inside.

She emerged moments later with a smile on her face and a bag stuffed with essential items.

Still laughing at her exchange with Mel, who worked the checkout, she paused outside Summer Scoop, the ice cream store. Lisa, the owner, was busy serving coffee and hot chocolate to frozen locals and winter sports enthusiasts.

Remembering how close Lisa had come to losing the business before Emily had stepped in to help, Sky was pleased to see the place busy.

The mural Sky herself had painted for the place in the summer had transformed the interior from drab and dull to cheery and bright.

Lisa passed two hot chocolates topped with whipped cream and chocolate sprinkles across the counter and then noticed Sky and waved.

Sky waved back and carried on walking until she reached her destination.

The store had no sign outside, and no decorations in the window.

Inside she could see Emily dipping a brush into a paint pot. One wall of the empty store was covered in haphazard stripes of paint.

Sky pushed open the door, relieved to escape from the cold. "Hi, do you know where I could find a new store called Something Seashore?" She put her bag down on the floor, making sure the contents were concealed.

"Sky!" Lizzy, Emily's six-year-old niece, shot across the store and Sky scooped her up.

"How have you been, my little popcorn pal? Is that a new tiara you're wearing?" She hugged her tightly. "And that's a great necklace. You made that?"

"I made it with Rachel last week."

"She's Miss Cooper to you." Emily put down the paintbrush she was holding. Her hair was caught in a ponytail and she looked harassed. "I hate this part. The decorating. I just want it done."

"Decorating is the fun part."

"No, the business will be the fun part. Where did you get that jacket? It's too big for you."

"It's Alec's. I borrowed it." Sky set Lizzy down gently. "Need some help?"

"Do you really need to ask? I've painted fifteen stripes on the wall and I don't like any of them. They all seem wrong."

"That's because they *are* all wrong." Sky squinted at the colors. "Grays and creams. You're playing it safe again, Em."

"The merchandise is going to be more important than the wall color."

"Agreed, but you want the wall color to set off the merchandise to its best advantage. The place is called *Something Seashore* not *Something Boring.* You need this place to feel like a trip to the beach." Sky slipped off Alec's jacket and put it over the back of a chair. "Is this all the paint you have?"

"I have a whole bag of samples. Help yourself."

Sky rummaged through the bag. "I thought you were talking to someone about designing the interior."

"I couldn't afford them. Ryan has someone who is going to help me fix the place up, but first I need paint color."

"You need to catch me up. I'm out of the loop."

"You were busy with your exhibition."

Sky felt a stab of guilt. "Well, I'm not busy now." She set all the blues out in front of her. "Do you have a bowl of some sort?"

"What for?"

"I want to mix these paints."

"Can't you just use a ready-mixed one?"

"No, because none of these are just right." Sky pushed up the sleeves of her sweater and knotted her hair at the back of her head. "When people walk through that door next summer, they're going to know they're at the beach."

"Are we going to paint a mural? Like we did with Summer Scoop?" Lizzy bounced with excitement. "Can I help?"

"I'm relying on it. But first I want to try something." Sky poured, mixed and experimented until she'd produced the shade she wanted. Then she painted a stripe on the wall next to the others.

Emily sighed. "For two days I've been painting stripes, and you walk in here and in one swipe of the brush you have the perfect color. I'd hate you if I weren't so grateful. You're brilliant."

"I haven't finished. We're going to do a paint effect."

"We are?"

"Yes, because block color is so hard. Something swirling, so that it feels as if we're under the water."

"Drowning? Because that would be appropriate."

Skylar smiled. "Not drowning. Think of me as your life preserver." She experimented and Emily left her to it and started unpacking boxes.

The afternoon passed quickly as they worked and caught up on the latest gossip.

"Where's Alec?"

"Working." Sky wiped a damp rag over the paint, smearing it. "Where's Ryan?"

"Working at the Ocean Club. The winter crowd is increasing. And Zach has flown Brittany to the mainland. She's talking to someone at the university. Lizzy, don't put painty fingers in your hair, honey. Go wash them."

Sky watched as Lizzy skipped over to the tiny bathroom at the back of the store. "How is she doing?"

"She's good." Emily mopped up the paint that Lizzy had spattered on the floor. "Better than I could have hoped for. She loves school, but that's mostly because of Rachel of course. And she and Lisa's twins are inseparable."

"It's good having two close friends—you always have one spare." She looked at Emily, noticing how tired she looked. "Is something wrong?"

"No! Nothing."

"Hey, this is me." Concerned, Sky put the paintbrush down. "Are you finding it hard? These past few months have been like a whirlwind for you and being responsible for a child is a huge thing." At least for her friend, who hadn't chosen this life.

"I'm tired." Emily picked at a smear of paint on

her hand. "And sometimes I'm scared I'm not a good enough mom."

"You're the best." Sky wrapped her friend in a tight hug. "No one could be better than you."

"Am I?" Emily's voice was muffled against her shoulder. "What if I'm doing it wrong?"

"You're not doing it wrong. Remember when you brought Lizzy here at the beginning of the summer? She was this pale, silent kid who wouldn't let go of that bear—Alistair—"

"Andrew."

"That's him. Andrew. You see? You know the name of the bear and I don't. She looks well, Em."

"She still has Andrew. And six stuffed puffins that Ryan bought her."

"Six?"

"One and five spares."

Sky grinned. "That's adorable."

"I lie awake at night wondering how Lizzy came to be living with me."

"She's lucky to be living with you." Skylar thought about her own parents and the way they'd raised her, and then thought about Alec's family and the way Suzanne had sat and talked with her. "There is no one way to be a parent. Just be the way that feels right for you."

"It's scary."

"Sure, but you're not on your own with it. You have us. And Ryan."

"Yes. Thank goodness for Ryan. So what's happening with you and Alec?"

"Nothing is happening."

"He was there for you when you were in trouble.

That's pretty powerful, Sky. But I'm worried. I don't think Alec is capable of happy-ever-after."

"I don't want happy-ever-after with Alec. Relax."

"His divorce had a bad effect on him. What if he hurts you?"

"He isn't going to hurt me—" She broke off as Lizzy came running back into the room.

The little girl screeched to a halt when she saw them. "Why are you hugging?"

"Because that's what friends do." Sky released Emily, who stepped back and smoothed her hair.

Lizzy giggled. "Sky has blue paint in her hair."

"Does it look good? Tell me it suits me." Sky picked up the paintbrush and advanced on Lizzy. "I think you need blue hair, too."

With a squeal of delicious panic, Lizzy raced toward the front door and ran slap into Alec.

"Whoa." He caught her before she could fall, scooping her up in an easy movement. "What's the rush?"

"Sky was going to paint my hair blue!"

He hadn't shaved and his weatherproof jacket brushed against his dark jaw. His shoulders seemed even wider than normal under the bulky material.

"Is that right?" His face was serious as he listened. "Want me to pin her down so you can paint her blue instead?"

"She's already blue."

Alec's gaze shifted to Sky's hair. "So she is." He met her gaze and Sky felt her insides tumble, free-falling and spinning.

Mr. Outdoor Guy, she thought, and felt something ripple through her. "Why aren't you working?"

"I came looking for you." His tone together with his penetrating gaze made her feel as if she'd been picked up and tossed around by the incoming tide.

They were in public, but the way he looked at her made her feel as if they were alone.

Had Richard ever looked at her with that degree of focus? As if she were the only person in the room?

He'd come looking for her.

"Oh. Well that's—" *Romantic*, she thought, and a delicious whisper of sexual awareness tickled her skin. "Great."

"I half expected to have to dig you out of a snowdrift." He lowered Lizzy carefully and Sky frowned.

Not so romantic.

He hadn't come looking for her because he'd missed her, but because he assumed she'd screwed up and fallen in a snowdrift.

Her false assumption made her prickly. And uneasy. Her relationship with Alec wasn't about romance. It was about lighthearted fun and lots of physical chemistry.

"If you were worried, you could have just called. You didn't need to climb in the car."

"I called. Your phone is switched off."

Her phone?

She scrabbled in her pocket, pulled out the phone and realized he was right. She'd forgotten to switch it on. It had been one of the many things about her that had driven Richard insane. "I'm sorry." She stammered the words, the apology instinctive. "I wasn't thinking. I mean I *was* thinking, but I wasn't thinking about the phone. That's just it. I was dreaming and miles away and—" Her flood of excuses tailed off as she noticed they were both staring at her. "What? I've said I'm sorry."

Emily touched her arm gently. "Sky—"

"I do it all the time." Alec's voice was calm and steady. "The last thing you want when you're thinking is to be disturbed by technology. You don't have to apologize."

"But it's irritating, I understand that. I should pay more attention to the real world and—" She gasped as Emily hugged her. "What?"

"Don't. *Don't*," she said fiercely. "Never apologize for being who you are."

Was that what she'd been doing?

She closed her eyes, drenched in embarrassment. "I know it's irritating when you can't reach someone, that's all." She was barely able to look at them. "You didn't need to come looking for me, Alec. I've been coming to this island since I was eighteen. I'm sensible and I'm hardly likely to fall down a hole in the middle of the day."

There was a pause.

"It's dark, Sky." His voice was as dark and soothing as rich chocolate.

"Dark?" She looked from his sympathetic gaze to the window and realized that at some point while she'd been talking to Emily and playing with Lizzy the sun had gone down. She let out a breath and pushed her hair back from her face. "I lost track of the time. Didn't realize it was so late. But you didn't need to worry. Em would have given me a ride home." Crap, she'd called his house "home." "I mean to your house. Obviously it's not *my* home, it's your home. Where I'm staying. For a short time." *Shut up, Sky.*

Caught in the beam of Emily's astonished gaze, she looked away just as Lizzy piped up in an innocent voice.

"You wouldn't hurt Sky, would you, Alec?"

Sky froze.

So did Alec. His shoulders tensed and his gaze fastened on her like a laser. "Why do you think I'd hurt her?"

"I don't know, but Emily said she was afraid you might."

Emily made a sound in her throat, somewhere between disbelief and acute embarrassment. "Lizzy—"

"You said he wasn't capable of happy-ever-after. I don't understand."

Sky and Emily were both mute and it was Alec who dropped to his haunches in front of the little girl.

"Emily is very wise," he said quietly.

"But why aren't you capable of happy-ever-after?"

"Because happy-ever-after is for fairy tales, not real life."

Lizzy looked him in the eye. "You're not happy?"

"Yes," Alec breathed, "I'm happy. But no one can be happy 'ever after.' Stuff happens. Life happens. Things change."

"I know. My mom died and now I'm living here with Aunt Emily. Did something sad happen to you?"

Alec held her gaze. "I hurt someone once. Your aunt Emily is worried I might do it again."

Lizzy stared at him. "Were you sorry?"

"Very sorry."

"So you don't want to hurt Sky?"

Alec hesitated for a fraction of a second. "No," he said gruffly. "I don't want to hurt Sky."

"I knew you wouldn't." Lizzy wrapped her arms round him and squeezed. "Come and see my painting. I did a picture of the *Captain Hook*."

Alec returned the hug and when he rose to his feet his face was blank of expression.

"Show me your painting."

Sky had never felt more awkward or uncomfortable about anything in her life.

"Alec—" Emily's voice was strangled but he gave her a brief smile.

"It's fine, Emily. You were looking out for your friend, and it's a legitimate concern." His tone was neutral and he followed Lizzy to the side of the room where she'd been painting.

Emily mouthed *I'm so sorry* to Sky, who gave a helpless shrug.

She didn't know which was worse—the fact Alec knew they'd been talking about him, love and happy-ever-after or the fact that he'd witnessed her emotional meltdown.

If she could have picked a moment for Puffin Island to sink back into the sea, it would have been now.

Alec studied the little girl's work closely, offering plenty of praise and some helpful observations.

Emily's expression softened and she glanced across at Sky again, this time with her hand pressed to her heart.

Sky rolled her eyes and went to wash the brushes and do what she could to remove the splashes of blue from her hair.

Emily might think everything was fine, but she now had to explain her way out of an embarrassing situation.

By the time she'd cleaned up, Alec was by the door.

"See you later." Sky bent to kiss Lizzy, postponing the moment of departure for as long as possible. Then she picked up her bag and followed Alec to the car.

The freezing air engulfed her and she snuggled deeper into the warmth of Alec's jacket, dreading the inevitable conversation.

"Maybe I'll just walk home."

"Get in the car, Sky."

If it hadn't been for the air temperature, she would have argued.

"All right, but for the record I don't see us dancing into the sunset together holding hands, so you really don't have to worry about me."

Alec opened the car door for her, his expression inscrutable. "Get in. We'll have this conversation somewhere there is less chance of developing frostbite."

Her heart sank. She didn't want a conversation. She wanted to forget the whole thing. "That sounds like something my mother might say. 'We need to talk, Skylar.' And we really don't. Emily worries, that's all."

"She's right to worry. Get in."

Sky glanced at his face, at the rigid set of his jaw, and slid into the car without argument. "You're not going to hurt me, Alec. I'm having fun, that's all."

"This morning I was grumpy and rude. How was that fun?"

"You had deadline panic. I get that. And I had a lovely, dreamy day. So dreamy I forgot to switch my phone on. I've already apologized for that oversight."

"And you shouldn't." His voice was soft but firm. "Don't ever apologize for being who you are."

Without giving her time to reply, he closed her door and moments later slid into the driver's seat.

Sky sat there, stunned.

Don't ever apologize for being who you are.

When had anyone other than her friends ever said that to her?

The answer was never.

Feeling ridiculously emotional, she was wondering how to respond when he lifted his hand and cupped her cheek. His fingers were warm, the slow stroke of his thumb deliciously suggestive.

The way he tilted his head meant that his mouth was dangerously close to hers.

Her need to kiss him, and be kissed by him, was almost painful.

She wanted to sink into his hard strength, slide her fingers into his silky hair and press her mouth to his.

She wondered if it was possible to be addicted to the way someone kissed.

"We shouldn't have started this." His voice was rough. "We should never have started this."

"Why?"

"Because you want love, and I can't give you that. Even your friends know it."

"I don't want love from *you.* All I want from you is what you're already giving me." Her gaze dropped from the perfect lines of his mouth to the hard planes of his jaw. The dark shadow told her that he'd been absorbed in his work all day. "You didn't shave."

"I forgot."

"I like it. It's sexy."

His eyes darkened. "You could stay with Emily

tonight instead of coming back to the cottage. You'd be safer."

"And sexually frustrated." She kept her tone light. Not for a second was she going to reveal how mixed up her feelings were. What his words had meant to her. "I don't want to be safe. A fun, exciting, adventurous life is never safe. You don't have to worry about me, Alec. I'm a big girl."

"Emily would disagree."

"She's a worrier by nature."

A muscle flickered in his jaw. "You're going to ignore the warning of a friend?"

"I am, just as you need to ignore that little voice in your head that keeps telling you that you were responsible for everything that went wrong in your marriage. Maybe your ex-wife was hurt by what happened, but you were hurt, too. She has destroyed your ability to interact with women normally without instinctively looking for an ulterior motive or some sort of subtext. Underneath that tough exterior you're a kind, decent guy, so stop all this 'I'll hurt you' bullshit." She tried to change the subject. "When I was in Harbor Stores I heard about the storm warning. Do we need to pick up food or anything? We might be trapped together for days."

He was silent for a moment and then his hand dropped. "We have everything we need."

She fastened her seat belt. "You do know the best way to warm up is to get naked, don't you? Flesh against flesh."

He sent her a look that almost blistered the flesh from her bones. "You're proposing we do that in Main Street?"

She grinned. “Maybe we should wait until we’re back at your place.”

“We’re not going back to mine. I’m taking you to the Ocean Club.” He dragged his gaze from her mouth to the road and pulled out into the snowy street.

“You need to see Ryan?”

“No. I’m taking you out.”

“Oh.” It was the last thing she’d expected him to say. “Why?”

“Because a relationship should be more than endless sex.”

Unless the point of it was endless sex. She felt a flicker of confusion.

“Our relationship is all about orgasms. Nothing else.”

“Tonight, it is not about orgasms. I’m going to buy you a meal. We’re going to sit across from each other like normal people and have a conversation.”

“So this is—” she blew on her chilled fingers “—a date?”

There was a brief silence. “You could call it that.”

“Are you doing this because of what Emily said?”

“No. I’m doing this because I want to get to know you. The real you. And we don’t have much in the way of conversation when we’re naked.”

The sudden lift in her spirits took her by surprise. He was taking her to the Ocean Club, that was all. The Ocean Club, where she’d been a thousand times before. It shouldn’t feel special. But it did. And it flustered her. “I hope you don’t expect me to sleep with you just because you buy me a chocolate milk shake. I’m not that sort of girl.” She hid her confused feelings behind a joke and the corners of his mouth flickered into a smile.

"I appreciate the warning. And you should have told me you wanted to go to the village today. I would have given you a lift."

"You were working and I was happy to walk. I enjoyed the fresh air. I spent the first part of the morning playing with designs for Laurel Ferrara."

"I saw them when I was looking for you."

The thought of Alec leafing through her designs made her feel breathless and vulnerable. "I don't normally show my early sketches to anyone."

"They were all over the floor of the garden room."

Her tendency to spread her work everywhere was another thing that had driven Richard crazy. And just like that the guilt and anxiety was back. "I'm sorry. I'll clear up as soon as we walk through the door. You'll never know I've been there."

He parked at the Ocean Club and killed the engine. "Let's get something straight—I'm not Richard." There was an edge to his voice she hadn't heard before.

"I know."

"Then stop apologizing for living life the way you want to live it."

"You do it, too. You warn me you're going to hurt me. If you can bring baggage to this relationship, then so can I." Everything about him flustered her. His words, his touch and the way he was looking at her. "We should have equal baggage allowance. I suggest one large case and a carry-on."

He smiled. "For the record my favorite was the seashell design. I think you should send her that one."

"I wasn't sure if it was a little fussy. Laurel likes to keep things simple."

"I thought it was clever and original. Would it be difficult to make?"

Richard had never discussed her work with her. She wondered if Alec was being polite.

"Part of it might be." She elaborated a little as they walked into the Ocean Club and Kirsti, the restaurant manager, found them a table by the window.

"Good to have the two of you back on the island." She handed them menus, gave them both a dazzling smile and then melted away.

Sky knew the menu by heart and didn't bother picking it up. "So how did your day go? Tell me more about what you're working on." She trawled her brain for what she already knew. She'd learned to file away details and bring them out when she needed them. After all, she'd been trained by the best. "Make any progress with your book?

"Some. But we were talking about you."

"I thought we'd finished talking about me. You're writing a naval history of the American Revolution, right? I confess I know nothing about that so you'll need to enlighten me."

He was silent for a moment, studying her. "So is this how it works?"

"Is this how what works?"

"The game of conversational tennis that your mother taught you. You forget yourself and focus on something you know interests me."

Flustered, she felt the heat rush into her cheeks. "I thought you brought me here for conversation."

"I did," he said slowly, "but genuine conversation.

The sort where we discover things about each other apart from what turns us on."

"This is a real conversation, Alec. I asked you a question. Now it's your turn. You're supposed to answer."

"I'm not a module to be studied. You're not going to pass or fail. If you're interested in something, ask. If you're not, don't."

He made it sound so simple.

"I'm interested." She glanced up as Kirsti arrived back at their table with drinks. "I'll have the gourmet burger with skin-on fries. Thanks."

Alec handed the menus back without looking. "I'll have the same. With extra fries. Is Ryan here?"

"On the phone with some rich dude who wants to park his yacht here over the winter." Kirsti tucked the menus under her arm. "I'll tell him you're here."

Sky gave Alec a questioning look. "You missed lunch, too? You ordered extra fries."

"Those are for you. To stop you stealing mine."

She peered at him and saw the smile tug at the corners of his very sexy mouth. "Smartass."

"Princess."

A week ago that term would have irritated her extremely. Now it made her smile. Or maybe it was the way he said it that made her smile. "How did you get the name 'Shipwreck Hunter'?"

"The first TV series I ever presented was about shipwrecks. They'd invited me to be an advisor, but I ended up in front of the camera. It went from there."

"But why shipwrecks? Was your uncle responsible for that?"

"Partly. He used to tell me stories that kept me

awake at night. I'm sure he exaggerated and elaborated to feed my imagination. And he succeeded." He reached for his beer. "There's something mysterious about a shipwreck—they're often shrouded by unanswered questions. Some ships become lost in the fog, others stray off course in bad weather and succumb to unpredictable swells or hidden sandbanks. This is the most hazardous stretch of coastline in the whole of the Eastern Seaboard. It was the coastline and shipwrecks that drew me here in the first place." His deep, dark tones made her shiver.

She could picture him, standing on the deck of a ship, absorbing the rise and fall of the water. "I'm imagining swashbuckling pirates who look like Johnny Depp."

"There wasn't much piracy on the Maine coast, although there was some. But there were plenty of shipwrecks. To a young, bloodthirsty boy it was exciting. I was hooked. I begged Harry to take me diving with him and eventually he did. We started with a few dives off the British coast. Those were dark, murky experiences. Then on one of his visits he told me about the HMS *Albany*, which ran on the ledges of the Northern Triangles in the middle of a winter storm in 1782, right at the end of the American Revolution."

"It was an American ship?"

"British. The enemy." His eyes gleamed. "Captained by Henry Mowat, who spent the best part of a forty-year career patrolling the North American coast. It was initially used to defend against the Penobscot Expedition, but it had been downgraded to a prison ship when it sank. There are hundreds of shipwrecks on this stretch of coast."

"So you studied—what? Maritime history?"

"Marine archaeology. Maritime history came later. I wanted to dive. A shipwreck is a time capsule full of hidden secrets. It was one big adventure for me."

She loved his enthusiasm. "Ever find any treasure?"

"Very few ships carried treasure. The galleons sailing from the New World to Spain carried gold ingots and coins and the Indiamen traded precious metals for spices in the Far East, but generally the value of most historic shipwrecks can't be measured in monetary terms."

"You sound like Brittany." She reached for her drink. "And now it's the American Revolution. So how do you decide what to write about?"

His gaze locked on hers. "How do you decide what to paint?"

"I paint what interests me."

"And I write about what interests me."

"I didn't even know there was a navy in the American Revolution."

"Sea power played a significant role in American Independence. The thirteen colonies would have struggled without maritime support. Am I boring you?"

"No. And when we get home I want you to tell me all this again, while wearing your glasses." She'd never particularly enjoyed history at school but somehow when Alec talked about it she could have listened forever.

The corners of his mouth flickered. "Glasses are a turn-on?"

"I think they might be." She looked at his smile

and wondered why she had ever thought him aloof and intimidating. Reserved, yes. Smart, definitely. But not aloof. "You were telling me about the navy. Carry on. Talk dirty to me."

"The Continental Navy was officially established in 1775. Its main role was to disrupt British maritime efforts by intercepting the supply of provisions and arms. Unfortunately many of the primary sources have been lost."

"Is that why you were in London last week?"

"Part of the reason."

"British Library?"

"The Caird Library and the National Archives."

Kirsti delivered their food but neither of them noticed and she slunk away, a smile on her face.

"I had so many galleries and museums on my list." Sky felt a rush of disappointment. "I had a whole itinerary for when I was in London and I barely did any of it. Still, at least I had a trip on the London Eye, thanks to you."

"You'll visit again."

She assumed it was a nonspecific comment rather than an invitation. "I wanted to visit the Tate Modern. Have you ever been?"

"Yes. I prefer the National Gallery."

"You like art galleries?"

"That's one of my favorites. Home to Turner's *The Fighting Temeraire*."

"You know that painting?"

"Of course. Turner is famous for his naval art. The *Temeraire* was a military ship. Played a distinguished role in Nelson's victory at the Battle of Trafalgar in 1805. Nelson was a brilliant strategist. He destroyed

Napoleon's maritime strategy and wiped out the biggest threat to British security for two hundred years."

She stared at him. It was like discovering another person was fluent in your language. "Turner was in his sixties when he painted that and he used a wonderful light, loose brushstroke. What I love most is the lighting. Of course the sun is setting in the wrong place in the picture, but who cares."

The food grew cold on the table between them as they talked.

"He was making a statement about the passing of an age," he continued. "Sail to steam and steel."

Skylar listened, fascinated as he added historical context to a painting she'd always admired on a technical basis. "He loved that painting so much he wouldn't sell it."

"Is that what happened with the bracelet you gave my sister? You loved it too much to sell it?"

"If you're asking if my artistic abilities are on par with Turner then the answer is no, but if you're asking me if I have ever loved a piece too much to part with it then yes. I have."

Richard's eyes had glazed over when she'd talked about art. Alec was not only interested, he had knowledge, but he wasn't one of those men who talked simply to show off what he knew. He had a sharp, questioning mind and enjoyed filling in gaps in his knowledge. He grilled her on all aspects of art and she responded, absorbed, enthused, until time and their surroundings blended into the background and her entire focus was him.

She couldn't remember when she'd enjoyed an evening more.

She would have carried on talking, except for the growling of her stomach. "I'm starving. I wonder where—" Her eyes widened as she finally noticed the food. "Did you see Kirsti deliver that?

"No." He was frowning. "We must have been talking."

Sky felt a little jolt. It was the first time in her life she'd forgotten to eat her food.

She stared at the burgers and then at Alec, thrown by the uncomfortable realization that she'd lost track of time with a man who at the beginning of the summer she couldn't stand. The realization made her uneasy.

It hadn't occurred to her they might have anything at all in common other than a desire to strike sparks off each other.

He'd surprised her, and she'd surprised herself.

It made no sense that part of her wished she still found him exasperating.

Or maybe it did.

She'd told herself it was just sex. That they had nothing in common. But it was hard to pretend a relationship was just about sex when you both had your clothes on and you'd just had the best night of your life.

"Why aren't you eating? Are you ill?" He pushed his bowl of extra fries toward her and she forced herself to take one because one sure way of alerting him to the fact that something was wrong was not to eat.

"I'm starving." She reached for her burger. "While we eat tell me more about your favorite paintings."

"I HATE TO SAY I told you so, but I told you so." Kirsti sneaked into Ryan's office. "I'm a genius. Not only do I make the best cappuccino on the island, but I can predict people's relationship future. I am going to set up a dating agency."

"There aren't enough single people living on the island to keep you busy so if I were you I'd keep making your incredible cappuccino." Ryan glanced up from the spreadsheet. "What were you right about?"

"Alec with Skylar. I told you back in the summer they'd be perfect together. And you dismissed me."

Ryan put his pen down. "They're not serious."

"Not yet maybe, but they will be."

"I hate to break this to you but it's just sex, Kirsti."

"Yeah? Because it wasn't sex that stopped them both from noticing me when I delivered their food a moment ago. I was thinking of sounding a foghorn to get their attention and then decided the food could wait."

Resigned to not getting any work done until the conversation was concluded to Kirsti's satisfaction, Ryan sat back in his chair. "So they were too absorbed in each other to notice you? That doesn't mean anything except that they need to get a room."

"You're missing the point. They were talking."

"It happens."

"Really talking, about—" she stumbled "—I don't know, some painting or other that I've never heard of. Naval art. And I don't think it had anything to do with strategic body piercing." She nodded sagely. "I didn't even know there was such a thing, but the two of them were so deep in conversation Napoleon himself could have walked right in here stark naked with Joséphine and neither of them would have noticed. So what's going on, Ryan? How did they get from naught to naughty in a few weeks?"

"They bumped into each other in London and spent some time together, that's all. I don't know the details."

"Then ask!"

"It's none of my business."

"Of course it's your business. Alec is your friend and he was glowering around here like a bad storm warning all summer. And the summer before that come to think of it. In fact as long as I've known him. Unless it's his divorce that's finally making him smile, I'd say Sky has had a positive effect on him. He looked *happy*, Ryan."

"Of course he's happy. He's having crazy, no-strings-attached sex with a stunning blonde. Men are simple creatures."

"So it would seem." She sighed. "Because for a very smart guy, you're clueless."

CHAPTER THIRTEEN

ALEC LIT THE woodstove while outside the wind howled and screamed around the cottage.

The National Weather Service had issued a storm warning that put the whole island on alert.

He wasn't worried. He had everything he needed in the event of a loss of power and even the prospect of sharing his space with another person wasn't bothering him.

Providing that person was Sky.

They'd been on the island for a week and she'd proved herself to be easy company.

She worked as hard as he did, was careful never to invade his space and didn't disturb him if he was in his study.

The fact that he still couldn't concentrate wasn't her fault.

He put in working hours, but spent most of them staring out of the window trying to think about the American Revolution and not the way Sky's face lit up when he talked or the way her slender curves fit perfectly against him.

Her favorite place was the garden room and she'd made it her own, spreading out her paints and covering the floor with her work.

Sometimes when he went in search of her he found

her absorbed in a drawing, other times he found her staring out to sea from the window seat.

Creative window gazing, she'd called it, delivering that trademark smile that he was fast discovering had the melting power of summer sunshine.

He rocked back on his heels and turned as he heard her walk into the room.

"Pinot noir or sauvignon blanc?" She held two bottles of wine in front of him. She was wearing jeans tucked into slipper boots and her hair streamed over her scarlet sweater.

Red for danger, he thought. "You bought wine?"

"Of course. The idea was to exhaust you physically, not financially. And anyway, with a storm warning in place it's important to stock up on essential items. I assumed by that they meant wine and condoms." Her wickedly sexy smile sent his libido soaring into the stratosphere.

"You bought condoms?"

"A truckload."

"In Harbor Stores?"

"Yes. I went there that day you picked me up from Emily's. It was hilarious. I picked up a few extra packets just because I wanted to see Mel's face. I wish you'd been there." She started to laugh, unable to hold it back. "I slapped the condoms down on the counter and Mel's eyes went the size of saucers. She asked me if I really intended to buy that many, so I thanked her and said that I should probably buy more, just in case." She was laughing so hard it made him want to laugh, too.

"You did that?"

"Yes. I added another three packets and pointed out

that they were predicting a major storm with power outages."

"You're shameless." Alec shook his head. "I'm never going to be able to shop in Harbor Stores again."

"Hey, I'm helping your reputation, Shipwreck Hunter. Thanks to me, you are now the island *stud.* You're welcome." She put the wine down on the table next to the bookshelf, still laughing.

Her smile was fast becoming one of his favorite things about her, along with the way she listened and her straightforward responses to everything.

She was the least complicated woman he'd ever met.

But that changed nothing as far as he was concerned.

It just made it easier, because she didn't want anything more from this than he did.

As far as he was concerned it was as close to a perfect relationship as it was possible to get. The sex was incredible, they were friends and they enjoyed each other's company, but it went no deeper than that.

She placed no demands on him, and that trapped feeling he'd had on the first day on Puffin Island had never resurfaced.

"The islanders will be talking about us. That doesn't bother you?"

"Why would it bother me what they think?"

"You care about what your parents think."

"That's different. They're my parents. We're unattached, consenting adults finding a legitimate way of passing the time in a Maine winter storm." She pointed to the bottles. "Pick one."

He could barely focus on the labels.

All he wanted to do was bury his hands in her hair and take her straight back to bed. “The pinot.”

“Good choice. It will go with the soup I’m making.”

“I thought you didn’t like cooking.”

“I can make soup. My specialties are lentil and smoked bacon, leek and potato, and, of course, chicken. I also make an excellent minestrone, courtesy of a lesson I had from an Italian when I was eighteen.” Picking up the wine, she walked back to the kitchen and he followed.

“I thought Italy was on your list of places to visit.”

“I’ve never been to Florence. And I really want to.” A loud crash from outside made her jump. “What was that?”

“Snow sliding off the roof.” He took the wine from her before she could drop it and put it down on the counter. “Are you scared of storms?”

“No. I love storms. The more howling, banging and crashing the better.” Her eyes sparkled. “Especially the banging part.”

He put the white in the fridge and opened the red. “I’ll try to make sure there is plenty of banging.”

“Good. I’ll have to go back to Harbor Stores and tell Mel we’ve run out. That would be fun.”

“You have a wicked sense of humor.”

She reached up and lifted two glasses from the cabinet. “I remember staying with Brittany once in a terrible snowstorm. It took three days to dig ourselves out. Kathleen must have been worried, but to us it was an adventure.”

“I never met Brittany’s grandmother. I wish I had.”

“She was the sort of person who survived everything. A pioneer." She put the glasses in front of him. "All summer she'd bottle fruit ready for the winter so in January we'd be eating blueberry cobbler and she made the most incredible ginger-topped apple cake. Brittany found her diaries in the summer. A New York publisher is interested in them. I hope it doesn't bring people flocking here. I know we need a robust tourist industry, but I wouldn't want it to change the character of the island."

He poured the wine. "I'm surprised you don't miss New York."

"I love New York, but I love this place, too. At some point I will have to go back to the city and put in some studio time, but right now I'm busy thinking." She pulled vegetables out of the fridge and put them on the counter. "I sent those early designs through to Laurel."

"How many ideas did you send her?"

"To begin with I gave her three. Not too many. I'll see what she thinks and we'll take it from there."

"At least you know that with 'Ferrara' in the name, they're not going to argue about money." He put the wine on the counter next to her.

"Yes. It's funny." She rinsed the vegetables and picked up a knife. "I know that in businesses these guys—both Cristiano and Nik—are ruthless negotiators, but when it comes to buying something special for the women they love they are marshmallows."

"You're envious of that?"

"Of the bottomless bank account? No. Of the depth of love—yes. I'm envious of that." Her voice softened and she stared out of the window at the falling snow.

She looked down at the vegetables. "This isn't getting the soup made."

"How did you meet Lily?"

"Brittany introduced us. She's a ceramics expert." She started dicing a carrot. "My collection was inspired by Mediterranean themes and she gave me some great ideas. I spent a few weeks in Greece with her and Brittany."

"How did you, Emily and Brittany become friendly?"

The wind screamed past the cottage, whipping angrily at the snow, but inside the kitchen they were cozy and warm.

"We met on our first day in college. We bonded over our disasters. Brittany had just emerged from her disastrous relationship with Zach, Emily had no one and she was so closed off it was like trying to break into a safe. And then there was me—" she paused to take a sip of wine "—I was in the biggest battle of my life with my parents, who wanted me to go to law school, not art college. It had been a dream for me for so long."

"Anyone can be a lawyer but not everyone can produce the quality and originality of the pieces you had in your show." He thought that confining Skylar to law school would be like caging an exotic bird. His admiration for her grew and he lifted his glass. "To dreams."

She put the knife down and lifted her glass. "To dreams."

"Were you ever tempted to do what they wanted you to do and choose law?"

"Not once. I knew what I wanted. That's what kept me going. If I'd had doubts, maybe it would have been different but I *knew.* You were the same. You listened to those stories your uncle Harry told you and you wanted to be part of it." Her phone rang and she reached for it in her pocket. "It's probably Brit." She glanced at the screen and then saw the number. Her smile vanished like the sun behind a cloud. "It's my mother."

The expression on her face made his insides knot. "Leave it."

"If I leave it, she'll call again. I've been anticipating this call for the past week so I might as well get it over with."

"You don't have to answer it, Sky."

"I do." Flustered, she paused and then put the phone down as if it were a poisonous insect. "You're right. I don't. I don't have to answer it." She stood with her hands hovering in the air for a moment and then clasped them behind her back as if that was the only way to stop herself from touching it.

She stared at the phone until the ringing stopped and the call went to voice mail.

"Right. Well, that wasn't so hard." She let out a shaky breath, her tension palpable. "Actually, it was hard. I feel guilty that I was here and I didn't pick up. How awful is that?"

What was awful was the fact that her parents tried to control her love life and worse, far worse in his opinion, was the fact that they trampled so roughly over her dreams. A less strong person would have given up and yet here Skylar was working her guts out and earning a living doing something she loved.

He eased away from the counter, wondering how to make her feel better about something that was manifestly unreasonable. "You can't always be expected to answer the phone."

"But I still have to listen to the message so all I've done is remove the confrontation part. On the other hand that does make the whole thing less stressful." She picked up her phone and listened to the message before he could suggest that she switch the damn thing off until tomorrow.

He assumed the message would be more of the usual. How selfish she was. How Richard was perfect for her. But then he saw her face pale and knew it was something more.

"Sky?"

She deleted the voice mail and stood for a moment, staring into space.

He felt a flicker of unease. "Sky?"

"Sorry about that." Her voice was bright and she reached for her wine.

He watched as she downed it. "Don't do that."

"What? Drink? Why not?"

"I wasn't talking about the drinking, I was talking about the fake voice. Be false with your mother if you like, but not with me. We agreed on honesty. Talk to me." He wondered why he was so keen for her to talk about her feelings when that was usually something he actively avoided. "What was the message?"

"You've dealt with enough of my crap, Alec." She picked up the knife and carried on chopping vegetables, each vicious slice cutting deep into the board. Carrot. Leek. Onion. Everything was diced to within an inch of its life.

He watched, concerned about her fingers, as the blade glinted in the light.

"Sky, maybe you should—"

"You eat lentils?"

"Yes, I eat lentils, but—"

"Good." She reached for a potato, dicing it with decisive strokes of the blade. "This is going to be the best thing you've ever tasted. It's a perfect winter comfort soup." Her voice was scratchy and raw and he sucked in a breath as he saw a gleam of moisture on her eyelashes.

During all the events of the past couple of weeks, the breakup, the accident, he'd never once seen her shed a tear.

He'd seen Selina cry a thousand times. He'd been sympathetic, made all the noises and moves that were expected of him, but her tears had never moved him. Toward the end they'd exasperated him. He'd assumed there was something missing inside him.

But watching Sky fight back that single raindrop of moisture made him feel as if he were being slowly unraveled. "Sky—"

"I need a moment, that's all. I'll be fine."

He reached for her and then withdrew his hand, feeling helpless. His chest felt tight. He tried to see her face, but she kept her head down as she sliced. And sliced.

Two minutes into her cathartic session of violent chopping, blinded by a veil of misery, she missed the potato and sliced into her finger.

"Crap. Alec, I—"

"Yeah, I know." Cursing himself for not having intervened earlier, he grabbed a towel and clamped it over her finger.

"The knife slipped."

"You couldn't see what you were cutting. For future reference, don't use a knife when you're upset." But the injury didn't bother him as much as her tears.

"You're right." Her voice was thickened. "I should have put the knife down and done something else to let off steam. I might go for a walk. Shovel some snow."

"There is a blizzard out there. You're staying right here." Ignoring the scent of her and the feel of her, he unwrapped her finger and held it under the running water. "It's not too bad. I can fix that."

She sniffed. "You're always fixing me."

He turned off the water and dried her finger. "Press hard and keep the pressure on. I need to find my first-aid box."

He delved into a cupboard and found it at the back. It hadn't been opened in a while. He hoped it still contained what he needed although he was pretty sure there was nothing in there that would deal with Sky's parental issues.

She stood, gazing out of the window. "Are you going to say, 'I told you so'?"

He opened the first-aid kit and delved through dressings and bandages.

"Why would I do that?"

"Because you told me not to answer the phone."

"You didn't answer the phone." He closed the wound with adhesive strips. "You let it go to voice mail."

"And then I immediately listened to it. Do you think I need an intervention?"

No. He thought she could do with a new set of parents, or at the very least giving the current set a serious shake-up. “They left you a message. Of course you’re going to listen to it. You did what felt right for you.”

“It feels like crap.” She winced as he pressed on her finger. “I’ve ruined the soup.”

“No, you haven’t.” He placed a sterile pad over her finger and strapped it into place. “But maybe we’ll skip the potato.”

She gave a choked laugh. “No matter what trouble I’m in, you always manage to make me laugh.”

“That’s because you laugh at anything and everything.”

“It’s either laugh or cry. You’re always so calm. Is there any situation you can’t handle?”

“Plenty.” He couldn’t handle her crying. He couldn’t handle seeing her upset or injured. “For a start I wouldn’t be able to handle what you’re handling.”

“What do you mean?”

“You deal with your family better than I would.”

“I don’t have a choice. If I want to keep them in my life, I have to do what I can to keep the peace. But right now—” She breathed. “My mother thinks I’m idealistic and romantic.”

Alec decided this was one of those occasions when it was better to listen than comment.

He secured the dressing and let go of her hand.

Her head was almost on his shoulder, her hair brushing against his jaw.

“Do you?” She spoke so softly he could hardly hear her.

“Do I what?”

"Think I'm unrealistic. I want this grand passion and my mother thinks that doesn't exist."

Alec stood still, breathing in the scent of her, blinded by how much he wanted her. He didn't understand how you could want something so badly when it was already yours. "I don't know," he said finally. "I don't know if that's unrealistic."

"I don't expect a life with no ups and downs, but I want to feel something with my whole heart. Not a relationship that looks good on paper, or seems logical. I want an emotional connection. I want someone who wants *me*. Not a version of me, but the real me. I want to be loved and accepted for who I am. Love with no reservations. Is that wrong?"

"No." His voice sounded rough. "It isn't wrong."

"But I'm asking a lot."

"I'm not an expert." All he knew was that he'd never felt any of the things she'd described.

"I never expected love to just land on my doorstep. That's why I date and go out and have a good time. You can't meet someone unless you get out there." She leaned her head on his chest and he hesitated, conflicted.

He'd convinced himself that their relationship didn't contain an emotional element but she hadn't stepped into his arms for sex, she'd done it for comfort.

He probably should have pushed her away, but instead he closed his arms round her, holding her tightly.

She was probably hoping for words of reassurance but he had none to offer.

All he knew was that he wanted to make her feel better.

Lifting his hand, he smoothed her hair. He wanted to slide his fingers through the silky strands and kiss her until she could no longer pronounce Richard's name. But that was sex, not comfort, so he took that urge and buried it deep.

He was barely breathing, doing his best to keep their contact low-key and under control, but then she pressed closer to him.

He breathed in the scent of her, felt softness and curves blend with the hard lines of his own body, and stilled.

Taking a deep breath, he tried to ease away from her but she pressed herself closer.

"Kiss me."

"Sky—"

Her arms were round his neck. "I want you to kiss me."

He should let her go. Nothing, he knew, had the potential to shift the delicate balance of a sexual relationship like strong emotions, but the strong emotions were the reason he couldn't let her go.

He slid his hand down her back, drawing her against him, and she rose on tiptoe and kissed him, the way she had that evening in the London Eye.

Her lips were soft and searching and he opened her mouth with his and heard her purr of pleasure as his tongue slid against hers.

The intimate contact changed everything. The kiss went from comfort to carnal in a single scorching breath. The blood pumped through his veins until the sheer heat of desire threatened to incinerate them both.

"Alec—" Her arms tightened round his neck and he nudged her back against the fridge.

His brain was screaming at him to stop. Sex with emotion wasn't what either of them had signed up for, but she was urging him on, her fingers in his hair.

"I don't want to hurt you." But he couldn't stop kissing her, couldn't stop tasting her. She was soft and sweet and sexy as hell and she pressed closer still, the heat of her driving every thought from his brain.

"You're not hurting me. You're making everything better." Her hands went to the front of his shirt, her fingers freeing buttons until it fell open and he felt her hands slide over his skin, stroking and exploring with fevered desperation. And then her fingers were on the snap of his jeans and his brain ceased to function.

He was so hard she struggled to free him and he covered her hand with his and helped her, his mouth greedy on hers as they kissed.

Her clothes proved easier, or maybe he was more desperate because they fell away under his impatient hands until she was naked from the waist down.

Without breaking the kiss, he lifted her and sat her on the counter.

She wound her legs around him, and he felt her fingers dig hard into his shoulders.

Still kissing her, he shifted position and buried himself deep.

Warmth closed around him and his mind blanked.

"Alec—" She breathed his name against his lips and met each driving thrust with subtle movements of her own.

Behind them the wind lashed at the window, but neither of them noticed and if they'd noticed they wouldn't have cared.

There was nothing for either of them but this.

She matched him kiss for kiss, her body moving with an erotic rhythm, her fingers hard in his shoulders as she urged him on. His thoughts blended together until his mind ceased to function and all his responses became physical.

He felt the first contractions of her body ripple along his shaft and groaned, trying to hold back, trying to still the writhing of her hips, but she couldn't keep still and every subtle movement ripped more layers from his self-control until release barreled down on him. They came together in a mind-blurring, dizzying climax that froze time and thought.

As his brain finally cleared, he realized that her breathing was unsteady and that her nails were digging into his back.

It bothered him that he'd been so out of control that for a few moments he hadn't known where he was. He could have been in the middle of Main Street for all the attention he'd paid to his surroundings.

Shaken by the intensity of it, he eased away from her and she gave a little whimper and clutched at him. "Thank you."

He didn't know whether to laugh or kiss her again. "Are you seriously thanking me?"

"Yeah." Her voice was husky. "I didn't think anything could make me feel better but you managed it."

There was a tightening in his chest.

Throughout his marriage he'd felt inadequate. He'd failed to meet almost all the demands made of him, fallen short of almost every expectation, until he'd convinced himself that he wasn't capable of making any woman happy.

And then Sky had come along, and made him feel as essential as sunlight.

"Sex has tremendous healing properties." Because she was still pressed against him intimately he felt the slight ripple of tension, a change in her that he knew he probably didn't want to question.

"Yes," she said. "It does."

He held her, breathed in the scent of her, felt the contrasts of soft against hard, revealing nothing of his own thoughts.

They'd promised honesty, but right at that moment he knew neither of them were being honest. Maybe sex did have healing properties but what they'd just shared, this new dangerous intimacy, felt a long way from "just sex."

A COUPLE OF hours later, the soup finally made and eaten, Skylar lay in the dark in Alec's bedroom, listening to the sound of the wind.

Snow fell beyond the window and an iridescent winter light sent a silver glow over their naked bodies.

She felt as if her bones had melted into the bed.

"Have I told you that you're good at sex?" It didn't begin to describe her feelings but it was the only sentiment she felt she could express. She knew he wouldn't want to hear anything else.

He stirred and pulled her closer. "So are you."

"We're good together." She realized how that sounded and felt a flash of panic that her thoughtless words might damage this new intimacy. "I didn't mean—"

"I know what you meant."

"When I picked up that message from my mother

I didn't think it was going to be possible to enjoy my evening, but I did. Lately you seem to always be there at my lowest moments."

"Tell me more about the message. I want to know what upset you."

She hesitated, but after everything they'd shared, not sharing this felt ridiculous. "She booked the church." She felt him shift onto his elbow.

"Who?"

"My mother. She put a reservation on a venue for a June wedding. Can you believe that? She actually booked somewhere." Sky still couldn't believe it herself. The frustration burned inside her, refusing to die.

"Without asking you?"

"Without asking or telling. She said that good places are often booked up years in advance and she was afraid by the time I'd made up my mind to do the sensible thing there would be nothing available." She gave a strangled laugh. "She booked it that first night I met Richard, because we seemed to get along so well. Of course we did, because she engineered it to be like that. Now she's facing a cancellation charge. According to her that's my fault, too. So apparently I need to make up my mind whether there will be a reconciliation. Good job she didn't tell me in person. Look what happened to the potato!"

He didn't laugh. Instead he drew her closer still and held her and she stayed there, against his chest, absorbing warmth and strength. It flowed through her, filling all the empty places inside her.

She wondered how he could possibly think he wasn't capable of making someone happy.

She felt his hand stroke her hair, slow and easy, and closed her eyes. “I envy you your family.”

“They’re far from perfect.”

“They seem pretty perfect to me.”

“Mine would be booking my wedding, too, if I let them.”

If I let them.

It was like being drenched by a bucket of cold water.

“It’s my fault, isn’t it?”

“They booked a wedding you didn’t want. How can that be your fault?”

“I’ve let this happen. I’ve never set boundaries. You adore your family, but you have boundaries and you make them clear. You love them, but you’re the one running your life. I’ve let mine interfere. I’ve let them have influence.” She eased out of his arms and sat upright, forcing herself to take a good, hard look at the truth. And the truth didn’t look good. “Choosing to study art, not law, was my decision and I knew how disappointed they were so I’ve been desperate to try to please them in every other way to make up for it.”

“Why do you have to make up for a decision that felt right for you?”

“Because it wasn’t what they wanted for me.” She thought back to her mother’s cold disapproval and her father’s exasperation. That constant feeling that approval was something she had to work hard to earn, like good grades.

“What about what you wanted for you?”

“That wasn’t relevant. Despite everything I love them, and I know they love me, but I don’t feel as if they know me. They have this vision of how I should be and I never fit that vision. I really admire you." She blurted the words out. "You have this wonderful relationship with your family, but when they try to overstep you manage to rein them in. They listen to you and respect you. Mine ignore me."

He drew her back down to him. "So maybe you need to find a different way of getting your message across."

"How? I don't want to fall out with them, I really don't. This is so pathetic." And she hated feeling this way. "I feel like a teenager, not an adult."

"That's because they're not letting you be an adult. They're afraid you're making a mistake and they're trying to stop that, instead of accepting that this is your life and your choice, mistakes and all."

"You're right. And choosing whether or not to answer the phone isn't enough." She lay there, wrapped in strength and warmth. "I'm going to spend Christmas here on Puffin Island."

He stirred. "Are you sure?"

"Yes. For once I want to be with my friends instead of a bunch of strangers. I'm going to tell my parents how I feel. Alec?" She could feel his hand in her hair as he gently massaged her scalp and knew that his pillow would be covered in long blond hairs in the morning.

"What?" His voice was rough with sleep and she nestled closer.

"I want this to be a perfect Christmas. When the storm ends, can we go and get a tree?"

She felt his fingers still.

"I don't have many decorations."

"I'm going over to Emily's in a few days. I'll make

some with Lizzy. Until then I'll scour the outdoors for inspiration." Her eyes drifted shut. "I want to go to the forest and choose one together. Can we do that?"

She wondered if it was too much. If her request was too personal. Maybe it felt too much like she was moving into his cottage, marking it as her territory.

"Yes." His voice was soft. "We can do that."

CHAPTER FOURTEEN

THE STORM CONTINUED for two days and then gave way to clear blue skies and bitter cold.

Alec dressed in thick layers and went outside to clear the snow while it was still soft and powdery.

Watching from the window, Sky decided outdoor gear suited him. He looked like a man who could take on nature single-handed. She indulged herself for a few moments, admiring sheer muscle power and masculine brawn, then she borrowed his spare jacket and joined him outside.

He looked surprised. "Are you sure you want to do this?"

"Are you kidding? Shoveling snow is better than the treadmill. And anyway, I just called my parents back and told them I'm spending Christmas here."

He straightened. "And how did that go?"

"Let's put it this way—I thought some snow clearing might lower my blood pressure."

He gave a sympathetic smile. "That bad?"

"Worse. But it felt good to tell them what I wanted for a change. They told me I was making bad choices and I pointed out that they were in fact my choices to make. And I felt—" she breathed "—strong. More in control. It was a good conversation."

And she knew he was the reason she'd found the courage to have that conversation.

Shoveling snow, she discovered, was a perfect way of working off a bad mood. They worked together, their breath forming clouds of vapor in the freezing air.

Alec gave her a long, searching look. "I should thank your mother for clearing my snow."

She eased upright, wincing. "I have a backache. That's what comes from taking your frustration out on a snowdrift."

"Welcome to Maine in winter. And we escaped lightly this time. We still have power and the plow came earlier so the road's clear at least." Alec unzipped his jacket a little way. "We can go on and find a Christmas tree later, but first I need to walk across to Hunter's Cove to check on Meg. I won't be long."

She wondered when he was going to get used to the fact she didn't need him to entertain her. "You can be as long as you need to be and do whatever it is you need to do. But who is Meg?"

"My nearest neighbor. Meg has lived on the island forever. Tough as they come and never asks for help, but she broke her hip last winter and isn't as mobile as she'd like to be."

"Does she have family on the island?"

"She has a son and a daughter, but not on the island. They live in Bar Harbor."

"That's not so far."

"They're busy with their lives and she doesn't want to bother them."

"So you watch out for her?" They didn't visit, so he did. Knowing that did something to her insides.

And she knew it wasn't just because he did the right thing, but because he did it quietly with no agenda or expectation of favors in return. He painted himself as selfish, and yet he always did what needed to be done, even when it inconvenienced him. He'd done the same thing with her. Her heart bumped against her chest. "I'll come with you and I'll put some soup in a flask for her."

"You don't have to do that. It won't be a very comfortable trek. The snow will be deep in parts and there will probably be some branches down."

"Deep snow is good. All the more for me to push some down your jacket when you least expect it. You're forgetting I have that gold medal in snowballing."

He gave a half smile. "You shouldn't have reminded me. Now I'll be ready for you."

"No, you won't. I'm cunning." Warm from the exertion, she unzipped her jacket slightly, too. "I'll wait until your guard is down and then I'll pounce."

"I like it when you pounce." He reached out and hauled her against him and because she didn't see it coming she lost her balance and put her hands on his chest to steady herself.

"I almost landed on my butt there. Do you always just grab what you want?"

"Sometimes. When it's worth grabbing." His mouth came down on hers, his kiss warm and skilled and she melted into him, clutching those broad shoulders. Her legs felt heavy and her breathing labored. She'd spent most of the past two days in bed with him, most of it awake, and still she couldn't get enough of him.

"Don't you need to work?"

He lifted his mouth just enough to answer. "Probably. But you're distracting me."

"Do not use me as an excuse. Go and work." She pushed at his chest. "Deadline."

He smiled against her mouth. "I love it when you talk dirty to me."

"I'm just pointing out that we've been indoors for two days and we've done nothing but talk and have sex. Neither of us has done any work."

He stilled and then slowly lifted his head, a frown on his face. "Two days?"

"Yes, Alec. Two days." And the fact that he hadn't registered the time passing sent a warm buzz through her body. "We need to go back in the house and warm up at least before we walk over to your neighbor."

"Sounds like a plan."

It was over an hour before they were ready to leave the house again and Alec didn't work. Instead he used the hour well, stripping her naked in the daylight and exploring every curve with slow deliberation. He knew exactly how to touch her, where to touch her, and he used that knowledge, swamping her with sensation.

She could have stayed there all day, but she knew Alec was worried about Meg, so she dressed in her warmest layers and went down to the kitchen.

She poured soup into a flask and put it in a backpack along with a loaf of crusty bread and some cookies Emily had made. "Do you think she'll need anything else? Canned goods?"

Alec shook his head. "If she does, then she can give us a list and we'll stock up at Harbor Stores. But she should be all right. Zach checked on her last week."

"This is one of the many things I love about the island." Sky fastened the backpack. "Does the island grapevine know that bad boy Zach is checking in on little old ladies?"

"Not sure." He zipped his coat. "I don't pay much attention to island gossip." He opened the door and Skylar gasped as the cold hit her.

"Funny, really, to choose to live in a place where it's so cold it hurts your face."

"You didn't choose to. You're my guest. You can leave whenever it gets too much."

Her heart gave a lurch. "Are you asking me to leave?"

He turned with a frown. "No."

"Because if the sex is distracting you from your work—"

"It is." He gave a sexy half smile that made her heart kick against her chest.

She tried to remember if this was the way she'd felt a few days ago but she couldn't remember.

"Don't worry. We'll be bored with each other soon."

He looked at her steadily. "What about you? Is it distracting you from your work?"

"No. I'm going to need to go back to the studio at some point, but right now I'm working on ideas for my next collection and I can do that anywhere." She wasn't ready to go back to New York yet. It was as if that part of her life was somehow connected with Richard and while she was here, he couldn't intrude.

Wishing she'd never mentioned it she looked across the sea. "Maine has extreme light changes. It's spectacular. I'd live here if I could."

"Permanently?"

They started to walk, trudging through the snow toward the road.

"Maybe." She wasn't sure exactly when the thought had come to her. All she knew was that life always felt better when she was on the island. "This place has always been special to me. It's a sanctuary, somewhere to escape to. Whenever I come here I leave my troubles behind on the mainland."

"You never thought of moving here before?"

"No. After I graduated I stayed in the city. My studio space is there. And then I started dating a guy who regarded a trip here as the equivalent of space travel."

"Richard never came with you?"

"No." And whenever she'd raised the idea there'd been the same tension. The same cold expression that was supposed to kill the conversation dead. "To begin with I didn't question it. I assumed it was because he was busy, and this place isn't exactly easy to reach, especially if the weather is bad. I made all sorts of excuses. The only thing I didn't consider was that the reason he didn't visit was because he didn't like my friends. And maybe to some people that wouldn't matter, but to me it is a deal breaker. I won't give up my friends for anyone. They're like family, only better because they accept me the way I am." She paused as a bird flew overhead. "What's that?"

"It's a dark-eyed junco. They're always hovering around bird feeders at this time of year."

It impressed her that he knew, that he could name it in the same way he could name every tree and every plant. He paid attention to his surroundings, took his time to breathe the air and enjoy nature instead of rushing past it on his way somewhere else.

"I miss the puffins. I always look forward to spring when they come back. I can never decide which is my favorite season on the island. I'm glad I'll be able to spend so much more time here next year."

And she wondered how he would feel about that.

Would it be awkward?

Deciding that they'd been serious enough for one conversation, Sky scooped up a handful of snow and advanced on him. "Are you scared, Shipwreck Hunter?"

His response to that was to hook his leg behind hers and land her in the snowdrift.

She screamed and then gasped as snow tumbled onto her, sliding in icy rivulets down the neck of her jacket.

"Holy crap, that is freezing." She tried to get up but the depth of the snow made it impossible. "If I die here, I'm going to come back and haunt you, Alec Hunter. I'll appear every time you want to work. Be afraid."

"I'm terrified." He held out his hand to help her up and she took it, picked her moment and then pulled him off balance.

Cursing, he fell into the snow alongside her. "Remind me why I brought you here?"

"To give me orgasms." Grinning, she pushed a handful of soft snow in his face.

THEY VISITED MEG and spent an enjoyable hour around the kitchen table drinking creamy hot chocolate and listening to Meg's stories of growing up on the island.

Sky was fascinated and it was obvious how much Meg enjoyed having someone else to talk to.

On the way home they found the perfect tree in the forest and dragged it back to the cottage.

Alec left her fussing over it while he went to work.

He dived into the world of the American Revolution and by the time he emerged the weak winter sun had melted into a sea of gunmetal gray.

The only light in his study came from the glow of the computer screen and he blinked and flicked on the desk lamp.

Checking the time, he saw that he'd been working for six hours straight.

His back ached, his neck ached and he was thirsty but he'd made a significant dent in his workload.

Aware that Sky had been on her own for most of the day, he saved his work and stood up, wincing as he rolled his shoulders.

He went downstairs and found his cottage transformed.

The staircase was wrapped with garlands of shimmering silver, interspersed with tiny bows and glowing lights.

Strolling into the living room, he breathed in the scent of cinnamon, cloves and orange. Light came from the flickering flames of the fire and the tree, now free of snow and tastefully decorated with tiny lights Sky must have unearthed from somewhere and twists of silver ribbon fashioned into bows.

Sky was on her knees, half under the tree as she fussed over a skirt designed to look like snow. The ends of her hair brushed the floor as she leaned forward, fiddling until she was satisfied.

He watched her for a couple of minutes. “You look good on your knees with your butt in the air.”

She gave a squeak of embarrassment and tried to wriggle out from under the tree, but her hair caught in a branch and she winced.

“Ow.”

He smiled, enjoying himself. “You seem to be trapped.”

“And you seem to be standing there watching instead of helping.” She tugged and cursed under her breath. “Now there will be hair in your tree. I like working with natural materials but my hair wasn’t supposed to be part of the decorations.” She tugged again and then batted her eyes at him and spoke in her most breathy voice. “Save me, Prince Alec, save me.”

He folded his arms. “I would, but my horse is stuck in a snowdrift.” Shaking his head, he watched as she tried to unwind her hair from the tree, making it worse in the process.

“That’s it. I’m cutting my hair short.”

“Don’t do that.” He dropped to his haunches. “Stay still.”

She stilled and he gently, methodically untangled her hair from the branch.

“Sorry. It gets everywhere.”

It was true, her hair did have a habit of getting everywhere. Over his chest when they made love, sliding past his face, adding a layer of silk to his pillow after she’d fallen asleep.

He let it glide over his hand. “It’s beautiful.”

Her glance was suspicious. “You think it’s beautiful?”

"Any guy with a pulse is going to think your hair is beautiful, Sky. It's fantasy hair."

"Even when it's blocking your shower?"

"Even then, especially if you're in the shower with it." He wound it round his hand and pulled her head toward him. Then he kissed her, his mouth lingering on hers before he released her and stood up. It was too comfortable being here with her. Too easy. "You're free, princess."

He reached out to remove a few pine needles that had tangled themselves in the soft strands. "You've been busy today. My cottage looks like a Christmas grotto."

Her smile widened. "I had fun. I found pretty much everything I need in the forest."

"Good." He glanced round, transformed by her innate talent. Her creativity and ability to make use of what the outdoors had to offer never failed to astound him. But the biggest transformation was her. For the first time, she hadn't apologized for doing the things she loved. "I don't usually decorate. Now I'm wondering why. It looks spectacular. If I ever decide to sell, I'll book you to show the cottage."

"You'd never sell this place." She eased away from him. "The bad news is I was so busy spraying your entire house with silver, I forgot to make us anything to eat. We could heat leftover soup?"

"I have a better idea. The Galleon has live music tonight. It's the start of the island Christmas Festival. I'm taking you dancing."

Her face brightened. "You dance?"

"No. I hate dancing, but I'm sure you love it."

"How do you know that?"

"Because you seem like the sort of person who likes to dance. And now you're going to accuse me of stereotyping you again."

She grinned. "No, I'm not. I am that person. I *love* to dance. And right now I'd grab any excuse to wear something other than thermals. Give me fifteen minutes to shine myself up and knock you dead." She flew across the room and he watched, thinking that her energy would make a perfect renewable power source.

"Sky?"

She stopped as she reached the stairs. "What?"

"Leave your hair down."

THE STAFF AT The Galleon had worked hard, having fun with Christmas and nautical themes. There were tiny lights twisted around lobster pots and wreaths decorated with seashells. The center of the restaurant had been turned into a dance floor, surrounded by tables that gleamed with silver and crystal.

On Puffin Island, businesses learned to be flexible and to cater to the needs of the local population, and Sallyanne Fisher, head chef of The Galleon, knew how to give her customers a good time while staying true to her goal—to deliver exceptional local food.

In honor of their third annual Christmas Festival, she'd prepared a feast.

During the summer the restaurant was booked months in advance by people visiting from all corners of the globe, but tonight's celebration was for the locals. Any money raised would be used to purchase rescue equipment for the fire department.

Alec had reserved a table for two, but the moment they walked into the restaurant they discovered that

Zach and Brittany had also bought tickets, and the four of them ended up sharing a table.

Brittany was looking sleek and pretty in a short blue dress that showed off her long legs.

Sky slid into the seat next to her. "You look great!"

"It's the only dress I own. And Zach is going to have to carry me through the snow because I cannot walk in these heels." She studied her friend. "You look incredible, but you always do. There's something different about you, though, and I can't work out what it is. It's not the dress—" she frowned and then her expression changed "—it's because you're wearing your hair down." She gave a smile of understanding and raised her glass. "To wearing our hair any way we damn well want to wear it. And to rebound sex, which is obviously doing you good."

Sky tapped her glass against hers.

Was it rebound sex? She almost wished they were alone so she could confess her changing feelings for Alec. "Where's Em? I tried calling her earlier and she didn't answer."

"She's not feeling too great. Ryan says she has a winter bug. Feeling sick and generally crappy."

"Oh, no. I'll call her tomorrow. We should get together, just the three of us." She put her glass down as Alec approached. She'd thought he looked his best in sexy outdoor gear, but now she decided that maybe she'd been wrong about that. He looked handsome and sophisticated in a tailored suit, the fabric skimming shoulders that were broad and powerful.

He had an indefinable strength and presence that set him apart from most of the men in the room.

She wondered whether that was one of the things

that had drawn Selina to him. Strength was an appealing trait to someone who was insecure and vulnerable.

"Dance?" He held out his hand and Sky felt her heart race like a teenager's.

She stood up and glanced at her friend expectantly.

Brittany laughed. "Are you kidding? Reindeer will fly across the sky before Zachary Flynn joins me on the dance floor." But there was a wistful note in her voice and Sky saw Zach frown slightly.

Leaving them to it, she took Alec's hand and sashayed onto the dance floor in time to the music.

They did it all. Jive, salsa, tango—the band, clearly motivated by the enthusiasm of the dancers, kept changing the tempo until Sky and Alec were the only two people dancing and everyone else was watching.

They carried on until her less than perfect attempt at an Argentinean tango almost resulted in an uncomfortable encounter between her high heel and a certain delicate part of his anatomy.

With an alarmed look, Alec scooped her up and carried her off the dance floor.

"It ends now," he muttered, "while I can still walk. When you threatened to put your stiletto somewhere it should never go, I didn't realize you intended to do it in public."

That awful night seemed like a lifetime ago.

Breathless and laughing, she slid her arms round his neck. "That was so much fun. I thought you said you couldn't dance."

"I said I didn't love it. I didn't say I couldn't do it. My mother sent me to dance classes with my sister when I was a teenager. At the time I hated her for it, until I discovered it gave me a head start over most other guys." He set her down gently and she saw that Brittany and Zach were dancing slowly in a corner.

Zach's hand was cradling her head and he was saying something softly in her ear that made her laugh up at him.

Sky's insides turned over. Zach hated dancing, but he was doing it for Brittany.

That was what love was, wasn't it?

It was doing something you didn't want to do, just because you knew it would make your partner happy.

Alec handed her a drink. "Thirsty?"

"Yes. And hot." She drank and swept her hair back from her face with her fingers. "Will we freeze if we go outside on the deck for a few minutes?"

"Probably, but we should still do it. Wait there."

He returned moments later with their coats and draped hers around her shoulders.

Leaving the noise and laughter behind, they walked out onto the terrace.

The snow had been cleared but the air was freezing, cooling her heated skin in seconds.

Alec was standing behind her and he wrapped her in his arms and rested his chin on her head.

She stared into the darkness, listening to the sound of the ocean, shaken by the realization that she hadn't been this happy in a long time.

And that was because of Alec. Not just his body, or his family, but *him*. The man.

Leaning against him, she felt safe and warm.

Alec Hunter was a man who could handle anything life threw in his direction.

Anything, she thought, except a serious relationship. He wasn't prepared to handle that again.

"What a perfect night. I feel very Christmassy. It's time to make plans and wishes for the next year." She slid her hands over his. "Tell me about your next big adventure, Shipwreck Hunter."

"Antarctica in January."

She gave a gasp and half turned. "Antarctica? It happened?" She thought back to the conversation he'd had with his father. How much he'd wanted it. "You weren't sure. Oh, Alec, I'm so thrilled for you."

"Are you?" He said it cautiously. "Why?"

"Because it's what you wanted more than anything." She turned so that she was facing him properly. "When did you find out?"

"I had an email yesterday."

"And you didn't share it with me? We should have opened champagne. We'll do it when we get home. I have a bottle in the fridge ready."

"Ready for what?"

She locked her hand in the front of his coat. "For occasions like this one. I happen to agree with your mother that we should celebrate small moments. In the meantime—we'll toast without the alcohol." She lifted her hand to his face. "To dreams coming true."

He looked at her for a long moment and she had a feeling she'd surprised him in some way, but before she could question him he cupped her face in his hands and lowered his mouth to hers.

"To dreams."

As his mouth touched hers she felt the punch of physical awareness and something else. Something indefinable but equally powerful.

It uncoiled deep inside her, warming all the chilled parts of her body.

It made her heart swell in her chest and her body feel as if she'd had a shot of adrenaline straight into the vein.

She didn't know what it meant, but she sensed it wasn't good.

Any feeling that went beyond the superficial wasn't good.

He'd made it clear this thing they shared would never go deeper and she not only understood but agreed with their arrangement.

Brittany and Zach came out onto the terrace to say that they were leaving and soon after Sky and Alec left, too.

To take her mind off the intimacy of the short car journey, she asked him more about the Antarctica trip.

"The BBC is making a documentary on Ernest Shackleton, the polar explorer. He planned to cross Antarctica via the South Pole, from the Weddell Sea to the Ross Sea. His ship, the *Endurance*, became trapped by pack ice and they couldn't free her. Ten months later she sank."

"Ten months? It took ten months to sink? So he didn't make it."

"He didn't succeed in crossing Antarctica, but he brought his men home. It's an incredible story. They couldn't drag their boats and stores, so they camped on the ice and drifted with it until the ice started to break up."

"Sounds precarious."

"They launched the boats and made it to a barren island. Shackleton knew their only chance of rescue was to reach the whaling station at South Georgia, an island eight hundred miles away, but that meant crossing one of the worst seas in the world in an Antarctic winter."

She didn't know which was more soothing and seductive, the soft purr of the car or the deep timbre of Alec's voice. She decided that he could read the telephone book and still keep an audience captivated.

"I'm guessing this didn't have a happy ending."

"Surprisingly enough, it did. He took one of the ship's boats, the *James Caird*, and a handful of men. They knew they'd be facing hurricane winds and high seas, so they reinforced the boat, did what they could."

"They made it?"

"Yes, and then rescued the men left behind. Shackleton showed tremendous leadership."

"You're going to talk about him?"

"I'm going to talk about the *Endurance* and the *James Caird*."

"So you're their go-to boat guy."

He smiled. "I suppose I am."

And he was good at it.

She didn't tell him that the day before when he'd been working, she'd sneaked onto the internet and watched him on YouTube. It had taken less than five minutes for her to see why he had such a large female following. She'd watched everything, sometimes twice, and it had been clear why he was in such demand as a presenter. "I'm envious."

He slowed as they reached the turning to the cottage. "Why? I can't imagine you'd particularly like Antarctica. Harsh, inhospitable, temperatures that make winter in Maine seem balmy—"

"It would be an adventure. And there's no such thing as bad weather, only bad clothing. And think of the light, the shadows, the luminous effect of low sun on ice—"

He was silent for a moment and then he killed the engine and stared out to sea. "You're a surprising person, Skylar Tempest."

She told herself that surprising could be good. So did that mean he'd just paid her a compliment?

It bothered her how much she hoped it did.

She was acutely aware of him. Of the power of his thigh so close to her own, of the strength of his hands and the width of his shoulders.

He'd go to Antarctica, he'd fly off on his next adventure, and then what?

He'd come back here and live in his cottage on the cliffs, buried in his books.

"Will you promise me something?" She felt the tension ripple through him and carried on quickly. "Don't shut yourself away here when you're back from Antarctica. Get out there again. You're a smart, interesting, fantastic guy and you should be with someone equally fantastic."

It was a moment before he replied. "You're taking over the role of mother?"

"No, I'm taking the role of friend. You shouldn't be using what happened with your ex-wife as a reason to avoid relationships."

"I'm not avoiding relationships, just a certain type of relationship."

She laughed. "The one that requires you to book early if you want the Plaza in June."

"That's the one."

Her laughter faded and she put her hand on his thigh. "You should get out there again, Alec. You should bury your cynicism somewhere in the bay along with all those shipwrecks and you should move on."

There was a long silence and then he turned his head to look at her. "Why?"

Because she couldn't bear to think of him alone, believing he wasn't capable of making someone happy.

Her heart thudded in her chest. "Because you deserve to be with someone. You deserve to be happy."

And with that she fumbled with the door and almost fell out of the car in her haste to escape before he asked her the question she didn't even dare ask herself.

CHAPTER FIFTEEN

THE SNOW BECAME their playground.

They wrapped up in layers of down and waterproof and explored the groomed trails through the forest, sometimes on Alec's snowmobile and occasionally on cross-country skis.

Apart from a couple of hardy outdoorsmen who passed them, they had the place to themselves.

Which was just as well, she thought, as she fell on her back again trying to balance on her skis while taking a photo.

Fewer people to witness her humiliation.

It made it worse that Alec was so competent at everything that had a physical element. She was convinced he could have been dropped anywhere in the world with nothing more than a backpack and survived.

"I'm crap at this," Sky said as she struggled with her skis. "I'm better at downhill." But she had to admit it was fun and she was laughing as she levered herself up again. "And how come you ski? You're British. You don't even have mountains."

"I was on the college ski team."

"Of course you were." She awkwardly rose to her feet, brushing off the snow. "Is there anything you're not good at, Shipwreck Hunter?"

"Marriage." He rescued her ski pole. "I was exceedingly bad at marriage."

The forest was still and quiet, the only sound the occasional rush of snow falling from the trees onto more snow.

She took the pole from him. "So when you're bad at something you give up on it? That's crazy logic."

"But it protects the innocent."

From what she'd heard his ex-wife sounded more manipulative than innocent, but Sky decided not to voice that thought aloud. "Well, you know what they say about being bad at something—you need to practice more." She wavered on her skis and he shot out a hand and steadied her, his expression amused.

"You need to get your skis into the tracks, then you won't lose your balance."

"Strangely enough I was trying to do that. You're probably thinking it would help if I stopped taking pictures."

"Why would you do that? For you, the pictures are the important part, not the skiing." He kept his hand on her arm, holding her securely. "Have you taken anything you can use?"

She still hadn't got used to the fact that he didn't mind her stopping all the time to take photos. "Possibly. I took a few of the sunlight through the snowy trees. I should have brought the Nikon but I can't ski with that round my neck." She shuffled back into the tracks. "You're very patient."

"I'm not patient."

"You are. You never complain when I stop to take photos."

"Why would I complain?" His eyes seemed darker

than ever against the untarnished white of the forest and she turned away and tried to focus on where she was putting her feet. She knew that if she kept looking at him, she'd fall over.

"Because of me you do a lot of waiting around."

"There's no point in being outdoors if you don't stop to breathe the air and enjoy the view."

He was so different from Richard.

"I'm very dreamy and unfocused."

"I think you have tremendous focus. Anyone who can turn a creative talent into a business has focus. You've achieved your dream. Tempest Designs."

"It's a work in progress. And it's not my whole dream." She breathed out, blowing clouds into the freezing air.

"You want love. I know. You want the sort of big love that makes you feel as if your heart is going to burst."

She laughed. "The sort that makes my heart feel too big for my chest. *Not* burst, thank you very much."

"That's a relief." He reached out and zipped her coat up to her neck to keep out the cold. "Because that option could be messy. You have a big heart, Skylar Tempest. I wouldn't want to be there when it bursts."

"You've already fixed my bruised head and my cut finger. I'll take responsibility for my heart myself."

His hand rested on her hip and his face was close to hers. "You," he said softly, "deserve to meet someone incredible."

He took her face in his hands and kissed her, and the contrast between the warm skill of his mouth and the cool bite of the winter air intensified every sensation.

All it took was that one slow kiss to make her head spin and her knees go heavy.

She felt his hands run slowly down her back, drawing her against him. Through the layers of clothing she could feel his body, hard and powerful, and then he deepened the kiss, searching and exploring until she was swamped with dizzying waves of pleasure. Desire sank its teeth into her and she pressed against him, frustrated by the layers of clothing.

"No one kisses the way you do." She murmured the words against his mouth. "If we get naked here, will we be caught?"

"No, but we risk getting frostbite in certain vital parts of our anatomy. It might make a stiletto through the balls seem like the soft option." He always managed to make her smile.

"We probably won't see each other once Christmas is over so maybe we should make a date for a hamburger in the summer." She hadn't intended to say it, but it slipped out, as if her subconscious was reluctant to let go of something that felt so good. "That was the wrong thing to say. Don't freak out."

"Sky—" he put his hands on her shoulders "—I don't ever want you to watch what you say with me. There is no 'wrong thing' between us, ever. And I'm having fun. More fun than I've had in a long time." He held her gaze, looking at her with such an intense expression that her heart started to pound in her chest and her palms grew damp.

Instead of making the situation easier, it made it more complicated.

"Right. Well—good. It's good that we've cleared that up." She peeped at him. "You're hard to read. You have a serious face. I guess it wouldn't do to be talking about some serious historical matter on camera and then suddenly collapse with laughter."

"It happens."

"It does? I can't imagine you losing control. Whenever I see you on-screen, you're very smooth and polished."

"You've watched me?"

It wasn't something she'd intended to confess. It made her feel like a schoolgirl with a crush. "I might have sneaked a little peep at that episode where you took your shirt off—just for research purposes. I can see why it has had so many views and why Liv's friend wants an introduction."

His eyes darkened. "You've seen more of me than that over the past couple of weeks."

Much more. And still it wasn't enough.

Her stomach flipped. "I wouldn't mind seeing it again, so let's get off this trail before I break something essential. You can tell me all about your embarrassing filming outtakes over a bowl of hot soup and a glass of good wine."

"Go ahead of me."

"Why? You want to look at my butt?"

"No, I want to be there to pick you up when you fall." His eyes gleamed. "But I can't promise that I won't look at your butt at the same time."

He always made her laugh.

"That would make a perfect alternative wedding vow, along with 'I solemnly promise always to remove strands of my hair from the shower,' or 'I solemnly promise to try not to sever parts of my body when I'm making soup.'" She saw his expression change.

He lost the relaxed, easygoing smile and she gave an embarrassed shake of her head. "Oops."

"I could probably come up with a few vows of my own." His tone was level. "'I solemnly promise to vanish at a moment's notice and spend weeks somewhere with no phone signal, thereby leaving you incandescent with rage.'"

She wondered if he was sharing that to make her feel better about her impulsive remark. "That made Selina crazy?"

"Everything I did made her crazy. Or perhaps I should say, everything I didn't do. Whenever I was offered a new project, she'd sink into misery until I began to dread telling her I was going away. If I'd told her I was going to Antarctica, she would have taken it as a sign I didn't love her and needed to travel to the nethermost reaches of the earth in order to escape."

"That doesn't sound like love to me. When you're in love with someone you should be their biggest fan. You celebrate each little success, and feel proud of everything they achieve. You encourage them and cheer them on."

"We've already established that you have high expectations."

"I don't think so. Not if you're truly partners."

"You believe in the 'two halves making a whole' approach."

"That isn't what I think. I think both parties are already whole." She pondered and tried to explain. "I believe love is a journey, it's an adventure you take together."

"Adventure?"

"Of course. I want someone I can support and encourage and who will support and encourage me back. I need someone who understands that there are going to be times when I stare into space and suddenly whip out a sketchbook or a camera. That there are going to be times when the journey is hard and we have to pick each other up. I want someone I can laugh with, and talk with in the middle of the night. I want to admire and respect them. Most of all I want someone who gets me. I can't take the journey of a lifetime with someone who doesn't get me."

The only sound was the lonely call of a bird somewhere in the forest.

She stood there, frozen into stillness, realizing that the only person she wanted to make that journey with was him.

She thought about how he'd been there for her every step of the way over the past few weeks. About the way they'd laughed and talked about everything. The way he was happy to be still and enjoy the outdoors while she took endless photos, and how he never complained about the way she looked or told her to hurry up.

Because she hadn't been trying to impress him or please him, never once had she tried to be anything other than herself. And that, she thought, was true intimacy. Revealing yourself fully, living life honestly with someone, was intimacy.

She'd stayed with Richard hoping she'd fall in love with him, even sometimes wondering if she was, but she knew now that falling in love wasn't about how much time you spent with someone but how being with them made you feel.

And being with Alec made her feel good.

He touched her face with his hand, his expression quizzical. “What’s wrong?”

It was typical of him that he’d noticed the shift in her mood and typical that he would ask.

There was so much she wanted to say to him, and she couldn’t say any of it.

She’d promised him, hadn’t she, right back at the beginning that she wouldn’t fall in love.

That this wouldn’t happen.

Her heart felt too full for her chest. So full it was almost too much to bear.

This was it. This was how it felt.

Now she knew.

And she also knew there was nothing she could do about it.

“Nothing is wrong.” She forced the words through dry lips, knowing that he’d be horrified if he could read her mind. “We should go back.”

ALEC SPRAWLED IN the chair in his office.

His laptop gazed back at him accusingly, the document untouched.

What the hell was he doing?

He should never have brought Skylar here. He’d been careful to avoid any romantic entanglements and keep his relationships simple, and yet somehow this “simple” relationship had turned into something different.

There was nothing simple about it.

Instead of working, he found himself thinking about her all the time.

Like now.

With a soft curse he hit a key and tried to focus

on the screen, but instead of seeing his work, he saw her face. Her smile.

It was supposed to be all about sex, but at some point that had progressed to fun and sex and from there it had moved on to fun and sex and friendship. And over that time he'd learned a great deal about her. He'd learned that although she was beautiful, she wasn't at all focused on her appearance. That she was equally happy in an oversize down jacket as she'd been in that incredible silver dress the night of her exhibition. That she was exceptionally creative, but lacked the basic insecurity that plagued so many creative types.

He knew she was happy in a crowd, but equally happy on her own and, like him, she could easily lose track of time when she was working on a project. Usually when he was with someone, he needed his own space, but with Sky he'd never once felt trapped.

She talked, sometimes with no filter, but she was also a good listener.

He'd shared with her, he realized, more than he'd ever shared with a woman.

And it was time to face the truth.

She had feelings for him.

He knew enough about women to know she had feelings for him.

Giving up on work, he went in search of her and found her in her favorite place—the window seat in the garden room.

"What are you doing in here? It's dark."

"I was trying to work but I couldn't concentrate so I thought I'd sit for a while." She moved her legs so that he could sit down. "Productive session?"

He noticed that she didn't meet his gaze. "No. I couldn't concentrate, either."

He wondered if she'd tell him how she felt.

He sat next to her on the window seat, his thigh brushing against hers.

It was a situation he'd never imagined, being here with a woman. Especially not one who induced such strong feelings.

"I expect you were too excited about Christmas." She nudged him in a playful gesture. "Don't worry, I've told Santa you've been a *very* good boy so I'm sure you'll get everything on your wish list."

He didn't smile. He no longer knew what his wish list looked like.

He wondered if she did.

What was she hoping for?

His stomach felt hollow because he didn't want to be the next person in her life to ruin her dreams. Enough people had already done that. He wasn't going to do it, too.

He knew he couldn't be trusted with her heart.

"What's on your wish list?" he asked.

"Nothing."

"Not even a new tiara or fairy wings? I gather from Ryan those are both on Lizzy's list."

She smiled and leaned her head on his shoulder. "It was never a tiara or fairy wings for me. When I was six I wanted to be a ballerina, but that was only because my parents took me to the Met and I fell in love with Degas's painting, *The Dance Class*. I wanted paints. Every year I asked for paints."

"I thought your parents didn't let you believe in Santa."

"They didn't, so I asked them directly."

"And that didn't work?"

"No. Eventually my aunt bought me paints. I spread them out in the kitchen on Christmas Day and incurred my mother's wrath because we had fifty guests coming for dinner."

"Fifty? That must have been a lot of studying. Did you ever get it all mixed up?"

"Oh, yeah." She sat up and removed a blond hair from his shoulder. "There was one Christmas Eve dinner when I asked the CEO of one of the banks how his new baby was doing."

"He didn't have a new baby?"

"No, but he'd recently borrowed someone else's wife. It was a big scandal. My mother had instructed us absolutely not to touch the subject of his social life. We were supposed to keep the conversation focused on his charitable interests."

He imagined her getting it wrong, stumbling over the awkward moment when she'd suddenly realized her mistake.

"So if you had to write to Santa now, what would you say to him?"

"Be careful not to get stuck in the chimney."

He laughed. "That's all?"

"Santa doesn't bring the things that are really important in life."

"Like what?"

"Friendship. Love."

It was a testament to her resilience that she still wanted that. "That would be top of your list? After everything that happened with Richard?"

"What I had with Richard wasn't love, but even

if it had been and my heart had been shattered into a million tiny pieces, I would still never give up on love. It's too important. In the end, love is the only thing that matters."

Alec stared at her fingers, which were now entwined with his. "Even when love causes pain?"

"You only feel that way because you had a bad experience, but what you had wasn't love, either. You weren't in love with Selina, and I don't believe she was in love with you. It isn't love if you feel you have to chain someone to you. And it isn't love if you want them to change, or be different, or give up everything they love. You fall in love with the whole person, so why would you want to change that? Take you for example—" she tightened her fingers on his "—you have an adventurous nature, but you're also academic so it's obvious you're going to want to spend time doing that. It's who you are. Take that away, and you'd be just as miserable as I am when I can't do what I love."

She was right that he'd been miserable.

"We made each other miserable." He hesitated, wanting to share as much as he could so that she understood. He needed her to understand. Needed her to understand that this was something he wasn't good at. "Her parents divorced when she was young and it left her with a chronic insecurity. When I wasn't with her, she wanted to know where I was and who I was with—not easy in a job like mine where I might be away filming for weeks. She wanted us to be together every moment of the day, but even when we were together we weren't happy."

"You've never told me how you met her."

"We were at a charity event and happened to leave at the same time. I was about to get into my taxi when someone knocked her over and stole her purse."

"So you were all dressed up in your tux, looking hot and sexy and you rescued her. You caught him? Of course you did." She didn't wait for his answer. "So you rescued her and then you took her home, and she wanted you to come up so that she could thank you properly but you said no, because you didn't want to take advantage of someone vulnerable. And that just about nailed it for her."

"How do you know that?"

"It was just a guess." She lifted her hand and touched his cheek. "You rescued her. You did the chivalrous thing."

"I did what anyone would have done."

"No. You did what you would have done. And I bet she loved being rescued, didn't she? And that set the pattern for your relationship. It's no wonder it didn't work, Alec. How could it? You weren't equals."

"Don't do that." There was a bitter taste in his mouth. It was so tempting to let her think that way, to bask momentarily in the warmth of her approval. But then what? That wasn't honest, was it? "Don't turn me into some sort of hero because that's what she did and it didn't take her long to find out how wrong she was and she's still dealing with the disillusionment. I don't want our relationship to be that way."

"It isn't. I don't think you're a hero. I do think you're a decent man, despite your attempts to persuade me otherwise. Why did she hate you going away? She was afraid you'd have an affair?"

"Yes, but in the end she was the one who did that."

It was something he'd never discussed with anyone, although his mother had guessed. When Sky made no comment, he glanced at her. "You don't seem surprised."

"When we were staying with your parents you said something about not everyone waiting until a relationship had ended to start another. You wouldn't have had an affair, so I guessed it was her."

"I walked in on them. She staged it that way. She wanted to make me jealous." He thought about that night. About the emotions that had flowed through him. "Why are you so sure I wouldn't have had one?"

"Because that's not your style. You're straight and honest. And you're an adult. If a relationship wasn't working for you anymore, you'd say so. You're strong enough to say and do the decent thing."

"I was a difficult person to be married to."

"Anyone would be difficult if they're married to the wrong person. She wasn't the only one who was hurt. You were hurt, too."

He sat for a moment, silent, knowing that it was important that she knew the truth. "I wasn't hurt, I was relieved, Sky. When I saw her with him, I was relieved. That was the moment I knew it was over and she knew it, too."

"You were hurt, Alec. Maybe not by the affair, but before that by all the small things she did—or didn't do. Somehow she managed to convince you that you can't make anyone happy. That you're better off on your own."

"I am. I'm selfish. Far too selfish to make a commitment like that. I don't want to be responsible for another person's happiness. I want to be able to leave at a moment's notice and travel wherever I want. I want to be able to spend a week with my nose in a book and not apologize for it. I want to work through the night when a book is going well, and I want to talk about travel, history, writing—the things that interest me, not parties and celebrities and who is dating who. That doesn't interest me." His voice was rough. Brutal as he spelled it out. "I really am better off on my own."

He was delivering a warning and he hoped she was listening.

"If you were selfish, you wouldn't have come looking for me that night in London. You would have carried on with your life, as Richard did. You only came to my exhibition to please Brit. You didn't even *like* me, but you refused to leave me. You stayed with me, and then you refused to let me stay on my own, and that was even though you were remembering what happened last time you helped a woman in trouble."

"You're nothing like my ex-wife." Now that he knew Skylar he couldn't imagine how he'd ever thought it.

"You are letting her affect the way you live your life, Alec. And that's crap. If you're caught in a storm when you're sailing, do you never take the boat out again?" She nudged him with her elbow. "So what do you think, Shipwreck Hunter? Maybe your New Year's resolution should be to get laid in as many positions possible with as many gorgeous women as possible in the hope you might meet someone interesting."

For some reason that didn't sound remotely appealing.

"I don't think so."

"Kirsti and I will vet them for you. Only women who love the outdoors and can wrestle a wild boar with their bare hands." She paused. "Promise me you'll get out there? I don't want you to live your life alone."

"What about you? What's your New Year's resolution?"

There was a brief silence and then she gave him her trademark megawatt smile. "I'm going to live life boldly, being me. And hopefully somewhere down the line I will meet a guy who thinks there are worse ways to die than being strangled in his sleep by my hair."

Alec found himself hoping she didn't meet that guy soon.

He wanted her to be happy, but he didn't want to think about her smiling and laughing with another man.

What did that say about him?

That he was exactly what his ex-wife had said he was.

Selfish.

HARBOR HOUSE GLEAMED with lights and festive greenery and Emily was deep in preparations for Christmas.

The kitchen smelled of baking and was covered with bowls, spatulas and trays of cookies cooling. The table was spread with paper and Lizzy was painting, her face a picture of concentration as she shook glitter over the page.

"I love that." Sky took a closer look. "It's the island. And there's the *Captain Hook*, all decorated for the holidays. And is this Alec's House?" She pointed to a lopsided house with a seagull next to it. "Do you need help finishing it?"

Lizzy reached for the pink glitter. "I'm running out of glitter."

"I might be able to help with that." Sky delved into her bag. "Glitter. In four different colors."

Lizzy's face brightened. "You're the *best.*"

Emily closed her eyes. "Have I told you lately how much I hate you? The last glitter you gave her ended up in the shower. Ryan sparkled every time he went to work."

Lizzy focused on the page, her tongue caught between her teeth as she drew carefully.

"But she's loving it." Sky spread the tubes of glitter on the table and put her bag down. "And creativity should never be stifled. Are you feeling better, Em?"

She was desperate to talk to her friend, but she knew there was no chance while Lizzy was there.

"Pretty much." Emily had her head down, helping Lizzy, and Sky reached for the bowl of cranberries from the table.

"These are pretty. Like jewels."

"Have you had any ideas for your new collection?"

"A few. Nothing final."

The next step was to get back to her studio in New York and start work.

But that would mean leaving Puffin Island.

And Alec.

And she didn't want to do that until the very last minute.

She wanted to make the most of every moment.

She sat down at the table, staring at Alec's cottage in the drawing.

Leaving it would be a wrench, but nowhere near as much of a wrench as leaving him.

The conversation the night before had been difficult because up until now she'd never had to hide her feelings from him. Their honesty was one of the things she'd loved most about their relationship.

What if he guessed? What if she couldn't hide the way she felt?

She'd made him a promise. She'd told him this wouldn't happen.

And she knew he wasn't going to change his mind.

He'd reminded her of that last night.

His words had been a warning.

She desperately wanted to talk to her friend but Lizzy was between them so she searched for something else to talk about instead.

"I met Meg Ferguson for the first time. Do you know her?"

"A little. She's a friend of Agnes's. She was part of the island woman's group that Kathleen used to belong to. I remember Brit telling us that they used to go on theatre trips to the mainland." Emily rescued the paintbrush Lizzy was waving around. "How did you meet her?"

"Alec checks on her when he's home. All summer he acted like an antisocial hermit, but when he's on the island he visits her every week and has done so ever since her husband died. That's a year, Em."

"I had no idea. He never said anything."

"He doesn't. That isn't his way. Richard used to do things based on how visible they were to the public, but Alec does it because it's the right thing to do."

Emily slid the top back onto a tube of glitter.

"That's good. So he's not as cynical and bitter as he appears on the surface."

"He isn't bitter." Sky leaped to his defense. "I think he blames himself and because of that he's wary."

"What's bitter?" Lizzy lifted her head from her painting and Sky realized they had to be careful what they said.

Emily provided an explanation while Sky stared into the bowl of cranberries.

"He loves art."

"Who?"

"Alec. I didn't expect that. I've never had anyone I could talk to about that before."

"That's good. I'm glad you're not upset about Richard." Emily ushered Lizzy to wash her hands.

"Actually, I'm happier than I've been in a long time. I'm having fun." *And I'm in love, and totally messed up. And I need to talk to you.*

Emily's head was close to Lizzy's as she washed paint from the little girl's fingers.

Sky swallowed. She *really* needed to talk.

Maybe she'd suggest a girls' night in. Just her, Emily and Brittany.

They could open a couple bottles of wine and chat.

"Are you free tomorrow night?"

Emily dried Lizzy's hands and lifted her down from the chair. "Sorry, no. We have a fund-raising concert at the school. You're welcome to join us. It's going to be fun."

But there would be no opportunity to talk. Sky shook her head. "How about the night after that?"

"We're helping Agnes decorate her flat. I've made a casserole and Lizzy has made decorations and next

on our list is chocolate cake. We're doing that now."
Emily cleared up the painting materials and then pulled eggs and butter out of the fridge and put them on the table while Lizzy found a bowl and a wooden spoon.

It was clearly a well-oiled routine and Sky thought how much her friend had changed since the beginning of the summer. She was so much more relaxed.

"You're happy," she said softly and Emily smiled as she weighed and measured.

"Yes, I am. Who would have thought it."

Lizzy picked up an egg and tapped it gingerly on the edge of the bowl. Half went into the bowl and the other half slid in a jellied mess onto the table. "Oops."

Sky watched as her friend wiped it up and showed the little girl how to do it.

She was patient and kind and Sky felt something uncurl inside her.

The best thing in the world was to see Emily with a family.

It wasn't just Emily who had changed, she realized with a pang.

All their lives had changed.

"You're brilliant. I love you."

Emily glanced at her in surprise. "I love you, too." She helped Lizzy stir the mixture and then spoon it into deep muffin cases. "Have you heard from Richard?"

"Nothing. And I'm relieved. We have nothing to say to each other." And they never really had. It unsettled her to think that not once in the time she'd spent with Richard had she experienced the intimacy she'd found with Alec. "Alec said the other night he thought

Richard might have a touch of narcissistic personality disorder. A lot of politicians do, apparently. It fits."

And she realized that all she'd done since she'd walked through the door was talk about Alec.

If she couldn't be with him, all she wanted to do was talk about him, as if a conversation somehow brought him closer.

She'd never felt this way about anyone before.

She put the bowl down, her hands shaking.

She had to get him out of her mind. She had to.

This was supposed to be lighthearted fun to take her mind off Richard. It was never meant to get serious.

Emily didn't seem to have noticed anything was wrong. She made coffee and put a mug in front of Skylar. "What about your parents? Are they still upset?"

"Of course." Sky had told Emily about the message from her mother and her friend had been horrified.

"I can't believe she booked a venue. That's appalling."

"My mother would think it was organized. She's probably going to bill me for the cancellation charge."

"I don't understand your parents. It's as if they don't care what you want." Emily looked puzzled. "They don't respect who you are."

"That's because I'm not who they want me to be."

Lizzy licked the spoon and looked at her solemnly. "Emily says you can be anything you want to be."

Sky smiled, remembering a time when she'd believed that. "And she's right." *Just not when you have parents like mine,* she thought. Then, you could be who you wanted to be but it came at a price, and that price was grim disapproval.

Emily wiped her hands. “I’m so glad we’re all spending Christmas together. Brittany has invited Agnes, too. It will be fun.”

“It will.” But somehow she was no longer looking forward to it.

What if she couldn’t pretend anymore in front of Alec? What if he guessed how she felt?

The cake in the oven, Lizzy went to play with Cocoa, their spaniel.

The moment she left the room, they both spoke at the same time.

“There’s something I need to tell you—”

They stared at each other and then laughed, remembering the number of times they’d done the same thing in the past.

“You go first.” Sky felt guilty that all she’d done since she’d walked into the room was talk about Alec. “Is it about Something Seashore? How is everything going?”

“Good. We’re all set to open at Easter—but no, that isn’t my news.”

“Then what? What’s wrong?” Sky picked up the mug, noticing for the first time the dark circles under her friend’s eyes. “You look really tired. Is it still that bug? Have you seen a doctor?” She leaned forward, worried. “Tell me. Is it Ryan?”

“No! He’s wonderful. I adore him. I— He’s the best thing that ever happened to me.”

“Is it Lizzy?” Seriously concerned, Sky went through the list of possibilities but Emily shook her head and tears suddenly welled in her eyes. “Now you're scaring me." Forgetting her own problems, Sky was on her feet and round the table in two strides. "Whatever it is, we'll fix it together. Do you want me to call Brit?"

"No." Emily wiped her face with her palm just as Ryan walked into the room.

His murmur of apology died the moment he saw the tears. "Em?" His voice was raw. "Are you ill, sweetheart? What's wrong?" He nudged Sky out of the way and took Emily in his arms.

Sky stepped back, feeling redundant.

This was how it was now.

Their friendship was changing, too. Things were different.

Brittany had Zach, Emily had Ryan and she had—

No one.

It would be foolish to pretend Alec was going to be in her life for long.

Her friends had both fallen in love with the right guys whereas she—she swallowed—she'd fallen for a man who didn't want anything to do with love.

Maybe her mother was right. She made crap choices.

Except love wasn't a choice.

Emily leaned her head against Ryan's chest. "Just being silly. I'm really emotional. Can't seem to help it, sorry."

"It will pass, honey." Ryan stroked Emily's hair. "I'm here. I'll always be here."

Feeling like an eavesdropper, Sky wondered what it was that would pass and then worked it out. "Holy crap—are you—?"

Emily eased away from Ryan, checking that Lizzy

wasn't in the room. "I'm pregnant. That's what I was going to tell you. I wasn't going to say anything because it's very early, but given that I'm always either sleeping or throwing up these days, it isn't going to be easy to hide it from the people close to me."

"Why would you want to hide something so amazing? Emily—" Sky's eyes filled and she pressed her hand to her chest. "Wow."

Ryan gave her a wicked smile. "Hey, she didn't do it on her own. I played my part."

"Yeah, I bet you did." Sky punched him on the arm. "Get out of here. This is a girl moment. It's not every day I learn I'm going to be an auntie. And don't look at me like that. She may not be my blood sister, but she's my heart sister and that's every bit as powerful." For a moment her own confusion was eclipsed by delight for her friend. Tears spilled over and she brushed them away with her palm. "Crap. Look at me. I'm a mess. Does Brittany know?"

"I do now." Her voice equally choked, Brittany walked into the room and wrapped Emily in a hug, ignoring Ryan. "You should lock your front door if you don't want eavesdroppers."

"This is Puffin Island. No one locks their front doors."

"No one needs to lock their doors." Zach followed her into the room. "There is so much snow no one can get anywhere near the doors anyway. Congratulations."

"Our first baby." Brit sniffed. "How long have you known?"

"A week or two." Emily was scarlet. "I was going to tell you."

But she hadn't, Sky thought. *Because now she has Ryan.*

"You don't share anything you're not ready to share," Brittany said softly. "You don't want people to know?"

"Not yet. We'll tell Alec of course, but other than that we're going to keep it to ourselves until after Christmas."

"I won't say a word. But this is Puffin Island. There's a strong chance everyone on the island is going to know the sex of the baby before you do."

"Sit down." Ryan urged Emily into the chair and squatted down next to her. "What can I get you, sweetheart?"

Seeing him so protective reminded Sky of Alec and she thought about the way he'd picked her up that night, when she was at her lowest point, and carried her to the taxi. About how he'd held her head when she was sick, and comforted her when she'd cried. She thought about his family and Church and Nelson.

She'd probably never see them again.

And her friends, who had been closer than family for so long, were embarking on a new chapter. There'd be a place for her, of course, but it wouldn't be the same.

It was pathetic to feel so teary, but fortunately she had Emily as the excuse.

And she could see Emily and Ryan didn't need her around right now.

She was going to have to handle her problem by herself.

Pulling herself together, she picked up her bag and

made for the door. "I'm going to leave you two alone. If you need anything, call me."

Brittany glanced at her. "How did you get here? Did you borrow Alec's car?"

"No, I walked."

"It's snowing again. I'll give you a ride back to Fisherman's Cottage."

"What about Zach?"

"He brought his own car. He's driving up to the airfield to fly a couple over to Bar Harbor. I'll give you a ride."

"Thanks." Her spirits lifted. She could talk to Brittany. Confide in her.

"Wait." Emily eased away from Ryan. "Wasn't there something you wanted to talk about, Sky?"

Yes, the fact that I'm in love with Alec and it's amazing and exciting and agonizing because he's not in love with me.

Sky smiled brightly and shook her head. "It was nothing."

"PREGNANT! WOW. Can you believe that?" Brittany drove carefully in the snowy conditions. "Talk about a steep learning curve. Em's has been more like a vertical cliff."

"But she has Ryan."

"Yeah." Brittany's voice was husky. "Those two are so cute together. And I take full responsibility. If I hadn't sent him to keep an eye on her—"

"I love seeing her so happy. And you with Zach."

"You'll be next. Now that you've finally dumped Richard the Rat you can find someone insanely hot who will appreciate you."

She'd found someone.

And he didn't want her. At least, not in *that* way.

"That's not going to happen."

"Hey, I know you're feeling bruised right now, but give it some time. I'm so glad you're having rebound sex with Alec. That's exactly what you need." Brittany slowed down as she approached a bend in the road. "All the fun, with no risk of emotion. Crap, these roads are slick."

There was plenty of emotion on her side. More emotion than she'd ever felt in her life. Her heart was full with it and she had no idea what she was going to do.

It was the cruelest irony that she'd found the one thing she'd always wanted with the one man who couldn't give it to her.

To Alec, a relationship was a cage. Something to trap him and prevent him from living the life he wanted.

It was no good telling herself that she wasn't like that, because in the end the only thing that mattered was the way he felt.

Emotion clogged her throat. "Brit—"

"I know you two don't have much in common outside the bedroom but it isn't as if you'll see much of each other once the holidays are over. He's off to Antarctica or something, isn't he?"

"Yes." And she was excited for him, but also sad and a little bit envious. She pushed that aside. "Do you think Em is all right about being pregnant?"

"You mean because she never wanted this? Yes, I do. It wasn't that she didn't want it exactly, but she was scared."

"We ought to find a time to talk to her. Give her a chance to talk about how she's really feeling." And maybe that would give her a chance to talk, too. "We haven't got together for ages."

"She has Ryan. Did you see him with her? It was adorable. She didn't notice us. Nothing makes me more mushy than a big strong guy being kind and gentle."

"A lot has changed since the beginning of the summer." Sky stared at her hands. "Have you noticed?"

"Yeah. Our friend has had a lifestyle and personality transplant. I'm living with my ex-husband and you're having crazy sex with a man you wanted to kill. No one can say we don't keep life interesting."

Sky turned her head and looked out of the window.

The island looked different, snow-covered, familiar and yet unfamiliar.

Like their friendship.

Everything had changed, except her. She'd stayed the same, hoping for something that was never going to happen. Trying to live her dream while also doing her best to please her parents.

Except she wasn't the same, was she?

She'd finally found the big love she'd wanted all her life.

Brittany pulled up at the end of the lane. "Can you walk from here? If I drive down there, I'll get stuck."

"Do you want to come in for a while?" The words rushed out of her mouth. "It would be great to catch up and talk." Did she sound desperate? Oh, God, she hoped not.

"Tempting, but I can't." Distracted, Britt glanced at her phone. "When Zach gets back from his flight we're meeting Philip. He saw the doctors again last week."

"Oh." Feeling selfish, Sky pushed her own uncertainties aside. "How's he doing?"

"They've changed his meds. Zach worries. Philip and Celia are going to Florida for a couple of months after Christmas in search of better weather. Spend some time together. We might even join them." She gazed at the cottage and the sea beyond. "I love this part of the island. The perfect romantic hideaway. Do you and Alec even find things to talk about when you're not having sex?"

They didn't stop talking, and the talking was almost as exciting as the sex.

She never had to apologize with Alec.

She'd stopped asking him if her hair drove him crazy.

She'd stopped excusing herself for the fact her work was spread all over his garden room.

She never paused before pulling her camera out of her pocket.

Finally, she felt as if she'd found someone who liked her the way she was.

She was about to say as much when Brittany's phone buzzed.

"That will be my honey, reminding me to walk Jaws. I get all the good jobs."

"How is Jaws?"

"As physically challenged as ever but healthy." Brittany read the text. "He is a success story."

"It was good of you both to take him in."

"Zach was the one who took him in and they came as a package deal, but Jaws is about as much responsibility as we can handle right now. He's our baby. We should have dinner sometime soon, all six of us."

All six of us.

"I'd like that. And maybe we could find some time on our own, too."

But Brittany didn't seem to hear her. She was busy texting Zach. She glanced up as Sky opened the door and let in a punch of cold air. "Hey, wait a minute—"

Sky paused, hopeful. "Yes?"

"I had this brilliant idea for Zach for Christmas. Did I ever tell you that when he was little he was never allowed to eat the chocolate from the Christmas tree?"

"I didn't know that."

"Probably not something I'm supposed to share, but Lizzy and I are going to hang so much chocolate from the tree this year he is going to feast for a week." Brittany was grinning, delighted with herself, and Sky smiled, too, pleased to see her friend so happy.

"That's great. He's so lucky to have you."

"I'm lucky to have him. You'll be next." It was a throwaway comment and Sky almost said something but Brittany had her head down, texting Zach.

Sky slid out of the car. "Thanks for the ride. Drive safely."

Brittany pulled away with a wave and Sky picked up her bag and walked to the door feeling lonelier than she ever had in her life before.

ALEC STARED AT the closed door to his garden room.

If Sky was working, he didn't want to disturb her. On the other hand she'd come back from a morning with Emily and vanished without saying a word and that was unlike her.

From the moment he'd rescued her—she'd kill him if she knew he thought of it as a rescue—from the gallery in London, she'd filled his world with bubbly conversation.

She overflowed with thoughts and ideas.

It was like living with a bottle of champagne that had been shaken around before someone had popped the cork. She was almost always upbeat and positive, she rarely whined and she saw the funny side of almost everything.

He'd learned that just because she was in a room with him, didn't mean she needed or wanted conversation.

Often she was away in her own world, thinking or drawing.

Her drawings were everywhere, left on every available surface of his cottage. Some were of jewelry, intricate in the detail, others were landscapes.

The scope of her talent never ceased to amaze him.

He stared at the garden room.

It was the first time he'd known her to close a door.

Had her parents called? Richard?

He still couldn't believe the guy hadn't once called to see how she was. If nothing else, it would have given her the chance to hang up on him.

He respected that closed door for two hours after dark and then picked up a bottle of wine and two glasses.

Opening the door, he saw her curled up on the window seat staring into the darkness. "Sky?"

"Hi." She turned her head and he saw the dark shadows under her eyes.

"Why are you sitting in the dark?" He flicked on

a lamp with his free hand and then set the bottle and glasses down. "What's wrong?"

"Why should anything be wrong?"

"Because you're like a bottle of soda that's been left with the cap off. You've lost your fizz."

She stirred. "It's nothing."

He wondered how it was that after only a short time together he knew she wasn't telling the truth. "I thought we agreed never to lie to each other."

"All right, it's something, but it's a stupid something."

"Tell me."

"I can't."

It shouldn't bother him that she wouldn't tell him, but it did.

"Is it about your parents?"

"No." There was something small and fragile about her. Because she was so energetic and bouncy she normally seemed bigger than she was, but curled up on his window seat she just seemed vulnerable.

"So what's wrong?" He poured wine into both glasses and handed her one. "Is it about Emily being pregnant?"

"You know about that?"

"Ryan told me. I'm not supposed to mention it, but there was no way Emily wouldn't have told you so I guessed that instruction didn't include you. Are you worrying about her?"

"A bit." She sipped her wine and he studied her face, looking for clues.

"Shall we invite them over? It would give you a chance to talk to each other."

"She has Ryan. Things are different."

Something in her tone caught his attention. "Different how?"

She gave him a wan smile. "Everything's changing. And I feel…weird." She shook her head and looked out of the window. "Ignore me. I'm feeling all sorts of stupid things. Selfish things. Go and work for a bit longer. I'll meet you in the kitchen in an hour and we can play raid-the-fridge." She'd given him an opening to leave, but instead of walking through the door he sat down next to her.

"Hey, I wrote the manual on selfish and I can tell you, you don't feature in it. And feelings are never stupid, they're feelings." Gently he removed the glass from her hand. "I hate seeing you upset. I may not be as good a listener as Brittany or Emily, but I can try. Tell me what's wrong."

"Our relationship is about sex. You're breaking your own rules."

It was true, but still he couldn't bring himself to walk away. Instead he put his arm round her. "Talk to me."

She turned and pressed her face in his chest. "Shit. Look at me. Crazy person. Push me away. Kick my butt. Whatever you do don't be kind to me. If you're kind, I'll cry and I'll drown you in emotion so fast you won't have time to call the emergency services."

He smiled. "I'm a good swimmer. I can handle deep water." He lifted his hand and stroked her hair. "What's changing, sweetheart?"

He felt her tense and then she eased back and stared miserably at the middle of his chest.

"Our friendship. It's been the three of us for so long. The three of us against the world."

"The three musketeers."

"At college we used to joke that we were like a three-legged chair. If one of us left, the others would crash to the ground. We were always looking out for each other."

"As far as I can see you're still looking out for each other."

"But Em has Ryan and Brittany has Zach. It's different. And it's not that I'm not pleased for them, because I am, but if I'm totally, truly honest I'm a little bit sorry for me. I miss talking to them." Her voice sounded clogged and he eased her back into his arms.

"Why can't you talk to them?"

"Because they have their heads full of other things and they don't need to hear me bleating."

"If they knew you were upset—"

"Who said I was upset?" She sniffed. "I'm not upset."

"What do you want to talk to them about?" He rubbed her arms gently and felt her still.

"Nothing."

"It's not nothing, Sky. Something must have brought this on. Whatever it is, you can talk to me."

"No." Her voice was muffled. "I can't. It's too—personal."

"Sweetheart, we are way past personal. After everything we've shared over the past few weeks I would have thought you could tell me anything." Amused, he tried to ease her away from him but she had her fingers bunched in the front of his shirt.

"Not this."

He frowned, wondering what "this" was.

"Want me to get them on the phone? Invite them for supper?"

"No." She pulled away and sniffed. "But thank you for offering. I'm being stupid. I know you can't freeze time. I know life has to change and I'm pleased for them, really I am, but—"

"Change is always unsettling."

"Not to you." Her indrawn breath was unsteady. "You're the sort of person who throws a saddle on change and rides it into the sunset yelling 'yee-haw.'"

"For me, the fear is being in one place. And I've never yelled 'yee-haw' in my life."

"You should add it to your bucket list." She slid off the window seat and stood up. "Don't say anything to them. I don't want them to know. I need to work this through by myself. It's inevitable that our friendship is going to change, and we all have to find our way through that. It's funny, because through my adult life we've always been there for each other. When my parents do something irritating, I call Em or Brit. When I'm dumped by a boy, I call them."

"A boy dumped you? Tell me his name and I'll steal his lunch money."

She smiled. "There is nothing you can do. I have to accept that I'm no longer the first person they're going to call when there's a problem." She paused. "And that they won't necessarily be available to listen when I have a problem. It doesn't mean that we're not still close, just that things are different."

"I'm available and I'm listening. Tell me the problem." He was surprised by how much he wanted her to confide in him.

He wondered why she wouldn't.

And then suddenly he knew.

He was the problem. She wanted to talk to her friends about him. And that was the reason she couldn't talk to him.

She shook her head. "That isn't what our relationship is about."

His mouth felt dry. "Is there a definition for our relationship?"

"Yes. It's physically based. Fun. No emotional ties. Angst-free. We are the diet version of a relationship. Relationship-lite. Nonfat. Call it what you like."

He had no idea what to call it.

No idea what to do in this situation.

All he knew was that he didn't want to make her unhappy, but it seemed he was managing to do that without trying.

"How about friendship?" he said softly. "Can we call it that?" He saw her swallow and look away.

"Yes." Her voice was barely audible. "We can call it that."

LATER, AFTER A meal they'd thrown together and eaten in the kitchen, they lay on the rug watching the snow drift past the windows.

Sky leaned her head on Alec's chest, feeling his arms tighten. "I need to go and tidy your garden room."

"Why?"

"My mess is strewn everywhere."

"It isn't mess, it's your work."

The only light came from the flickering fire and the twinkling lights on the Christmas tree.

"You're very patient."

He laughed. "You're the only one who thinks so. You're a talented artist. Ever thought about doing more of that and less jewelry?"

"I like mixing it up. I like variety. Next time I'm in London I'm going to go to the National Gallery and see the Turner you talked about."

"You live in New York. You have plenty of your own galleries. Do you ever go to the Met?"

"Of course. All the time."

"Favorite painting?"

She smiled. "That's easy. *Portrait of Madame X*."

He nodded. "John Singer Sargent. He thought it was possibly his best work."

"You know it?" Yet again, he surprised her. "There were already nudes, but that painting created a *huge* scandal." She lifted herself onto her elbow so that she could look at him. "It was the dress and the way she held herself, she was sexy. I love that painting."

"I confess I've only ever seen it in pictures."

She opened her mouth to say that she'd take him and then realized that an invitation like that was out of place in their relationship so she lay back down and snuggled close. "This is perfect. I wouldn't care if we were snowed in for a month."

She wished they would be, because then she'd be trapped with him and she'd have more time.

"You'd miss Christmas with your friends."

"Staying here would be the perfect Christmas for me."

Crap. She shouldn't have said that.

Now he was probably thinking he'd never be able to get rid of her. That she'd broken their deal.

She kissed him, desperate not to let him speak.

She didn't want to hear him remind her that this was supposed to be lighthearted fun and nothing more. She didn't want him to remind her that after Christmas they probably wouldn't meet up again for several months and when they did it would be as nothing more than casual friends.

She slid her hand over his chest and unbuttoned his shirt.

He raised an eyebrow, his hard features softened by a smile. "What are you doing?"

"I'm being bad. Let's just hope Santa isn't watching or I'll be put on the naughty list." She opened his shirt and kissed her way down his body, dealing with the snap of his jeans.

She freed him and heard the soft hiss of his breath.

"Sky—"

"I can't think of anything I'd rather find under the Christmas tree. Merry Christmas, Alec." She slid her mouth over him, over velvet and steel, felt hard hands grip her shoulders and then sink into her hair.

In a smooth movement he rolled her onto her back, trapping her with the weight of his body.

For a moment he stared down at her and then he lowered his head and all she could feel was the hot glide of his tongue and the hard heat of his body.

He eased his hand under her hips, his mouth still on hers.

It was like being caught in white water. She was swept away, engulfed, submerged by the power of her own feelings.

She felt the ripple of muscle under her fingers and the swell of emotion in her heart.

Dizzy, disorientated, the words floated to the surface.

I love you.

I love you.

The need to say it aloud was so great that she turned her face into his bicep, mouthing the words against the hard swell of muscle.

I love you.

His rhythm didn't alter and with each skilled thrust of his body he drove her higher until the pleasure reached screaming pitch.

He caught her face in his hand and looked down at her, kissing her, sharing every breath, every quiver, every trembling rippling contraction, exposing all her secrets. Except one.

That one remained inside her. Just.

As the ripples of pleasure gradually eased, she closed her eyes, shaken by how close she'd come to saying it aloud.

The thought of how he would have reacted made her dizzy with horror.

She'd never be able to look him in the eye again.

Worst of all, he'd feel sorry for her.

What if it slipped out in the future?

What if he noticed something in her eyes? She'd always been hopeless at hiding her feelings.

And even if she somehow managed it, did she really want to live like that, subduing everything?

He rolled onto his back, gathering her against him. "What are you thinking?"

She was thinking about him.

Her mind kept circling round all the reasons that she shouldn't feel this way and it always came back to one thing.

He didn't want what she wanted. And if he knew

the truth he'd feel bad about himself again. He'd blame himself. He'd feel as if he were somehow responsible. There was no way she was doing that to him.

"Nothing," she said. "Nothing at all.

CHAPTER SIXTEEN

SKYLAR LAY IN bed with her eyes closed, pretending to be asleep until she felt Alec get up and heard him move into the study.

The temptation to stay in his bed and never move again was great, but she knew that wasn't an option open to her.

Forcing her limbs out of the bed, she dressed quickly and pushed her clothes into a suitcase. If she was going to do this, she needed to do it now. The longer it lasted, the harder it would be.

To make sure she couldn't change her mind, she made two phone calls.

The first was to her parents.

The second was to Pete, who ran the local cab firm.

She carried her case downstairs, then poured herself a cup of fortifying coffee before going in search of Alec. It was the first time she'd disturbed him while he was working.

Her knees shook. Her palms felt sweaty. Because she had never felt less like smiling, she compensated by doubling the size of her smile.

"Good morning." She placed a mug of coffee on his desk. "Sorry to disturb you, but I wanted to say goodbye before I leave."

"Are you going to see Emily?"

"No. I'm going home."

"Home? Home to your parents?" The shock in his voice threw her.

"Yes." She shrugged. "It's Christmas. If I don't go home it will make things worse than they already are. And they're still my family even though they're far from perfect."

"But you'd made the decision to stay here." He put his pen down. "You've always wanted to spend Christmas with your friends."

"Maybe next year. Right now Em and Brittany are both wrapped up in their new lives. They won't miss me."

There was a long, loaded silence.

"What if I said I'd miss you?"

Her heart felt like a lead weight in her chest. "Oh, come on, Alec. We both know what this was. Just fun, right? Great sex, a few laughs and no strings or promises on either side."

His level gaze was disconcerting. "So that's it?"

What else was there?

One day, maybe, there would be real friendship but right now she wasn't sure she could cope with a half measure of something she'd rather take as an overdose.

"Next time I'm on the island I'll send you a text and we can hook up for a drink or something." Knowing she had to get out of there, she walked over to him and kissed him on the cheek. "Thanks for everything, Alec. You've been a real friend. I owe you." Before she could step back he clamped his arm round her waist and pulled her back to him.

"Wait." His voice was thickened. "This is sudden."

"Not really."

"It's sudden. And it doesn't feel right. What aren't you telling me? Did your parents call again? Did they say something?"

"Yes. And it was awkward." Better for him to think that than know the truth. "And I really need to go home and clear the air."

"Is Zach flying you?"

"No. I don't want Emily and Brittany to know because they'll try to talk me out of it. I'm taking the ferry."

"I'll drive you to the ferry."

And she'd be trapped in the car with him, in that close, secluded intimacy that would somehow make her feelings feel huge. "No need. Pete is on his way."

"You called Pete? Why?"

"Because you have a deadline."

"I would have driven you."

She eased away from him. "I probably won't see you before you go to Antarctica, so have a great trip. Post some photos. I'm following you on Twitter and Instagram now, along with half the female population."

"Sky—"

"I hear Pete." Choked, she grabbed her case and walked quickly to the door. "You should probably spend Christmas Eve at Harbor House because there's another storm forecast and you don't want to be snowed in here with no turkey."

She dragged open the door and gasped as the freezing air hit her.

The sky was gray and overcast, threatening more snow.

She paused, torn between stealing a last look at

him and wanting to run. She'd wanted love for so long. She'd had no idea it would feel this painful.

"Merry Christmas, Alec."

"What do you mean she's gone? How can she have gone?" Brittany stared at him the next day when Alec headed over to Harbor House for some lunch. "What the hell did you do to her?" Her anger scraped over him like fingernails on a blackboard and Alec gritted his teeth.

There was no blame she could direct at him that he hadn't already directed at himself. "I didn't do anything."

"She was going to have Christmas with us for the first time." Brittany stalked around him, eyes flashing. "What happened?"

He'd asked himself the same question repeatedly. Looked at it from every angle. "Nothing happened."

"Something must have happened to make her change her mind."

Zach frowned. "He's told you nothing happened."

"I don't believe him." Brittany planted herself in front of him like a warrior confronting the enemy. "So you woke up and found her gone? She left a note?"

"No. She told me she was going."

"And you didn't call us?" Emily's tone was reproachful. "Why didn't you call us? If we had known, we might have been able to stop her. Did she seem upset?"

He'd asked himself that, too. Gone over and over that morning, as if repeatedly streaming the same movie, looking for something he'd missed.

"No. It didn't occur to me that she was upset until after she'd left."

"So what happened after she left?"

Alec breathed. "I found all her paintings in my garden room. She left them there. Every one." Including one of him, naked, that she must have painted at his parents' house.

He'd spent an hour looking at it, wondering what she had been thinking when she'd painted it.

Emily pressed her hand to her chest. "There is no way she would have left without those. Unless— Did she say she'd be coming back?"

"No. She told me to have a good time in Antarctica." And that, he thought, had been the worst part. Her words had left him feeling hollowed out, as if someone had removed all the important parts of him, leaving only the outside.

Brittany cursed under her breath, dragged her phone out of her pocket and dialed Sky's phone again. "I've been calling and calling and it just goes to voice mail. Why isn't she picking up? Even if she was upset with you she should be calling us." Misery rippled through the anger and frustration. "Alec, *please.* You have to tell us. Did you fight? Tell me exactly what happened the last time you were together."

Alec held her gaze. "We had sex four times in the living room and twice more in the bedroom. Is that enough detail or do you want more?"

Emily turned scarlet and Ryan gave a choked laugh and headed for the kitchen. "Time for a beer or ten."

"You can't drink ten by yourself." Zach virtually sprinted after him.

Brittany didn't move, but all the anger in her eyes had faded and now she just looked deeply unhappy. "I'm sorry." She murmured the words and then slid her arms round Alec and hugged him. "I'm sorry to be such a witch, it's just that I'm worried about her and I don't know why she didn't call us. We talk all the time, about everything."

"Do you?" He hadn't meant to say it but he was feeling as raw as she was.

Brittany stepped back and gave him a questioning look. "What's that supposed to mean?"

"Nothing." Regretting his words, realizing that there was nothing to be gained by taking his frustration out on them, Alec went to follow Ryan and Zach to the kitchen, but Brittany blocked his path.

"Hold it right there, Shipwreck Hunter. What do you mean?"

Alec sighed. "I don't mean anything. But if you talk all the time then you should have more of an idea of why she left than I do."

"We do talk all the time, although obviously not so much lately—" Brittany stared at him and her color rose. She bit her lip and glanced at Emily. "When did you last talk to Sky? Properly, I mean?"

"I talk to her all the time. Lizzy is often with us of course, but—" Emily broke off. "And now that you mention it she said she had something to tell me when she came over here the other day. But then she found out I was pregnant and somehow the conversation never happened."

That was the day she'd arrived home and locked herself away, Alec thought. "She didn't give you any clues?"

"No."

Brit was still staring at Emily. "You never told me that."

"It slipped my mind. I guess I didn't realize it was significant. She didn't seem unhappy. And how about you? You gave her a ride home. Did she say anything then?"

"No. We talked about things—" Brittany frowned. "She seemed fine. Maybe a little distracted. She asked me in for a coffee but I had to meet Zach."

"She asked me if we could have dinner, the three of us." Emily looked troubled. "I assumed she was being sociable."

"Shit." Brittany stared at her, anguish in her eyes. Then she pulled her phone out again. "All we can do is keep calling. We've left a hundred messages. That's the best we can do. Let's eat dinner and hope she calls later."

"You should stay tonight, Alec."

"It's only lunchtime."

"I know, but if she calls you I want to be here to listen. We're going to curl up and watch Christmas movies."

Ryan stuck his head round the door. "Zach and I are planning on finding alternative entertainment. Join us."

It was either that or go back and spend a night on his own in Fisherman's Cottage, surrounded by memories of Sky. The decorations she'd made filled his house. Her scent still clung to his pillow and he'd found two blond hairs clinging to the sweater he'd pulled on that morning.

"I'll stay."

AFTER LUNCH BRITTANY joined Emily in the kitchen and closed the door.

"What do you think?"

"I have no idea." Emily stacked plates into the dishwasher without concentrating. "I feel terrible. I was so wrapped up in myself I didn't ask the right questions. Does it sound awful to admit I'd almost forgotten she's only just broken up with Richard? She seemed so normal and fine about it."

"She did seem fine. Those plates are covered in food, Em. You need to rinse them."

Emily stared vacantly at the plates. "But what if she wasn't? What if she was traumatized and she didn't tell us?"

Brittany shook her head. "You saw her and Alec the other night—they were laughing and having a good time. She didn't look traumatized. She looked happy."

"So why did she leave? And what did she want to talk about? Breaking up with Richard definitely had an impact on her relationship with her parents. She must have been worried about that. That must have been why she went home instead of coming here. They probably put pressure on her."

Brittany flopped into a chair. "I wish she'd told us."

"Me, too."

"If we don't hear from her tomorrow I'm calling her parents. And it won't be to wish them a Merry Christmas. Do I smell burning? You need to remove whatever is in the oven."

"Oh. I forgot the cobbler." Emily was pulling dessert from the oven when a phone rang.

"It's mine." Brittany made a grab for the phone. "It's her! Sky? Holy crap, we've been worried about you. Why didn't you call?"

Emily put the cobbler down. "I want to talk to her, too. Put her on speaker."

Brittany put the phone on the kitchen table so that they could both hear.

"I'm fine." Sky's voice echoed round the kitchen. "I'm at my parents' house."

Brittany swore under her breath. "Sky—"

Emily put her finger to her lips and shook her head to silence her. "Why, honey? I thought you were going to spend Christmas here, with us."

"That was the plan, but, well, things changed."

"What changed?"

There was a silence. "There were things I needed to do. I needed to get away for a while."

Brittany frowned. "I thought you loved the island in the winter, and we had so many plans for Christmas. We've all been cooking and I even made you a stocking and stuffed it full of presents. Real presents, not empty ones. It was going to be our first Christmas together. What the hell is going on? What aren't you telling us?"

"It's not the island." Her voice was strangled. "I needed to think. There are things I need to sort out."

"Is this about Richard?" Brittany looked at Emily for inspiration. "Is he there?"

"Yes."

Brittany's face darkened. "Has he upset you?"

"No. In fact we cleared the air. It was probably the best talk we've ever had. Look, I can't really talk now, but you left a ton of messages and I didn't want you to worry. I'll call you soon."

"We're officially worried." Ignoring Emily, Brittany dragged the phone toward her. "Something's wrong. Why won't you talk to us? Since when don't we talk to each other?"

There was a silence. “You’re both busy with other things.”

“We’re never too busy for our friendship. Except—” Brittany hesitated. “You suggested having a coffee and I didn’t realize— I didn’t know you wanted to talk.”

“You don’t have to apologize. Everything is changing—our lives are changing.”

“But we’re still there for each other. Always.” Emily spoke quietly and Brittany cleared her throat.

“Sky, please. Whatever it was you wanted to talk to us about and we were too stupid and self-absorbed to listen to, tell us now.”

There was silence. “My whole life I’ve wanted to be in love. Really in love.”

“We know.” Emily bit her lip. “Is it hard for you, because Brittany and I are with Zach and Ryan?”

“No! I’m happy for you.”

“But it has made it even more difficult that you don’t feel that way yourself.”

“I do feel that way. That’s why I had to leave.”

It was their turn to be silent.

Brittany glanced at Emily, who gave a bemused shrug.

“Sky, if you’re going to tell us you suddenly woke up and realized you were in love with Richard—”

“No.” Sky’s voice was barely audible. “Not Richard.”

“But—” Brit transferred her gaze from Emily to the phone. “Are you saying—?”

“That big love I wanted to find? I found it. Except that it isn’t how I imagined it because he doesn’t love me back.”

Emily dragged the phone back toward her. "Are you crying?"

"No! I'm not that pathetic. But I needed to get away while I sort my head out because I don't want him to know and I wasn't sure I could hide it."

"Why would you have to hide it?" Brittany's gaze locked with Emily's. "Are we talking about Alec?"

"Yes. But I don't want him to know. It's very important he doesn't know."

"Why?" Emily rubbed her fingers over her forehead. "Maybe he feels the same way."

"He doesn't. You know he doesn't. You were the one who warned me to be careful. And I wasn't worried, because to begin with I didn't think this could possibly happen. We were only ever having fun, that's all. That's what we agreed. I'm the one who changed the rules."

"Rules?"

"It was never supposed to be serious. And I know it doesn't make sense, so don't waste time telling me that. You'll say I'm on the rebound, or you'll point out that we spent all summer sniping at each other, but these last couple of weeks…well, it's been the best time of my life."

"We could see you were having fun, but—" Emily swallowed. "You love him?"

"Yeah. And I know it's crazy because back in the summer I would have killed him as soon as kissed him but now…because I wasn't trying to please him, I was myself. Really myself, for the first time ever. And I had fun. I felt *free*. I love him for so many reasons, but the biggest one is because he makes me happy."

A sound in the doorway made both girls turn.

Alec was standing there, his face white as he stared at the phone on the table.

Brittany made a grab for it but he crossed the room in two strides and trapped her hand in an iron grip, shaking his head.

Emily swallowed. "Sky, we should talk about this another time—"

"No. I want to talk about it now. I can't tell him, but if I don't tell someone, I'll go mad. The crazy thing is that all the things he keeps apologizing for are the things I love about him. I love that he gets so absorbed in a piece of work he forgets that I'm there. I'm exactly the same. It used to drive Richard crazy because I'd get an idea and instantly want to work on it and he wasn't like that. I'm a spontaneous person. And Alec is like me. He's spontaneous. He hates to be trapped and so do I. That's how it felt with my parents all these years. They made me feel trapped. I was trapped trying to be this person they wanted me to be and I'm just not that person. And I don't want to be that person anymore."

"That's great," Brittany said, her eyes on Alec's ashen features. "But—"

"There are no buts. You can control a lot of things, Brit, but you can't control your heart." Her voice broke. "You can't control that. And my heart belongs to him even though he doesn't want it. It may have been a short relationship, but it was the most honest, true, *real* relationship I've ever had. With him, I never felt like I should try harder to be something different."

Emily's cheeks were wet. "Why would you? You're wonderful."

"But I'm not easy to live with. I can't be with him,

but spending time with him showed me that I like being myself. And maybe I will never find another person who likes me the way I am, but this is the way I want to be now. It's like being liberated. It's—it's like wearing control underwear and suddenly taking it off."

Brittany frowned. "When have you ever worn control underwear?" She shook her head. "Never mind. So what happens now?" She was looking at Alec as she spoke, but his gaze was fixed on the phone.

"I talked to my parents today. I had a proper talk, where they did the listening for once. Watching the way Alec was with his parents made me realize that some of the blame lies with me. I've been allowing them to interfere with my life. I told them how I felt. And I can't honestly say it was well received, but the ball is in their court now. I don't know what will happen, but they either accept me or they don't. Living with them made me feel like a flower deprived of water. Tomorrow I'm coming back to the island and spending Christmas where I want to spend Christmas—with people who love me the way I am."

Brittany stared at the phone. "You're coming back?"

"Yes, I wasn't going to, because I wasn't sure I could hide how I feel about Alec, but then I realized that I want to spend Christmas on Puffin Island with all of you. If I stop coming to the island because I'm afraid to bump into him, then I won't ever see you and that's too high a price to pay. I've worked out a lot of things today, and I think I can handle it. I'm not the world's best actress, but I can do this. I can act as if nothing has changed and he is never going to know."

Brittany covered her face with her hands. "Kill me now."

"You're worried it's going to be awkward, but I promise you it's not."

"Good." Brittany let her hands drop, her expression resigned. "See you tomorrow. Have you hired a car? Zach will fly and pick you up."

"Thank you. You promise you won't tell Alec?"

Brittany's gaze locked with Alec's. "I won't tell him. But I think he might know."

"He won't know." Sky's voice sounded muffled. "I've been practicing in front of the mirror. There is no *way* he is going to find out. Just watch me. My smile is going to be bigger than Alaska."

Emily cut the connection and gave Brittany and Alec an agonized look. "What happens now?"

Brittany rolled her eyes. "We're screwed. Completely, utterly screwed." She glared at Alec. "This is *all* your fault. Why did you have to walk into the kitchen at that point?"

"It's not his fault," Emily said reasonably. "You put the call on speakerphone."

"Because we both wanted to talk to her! We didn't know we were going to have an uninvited guest. Since when did men ever show themselves when there is work to be done in the kitchen?" Brittany said testily. "You'd better pretend you don't know, or I will kill you with my bare hands and bury your body so deep you'll be oil before anyone finds you. If she finds out you heard that conversation, she'll be mortified."

Alec said nothing, just gripped the table until his knuckles were white.

"Alec?" Emily's voice was cautious. "Say something."

"She said that I make her happy." He sounded like a robot and Emily looked at him with concern.

"Yes, she did. What are you going to do, Alec?"

He stared at them for a long moment.

Then, without answering them, he turned and strode out of the kitchen.

Moments later they heard the front door slam.

"Crap, crap, crappity, crap." Brittany lowered her head onto the table. "What the hell do we do now? Think we should tell her?"

"No! If you tell her, she won't come home." Emily stood up and paced the kitchen. "We're all going to have a lovely friend Christmas for the first time in our lives and nothing is going to spoil it."

"Is Alec even coming back?"

"I have no idea. But even if he does—" Emily looked at her in despair "—we need a miracle."

Brittany shrugged helplessly, clearly unconvinced. "It's the season for it."

CHAPTER SEVENTEEN

HI, ALEC, GREAT to see you again.

Should she kiss him, or not?

Yes, but maybe just a kiss on the cheek, as friends would.

On the other hand, was that weird given everything they'd been doing together for the past few weeks?

She tried not to feel disappointed that she hadn't heard from him.

It had only been a few days. And he had no reason to contact her.

Hi, Alec. Merry Christmas. I hope all your Christmasses are white.

Well, of course they were going to be white. As long as he was living in Maine, there wasn't much doubt about that.

Exasperated with herself and exhausted from contorting her face into a variety of happy smiles, Sky arrived at the airport in Boston and found Zach waiting for her.

"It's Christmas morning. You're not supposed to work on Christmas morning." She kissed him and was surprised when he returned her hug.

"I only do special deliveries. Brit is with me. She's in the plane. Emily would have come, too, but she's cooking."

"Of course she is." Part of her was touched that Brit had come, too, but another part of her would have liked to use the time to further her plan of how she was going to greet Alec.

She'd been bracing herself to do this alone.

Was it better to do it in front of her friends, or worse?

Nerves fluttered in her stomach like a flurry of snowflakes dancing in the wind.

Should she kiss him? Cheek or mouth? What was appropriate for two people who had been intimate but not committed in any way? What was off-limits?

Hauling her bag over her shoulder, she followed Zach.

She was overthinking this. With the six of them, Agnes, Lizzy and two dogs it was going to be mayhem, and mayhem would mean Alec was less likely to notice any subtle differences in her interaction with him. Ironic, she thought, that this was the Christmas she'd dreamed of having for so long, and now it promised to be more stressful than anything she'd experienced with her family.

The weather was bitterly cold and she followed Zach up the steps of the plane and was immediately enveloped by warmth and a hug from Brittany.

"Merry Christmas."

"You should be home playing with Jaws under the Christmas tree. You didn't have to come."

"I wanted to see you. I've been a crap friend."

"You're never a crap friend."

Looking alarmed, Zach vanished to the cockpit.

"Yeah, I was." Her voice husky, Brit pulled away. "I was so wrapped up in my own world, thinking about the camp, Philip, Zach—I didn't pay attention. Do you forgive me?"

"There is nothing to forgive. How is Philip?"

"He's doing well, thanks, but I don't want to talk about him right now. The only person I want to talk about is you. I'm officially worried."

"You don't need to be. And I'm glad you're busy and happy." Sky stood for a minute, absorbing warmth and friendship.

Different, she thought, *but no less genuine.*

She'd been silly to think it. Whatever life threw in their direction, they weathered it together and they'd weather this.

The flight was short and uneventful and Zach drove the short distance from the airfield to Harbor House.

The island roads were empty, the snow banked high on either side. They passed a few houses, lights sparkling in the windows, their gardens plunged under mounds of snow and ice.

As Zach pulled up outside Harbor House Sky felt so nervous she was sure her hands were shaking.

She told herself it would be fine once the first awkward meeting was over.

And it wasn't awkward for him, of course. Just her.

The door opened before they'd made it up the steps and Emily hugged her and pulled her inside. "Merry Christmas. I'm so glad you made it. All of us together!"

Cocoa hurled herself across the room and licked her while Jaws glared at her from his post at the foot of the stairs.

Sky made a fuss of Cocoa and summoned up the

smile she'd been practicing. The one that said nothing was wrong.

"I brought gifts!" She waved the bags she was carrying. "Real ones, not empty ones."

"Come and put them under the tree. We're doing gifts later."

Sky walked through to the living room. Candles flickered on the high surfaces and the lights on the Christmas tree glowed like tiny fireflies. Lizzy crawled under it, rearranging gifts and adding the ones from Sky's bags.

A large bay window overlooked the sloping garden, now hidden under a thick blanket of winter white. On a clear day there was a perfect view across the bay to the mainland.

Children, dogs and good friends, she thought. The perfect Christmas.

If you ignored the fact that she felt as if she'd been crushed by a heavy object.

She couldn't breathe. She ached all over. Maybe she was coming down with the flu.

There was no sign of Alec.

She hoped he wasn't staying away because of her.

"Don't eat the chocolate on the Christmas tree," Lizzy said solemnly. "It's for Zach."

Grateful for the distraction, Sky raised her eyebrows. "All of it?"

"He never had chocolate on the tree growing up. This is all his. Brittany and I fixed it for him."

Sky saw livid color highlight Zach's cheekbones and then he dropped into a crouch in front of Lizzy.

"You did that for me?"

Lizzy nodded. "Brittany and I chose the chocolate together. You can eat all of it if you like. It's yours."

Zach looked at the tree and then at Brittany and something passed between them.

A wordless, intimate exchange that excluded everyone else in the room.

Then he rose to his feet. "That is a lot of chocolate. I think I'm going to need some help."

"That's cool." Lizzy slipped her hand into his. "If you're sure."

"Champagne time." Ryan disappeared into the kitchen and emerged moments later with two bottles. Emily followed with glasses just as Alec walked into the room.

Sky felt her heart accelerate like a racehorse out of the starting gate.

She was so pleased to see him she wanted to hurl herself across the room like Cocoa, wag her tail and lick him all over. Instead she gave him a smile that she hoped was natural, and then turned to Ryan.

"Champagne! Great idea. Just hand me the bottle and a straw," she said and then gave a weak smile. "Just kidding."

Emily shot her a concerned look and she realized that both her friends appeared more jumpy than usual.

They were probably worried she was going to cause a scene with Alec.

Had it been unfair of her to be honest with them?

"In a minute." Alec's gaze was fixed on hers. "First, I want to talk to Sky alone. Could you all give us a moment?"

"No, we couldn't." Brittany sat down on the sofa with a determined thump. "It's Christmas, Alec. I don't see what you could possibly want to say to Sky that we can't all hear."

Sky wondered why Brittany was glaring at him. "Have you two had an argument or something?"

"No." Alec turned to look at her. A muscle flickered in his jaw and his eyes were dark and serious. "If they won't leave, then we'll leave. Come into the kitchen."

She had no idea why Alec wanted to be alone with her, but she knew she didn't want to be alone with him.

He was far less likely to notice a change in her when they were surrounded by people.

"Why the kitchen? I like it here, with the lovely tree."

His gaze was steady. "I need to talk to you, Sky. And I'd rather do it in private."

"It's Christmas," Emily said desperately. "This is family time. Friend time." She stumbled. "Whatever you have to say, Alec, can wait."

"Time to open that champagne, Ryan," Brittany said brightly, but Ryan didn't move.

"What they're not telling you," Alec said slowly, "is that I overheard your conversation."

Sky frowned, puzzled. "What conversation?" And then she knew and her knees turned to water. "You mean—?"

"Yes, that conversation. The one where you told them that you love me and you didn't want me to know."

All sounds faded into the background.

If she'd ever been in a more hideous, uncomfortable situation she couldn't remember it.

She felt the hot scald of humiliation darken her cheeks. "But how—?"

"I put you on speakerphone," Brittany muttered. "Em wanted to listen, too. We didn't know we had a third pair of ears. You can kill us anytime you want. Advertise for new friends. I'll pay for the ad myself."

Sky dug her nails into her palms. "You heard?" Her mouth was dry. "How much?"

Alec held her gaze. "All of it. Every word."

She wanted to crawl under the Christmas tree and hide among the presents. She felt more exposed than she ever had in her life before. "Right." Trying to maintain her dignity, she gave what she hoped passed as a casual shrug. "Well, we said we wanted an honest relationship, I guess that's what we have. You know how I feel." And she knew how he felt. "And I'm sure hearing that scared the crap out of you."

"Is that why you went home? Because you were in love with me and you were afraid you couldn't hide it?"

"To begin with." If he'd heard the conversation then he already knew everything. She figured that more honesty couldn't make her feel worse. "I was afraid you'd guess, and that wasn't fair to you. But five minutes with my parents was all it took for me to realize that avoiding you would mean losing the most important people in my life. Don't feel awkward, honestly. It's fine." She turned to Ryan, desperate to shift the focus. "Let's open that champagne. Em can't drink so I'll have hers, too."

"Not yet." Alec stepped toward her. "You've told me the truth, so now it's my turn."

That was one thing she really did *not* want to hear.

She could just about cope with telling him the truth of how she felt, but she couldn't cope with hearing how he felt spelled out. "I know I broke the rules," she said. "I know I said this wouldn't happen and I really believed it at the time—I didn't lie. None of this is your fault, and I promise it won't be awkward. After Christmas I have to go back to New York and you're off to Antarctica so we won't even see each other for months."

His response to that was to hold out his hand to Lizzy.

"Now?" She hissed the word in a theatrical whisper, and when he nodded she scrambled out from under the tree carrying a large parcel. She handed it solemnly to Alec, who in turn handed it to Sky. "Merry Christmas."

Emily looked puzzled. "I thought we agreed to do presents after lunch?"

"This isn't a Christmas present." Alec had his eyes on Skylar. "Open it."

Wondering why he was giving her a gift now, and why Lizzy was involved, Sky slid her finger under the tape and opened the present. It was soft and bulky and the paper fell away to reveal a down jacket in a pretty shade of blue.

"Oh. It's great. I love it. Thank you. It will be useful for Maine winters, especially if I can't borrow yours."

"You won't be wearing it in Maine." He was talking just to her, as if no one else was in the room. And no one said anything. No one moved. "You said there is no such thing as bad weather, only bad clothing. I hope you still think that when you're shivering with me in a tent in Antarctica."

Her brain was having trouble making sense of what he was saying. "Why would I be shivering with you in a tent?"

"Because you're coming with me. At least, I hope you are. You said you wanted adventure. I'm offering you adventure. It's only for a few weeks, but after that I'm going to Iceland with a film crew to make a documentary on the Vikings. If it fits with your own plans, I hope you'll come with me there, too. Jewelry was important to the Vikings. I think you'd be interested."

Antarctica? Iceland?

"You want me to come with you?" Her head was full of questions, but she was afraid to ask any of them in case she humiliated herself more than she already had. "But you do these things by yourself. You don't like feeling trapped or restricted."

"I never feel restricted with you, and if I was ever trapped, I hope you'd be there with me. In fact I'm adding you to my list of essential items to have with me next time there's a storm warning."

To her acute embarrassment she felt her eyes fill. "Alec—"

"You said that hearing that phone call scared the crap out of me, and it did. But not because I heard you say you loved me. I already knew that. I knew you loved me, but I didn't trust myself not to hurt you. I didn't trust myself to be able to make you happy. After everything that has happened with your parents and then Richard, you didn't need another person crushing your dreams. And when it comes to love, you have big dreams, Sky. I'd convinced myself that the best way of helping you to be happy was to stay away. So when you said you were leaving me, I didn't stop you even though watching you leave was the most painful thing that has ever happened to me."

"Alec—"

"I proved to myself that day that I'm not as selfish as I thought, because if I was I would have stopped you going. Letting you walk out of that door almost killed me." He took a deep breath. "And then I heard that phone call. I heard you tell your friends that being with me was the happiest time of your life. I heard you tell them that I made you happy and those were, without doubt, the best words I'd ever heard. The second best was hearing you say you were coming back for Christmas Day."

"You went dashing out of the house," Brittany muttered and Alec nodded, his gaze still fixed on Sky.

"Because the shops were only open for a short time. I needed to do something to convince you that you aren't the only one with strong feelings. Words aren't enough, we both know that."

From him, words would have been enough.

"You have strong feelings?" She didn't dare believe it. She didn't dare. "How strong?"

He strode toward her and her eyes widened as she saw the look in his eyes.

"Oh, Alec—"

He kissed her.

His mouth was warm and sure and he kissed her as if she were as essential to him as breathing. She could feel the strength of him, the hard power of his body as he wrapped his arms around her and drew her close.

They'd shared hundreds of kisses over the past

few weeks, but this one felt different and she couldn't work out why. Her brain tried to decipher the signals, to understand, but it was like reaching up to touch a cloud. There was nothing she could grab.

Through the mists of her brain she heard Lizzy giggle and Brittany clear her throat.

Finally, Alec eased her away from him.

"Put the jacket on, sweetheart." His voice was husky and she was shaking so much she dropped it twice.

She still wanted to know why the kiss felt different.

"Sorry. I feel like jelly."

Smiling, he took it from her and fed her arms into the sleeves. "Put your hands in the pockets."

His eyes were warmth and darkness and she couldn't look away.

She fumbled and drew out something from both pockets, a box from the left and an envelope from the right.

She heard Emily gasp and Brittany give a choked laugh.

"Go, Alec. Ignore the envelope, open the box, Sky."

"The envelope is a ticket to Antarctica." Alec took the box from her shaking hand before she could drop it and flipped it open.

Sky stared down at the huge diamond, sparkling like the lights on the Christmas tree.

"Oh—oh, Alec—"

"Do you have any idea how terrifying it is choosing jewelry for someone as talented as you?"

"I love it. It's stunning. But—"

"I didn't want to propose to you in public," he

said softly, "but given that our friends won't leave the room, I have no choice. I hope you'll forgive me."

"Y-you're proposing?"

"Why would I leave?" Brittany grinned. "This is the best thing I've seen in a long time. And, Sky, if you don't say yes in front of me *I'll* never forgive you." She snapped a photo on her phone. "I'm tweeting this to your hundred thousand followers, Alec. Tough, cynical Alec Hunter is now soft, marshmallow Alec Hunter."

Sky saw his mouth flicker at the corners.

"Children are present," Emily said hastily, and ushered Lizzy toward the kitchen. "Come and stir the cranberry sauce. We'll be in the kitchen when you're done. Brit, I need your help. Ryan, Zach—"

With a sigh Brittany rose to her feet. "Okay. I guess you're right. But I want a full report later. No detail left out."

Their friends melted away and finally Alec and Sky were alone with the flicker of the fire and the scent of the Christmas tree.

Alec took her hand. "When we went for that walk that day at my parents' you told me that jewelry had meaning. That it was an expression of emotion." He slid the ring onto her finger. "This tells you that I want a lifetime with you. It says I love you and that I want you by my side for every adventure life offers us. Forever." He took her face in his hands and kissed her gently. "Say something. Anything. As long as it's not *no*."

She felt the heavy, unfamiliar weight of the ring on her finger and the swell of emotion in her heart. "You really are proposing?"

"I'm telling you I want to spend the rest of my life with you and I don't mind whether we make that official or not. It's you I want, not a ceremony or a piece of paper. I don't care about any of that. We're going to be together because it's what we both want. Because there is no one else we'd rather take this adventure with." He stroked her hair away from her face, his eyes gentle. "Of course, if you married me it would stop your parents plotting your romantic future and it would make my parents' day, but every decision we make is for us, not for anyone else."

Us.

If any word had ever sounded as good, she couldn't remember.

Her heart felt huge in her chest. "I like the sound of *us*."

"I like it, too. I love it." He smiled against her mouth. "I love you. And we're going to make a great *us*."

Part of her, the part that knew life didn't usually turn out fantasies, still didn't dare believe it. "I never expected to fall in love with you. I was having fun, that's all, and suddenly in the middle of having fun, and talking to you, I realized I wanted to carry on doing it."

"So do I."

"Are you sure? You said—"

"I know what I said. And that was the way I felt to begin with. When Brit texted me and asked me to go to your exhibition, I tried to find a reason not to go."

"I reminded you of Selina."

"A little. I found you very attractive, and I didn't trust the feeling. In the summer I was rude to you—"

"You were keeping me at a distance." She understood that now. She understood all of it.

"I used to think that being in a committed relationship meant sacrifice. That it forced you to make difficult choices. Then I spent time with you and realized that it's not about choosing one life over another. It's about sharing that life with someone you love. You were the one who showed me that was possible. I want that someone to be you."

She listened, still afraid she was dreaming. That this was another one of those scenarios spun into reality by her creative brain. "When I was with you, I was me. Because I wasn't trying to impress you, I didn't feel the need to be anyone other than who I am. I didn't care if you judged me, and it turned out that you didn't. You taught me to accept who I am. You taught me that having a passion and wanting to pursue it is valid. You were never impatient about what I did. You made me so happy."

"I was so scared of hurting you." He groaned the words against her lips. "I don't ever want to hurt you."

She wrapped her arms round his neck. "I'm not some vulnerable flower, Alec. I'm not going to blow over in the wind or wilt if you leave me at home unwatered."

"I know. I discovered that on that night when you threatened to put your stiletto through my balls."

She grinned. "In the circumstances, that was very rude and ungrateful of me. I'm surprised you didn't leave me there."

"I would never have done that."

"I know. You refused to leave me." It choked her to think of it. "You behaved like a real hero."

"Don't put me on a pedestal."

"I'm not. I know who you are, Alec." She touched his face gently. "I know you're single-minded and focused when it comes to your work. I know you have bursts of enthusiasm for what you're doing that makes any intrusion from the outside world unwelcome. When you're working on a project that's all you think about. You give yourself totally to it and even the thought that something or someone might intrude on that makes you irritable. I know you think that's selfish, but I think it shows focus and commitment and a drive to do the very best you can, and I understand that. It doesn't irritate me. On the contrary, it's one of the many things I love and admire about you." She paused, trying to explain. "If I'd been on my own that night...well, it wouldn't have been pretty. You did what needed to be done, even though it inconvenienced you. I think that's heroic. And you were kind. You didn't even like me, and you were kind."

He inhaled deeply. "I liked you. In fact I liked you a little too much. I liked your fire and energy and your ability to laugh at everything, even yourself."

"You took me to your home, even though that must have been the last thing you wanted to do." She swallowed. "I think I fell in love with your family before I fell in love with you."

"It was mutual. They love you back. They're going to love you even more now."

"Let's call them. I want to tell them. And after that we'll call my parents."

He eased away from her, his gaze searching. "Are you going to tell them not to cancel the Plaza for June?"

"No. We're not getting married at the Plaza. We're getting married on the beach. A lobster bake, catered by the Ocean Club, followed by ice cream from Summer Scoop. All of our friends and the people we love. Guests can arrive on the *Captain Hook* and we'll ask John if we can decorate it." She hesitated, wondering if she'd misread him. "Unless you'd rather have the Plaza?"

"A beach wedding sounds perfect to me." He lowered his head and kissed her. "You," he said slowly, "are the most generous, unselfish, beautiful person I have ever met."

There was a sound behind them and both of them turned.

All four of their friends were hovering in the doorway.

Emily's cheeks were wet, Brittany was blinking rapidly and Ryan was grinning at him.

Alec rolled his eyes. "Is anything around here private?"

"Not much." Zach moved to one side as Lizzy wriggled through.

"Can we open our presents now? That pile there is for you, Sky."

Still dizzy from everything that had happened, Sky looked toward the tree. "You all bought me presents? Oh." She was immensely touched but then she saw Brittany shake her head.

"That pile is from Alec. All of them."

"A bit over the top if you ask me," Ryan muttered. "Puts pressure on the rest of us."

Emily slid her arm into his. "Is that your way of saying you forgot to buy me a present?"

"I might have bought you a couple of things. Token gestures. But nothing like the Mount Everest of gifts Alec has produced, so don't get your hopes up." But Ryan was grinning and Lizzy was dancing on the spot like a flea.

"He's bought you *tons* of things. We chose some of them together. I can't wait for you to open them, Mom." The word slipped out naturally and Skylar looked at Brittany and then at Emily.

Her eyes were glistening and she stooped to hug Lizzy. "In that case I think we should open them now. I don't want to wait a moment longer. I want to see what you chose."

Another change, Sky thought. Another shift in their relationship. And it was a good one.

She knew how much that word would mean to her friend.

As Lizzy extracted herself from the hug and dived under the tree to start opening presents, Brittany walked across to Sky and Alec and hugged both of them. "That ring is amazing. I'm so happy for you both. Can you believe this? It used to be the three of us against the world, and now we're a six."

"Seven," piped up Lizzy, half-buried under wrapping paper, "nine if you count the dogs."

Emily exchanged looks with Ryan and Sky knew what they were thinking.

Soon they were going to be ten.

Brittany gave a soft smile. "Our little circle has grown."

Our circle.

Sky's skin tingled. Friendships changed, but that

didn't mean they were less meaningful or genuine. Just different.

She glanced at Alec and saw him smile with understanding.

He drew her back to him and lowered his mouth to hers, kissing her gently. And this time when it felt different, she understood why. He'd kissed her so many times, in friendship, in passion and for comfort, but he'd never kissed her with love.

Until now.

It melted over her, sliding into every part of her, warming every corner of her body, and she knew that this was the feeling she'd been waiting for all her life.

Her heart felt too big for her chest.

She was dimly aware of laughter and the tearing of wrapping paper as her friends gathered round the tree and she drew away just enough to speak, whispering the words just for him.

"I always wondered how love would feel."

The look in his eyes was just for her. "How does it feel?"

"It feels amazing. Like waking up to a perfect winter day of blue sky and crisp white snow." She smiled, because now she knew the truth. "It feels like Christmas, ever after.

* * * * *

ACKNOWLEDGMENTS

I'm grateful to all my readers. So many of you take time to email and chat to me on Facebook and your kind comments and supportive messages always make my day. Keep talking to me!

Seeing my books on sale around the globe is a dream come true for me, made real by the team at Harlequin. Thanks to Loriana Sacilotto, Dianne Moggy, Margaret Marbury and Susan Swinwood for their encouragement and support, and to the global editorial team who have embraced my single-title career. The team in the UK have done so much to deliver my books to the widest possible audience and I'm truly grateful. It all started with you!

I'm lucky enough to have Flo Nicoll as my editor and I'm thankful for the vision, patience and enthusiasm she displays as we work together on each book.

I'm grateful to my agent Susan Ginsburg and the team at Writers House for everything they do.

I have the best family in the world and I'm continually grateful for their unwavering support and all the delicious meals they produce when I'm on a deadline. You're the best!

We hope you enjoyed reading

IN TOO DEEP

by *New York Times* bestselling author

LORI FOSTER

and

ONE ENCHANTED MOMENT,

an original ***Puffin Island*** story

by *USA TODAY* bestselling author

SARAH MORGAN

IN TOO DEEP was an original **Harlequin® Blaze®** series story!

Harlequin® Blaze® stories sizzle with strong heroines and irresistible heroes playing the game of modern love and lust. They're fun, sexy and always steamy!

Red-Hot Reads

Enjoy four *new* stories stories from **Harlequin Blaze** every month!

Available wherever books and ebooks are sold.

www.Harlequin.com

NYTHB0516R

SPECIAL EXCERPT FROM

HARLEQUIN *Blaze*

Aria Danes puts her dreams on hold to help her injured brother. A foal will be just the therapy he needs. But when she meets horse trainer Brant Ellison, the chemistry between them may derail all her carefully laid plans...!

Read on for a sneak preview of COWBOY ALL NIGHT, the first story of 2016 in New York Times *bestselling author Vicki Lewis Thompson's sexy cowboy saga* ***THUNDER MOUNTAIN BROTHERHOOD***.

He longed to reach for her, but instead he leaned into the van and snagged her hat. "You'll need this."

"Thanks." She settled the hat on her head—instant sexy cowgirl. "Let's go."

Somehow he managed to stop looking at her long enough to put his feet in motion. No doubt about it, he was hooked on her, and they'd only met yesterday.

If she was aware of his infatuation, she didn't let on as they walked into the barn. "I'm excited that we'll be taking him out today. I thought he might have to stay inside a little longer."

"Only if the weather had been nasty. But it's gorgeous." Like *you*. He'd almost said that out loud. Talk about cheesy compliments. "Cade and I already turned the other horses out into the far pasture, but we kept these two in the barn. We figured you should be here for Linus's big moment."

HBEXP0516

"Thank goodness you waited for me. I would have been crushed if I'd missed this."

"I wouldn't have let that happen." Okay, he was grandstanding a little, but it was true. Nobody at the ranch would have allowed Aria to miss watching Linus experience his first time outside.

"How about Rosie and Herb? Will they come watch?"

"You couldn't keep them away. A foal's first day in the pasture is special. Lexi and Cade are up at the house having breakfast with them, so they'll all come down in a bit." And he'd text them so they'd know she was here.

But not yet. He didn't foresee a lot of opportunities to be alone with her unless he created them. He wanted to savor this moment for a little while longer.

"Brant, can I ask a favor?" She paused and turned to him.

"Sure." He stopped walking.

Taking off her hat, she stepped toward him. "Would you please kiss me?"

With a groan he swept her up into his arms so fast she squeaked in surprise and his hat fell off…again. His mouth found hers and he thrust his tongue deep. His hands slid around her and when he lifted her up, she gave a little hop and wrapped her legs around his hips. Dear God, it felt good to wedge himself between her thighs.

Don't miss COWBOY ALL NIGHT
by New York Times *bestselling author*
Vicki Lewis Thompson, available June 2016 wherever
Harlequin® Blaze® books and ebooks are sold.

www.Harlequin.com

Copyright © 2016 by Vicki Lewis Thompson

HBEXP0516

HARLEQUIN®

Blaze®

Red-Hot Reads

Use this coupon to save

$1.00

on the purchase of any Harlequin® Blaze® book.

Available wherever books are sold, including most bookstores, supermarkets, drugstores and discount stores.

Save $1.00

on the purchase of any Harlequin® Blaze® book.

Coupon valid until July 31, 2016.
Redeemable at participating outlets in the U.S. and Canada only.
Not redeemable at Barnes & Noble stores. Limit one coupon per customer.

Canadian Retailers: Harlequin Enterprises Limited will pay the face value of this coupon plus 10.25¢ if submitted by customer for this product only. Any other use constitutes fraud. Coupon is nonassignable. Void if taxed, prohibited or restricted by law. Consumer must pay any government taxes. Void if copied. Inmar Promotional Services ("IPS") customers submit coupons and proof of sales to Harlequin Enterprises Limited, P.O. Box 3000, Saint John, NB E2L 4L3, Canada. Non-IPS retailer—for reimbursement submit coupons and proof of sales directly to Harlequin Enterprises Limited, Retail Marketing Department, 225 Duncan Mill Rd., Don Mills, ON M3B 3K9, Canada.

U.S. Retailers: Harlequin Enterprises Limited will pay the face value of this coupon plus 8¢ if submitted by customer for this product only. Any other use constitutes fraud. Coupon is nonassignable. Void if taxed, prohibited or restricted by law. Consumer must pay any government taxes. Void if copied. For reimbursement submit coupons and proof of sales directly to Harlequin Enterprises Limited, P.O. Box 880478, El Paso, TX 88588-0478, U.S.A. Cash value 1/100 cents.

® and ™ are trademarks owned and used by the trademark owner and/or its licensee.

© 2016 Harlequin Enterprises Limited

NYTCOUP0516

THE WORLD IS BETTER WITH *Romance*

Harlequin has everything from contemporary, passionate and heartwarming to suspenseful and inspirational stories.

Whatever your mood, we have a romance just for you!

Connect with us to find your next great read, special offers and more.

/HarlequinBooks

@HarlequinBooks

www.HarlequinBlog.com

www.Harlequin.com/Newsletters

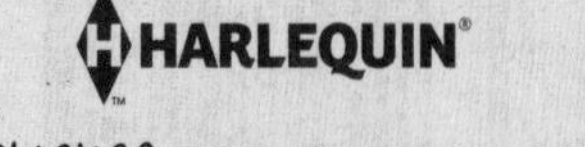

www.Harlequin.com

SERIESHALOAD2015